Chapter One –The Sight

Rhana - July 1966

There it was again, that cold sadness making Rhana shiver. She had never experienced anything like this and it scared her. She moved away from her table to the tent's opening. The throb of the fair filled her ears. The familiar smells and sounds didn't calm the eerie feeling that swept over her. What was it? Something was here, but she could only feel it.

She stepped out among the crowds. The wind whipped at her long frizzy auburn hair. This reminded her she had not tied it back in its tight plait like she normally did when she left the tent. As she turned to go back in, a child ran at her and clung to the back of her legs. Without turning she knew it was her daughter, Rainbow, the child she had conceived through force.

"Mummy, have you finished?"

"No darling, I wanted some fresh air," lifting the child she was reminded of Flynn and the Apple Fair five years ago, "Where's Uncle Jimmy?"

Jimmy loved Rainbow, he loved Rhana too, but there was never to be a man to tie Rhana down now. "He saw you mummy, and said to come and see what's wrong."

"Nothing's wrong, darling, I just wanted to move with the people."

Rainbow wriggled out of her mother's arms, ran to the carousel, and climbed onto the big horses before the ride started.

Rhana cast her mind back. Flynn had been one of the travelling families that gathered for the Apple Fair every year. It was a huge event where, come autumn, they raced and bred their horses giving them the distinctive broken colours. The locals kept out of the way, it was well known the two didn't mix.

1

Flynn Murphy had just won a bare-knuckle fight against one of Rhana's lot when he caught her eye. He'd winked and she had gone all shy, and looked down. She couldn't remember a time when she hadn't loved him. She had been fifteen when they'd shared their first kiss. It was in a sheltered bank that looked a bit like a shallow cave. They had met there regularly for the next four years.

Rhana at nineteen years old, had blossomed with time. Her hair was auburn, wild and so long she could sit on it. Her green eyes darkened with her mood. Her pale face had a sprinkle of freckles which she had hated.

He had been washing his bloodied knuckles in the cool water of the brook by the time Rhana had met him. She knew immediately something was different. His kisses were rough and demanding. When she had tried to pull away to slow down his urgency, it seemed to increase his determination and excitement. Flynn had denied Rhana the pleasure of loving, as he forced his way between her legs taking his own pleasure.

He had raped her and walked away doing up his trousers. To anyone else it might have looked as if he had stopped to urinate. She had lain feeling sore and dirty.

Once he was out of sight she had waded into the water of the brook to cleanse herself. The desire to end it all had come over her. Lying face down she had let her arms float at her sides waiting for darkness to take over and numb the pain. It was then she had had a vision, she had seen Rainbow, a girl child had been planted in her womb. She'd coughed and spluttered as she'd scrambled back on to the bank.

Through fear of her drunken father she had run to her Nana Jay. Nana Jay had given Rhana what looked like her life savings, seventy two pounds.

Rhana had walked through the night, frightened only of what she was leaving behind. She caught the first bus that came along and two days later arrived in Cornwall.

The fete in the village of Port Isaac attracted crowds - including 'Farley's Fair' - it was here she'd looked for work amongst what looked like her own people.

Watching Jimmy give out the mats for the Helter-Skelter while laughing with the children, had given her the confidence to approach him. They had met that evening at 'The Mote' where she had poured out her heart. She had told him of her unusual insights, she didn't like to describe them as feelings as they were more vivid with visions. When Jimmy listened without mocking she told him how she knew she was with child. Rhana had joined Gloria.

Gloria was the fair's fortune teller, and had been for fifty nine years. She read the tarot cards, and looked into a wired up ball. It would flash different colours giving the appearance of reacting to a predicted vision. It was all pretence but it added a little excitement and mystery to the reading.

Gloria had resented Rhana's lovely young presence right up until Rainbow had been born. It was then that things had got easier between them. Through Gloria's love of the new baby a close friendship developed between Rhana and herself.

When Gloria died four years later she had taught Rhana to read the tarot cards, work the ball, have a good understanding of money and speak the Queen's English, but Rhana still wanted better for Rainbow. She wanted her to learn her letters, to be able to read and have the opportunities she had never been given herself. Very few could read or write at Farley's Fair and those that could did not have the patience for teaching. So Rainbow now ran wild, barefoot in summer jumping from ride to ride as the fancy took her. She was well loved among them all, these people were Rhana's family now, and the only family Rainbow knew.

*

"Come on, Tilly, run, we can make the big horses."

Tilly and Ed ran, just catching hold of the ride as it started to move. They sat giggling as the music started and the Fairman came and took their money.

A skinny child with brown wavy unkempt hair sat beside them. One hand held the pole while the other was held out as if catching the wind.

Tilly put her lips to Ed's ear trying to be heard above the music,

"Look, Ed, that poor child. She's got no shoes on, and looks like she could do with a good bath too."

Ed leant back laughing, "Mrs Barrett, really! You're already sounding like my mother."

Tilly pushed him in the back, "Heaven forbid, I'm just saying."

"That's what she would say, Tilly, watch out now."

As the ride slowed, Ed slid off his horse and gave Tilly a hand down. She was still laughing at the insinuation of her being like his mum. Ed held his arms out to the little girl offering to help her too, "Come on, little one. Let me help you."

Her grey eyes twinkled with mischief, "No ta, mister, I can do it meself."

She ran off towards the chair-planes, managing to catch an empty seat before it started.

"Tilly let's have a go on the bumpers."

"I want my own."

The pair of them laughed their way round, bumping each other rather than avoiding. When they got off Ed slipped his arm round Tilly's waist, kissing her ear,

4

"Are you glad you married me, Tilly?"

"Give me time, as my gran would say, wait until the honeymoons over."

They had a go at the rifle range with 'shoot the duck', and Ed won Tilly a teddy. It was bright orange with a blue ribbon. She kissed its nose saying,

"If I see that little vagabond I'm going to give it to her."

"I wouldn't worry, Tilly, she belongs here. I saw her trying to get on the bumper cars after us. The chap held her back while the cars were taken. I think she just roams around from ride to ride."

"I'm not saying anything. I don't want to get accused of sounding like your mother, but it's a shame, that's all."

"There she is, Tilly, standing by the candy floss. Go on, give it to her, but she probably has loads."

The two of them moved across and Tilly got down with the bear,

"Would you like this teddy? He needs a good home."

"No ta, me mum says not to speak to you lot."

The attention was broken when she shrieked out, "Uncle Jimmy."

The child jumped into his arms. He put her on his shoulders saying, "What's going on here then?"

"She tried to give me that teddy, but I said no, just like mum says."

Jimmy turned to Ed and Tilly. His eyes looked threatening, making them both feel uneasy. It was Tilly who spoke, "Nothing's going on. I won a teddy and have no use for it whatsoever."

Still looking threatening he said, "What did you play for then?"

Ed spoke up, "Fun, isn't that what you come here for?"

Jimmy turned his back on them, and walked away with the child still up on his shoulders.

Tilly linked arms with Ed, relieved he had gone, "Ooh that was uncomfortable. At least she's looked after... in a fashion."

Ed draped his arm round Tilly unperturbed. They spotted a brightly coloured tent. It had a lot of coloured streamers flying from the top in an arch like a rainbow.

"Come on let's get a cuppa, that looks like a tea tent."

As they got closer they saw it was for telling your fortune. "Go on, Tilly, in you go, see what our future holds."

"No, after you, if it's all honey and roses I might be tempted."

*

There it was again, that feeling, the cold chill. Rhana sat still waiting for it to pass, but it didn't. It was closing in. It was here.

Rhana looked up and knew it was him. Ed stood in the flap of the tent. This was the force she had felt. He moved in towards her filling the tent with his presence. His green eyes shone like emeralds, they matched her own. His hair had a wave, and was dark like a raven. Her heart thumped, she could count the beats, and goose pimples crept over her body. She had never felt such fear... she questioned the feeling, *'Is it fear?'* She found her voice, "So you have come."

Ed thought this was part of her little speech, he had only gone in for a giggle.

"Yes I've come, what can you tell me?"

"Sit."

The command sounded tinny to Rhana's ears and from nowhere came the words; "You're one of a pair."

6

Ed paled, "I had a twin but that was a long time ago. I want to know about now."

"Give me your hands, let me feel."

Ed placed his hands on top of Rhana's, and she felt it. The pain, the loss, the darkness, it was all here.

"You have troubled water around you."

Rhana knew she should say something positive, what was wrong with her, starting a reading like this? Before she could go any further he spoke, "I've been in troubled water, but I want to know about the future, not my past."

Rhana took hold of the cards holding them out to him, "Cut them in three places and hand me the pile you want me to work with."

Ed liked this. He laid them out in front of himself and picked the pile to the left.

"You have picked the highest card for love. Someone loves you very much. You love back too. I can see great wealth… yes you will be very wealthy, and I see children."

Rhana was brought out of the reading when Ed broke the silence, "Children, are you sure?"

"Yes, I see two girls."

Ed had had enough. He was convinced now that she was seeing the two babies Tilly and he, had had aborted, "You are good, very good, but you are not seeing my future. You are seeing what I was, I wanted to see what is coming."

"It is a forward reading, Ed, I can see it is."

Ed stood backing away. She was frightening him. He was sure he hadn't told her his name, yet she had just spoken it.

7

Rhana could see she had unnerved him, "Don't fear me…" It was too late, Ed had gone.

Rhana looked at the cards. What was it, what was the connection? She turned the unread card over and over between her fingers, staring at the two wands. *What could the connection be between us? I've never set eyes on that man in my life.*' She scooped up the cards and shuffled them. Cutting them in three places she picked the pile to the left. There they were again, the wands. Feeling restless, she lay back letting her arms fall at her sides willing a vision to come. She was desperate to see the connection between herself and the young man who had just left, but nothing came. Jimmy broke her concentration, "What's up, Rhana, are you okay?"

Rhana opened her eyes, "Yes I'm okay. Troubled by a reading that's all. I'm feeling restless. I can't pinpoint it, but I feel scared."

"What did that fella want?"

What fella, where?"

Jimmy sat, taking hold of her hand he said, "You alright, love? You look pale."

"I feel uneasy, Jimmy, I've done a reading and can't see the significance of it, but I can feel it."

"What, with that fella that just left?"

Rhana pulled her hand away, "Yes it was probably him, if he had dark hair, shorts and yellow shirt. Why, did you see him?"

"He was trying to give Rainbow a teddy bear, I warned him off."

Rhana closed her eyes and let these thoughts flow through her. Strangely they brought a calmness, but it was clouded by fear. Rhana's voice came out in a whisper, but she didn't feel like it was her speaking, "There's a thick coloured mist. It's black, no dark… green, so dark almost black but it's not black and it's not green."

8

She opened her eyes, "Jimmy I'm scared, something's wrong here and I can't settle."

"Shall I deal with him for you, Rhana?"

Rhana leant back in her chair, "No, Jimmy, leave it. I don't know what it is. There is nothing wrong with that young man, but he has a place in something I can't understand. I can't see anything, but I feel danger. Something is going to happen, yet I can't foretell it."

"Well if I get rid of ..."

"Stop it, Jimmy, he's harmless, that is something I can feel. Somewhere, somehow though, he will fit into this puzzle. I can feel that too. I sensed his presence before he even came."

"Bloody hell, Rhana, you're scaring me now."

Rhana attempted to laugh to lighten the mood, "Don't be silly, Jimmy, it's probably me being over sensitive. I'm going to pack up now, I'll walk with you and find Rainbow."

*

Tilly lay back in Ed's arms content in their love making. They had been married just over a week and had spent their honeymoon in a boarding house at Falmouth, paid for by Tilly's gran as a wedding gift. They had had a lovely week with just one day left of their holiday, but the day at the fair had cast a shadow over Ed's mood leaving him troubled, and she couldn't get him to share the problem. "What is it, Ed, you haven't been the same since you went into that fortune telling tent. What did she say? Apart from - you'll be wealthy and someone loves you."

"Nothing really, Tilly. It was more about what has been, she could see Luke..."

Tilly noticed the hesitation, "Ed, tell me what she said, then we can laugh it off together."

"It was nothing, honestly. Nothing we don't know anyway."

"Tell me then."

Ed rolled over on to his side propping himself up on one arm. He pushed her blonde hair off her face with his free hand and looked into her piercing blue eyes. He never tired of looking at her, he loved her so much. "Tilly she could see our children, the ones we got rid of. They were girls."

"Did she say that?"

"No… she said we would have two girls. I just know it was the ones we got rid of."

Tilly moved away, "Don't say that, Ed. It was a decision, made - that seemed right at the time, it cost us both dearly. Anyway who knows?"

Ed moved her back in his arms stroking her hair, and kissing the top of her head, "That's the problem, Tilly, we both know. I was told you'll never be able to have children, so how can she see two girls? It has to be what we got rid of. I'm sorry, Tilly, but there's no other way of saying it."

Tilly ignored his explanation, "Well, maybe with medical discoveries moving forward I just might get fixed."

"Oh Tilly that would be wonderful, but unlikely, you know that, and so do I."

"Well tomorrow I shall go. You go off for that fishing trip you fancied, and I'll wander along to the fair again on my own, just in case she's for real."

Ed didn't like it, "Tilly, she's scary, I can't explain it. It was like she knew me, and could see inside my soul."

Tilly pushed him away, "Ed Barrett, that woman has bewitched you, it's just a bit of fun, but I won't go if you'll feel easier. I shall do some shopping. I promised Rachel we'd bring her back a stick of rock and I'll get your mum and my Gran some fudge."

The atmosphere lifted as Ed said, "You love Rachel too, don't you?"

"How can you not, she's infectious. I'm still amazed your mum took to her though."

She caught the hurt look flicker across Ed's face, and added, "I didn't mean that in a nasty way, it's just that your mum is so judgemental and likes to think her family are so perfect, and then she adopts a child with a disability."

"Rachel's not disabled, Tilly, she has Down syndrome, a condition."

Tilly felt like she was digging herself a hole, "Forget it, Ed, I love Rachel. I can see you all love her. I was just trying to say that knowing your mum and what she was like to me for all those years, I'm surprised, that's all."

"Don't be too hard on mum, she's changed, Tilly. What with me going off the rails like I did, I think she found herself. She came down off the high horse she had put herself on, and found a much better place to live in."

Tilly wasn't wholly convinced, but gave up on the conversation, it was a touchy subject with Ed. Gone were the days when the two of them would rip May to pieces for her spiteful tongue. Ed had a huge respect for his mother these days, and as for Rachel she might just as well be his blood sister because he defended her fiercely. Tilly felt a pang of jealousy, never before had she had to fight for Ed's affection, she had always been his one and only. As she turned over to settle down to sleep she chastised herself for her childish thoughts.

11

Ed draped his arm over her waist, she nestled into him feeling happy and content letting her thoughts drift to her own fortune being told tomorrow.

*

Tilly stood waving as Ed sailed off for a morning of fishing. She would buy a few goodies to take back home later, first she wanted to get to the fair.

The big white hand that hung over the gate was gone, and it looked like they were moving on. Disappointed, Tilly slipped inside the gate making her way round appearing to go unnoticed. There was a lot of shouting, and rides were coming down. She spotted the Rainbow tent rolled up on the ground, but there was no one there.

She wandered over to the caravans, moving with the people – no one seemed to take any notice of her, they were all busy unscrewing bolts and lifting heavy equipment onto the back of trailers.

There it was, a caravan with a rainbow painted over the door. A dog was barking wildly at the side, but lucky for Tilly it was tied up. As she neared the van she could hear raised voices, hesitating at the door, trying to pluck up the courage to knock, she heard, "You fucking bitch, my kid's here somewhere, and I'll find it, and when I do it'll be coming with me."

The sounds coming from the van indicated violence which unnerved her. As she backed away she nearly stepped within reach of the dog that seemed desperate to break free. She started to run, wanting to be away from this place, it no longer felt safe. Not looking where she was going she ran blindly struggling to recognise her whereabouts. A hand grabbed her, "And what do you think you're doing sniffing round here again?"

Tilly recognised him as the man that had threatened them yesterday over the teddy bear incident. She was breathing fast but managed an

12

indignant, "Let go of me, I'm not doing anything. I just wanted to have my palm read but you're all going. I found the caravan with the rainbow and knew it was her, but there's trouble in there so I ran."

His grip tightened, "What trouble, is it your fella?"

His hold on Tilly was painful as he dragged her towards the caravan, "I'll kill him if he hurts Rhana."

Tilly managed to pull free of his grip and stood her ground, "My husband is fishing. I'm only here because she gave him a strange reading. I wanted mine done, that was all. I didn't knock on the door because someone's in there now, swearing at her, about it being his kid. I was scared…"

At that moment the child Tilly recognised from yesterday ran up to Jimmy, she was hysterical, "Uncle Jimmy, help me mummy, he's got her by the hair, she's…" Before the child could finish he was running, shouting to the others to head for Rhana's van.

Tilly got down and cradled the child in her arms speaking in a soft voice, telling her over and over that everything would be alright.

Rainbow clung to Tilly like her life depended on it. A woman from the win a gold-fish stall approached, trying to prise Rainbow out of Tilly's clutch. Rainbow hung on tight, hiding her face in Tilly's neck.

When Tilly saw Rhana running towards them with blood on her face and hands she tightened her grip on Rainbow. Rhana's hair had come free of its plait and hung loose, her eyes were wide with fear, making her look wild. When Rainbow heard her mother's voice Tilly could no longer hold her. She watched as Rainbow ran full pelt into her mother's arms.

Rhana hugged the child to her, she was frantic. Tears poured down both their faces, and there it was, it came to her. Rhana felt it – the connection. It was as clear as if she had seen it on screen.

Tilly was leaving, she had seen enough. She made her way to the gate where she had entered about half an hour ago. The sound of a desperate cry caused her to stop and turn. Rhana was chasing after her with the child trailing behind clutching her mother's long skirt, "Wait! Please wait." Tilly felt uneasy, she wanted to be away from here. These were not her kind of people. Having her fortune told was long forgotten.

When Rhana caught up she grabbed Tilly by the arm. Words spewed from her mouth like an explosion from a shaken bottle of fizzy pop. In her frenzy, her voice lost the accent Gloria had instilled in her, making her sound common. She asked Tilly her name and what was her business here.

Tilly didn't like Rhana touching her, her hands were bloodied and sticky. She pulled away from them, "My name is Tilly, Tilly Barrett, I came because you unnerved my husband with a reading yesterday, and I wanted you to read mine, but now it's not important."

She watched as Rhana closed her eyes saying her name on a whisper.

"'Tis Tilly, 'tis very important. I need 'yer. I need 'yer help."

"You don't need me, you have your people. I must go, my husband will be waiting."

Rhana, with Rainbow hidden in her skirt, fell to her knees begging Tilly, "Please help me, 'elp us both. That man has come for Rainbow, she needs to get away, take 'er with you please. I felt it in 'yer 'usband's presence yesterday, but didn't understand it then."

Tilly stared, saddened at the sight before her. Rainbow, just a lump draped in material hidden from view, and Rhana behaving like a beggar woman desperate for money. Tilly couldn't believe what was happening. She tried to explain that she couldn't possibly take Rainbow, which caused Rhana to become hysterical, "Oh, Tilly please, that man's bad, and when I say, bad, I means bad. He tells me

14

he killed me dad and they buried him in a sheep field. Beat him to a pulp and buried him."

This was horrific for Tilly. She wanted to be away from here, she was frightened now. These were nasty people that seemed to be a breed all of their own.

Rhana was on all fours. Tilly could see the fear in the fixed stare which caused her green eyes to flash. This reminded Tilly of a wild cat watching its prey. With both hands Rhana grabbed hold of Tilly's ankles.

"Tilly I 'ave the sight, it frightens some people – me too at times, but I know this is right. Please, please take Rainbow. She'll be safe with you. 'Yer can teach 'er to read and write, all the things I never 'ad. I'm begging 'yer."

People were starting to mill around the grounds again, and Tilly felt conspicuous with this woman on her knees in front of her. She leant over, pulling at her arms, trying to encourage her to stand, "Look, I want to help, but we've only just got married. I'll need to speak to Ed. I don't know what people will say back home…"

Tilly didn't get a chance to finish because the man who Tilly now recognised as Jimmy approached, "Come on, Rhana, get your things, we need to get going. We'll leave this lot, they'll catch us up on the road."

She got to her feet with Rainbow still rolled up in the skirt, making it look like Rhana had a bustle.

"Rainbow's staying 'ere with Tilly. She'll look after 'er, I know she will, until she's old enough to find me."

Rainbow started crying, begging her mother not to go, it was like a nightmare for Tilly, she wanted to wake up. She had to make herself heard, if only for the child's sake, "I want to help you, but I can't take your child, it isn't right, I'm sorry."

15

Rhana's desperation was reflected in her high pitched voice, "Yes yer can I saw it in the cards yesterday, I didn't understand it then, but now I see it. You'll raise Rainbow for me, she can't stay 'ere now. That man'll take her if you don't."

Jimmy became impatient, "Rhana, come on, we'll sort this out, I'll protect Rainbow, but we've got to get going, you can see she don't want her."

"No, Jimmy, 'yer don't understand, he'll come for her, he'll not rest now till he takes her from me. Rainbow must go with Tilly."

Without answering he unravelled Rainbow from Rhana's clothing, holding her out to Tilly. The child wriggled in his grip screaming. She leant forwards trying to grab her mother, but was thrust into Tilly's arms. Tilly had no choice but to hold on to Rainbow for fear of her falling, "How will I find you? You'll want her back."

Rhana reached out to Rainbow wiping her tearstained face, "You go with this kind lady, she'll teach yer yer letters. If yer ever need me, remember what I've always told yer, look for the rainbow."

Tilly, as if bewitched, left with the child clutching her round the neck. She had nothing for her, only what she was wearing. Tilly wondered how she was going to explain it all, and could she get away with it?

Tilly found a seat looking out to the sea. She moved the child on to her lap, but she buried her head in Tilly's chest refusing to look at her, her shoulders shook in sobs. Tilly rubbed her back, talking to her in a gentle voice, trying to coax and soothe her. "Come on now, nothing's ever as bad as it seems. You heard your mummy, if we need her we'll look for the rainbow, but for now until that scary man has disappeared let's do what mummy says and all get along together."

Rainbow didn't answer.

"Come on let's dry those eyes. Blow your nose in my hanky, and we'll go and buy you some clothes." She stood placing Rainbow on the ground holding out her hand, "Come on, there's a good girl." Tilly was surprised when not saying a word she took it, and the two of them walked towards the town.

"We'll go to Woolworths, you can choose… would you like that?"

There was no answer, but the further they walked a tingle of excitement bubbled in the bottom of Tilly's stomach. The child was going to live with her, her and Ed, they would be a family. The idea warmed Tilly's heart. *'I just have to convince Ed.'*

Tilly could just see the boat coming into shore. Clutching her shopping in one hand and holding onto Rainbow with the other, nerves replaced her earlier excitement as Ed jumped onto the jetty.

She had spent the last of her holiday money on Rainbow, who had come to life when choosing a white dress with buckets and spades running along the bottom of the skirt. Tilly bought a night shirt, socks and underwear and a pair of bright pink jelly shoes, with a pair of little school plimsolls. She knew her gran would soon sew a few bits up in a flash for the new arrival despite her failing eyesight.

Ed seemed to pale at the sight of Tilly with the child they had been warned to stay away from. Kissing her cheek he raised an eyebrow, saying one word, "Tilly?"

She widened her eyes at him as if to halt his questioning, "This is Rainbow, her mummy has asked if we can look after her for a while as there was a little disturbance at the fair, and people got frightened." Turning her attention to Rainbow she said, "And when we need mummy we know how to find her… don't we?"

Tilly held her breath waiting for some sort of resistance. Ed got down on one knee and said, "Well that's alright then isn't it? When he got no answer, "We'd better think about getting you home, hadn't we?"

As if by magic, Rainbow let go of Tilly's hand, took the bag off her and said, "Look mister, Tilly got me a dress, it 'as boats on it."

Tilly brushed the top of her head, saying, "Not boats, darling, buckets and spades…remember?"

Ed held the dress out in mock admiration, telling her what a pretty girl she would look. They walked back to the boarding house as if it had always been the three of them.

Little was said at Rainbow's arrival at the boarding house, but both Tilly and Ed could sense their curiosity. Tilly packed up their things to go home that evening, leaving a day earlier than planned. Ed made a phone call to his parents, relieved to hear his dad's voice and not his mum's on the other end of the line.

The Rainbow

Chapter Two

Little Acorns

May cleared away the dishes from the breakfast table, puzzling over Ed's phone call. *'How can they be coming home with a child? Trust Norm to take it in his stride and not ask questions. I wished I'd got to that phone – what was it Norm said? Don't ask, well of course I'm going to ask, if I don't the street will. Who do they think they're kidding to think they can waltz back from their honeymoon with a kiddie in tow, and think no one will wonder where she came from?'*

Catching sight of Rachel sitting on the floor playing with a doll, she took her irritation out on her, "Rachel, will you hurry upstairs and get your teeth cleaned, the bus will be here in a minute."

"You help me, mummy, I can't do it."

May took hold of Rachel by the hand, a little sharper than she intended, "Now missy you can do this well enough on your own, you're a big girl now."

Rachel started to cry, she sensed May's annoyance, "Stop that silly noise." May put the paste on the brush, giving it to Rachel, trying to take the anger out of her voice. "Come on now, the bus will be tooting in a minute."

May went into the bedroom to get Rachel's school blazer. She went to a private school in Chichester called Little Acorns. It was costing a small fortune, but May and Norman decided she needed the best start they could give her. May thought about the child that Tilly and Ed had brought home, annoyed that she hadn't heard anymore. They came home Saturday night and hadn't been near yesterday. It felt wrong to May, she didn't like it. Making up her mind to phone Agnes once Rachel had caught the bus, she thought, *'I hope Tilly doesn't answer it.'*

Attacking the bed sheet and covers her mind stayed with Tilly, she had always been a problem. How she wished Tilly wasn't related to Agnes. May had a warm affection for the old lady, and had had to hold her tongue on many occasions. It also rankled that Ed and Tilly had started their married life living with Agnes too. This had caused Alf to move out earlier than planned, to live with Brenda before their November wedding. *'Honestly what is the world coming to?'*

The sound of the bus brought May out of her reverie and she hurried Rachel down the stairs trying to put the straw boater on as she went. Rachel pulled at it "I don't want to wear a hat, I want to hold it."

"Put it on your head, young lady and do as you're told, it's your uniform and if you don't wear it Mrs Waters will have something to say to you." With that said Rachel left it on her head and climbed the steps on the bus chatting to the driver.

May waved Rachel off, and was delighted to see Ed's van coming up the road. She went inside to put the kettle on. She had lots of questions that needed answers, her intentions to phone Agnes forgotten.

"Morning, mum." Ed kissed May's cheek as she lit the gas.

"Cuppa, tea or coffee?"

Telling May he would have a quick tea, he explained he had to be back in Chichester before ten, they were busy, especially as he had had a week off. May became impatient, she didn't want all this polite chit chat, her old self reared up as she went in with both feet, "What's all this about a child, honestly when are…"

She didn't get to finish. Ed interrupted, ready for the onslaught, "What is it with you, mum? We're looking after a child that needs a home that's all, there's no crime in it and we're not hurting anyone, just helping. How can that upset you?"

"What do you mean? How can you have a child, who does she belong to?"

"It isn't important, mum, you'll meet her soon enough. Why can't you be more like Agnes? She has just taken it at face value, welcomed the child in, and she loves her already."

"Child, doesn't she have a name?"

"We've called her Rosie, she seems to like that."

"Rosie! Rosie? Didn't she have a name then?"

"Yes she did, but it was unusual so we changed it. Then, if needed - she wouldn't be found easily."

"Oh my god, have you stolen her?"

She watched as Ed pulled his hand through his hair in frustration, "Look, mum, we haven't stolen her. She was given to us by the mother. By what Tilly told me, I think the father was after her. She said it'd got nasty, but whatever it is it's not important. Rosie will live with us while she needs to. No one asked you questions when you came home with Rachel, did they?"

"That was different, Ed, you have only just got married. People will wonder and talk..."

"I haven't got time for this, mum, I popped in just to fill you in. Rosie's her name. She's living with us for a while, and will be starting school after the summer holidays."

May had so many more questions, and as Ed stood to leave, she managed to delay him a few more minutes, "How old is she then?"

"We don't know, mum, she says she'll be six in July, but we'll start her at school as a first year, she's had no education from what we can gather - She's what you call a traveller."

May forgot her good resolve to hold her tongue and be tactful, "Bloody hell Ed, she's not a gypsy, is she?"

"Could be, mum, she travelled with a fair, but I don't care. Rosie needs a home and she's being given one, with us."

"Rosie, bloody Rosie, of all the names you could have chosen, you had to pick one that says gypsy Lee. For God's sake, Ed, call her something like Linda or Susan, anything but Rosie."

Opening the door Ed's last words were final, "She chose Rosie, Tilly likes it and so do I."

As the door closed May thought, *'Tilly liked it, well yes she would wouldn't she.'*

May sat and mulled over the thought of having some gypsy child connected to her. *'Whatever next will that girl bring to our doorstep?'*

*

Rosie sat watching Agnes sew on her machine. She rested her chin on the table, fascinated at how the material was threaded through and came out stitched.

"Is that for me too?"

Agnes stopped sewing and brushed her old hand over the child's head, "No, love, this is a pair of curtains for a Mrs Oliver. I do this as a job."

"My mummy reads people's 'ands. She can see what's going to 'appen to 'em."

Rosie looked up as Tilly came in, "There you are, are you coming round with me to meet Ed's mum, Mrs Barrett?"

Rosie sensed an atmosphere between her Granny A and Tilly at the mention of Mrs Barrett, but said nothing.

"Do you want to come, Gran, moral support?"

"No thanks, love, I'm busy here. These days it takes me longer and longer.

"You know what Ed said, there's no need for you to do it now. He earns enough for us all."

"Go on with you, what would I do all day if I didn't sew? It's all I know, I'll die at this spot."

"Gran, don't say such things."

Rosie took hold of Tilly's hand, and they both kissed Agnes goodbye before leaving her.

*

Once they were out in the fresh air, Tilly's stomach turned with butterflies. She knew Ed was right it would be better if they went round together, but Tilly thought it would be a good bridge builder if she braced the ordeal herself.

Knocking on May's door she could hear the old dog barking in the back garden, and May's voice.

"Coming, give me a minute."

May's shock didn't go unnoticed but she recovered well. "Tilly, you should have come round the back, no need to knock."

Tilly didn't call May mum, even though she was now her mother in law. May had said after the wedding to just call her May. This had hurt at the time, but now Tilly preferred it, it was easier.

"I've brought our new addition round to meet you, May, her name is Rosie and she's nearly six, a playmate for Rachel."

May ignored the introduction, putting on the kettle. Giving no thought to Rosie's feelings, she blurted out, "Ed's been round this morning, said the child's from a gypsy background."

Tilly's back was up, "No, May, Rosie is a fairground child, she needs protection for a while. We're just helping out." Tilly looked down at Rosie trying to soften this attack, "This is Ed's mum, Rosie, they too have a little girl they're looking after, but she doesn't know her mummy."

May undid her apron puffing out her bosom, Tilly could see she had rankled her. "It's a bit different, we've adopted Rachel, Tilly. She's now ours."

How Tilly disliked this woman, *'How could everyone say she'd learnt hard lessons, she was still an old battle-axe.'* Wishing she had listened to Ed and left the meeting till it was the three of them. The awkward silence was broken by Rosie, "I don't like it ere. I wanna go 'ome with Granny A, she's nice, and she smells nice too."

Tilly knew Rosie loved the smell of her gran. It was the lavender. Gran made lavender bags for her drawers, she hung lavender in bunches in the wardrobe and even wore lavender cologne.

Tilly remembered Rosie's first night at home. She'd tucked her into bed, amused as she sniffed the sheets saying, 'I like it 'ere, it smells real nice. Yer gran smells like flowers, I just wanna keep sniffing 'er. Tilly had laughed out loud, telling her it was the lavender, and showed her the little bags everywhere, explaining that her Gran believed it kept away the moths.

Tilly could see May was put out by Rosie's comment, her cheeks were flushed and her lips were pursed like she had tasted something bitter. She didn't know though, just how annoyed May was at the impudence of the child, and that May felt shamed at her insight, "I'm just putting on the kettle, if you want you can go through to the sitting room." She pointed to the lounge, "Rachel has left some toys out this morning, you can play with them, she won't mind."

"Tilly I wanna go 'ome, I don't wanna play 'ere, I like your 'ome, not the Mister's."

"We won't stay, May, we'll come again with Ed. I should have waited."

May looked desperate, she'd tried to back track, but Tilly stood with her shoulders back, and her head held high. She was enjoying watching May trying to repair the bad feeling that had been created. "Come now, it's a shock for me, that's all." She sniffed at her arm pits, "I don't smell, do I?"

Rosie was not easily won round, and buried her head in Tilly's skirt, refusing to look at May.

Tilly lifted her up, saying, "There's a dog in the garden, do you want to see him?"

That clinched it, Rosie wriggled out of her hold and ran to the back door. Within minutes May appeared in the garden with a tray. There were two glasses of orange and a plate of cream biscuits.

Rosie was now up the garden on the swing Norman had erected for Rachel, and was swinging her legs frantically backwards and forwards enjoying the sensation of flying, showing no signs of fear.

May whispered. "She's a little wild, don't you think?"

"No, May, I don't. She was brought up on a fair, she's ridden rides since she could walk. Of that I'm sure."

May's next words made Tilly pale. "I hope her lot had nothing to do with that violence where you were staying in Cornwall? I heard it on the news, they say it was the show men and the travellers."

Trying to look nonchalant, Tilly asked, "What violence, May? I haven't heard anything."

"There was a big fight that broke out. Axes and meat cleavers. People have been hurt, badly. You know what they're like. The

25

police are involved, not that they'll do anything, they're a law unto themselves that lot."

Despite the uneasy feeling in the pit of Tilly's stomach, she paled saying as blandly as she could, "That's awful, May, but no, we haven't heard anything."

Tilly could see May knew she had unnerved her, and was enjoying having the upper hand as she added, "Ed said earlier there was trouble, I just thought, that was all. You don't want to be harbouring a child involved in that sort of violence."

"Trouble, yes, but not that sort of trouble." Wanting to change the subject she reached for the orange on the tray, calling up the garden, "Come on, Rosie there's a drink here for you, then we must get home, Granny A will wonder where we are."

Tilly watched as May bristled at the mention of Agnes being referred to as Granny A, and smiled inwardly as May tried to endear herself to the child, "Did you like the swing, Rosie? That belongs to Rachel, Ed's daddy put it up for her. You can come and play one evening, have some tea with us, and meet her if you like."

"Yeah may do."

Tilly took hold of Rosie's hand, and the two of them made their way home. Without looking round she knew May was watching them from the kitchen window.

May's news of the fight and the reports of such shocking violence made Tilly feel uneasy. Aware she was still being watched, and not wanting to give May the satisfaction that she had succeeded in unsettling her, Tilly started pointing things out to Rosie, laughing with her, trying to look like she had not a care in the world. Rosie shattered this act of bravado when she said quite simply, "The mister's mum don't like you, Tilly."

*

26

Tilly brushed Rosie's hair, pulling it into a ponytail, "I used to wear my hair like this at your age, sometimes I'd have pigtails."

"I like one tail, like a horse. I can feel it bounce."

The phone ringing in the hall caused Tilly, to shout to her gran, "I'll get it, gran, don't worry."

"Hello, Bognor 3125."

"Hello, Tilly, it's May. Rachel said this morning she would go to Sunday school after all. Can you pick her up for me on your way? Norman's gone to the allotment, and you're passing..." She didn't get to finish.

"Yes, May, that won't be a problem. Rosie 'll be pleased of the company."

"Lovely, thank you. See you soon then."

The phone went dead. Agnes had made her way to the hall, "Who was it, love?"

"Only May. She wants me to pick Rachel up when I take Rosie to Sunday school. I didn't think she liked it, but there you go. Who am I to question anyone?"

"Now, now, Tilly, don't be like that. It doesn't become you to be sarcastic. May has been a lot better with you lately."

Tilly knew this was true. She couldn't be sure if it was the fact they now had Rosie, and Rachel loved her, or the fact that their Sunday afternoons were now spent at May and Normans so the girls could play. Either way Agnes was right things were getting easier. There was still the odd spat between the girls, but in general they seemed to have found a friendship. May and Norman shied away from being called Nanny and Grandad and had adopted the names of Auntie May and Uncle Norman.

27

"Do you want to come round with us, Gran, you can wait with May and have a cuppa?"

"No, love, I've got curtains to finish. It takes me longer and longer these days. I can't keep drinking tea either, I can't hold my water like I used to."

"Oh gran, you do say funny things."

Tilly wished her gran would give up the sewing, it seemed too much for her these days, "Did you know, Gran, they're building more bungalows off the Fairlands estate? You could sell up here. Ed and I would manage to find somewhere."

"Stuff and nonsense, I love living here with you, especially having Rosie join us. That was a stroke of luck you were there like you were."

At the mention of that fateful day, thoughts of moving were forgotten. "Oh Gran, it wasn't lucky at the time, I was terrified. I'm only glad that trouble May went on about has not come to anything. I bet it was Rosie's lot though."

"Now you don't know that. I told you at the time not to worry. Even if it was Rosie's family it wouldn't affect us. Rosie's safe with you, and she's settling in much better than we could have hoped for. When you first brought her in, her eyes were as wide as saucers in her little face, she looked so frail and frightened."

Tilly laughed at her Gran, she was always so positive. "Gran, one thing Rosie isn't, is frail and frightened. She has been raised as a wild child, but I love her, Gran, I love her already."

"I know, love, so do I, and so does Ed."

Rosie came down the stairs with the belt of her dress dangling at her sides, "I can't do it, Tilly."

"Come here, turn round." As Tilly tied a bow in the frock she told her they were going to pick Rachel up for Sunday school.

Rosie, turned round, face indignant, "I don't want her to come, Tilly, not to school."

Tilly, knew Rosie loved Sunday school. Mrs Parry the teacher, had said Rosie was enthralled by the stories and the pictures she put out to colour.

"Rosie don't be unkind. Rachel has not gone with Uncle Norman today so she can come with you as your friend.

"Well I don't want to sit with her. She keeps touching me and trying to kiss me. She's alright when we're playing, she forgets, but when we're listening to stories she can't leave me alone."

Tilly ran her hand down Rosie's ponytail like her own mother had done to her, laughing, "You're a funny little thing. Is that why you pushed Rachel off the sofa the other day?"

"Yes, I told Auntie May what she's like, but she still told me off."

Tilly was lost for words. Rosie wasn't one for cuddles and kisses. She would accept a kiss from her, Ed and her Gran, but that was about it. Of an evening Rosie would rather sit curled in a chair on her own rather than perched on someone's lap.

Agnes had taken herself back to her sewing. Tilly called out, "We're off now. I won't be long. I'll not stay at May's."

Rosie broke free of Tilly's grip, "I want to show Granny A my dress." She rushed into the sewing room to do a twirl. She kissed Gran's cheek, saying, "Bye, see you later. I'll do you a picture."

Sunday school was held in the hall at Westloats. Tilly pushed Rosie round to May's, sat on her bike. It was difficult as Rosie kept leaning to one side making the pedals hit the side of Tilly legs. Tilly could drive now, having passed her test. It was at times like this she hoped Ed would either sort her out a car, or put a child seat on the back of her bike.

May was waiting at the gate with Rachel. "Thanks, Tilly. I could get Norman to pick them up if you want?"

"No it's okay, May, I'm not busy. Ed's sorting out the garden with Ken. They're moving the last of the stuff to Chichester."

"You are still coming for tea? We've been baking, haven't we, Rachel?"

Rachel ignored the question, so busy was she trying to climb on the bike that she just called out, "Bye, Mummy. Come on, Tilly, it's my turn." Rachel was already trying to climb up on the saddle.

"Don't worry, your cooking won't go to waste, May, Ed's almost finished and I'm sure we'll make yours by the afternoon."

Once the girls were settled in the hall, Tilly rode home.

*

"I'll put the kettle on, Gran. Do you want a cuppa?"

"No ta, love, I've got a bit of indigestion."

Watching Agnes rub her shoulder caused Tilly alarm, "Are you alright, Gran?"

"I've got a bit of a pain, too much sewing over the years I think."

Tilly didn't like the sudden loss of colour from her cheeks. "You don't look so good, Gran, you look a bit grey. Shall I open the window, or get a drink of water?"

Agnes attempted to laugh, "Grey by name, love…"

Tilly watched in horror as Agnes buckled over gasping for breath, unable to finish her sentence. Tilly leapt to her feet, giving Agnes' shoulder a gentle shake, saying over and over, "Gran, Gran - Gran…"

Tilly managed to get Agnes through to the lounge, and settled on the sofa, but the pain was persistent, which showed in her struggle to breathe.

"Lay still, gran, I'll phone Geoffrey."

Tilly was glad at times like this that she had worked for the doctor's family. She was on first term names with both the doctor and his wife, Dorcas. Tilly knew Geoffrey would be happy to give advice. Once she had placed the phone back down she sat at the side of her Gran, "Come on, Geoffrey says to loosen your clothing and sit you up. He's going to pop round. Are you feeling better?"

When Agnes made no comment Tilly added, "If the pain doesn't go off Geoffrey says I'm not to wait, but to phone an ambulance."

Tilly wasn't sure if it was the threat of the ambulance, or she really was feeling better, but the colour came back into Agnes' cheeks as she found her voice, "Nothing wrong with me that a good dose of Andrews won't cure. It's my own fault, I shouldn't have eaten those hot jam tarts out of the oven earlier, they must have given me indigestion that's all. Now don't go making a fuss please."

Tilly brought in a cup of sweet tea, "Has the pain eased, Gran?"

"Yes, love, don't you go worrying about me, you go and get Rosie. You don't want her left at the hall like unwanted baggage."

"No, Gran, I'll wait for Geoffrey. Dorcas said she'll pick Rosie up with her brood, and get a lift back home with Geoffrey when he's examined you."

Agnes started to protest, "What about Rachel?"

"Gran, it's all sorted - stop worrying."

Within minutes Geoffrey arrived. Tilly hovered in the doorway wanting to hear first-hand what was said.

"Your pulse is a bit fast, but that could be the excitement."

He gave Tilly a wink as he took her blood pressure, "Agnes, have you had many turns like this?"

Tilly was alarmed to hear her gran say that of late she had been struggling. She put it down to the position of leaning over the sewing machine. She explained her eyesight was really deteriorating these days, which meant she leant over at an awkward angle for long periods of time.

"I think, Agnes, your sewing days are numbered."

Tilly remained silent as Geoffrey got out a light and shone it in Agnes' eyes, one at a time, "You've got cataracts on both eyes, Agnes. I'm surprised you can see what you've made, let alone make it."

Tilly interrupted, "I have just told her there's no need for her to keep working. Ed earns enough for us all now."

"Well let's get Agnes settled in bed. The afternoon up there will do her good. Tomorrow I'll organise for her to see both the cardiac and eye specialist. We'll make a new woman of you yet, Agnes, you'll see."

With Agnes settled upstairs, Tilly had questions of her own, "Geoffrey, is gran going to be okay?"

"I think, Tilly, her heart is giving her a warning. She'll need monitoring, but don't worry, I'll sort out her having a full medical tomorrow. As I said we'll make a new woman of her."

"Is it serious though?"

Geoffrey's frown made Tilly nervous, "Well obviously it's not good, Tilly. The heart is a major organ, and when it isn't working properly you have to be concerned. I do think though, her sewing days should be over. Could you really manage on just Ed's wage?"

"Yes of course we will, I don't know what mortgage is left on this house, but we'll manage."

"What about your new addition? I hear you're looking after a little girl for a while. Surely that'll mean you won't be able to work. Will you?"

"No, Geoffrey, I wasn't planning on it, but if I need to I can. I could get something at the school. I'll speak to Ed first, he'll know if it's necessary or not."

"Our Gordon's smitten with this little girl you have acquired. Dare I ask how you came by her?"

Tilly was pleased to have this conversation, she wanted the doctor on her side. "Oh Geoffrey, when we were on our honeymoon we met this fortune teller, I won't go into it all but she seemed to take a liking to Ed, she said she could see things. I know it sounds crazy but the next day I went too. There was trouble there, big trouble. Cutting a long story short, she ended up begging me to take her daughter for her, to keep her safe."

"How, and when will she get her back, Tilly?"

"I don't know really. She told Rainbow to look for the rainbow. She has a very colourful tent with brightly coloured streamers flying from the roof. It's where she reads people's hands."

"So her name is Rainbow, the child."

"Yes, but we changed it to Rosie. While she's with us we thought it would help her fit in. Don't you agree?"

"I do, yes. Are you happy having someone else's child, Tilly? You've only just got married."

"I love it, Geoffrey, we both do. Rosie's lovely." Tilly looked embarrassed, "You know I can't have any of my own… you know… after what we did. This is like a second chance."

"Tilly, you could adopt, have a baby from six weeks old. It could be legally yours and Ed's. Wouldn't that have been better?"

"It sounds perfect, Geoffrey, but Rosie needs us. I want her now. It probably sounds silly to you, but we love her already. All of us, even Ed's, mum and dad have accepted her now."

"I can see you do, Tilly, but you love all children. Look what you were like with our lot."

"Geoffrey, I want to do this. I want to settle her into school as a first year, even though she's six next month. She's never been to school and I want her to start from scratch. Can you help me?"

"Of course I will, but how can I help?"

"I need some sort of form to say she's ours, for a start."

Tilly watched as Geoffrey scratched his head and pushed his hair behind his ears, "I'll get you a written document of guardianship. I'll do it tomorrow when I sort out your gran. If you pop to the surgery I shall have a look at the child medically, and ask a few questions. If all seems as you say, she'll be yours, Tilly. That is, until her mother comes looking for her, whenever that might be."

"Thank you, Geoffrey, thank you so much."

The noise from outside indicated Dorcas was making her way with the children.

*

Agnes stayed in bed for the rest of the day. Tilly phoned May, explaining why she couldn't leave her gran. She went on to say they were welcome to come round to theirs if they wanted. Tilly had

34

expected May to decline, giving a polite excuse but was surprised when she had accepted, saying, "We'll be round about three. Norman says he'll help Ed and Ken with any clearing left to do."

They arrived on the dot of three. May had brought a Victoria sandwich which she had baked that morning, along with some scones. Rachel had two gingerbread men she had made, one each, for herself and Rosie.

The two girls went off together, content to play in the back garden unperturbed by Agnes' heart scare.

Tilly knew the change of plan suited Ed. He and Ken had almost finished the clearing, and both were grateful of Norman's help. The business was now run from Chichester, making Agnes' back garden redundant. Ed and Ken had a warehouse with Barrett and Jarmes Wholesale Fruit and Vegetables printed across the door in bold blue letters. They sported a logo on the back of their lorry that read 'For Barretts Best and Jarmes Juiciest Buy Locally.' Their telephone number was printed underneath and orders came in and work flourished.

Tilly made sandwiches with May's help. The plates of food were placed on the small table in the kitchen. She felt a prick of embarrassment when May said, "Shall I lay up the dining table and take some of this food through?"

Tilly could only ever remember the dining room being used as a sewing room, and her mum, gran and her had always sat round the small kitchen table for as long as she could remember.

Rising above the awkwardness, she told May they would have to eat with their food on their laps in the lounge, adding, "Can you lay a blanket on the floor for the girls, please?"

If May thought it was undignified she never made a comment and no looks were noticed. Agnes ate very little, but conversation flowed. The afternoon passed in pleasant tones.

Chapter Three

The Birthday – July 1966

Tilly hung out the washing, she was pleased with the garden. It was now laid to lawn with a little area of paving slabs outside the front of the French doors.

There was only one greenhouse left now, a reminder of Ed's early dreams of a market garden. These days everything Ed and Ken sold was bought in from the London market.

Carrying the empty washing basket down the path her mind wandered to Rosie's party. They were to believe from Rosie her birthday was in July, and Tilly and Ed had decided it would be the Sixteenth. It fell on a Saturday this year, but it suited them all to celebrate it on the Sunday.

Tilly was hoping to hold the party outside. She had turned her hand to making bunting, which she was going to hang on the side of the shed and across the French doors. They had managed to borrow a pasting table so the children could be seated and The Newtown had lent them a few chairs.

*

Tilly sat with Rosie, pen and paper in hand, "Who do you want to invite to your party, Rosie?"

"I don't want Gordon, but I'll have Mandy."

"No, darling, there are some people that have to come. Mandy is fine, but you can't exclude Gordon or the twins."

"I want Hannah."

Tilly was pleased. Rosie and Hannah seemed to have clicked together like Tilly had done with Cathleen so many years ago.

Tilly folded the invites and handed them to Rosie to put in the envelopes, "Is there anyone else you would like?"

"No, just you, Granny A and Ed."

"Darling, there will be other adults. Auntie May and Uncle Norman. Hannah's big sister, Cathleen. She was my best friend when I was your age and still is. Not forgetting Ed's friend Ken, who's also Cathleen's fiancé, she'll want him here, too."

"What's a fincy?"

"Not a fincy, a fiancé. It's someone who you've promised to marry."

The party forgotten Rosie was curious to know about Cathleen and marriage, "Why do you get married?"

"So you can live together and have children."

"My mum didn't get married, and she had me."

"Well, Rosie, my mum didn't get married and she had me too. Perhaps we get married because we love the person so much that we want to belong to them, I don't know. I married Ed because I loved him."

"Do you want children too?"

"I've got you, Rosie… for now, and of course I would love to have children, but we can't always have what we want." Trying to distract her she said, "Come on, let's get these invites done and prepare some games for the party.

*

The Birthday Party - Sunday 17ᵗʰ July 1966

Agnes stood in her old sewing room, it was unrecognisable from her working days. Gone were the machines, free standing hangers and materials. In its place was a long dining table laden with party food.

She had given up the sewing on doctor's orders. Ed had bought the table second hand, and it had come with six chairs. This action had wiped out so many of Agnes' memories of her years toiling over a sewing machine. She wasn't sorry, she was already feeling the benefit to her health at not having to stoop over, trying to thread needles and bobbins. Agnes rubbed her fingers, *'Yes, it's a relief those days are gone."*

Tilly broke into her thoughts, "Are you alright, gran?"

"Yes, love, I'm fine, you've made a good job of clearing out this old room."

"No more pains in your chest, I hope?"

"No, love, Geoffrey's given me those pills, they work like magic. You enjoy the party, don't you go worrying over an old woman like me."

Tilly moved over to take Agnes in her arms, "Gran, you mean the world to me, I shall always worry about you."

Agnes returned Tilly's hug. Rosie interrupted the moment, "Tilly where's that big parcel with all the newspaper wrapping?"

"I've got it all sorted, you just worry about welcoming your guests and being on your best behaviour with Rachel and Gordon, no fighting, remember."

Agnes listened as Tilly told her how Rosie said if Gordon tries to kiss her today she was going to punch him, "Honestly, gran, you should have seen her dancing on her toes with her little fists up. She said, Me Uncle Jimmy taught me." Tilly did a little demonstration

39

for Agnes causing her to laugh out loud. She was so pleased to have her granddaughter living with her again. Having Rosie join them as a family had been a bonus too.

Rosie was on her best behaviour, and the party went well. The weather remained sunny and all the party games were played outside.

Rosie relished in the attention, and the little gifts she received all caused a lot of excitement. When they did the egg and spoon race, Rosie was delighted to beat Gordon, who seemed to drop his egg more times than he managed to carry it.

Rosie and Rachel paired up to do the three-legged race, they fell over within the first few steps tangled together giggling. May stood at the side laughing at the chaos, she seemed relaxed with the happy atmosphere. The garden was alive with cheering and laughter. Ed, caught up in the moment, wrapped his arms round Tilly and kissed her ear.

Once Tilly had got Rosie to bed she joined Ed and Agnes, who were busy tackling the clearing up.

"That went well, everyone seemed to enjoy it."

Ed held out the tea towel to her, "It did, Tilly, you did us proud, didn't she, Agnes?"

"Yes you did, love, that'll certainly be a day to remember. Rosie appears to be warming to affection too. She seemed quite happy holding hands and running with the others, in, 'What's the time Mr Wolf?'"

"I know, gran, those games never seem to go out of fashion. I can remember playing them in the playground too."

Ed broke into the memories, saying, "I'm going on up. I've got an early start, it's my turn to go to London. It's alright for some" He kissed the top of Tilly's head saying, "Night, my lady of leisure."

Tilly returned his kiss, saying she'd be along once she'd cleared the kitchen of uneaten food. She turned to Agnes, "If you're tired, I can manage here, gran. It's been a long day for us all."

"Nonsense, I'm fine. You're all treating me with kid gloves these days. I'm not going to collapse with a little washing up you know."

Tilly put uneaten food into boxes, "I'm hoping to take Rosie to the beach tomorrow if this heat continues. Do you want to come? You can sit in a deckchair."

"No ta, love, I can't bear sitting in the heat. I shall be fine here. You go off and enjoy the beach while it's quiet. The kids will be breaking up soon.

＊

Pam could see May making her way up the garden, it looked like she had stripped the bed sheets. The linen was spilling over the wicker basket.

"Morning, May. Glorious, isn't it?"

"It is that. My new neighbours are moving in Friday. A George and Florrie Coffin."

"That's good, May. I bet you're glad it's not some young, rowdy family?"

"I am, Pam, but these old houses have solid walls. It probably wouldn't have been a big problem. George and Florrie are brother and sister, they seem a nice couple."

Pam got to her feet, "How old are they?"

"I'd say they're both in their sixties."

Pam, changed the subject. She pushed her hair out of her eyes with her forearm, and said, "This is hard work, I've never been one for the garden."

May puffed out her bosom. "Give me the garden any day, I love it. I'd rather be outside than doing house work. The upstairs needs a good dusting too."

Hannah was happy running up and down the lawn with a hoop. This action changed Pam's train of thought. "Wasn't it a lovely party Tilly did, May? Hannah loved it. Rosie's such a little love, isn't she? Your family's growing."

"She's not really my family. They're only looking after her. I'm hoping her mother will come and claim her soon. It doesn't feel right to me. I can see a lot of pain down the road, can't you?"

Pam sighed, "Yes that must be a worry for you, May. But they'll cope, I'm sure."

May seemed genuine with her concerns, there didn't appear to be any nasty jibes when she added, "Yes, you're probably right, but it feels so unnecessary to me."

"Oh May, Rosie's an infectious little thing, everyone loves her. Even my Cathleen's taken to her. I think she's going to ask Tilly if Rosie can be a bridesmaid with Hannah. Now that says something doesn't it?"

As soon as the words left Pam's mouth, she could have bitten out her tongue. Her neighbours face said it all. Pam tried to back track, "Nothing's settled of course, it was just a thought."

She knew what was coming before May opened her mouth, "Rachel would like to be a bridesmaid, I'd be happy to pay for the dress. It wouldn't be fair on Rachel if only Rosie was chosen."

Pam's heart sank, how could she say what she knew without causing more pain?

"It isn't for me to say, May. You know how headstrong Cathleen is. I'll mention it to her, but it's her day, remember."

This comment had May throwing the peg bag in the wash basket without saying goodbye, Pam caught May's angry retort as she turned her back "I can't stand here all day. I've got bedrooms to clean."

Pam knew she had upset her neighbour, her body language said it all. She was annoyed with herself, she had hurt May's feelings. The trouble was, she knew Cathleen wasn't planning to have Rachel as a bridesmaid. The subject had already come up before Rosie's arrival.

Pam knelt back down to tackle the weeds again, Hannah jumped on her, clinging to her neck. "Careful, darling, Mummy's back can't take it."

"I want a party like Rosie, mummy, can I?"

Pam was aghast at this sudden thought. She knew Hannah would be four on the 30th July, and the day after, Cathleen would be twenty. What with Cathleen's wedding in October, she was hoping to get away with a small family tea, "Not this year, darling. Rosie only had a party like that because she'd never had a birthday before. We'll do you one like that when you're five."

Seeing the disappointment on Hannah's young face made her feel guilty. *I'm not having a good day today, I'm upsetting everyone.'* Pam decided to give up weeding, 'Come on, love, let's go round to Tilly's, you can play with Rosie. She said yesterday that we might go to the beach, that'll be good, wont it?"

"Can we go to Cathleen's shop and have a drink with her?"

"We'll see what Tilly's doing first, and if the café isn't busy we'll try." Pam was pleased the talk of parties was forgotten for the moment.

*

Cathleen wandered into the garden to find her mum and Tilly sitting in deckchairs. Tilly was dressed in short shorts, a little vest top, and bare-feet with a silly sun hat perched on her head. The seaside shells, pebbles, buckets and spades that lay scattered on the lawn told Cathleen they had all been to the beach. Tilly's sandy feet and sun kissed glowing face gave Cathleen a pang of jealousy. Hannah and Rosie were playing on the slide, still wearing swimming costumes. She was feeling hot and tired, and seeing Tilly playing happy families made her snap, "What's all this then? It's alright for some, I've been flat out in that café and in this heat too."

"It's only just gone four, love, you're early."

"No I'm not, mum. I told you this morning I'm working another one of those dinner dances tonight. I've got a couple of hours off, then I'll be going back."

"How will you get home? They don't finish till eleven."

"If Daisy's boyfriend picks her up, I'll cadge a lift with them, failing that, Ken'll pick me up."

Before anyone could answer, Hannah came rushing down the garden throwing herself at Cathleen's legs, "We've been to the beach, and had ice creams. Rosie can swim. She went in right up to her tummy, but I just paddled."

Cathleen softened, she loved her little sister. Then, looking across at Rosie who had wriggled between Tilly's legs, said, "That's clever, Rosie, who taught you to swim?"

Rosie promptly jumped up, rolling her arms giving a demonstration, "Me uncle Jimmy showed me. You've to pull your arms like this, just like a doggie."

Cathleen was going to correct her English but held her tongue. Not because she didn't think it her place, but she was so hot she couldn't be bothered. She flopped down on the grass in front of the deckchairs saying, "I'm glad you're here, Tilly, I wanted to go over some plans for the wedding. I've…"

Pam interrupted, "Not out here, Cathleen, I've something to discuss with you. I think I put my foot in it earlier with," Pam lowered her voice, "next door."

"Let's go in then, it's too hot for me out here in this overall."

The girls disappeared up the garden again, and Cathleen, Pam and Tilly went inside. No sooner they were all sitting in the cool lounge Pam explained how she had told May how Cathleen wanted Rosie to be a bridesmaid. Cathleen couldn't see the problem, shrugging her shoulders she asked, "So, why should she care?"

"She was hoping Rachel would be asked too. She even offered to pay for the dress, saying Rachel would love it."

"Oh god! What did you say?"

"Don't take that tone, Cathleen. It's obvious she wouldn't want Rachel to be left out, especially if you're asking Rosie."

"It's my day and I shall have who I want. Tilly do you want Rosie to be a bridesmaid?"

Tilly looked uncomfortable, "It would be lovely, but I don't want to stir trouble, Cathleen. I'm sorry but I can see why May wouldn't like it."

"Well you've changed your tune, I thought you hated the old bag and would love to give her some grief."

"Come on, Cathleen, things are a bit better between May and me these days. Think how upset Rachel would be too. Would it be so bad to have them both? The three of them get on well together, don't they?"

Cathleen's cheeks looked like they were slowly bleeding as her face seemed to change colour with the return of her earlier bad mood, "Is no one listening to me? I don't want her. And yes, Tilly, it would be awful. It's my day and I want it to be perfect. She would ruin the photos and…"

Before she could utter another spiteful word Pam stopped her in her tracks, "Cathleen! That's a horrible thing to say, you should be ashamed of yourself. And if you aren't, I'm ashamed for you."

Cathleen burst into tears, "I'm sick of this already. Why are there so many problems to getting married? Ken said yesterday that we could live at his mum's house when she moves to the Lake District in November, take over the tenancy. Yuck! Can you imagine it? Living in Collyer Avenue in that ghastly…"

"Go, Cathleen, get out of my sight until you calm down. I can't believe you could say such things. It saddens me. I knew we'd spoilt you, but I really thought since Hannah arrived you'd softened a little. I can see I've been wrong."

Cathleen stormed up to her room, not saying good bye to Tilly or acknowledging her mother's harsh words.

*

Seeing Pam's distress Tilly moved across and draped her arm across her shoulder, "Don't worry, Pam, she'll cool down, I've heard you say it's that red hair."

46

"I don't know, Tilly. What sort of a marriage are they going to have if she's too proud to live in Ken's childhood home? What must he think?"

"You know Ken, Cathleen can't do any wrong in his eyes, he's probably already trying to find somewhere that will make her happy."

"When I married Hal I would have lived on the moon if it meant we could be together. We've spoilt her and it's at times like this that we can both see the damage it's done."

Before Tilly could answer, Pam moved away to see what the commotion was down the end of the garden. "Look at them, Tilly, Rachel's joined them."

They were sat on top of the old rabbit hutch. The three of them looked like they were making believe they were on a ship. "I can't get over the wicked things Cathleen's said this evening, can you?"

"Come now, Pam, don't be too hard on her. I'm sure when she thinks about it she'll be the first to say it was not very kind. I suppose having such a big white wedding causes problems. It was easy for me, just a small do, with not even my mother attending."

Tilly, could see Pam felt guilty, "Don't worry, I was happy with my little wedding. Mum couldn't possibly fly all the way from Canada for the small gathering we chose to have."

"You're a good girl, Tilly, June did you proud. It's at times like this I feel Hal and I ruined Cathleen to the core."

Tilly looked at her watch, it was nearly five. "I must go, Pam, I've had a lovely day, but I must get home to gran, and start some supper for Ed. He shouldn't be too late. We have an appointment at seven with a Mrs Stroud, a teacher from the school in North Mundham."

"Really, aren't you sending Rosie to Bognor?"

"No, Pam, we've decided to send Rosie out of the area so she has a real fresh start without anyone knowing her. Both you and I know how tongues wag, and how cruel children can be. I think Rosie will do well there."

Pam laughed out loud, "Oh, Tilly, Rosie's able to hold her own. I think she'll do well anywhere."

Tilly called to Rosie that it was time to go. Rachel came running up for a cuddle asking if she could come too. Tilly returned the affection saying, "Another time, darling, I've got a lot on tonight and we've been out all day." Seeing the cross look on Rachel's face she added, "It's only one more week and you'll break up from school yourself, then we'll all go out."

"Mummy too?"

Tilly didn't relish the idea, but managed to smile, saying, "Of course, darling, if she wants to." Before any more awkward questions could be asked Tilly held out her hand to Rosie, "Come on, we must get going, Gran will wonder where we've been all day."

*

Cathleen could hear her mum and dad downstairs and guessed they were discussing her. They had called her for dinner but she had ignored them. *'Hurry up, Ken. I can't be late for the café.'*

As if her thoughts summoned him she heard the front door knock. Cathleen ran down the stairs calling, "Leave it, it's for me." She grabbed a light jacket from the peg, Pam met her in the hall, "About earlier I…"

"Not now, mum, I shall be late for work."

Cathleen closed the front door behind her without a goodbye to any of them. As she climbed in the car she leant over and kissed Ken.

"Evening, you're pushing it a bit tight. I'm not meant to arrive at six, I'm meant to start at six!"

"I'm busy, Cath, its summer. You should learn to drive like Tilly. You could use the van when it's not needed like she does."

"Don't call me Cath, I'm Cathleen. Don't start on me either, I've had an evening of it."

Cathleen was annoyed as Ken laughed, "You're touchy tonight. What's eating at you?"

"That stupid May Barrett wants me to have Rachel as my bridesmaid. I've said no I don't want her, but you would think I'd committed a crime."

"What's the big deal in having Rachel, Cath?"

"Cathleen! I'm not going to answer you if you call me that, I hate it. I don't want Rachel. She'll spoil my photos. I want my day to be perfect. I've said Rosie can if she wants, but Tilly said it wouldn't be right without - her next door."

"I'm sure Tilly didn't use those words, Cath-leen. But I think you're being mean. There, I've said it, and while I'm on it, it's my day too not just yours."

"Let me out here, I'm sick of all this. At this rate you'll be lucky enough if I even marry you at all."

"Come on, Cathleen, calm down. Mum say's everyone argues over their wedding day, and it'll all unfold, you'll see. We'll have a perfect day."

Cathleen knew when she threatened not to go through with the wedding Ken softened. She gave way to tears causing Ken to pull over, "Now, now, come here."

Cathleen rested her head on his shoulders, "Everyone thinks I'm being mean. I'm not, Ken, the thing is I just want my sister as a

49

bridesmaid. I only asked Rosie, what with Tilly being my friend and all. I was trying to be kind."

"I know, sweetheart, I know. Come on, dry your eyes."

Cathleen felt Ken's hand brush above her skirt, finding the soft flesh of her inner thigh, "Stop that, it's no good teasing yourself. I'm saving myself for the wedding night."

Cathleen knew she was driving Ken mad. She couldn't be like Tilly and give herself to Ken before she had a ring on her finger. She wanted it to be a true white wedding in every sense of the word. When Cathleen had told Ken that her mum would take her to the family planning clinic before the wedding there had been another row. Ken had said it would be nice to just see if a little one followed. Cathleen had reared up saying she didn't want a family for at least five years, telling him she had only just got her figure the way she wanted it.

Ken persisted in his plight up Cathleen's skirt. She pushed his hand away, "Stop it, Ken, I'm going to work. I'm not in the mood anyway."

"No you never are. Sometimes I don't think you love me like I love you. I ache to hold you and love you. This waiting is driving me insane."

"Don't start that old trick, trying to blackmail me into it. I'm waiting till after the wedding, and if you love me like you say, you'll feel honoured that I'm not easy."

"Easy, Cathleen, you could never be called easy on any front."

"Just take me to work, Ken. I've had enough."

Ken pulled up outside the café. "I'll pick you up at eleven."

"Don't bother, Daisy's in tonight. I'll cadge a lift home with her and her boyfriend."

She leant over and kissed his cheek. He looked sad but she didn't care. He was like an adoring puppy dog. She looked over her shoulder and gave him a brief wave as she walked in with Daisy.

*

There was a big crowd in with every table taken. It was Mickey Millers band and they were always popular.

Cathleen was busy filling coffee and tea pots when Daisy came into the kitchen calling, "There's a chap at the far table near the band asking about you, Cathleen. Say's you used to jive with him?"

Cathleen pushed open the kitchen door to see if she could glimpse who she was talking about, but the room was filled with people and smoke.

"What did he look like?"

"Blonde straight hair, swept back with cream. Good looking, Cathleen, I know that!" Daisy plated up some mints that were to be served with the after dinner drinks, "Here, take these out and see for yourself."

Cathleen took her hairband out and pulled her fingers through her red wavy hair. She placed the band back on her head, pushing it forward giving a pretty kink at the front. She tweaked her cheeks, which brought a bit of colour to them. Taking the plate from Daisy and holding her head high with an air of importance, she made her way across the room. As soon as she got within sight of the table she knew it was Michael from the Newtown jive classes. She hadn't seen him for about three years. Michael and Joe had ridden scooters back then, and she had once got on the back of Michael's, while he sped up and down South Way breaking the thirty mile speed limit by far. Before she could place the mints on the table Michael looked up saying, "Well, well, our waitress. What a nice surprise." He looked at his mother who had stopped her own conversation to see who her son was speaking to, "Mother, this is Cathy Kay, as I call her. We used to dance together at the jive classes in Bognor. You remember? Me and Joe used to go every Friday night."

Cathleen witnessed the look of dislike cross the snobby looking woman's face, "Yes, I sort of remember." Looking at Cathleen she said, "Put the plate up here please, thank you, dear. If you don't mind could you run along and bring a bottle of champagne for later. We're celebrating Michael's forthcoming engagement to Christine."

Cathleen felt a pang of disappointment. She glanced up and down the table. There didn't seem to be any spare ladies, everyone seemed to be in couples. Not wanting, nor liking the put down she said, "Really! How exciting, where is this lucky lady, I ask?"

Her comment fell on deaf ears, Michael's mother had already dismissed her.

Cathleen felt a pinch on her bottom, she jumped turning round to see Michael smiling, "Christine's poorly. We're here with the family. The plans are we'll be married next spring. They own stables in Petworth. What about you?"

"I'm marrying Ken, do you remember him we were dance partners. He runs his own fruit and…"

"Not curly Shirley?"

Michael's laughter rang down the table. This not only angered her but embarrassed her too. Cathleen's cheeks flushed red as she jumped to his defence, "He's done well for himself actually. We're getting married at the end of October."

"Touchy, touchy. I was only teasing." Changing the subject he said, "Didn't your mum have a baby?"

"Yes, Hannah, she's lovely. She'll be four at the end of the month."

"Does she go riding?"

"What, horses?"

"Der… yes, horses! What did you think I meant?"

Cathleen hated the way he made her feel foolish, when all she wanted to do was impress him, "I don't know… no, she doesn't ride. Why do you ask?"

"Bring her down to my stables, I'll give her a ride on one of the small ponies. She'll love it. You too if you like."

The thought that he wanted to see her again caused goose pimples to spread over her body as excitement replaced anger, "I just might do that. You're in Hunston, aren't you?"

"That's us – Forresters'. You can't miss us, it's on the main road."

Cathleen caught sight of him looking down the table at his mother's frown. Not wanting another run in with her she said, "I'll catch you later."

Cathleen went back to the kitchen but she couldn't settle. Her hands shook, and her stomach jiggled with nerves. She felt sixteen again.

By ten o'clock the work was done and the girls were allowed to go and have a dance. Cathleen grabbed Daisy's hand, "Come on let's show those old 'Fuddy Duddies' how it's done."

Cathleen took to the floor. She was a good dancer, ballroom and jive. She knew she moved well, and had a good figure. Daisy was shorter and plumper which made Cathleen stand out as stylish and elegant. Cathleen could feel Michael watching her from his table, which made her wriggle her bottom in her tight skirt in an exaggerated way. The song hadn't finished when she saw him making his way over.

"Excuse me, young lady, can I take over?"

Cathleen felt her knees go weak as he took her in his arms for a waltz. She nuzzled in his neck. The smell of him was nostalgic, and it felt good. She had the urge to look up into his eyes so their lips could meet, but she guessed his mother was watching them.

"We dance well together, Cathy Kay, don't you think?"

His use of shortening her name pleased her. It gave them more familiarity, and she loved it, "We do, Michael, we always did."

"Have you thought anymore about coming to the stables for some riding lessons? I'll give you the first hour free, you and your kid sister."

"I don't know, Michael. You're engaged and I am too, it feels a bit dangerous."

"Live dangerously, Cathy Kay, it's what makes for a fun life. We're only young once. Don't you believe what the eye doesn't see the…?" He didn't finish his quote. Cathleen interrupted him, "Can I bring Tilly? You remember her, she was my best friend. Tall, Blonde, much quieter than me."

"I do, yes. Joe liked her for a while. Didn't she go off the rails a bit?"

"No, not Tilly. She went to Canada to find her dad. She's married to Ed, Ed Barrett. They have a little girl they're looking after, Tilly could bring her with Hannah."

"Oh bring who you want, it'll be good to see you out of here."

The music changed and they played The Seekers 'I Know I'll Never Find another You' Michael edged them out of sight of his mother's table. They started jiving, and every time the song got to the lyrics, 'I know I'll never find another you' Michael sang it in Cathleen's ear. She felt alive for the first time in ages. She wanted Michael to kiss her. Good sense deserted her as the music filled her ears. The two of them swirled in time to the music as if they were the only couple on the floor.

"When will I see you again, Cathy Kay? Will you make Saturday? I'll be at the stables all day, please say you'll come."

Cathleen leant her body into his, she felt the need for support. The excitement that swept over her made her legs turn to jelly. She wanted the evening to last forever. She hadn't felt like this with Ken - ever.

"I'll sort something out. Tilly can drive now, she'll bring us down if she can get the van. If not we'll catch the bus."

When the music stopped Cathleen knew she should return to her work. There was nothing she had to do until the room cleared, but she felt they were all watching her. They knew she was to be married in the autumn, she could imagine their whispers already.

"I'll see you Saturday, Michael, promise."

"Give us a kiss, for old time's sake? Just a quick one, no one's looking."

Cathleen ached to kiss him, to feel his lips on hers. Her body felt like it was already his. These were new feelings for her. She now understood what Ken meant when he said, 'the want is painful'. Michael made Ken seem dull and boring in comparison. Lifting her head to Michael's, their lips met in the dark corner of the room. If anyone could see them, at that moment Cathleen didn't care, she couldn't care if the whole world watched. It felt like fireworks were going off in her chest. *This is what love feels like. I just know it.*

When his hand moved round and clasped her breast she tilted her hips in to his, feeling the arousal between his legs. In that split second she felt everyone vanished, they were the only people in the room.

Cathleen kept herself busy clearing the now empty tables. Michael had left taking the excitement with him. A pang of guilt and embarrassment washed over her. *'What will the girls be saying about me in the kitchen?'* Cathleen now wished Ken was picking her up. She knew it would be awful sitting in the back while Daisy's boyfriend drove her home. *'I bet she'll tell him about me. Say Ken hears, oh god this is awful.'*

Before Cathleen could torture herself any longer she heard Daisy call, "Come on, Cathleen, you can see your face in those tables. Ron's waiting outside, and we've finished for the night."

Cathleen was glad of the quick escape. She ran to the cloakroom, grabbed her coat and met Daisy in the doorway, "Thanks, Daisy, this is really good of you."

"Don't be daft, girl, we're going past your road."

Cathleen sat in the back listening to Daisy talking about the evening. Not one word was said about her behaviour. It felt like Daisy had forgotten she was in the back.

Ron pulled over, right outside her house, "There you go Missy."

Daisy opened the door, pulling the seat forward so Cathleen could climb out, "Cheerio now, see you tomorrow."

"Yes, thanks, Daisy. Thanks for the lift, Ron."

Laying in her bedroom she replayed the events of the evening. The excitement didn't return with the privacy of her room. She groaned as she thought how she had behaved, *'How could I? Jesus I must have looked like a right old slag.'* Shame lay like a sack of potatoes, heavy on her chest. She rarely prayed, and only if she wanted something. Tonight was one of those nights. She put her hands together and clasped them under the covers, 'Dear God, please, please don't let Ken hear how I've behaved tonight, and I promise I'll never ever see Michael again. I won't go to the stables on Saturday. God please let this be forgotten by everyone at work too. Please let them not have noticed, and if they did, let them think I'd just had a bit too much to drink.'

When she had finished she felt just as wretched. Thinking God would listen better if she wasn't under the covers, she got out and knelt down by her bed repeating her prayers over and over until she felt calmer.

Cathleen arrived at Lesley's Café early. If the girls were talking about her behaviour last night, she didn't want to witness the sudden silence as she walked in.

By mid-morning nothing had been said and Cathleen began to think perhaps her feelings of guilt were unwarranted. The question that plagued her, was, should she go on Saturday or not? She wanted to but her conscience pricked. *'I could just go and explain that I'd had too much wine with the girls and got a little tipsy.'* Then she asked herself *'Why do I have to give an explanation? Michael's a stranger to me these days. I'll just forget all about him, that's it, end of story.'*

"Penny for them, Cathleen" Daisy stood before her, "Come on, it's our tea break. You're normally the first one up there."

"Thank you very much, you make it sound like I'm a right ole shirker."

"Truth hurts."

As they made their way up to the tea room, she was sure Daisy's laughter would be heard in the shop.

They sat eating iced buns, and drinking tea when Daisy said, "What's going on between you and that fella who was here last night?

It felt to Cathleen like her eaten iced bun had found its way back to her throat, this made her gag, "We're just friends, we go back a long way." Feeling uncomfortable she picked up a teaspoon and stirred her tea even though she didn't take sugar, "It was good to see him, but I was never keen on him like that. It's always been Ken."

"You could have fooled me, I thought you were going to eat him."

Cathleen was always pale, her red hair determined that, but she paled even more, "Don't say that, Daisy, someone might hear. I had a little too much to drink. I can't remember much. Was I that bad?"

"No, I'm only teasing. Jealous more like. What a dream. I was hoping you were going to tell me some juicy gossip."

Cathleen decided to keep her hand close to her chest and say no more on the subject. It didn't stop her mind see sawing with, should she go on Saturday or shouldn't she? No sooner had she talked herself into not going she thought about why she should go. The decision was taken out of her hands when Daisy said, "I have a great whacking big favour to ask of you, Cathleen. I know it's your weekend off but I'm desperate for Saturday this week. Please say you'll swap with me, you can have my Friday, and my weekend next week."

Cathleen's mood changed from excited turmoil to disappointment. Her mind had been made up for her by the powers that be. Trying to keep her voice light, "Yes that's okay. It won't be a problem. Ken works Saturdays anyway."

Cathleen didn't know whether to be pleased or not. The nervous energy that had had her running around like a cat on hot bricks, dropping and spilling things, had finally disappeared over her cup of tea and iced bun. She only knew one thing for sure, and that was all her earlier anticipated excitement had been replaced with what felt like a gloomy black rain cloud.

The Rainbow

Chapter Four

The Forresters'

Cathleen's deflated mood would not lift. It didn't matter how many times she told herself it was for the best, she couldn't quell the deep yearning to see Michael again. To feel that thrill of being kissed. Ken kissed her but not like that. He was always trying to maul her, which of late had started to feel revolting. With Michael it had been different. The evening of the dance, she would have given herself to him if the setting had been right. When her good sense returned she had asked herself over and over, *'How could I have behaved like that?'*

It wasn't until the weekend, when she had overheard her parents discussing Hannah's birthday that a little excitement returned. Cathleen's mother had said, 'what with the wedding round the corner, Hannah could just have Rosie and Rachel for tea.' It had given Cathleen the opportunity to say she would take them all horse riding at The Forresters'. She had sensed her mother's delight at this show of kindness. Even more so because she had included Rachel. Cathleen knew it helped in a small way towards forgiveness over her not wanting Rachel as her bridesmaid. She had tried to explain it had nothing to do with Rachel's condition, and that she only wanted her sister behind her on her big day, Rosie had only been an option because Tilly was her best friend, and she had wanted to please her. Cathleen had stressed how sorry she was if she had offended anyone, but if it was going to cause all this trouble she would just have her sister, Hannah.

Her idea to take the girls riding had helped heal the bad feeling enormously. She only hoped Michael hadn't written her off when she hadn't shown up yesterday.

Hal had offered to drive them all there, saying how pleased he was that she was prepared to give up her weekend off, for her sister.

Cathleen had declined not wanting her father anywhere near the place. "Tilly will drive us, dad. They'll enjoy that, all in the back of the van."

When Cathleen ran her plans by Tilly, it turned out that they couldn't use the van, it would be needed for the Saturday deliveries. They had decided it would be fun to catch the bus and get off at Mundham corner and walk down. It wasn't far, and the excitement it had caused between the girls was amazing. Rosie had claimed that she could ride a horse already, and that her mother owned a horse called Black Jack. She had given them all a hilarious demonstration by using the arm of the chair as a pony. No one could say whether this was fabrication or not, but as Tilly had said, one thing Rosie didn't seem to do was tell falsehoods.

Cathleen's nervous excitement made her tongue sharp, and guilt made her feel low. But the thrill of seeing Michael again drowned out the opposing feelings, causing her to flit about unable to sit still for two minutes. Time had dragged, and the nervous energy she had used up on this dilemma had taken her appetite. Her sudden weight loss was put down to pre wedding nerves.

The week dragged and when Friday night arrived, Cathleen hadn't been able to sleep. She had chastised herself, '*What's wrong with me?*'

She had eventually drifted off to sleep, only to wake before day light with the feeling that she was about to sit an exam. She hadn't managed any breakfast, and her stomach rumbled as they waited at the bus stop. The girls held hands skipping in a circle, unable to contain their excitement. When Tilly said, "You look nice, is that a new pair of jeans?" Cathleen had felt uncomfortable.

They were flared at the ankles, and tight on her slim hips. Her beige and cream checked shirt went well and she wore a waist coat that had an orange flower stitched on the pocket, it matched her orange belt. Cathleen had always been a follower of fashion, so it was easy to pass off her smart appearance. "No, I bought them for a party,

61

but we didn't go. This is all I had that was suitable. I don't look over dressed, do I?"

"No, you look lovely. You make me feel a right scruff though." Tilly changed the subject, "Is this the stables that Joe and Michael used to talk of at jive classes?"

Cathleen's heart skipped a beat. She tried to sound nonchalant, "Yes, Michael's family own them. It's funny, I bumped into him at the dance a couple of weeks ago. He said we could have some lessons, it seemed like a good idea for Hannah's party treat. Mum had said she couldn't be doing parties this year what with my wedding."

"You didn't say you'd caught up with him. Do you remember when Ed and I split for a while? It feels like years ago now, I must have been about fourteen, fifteen. Not waiting for an answer from Cathleen, "I think Joe was quite keen on me."

"Do you know, Tilly, Michael said that. Did you like him?"

"Oh Cathleen, Ed is my one and only, you know that. I was in a state of depression back then, all because Ed didn't ask me to help him in the garden when I left school?"

"What was the big deal in that?"

Oh god, I sulked for weeks. Then we had that blow up and parted, but I never stopped wanting him, never."

"You had it bad, Tilly. I was always out for a bit of fun. Ken sort of grew on me."

"He thinks you walk on water, Cathleen. He thinks the world of you, you know he does."

Cathleen wanted to say she thought the same about him, but the words stuck in her mouth like a sour grape. Luckily the bus came at that moment and the conversation changed as the girls scrambled on the bus, heading for the back seat, pushing each other as they ran.

If Michael was shocked to see Cathleen, he hid it well.

"Oh, so you decided to come after all. Which one is your kid sister?"

"This one here." She pushed Hannah forward. "It's her birthday today." She then introduced Rosie and Rachel, and was also impressed that Michael appeared to take Rachel's Down syndrome in his stride, and when Rachel took hold of his hand he led her towards the horses, saying, "You can ride Smokey, he's one of our favourites." He gave Cathleen a wink, which caused her to hold on to the gate post for fear her knees might buckle under her.

The girls were all on horses, including Tilly. Cathleen chose to watch, she was hoping to have some time with Michael alone to explain that as lovely as it was to see him the other week she wouldn't normally behave so wantonly. She questioned whether she was planning to bring it up for the right reasons. Part of her wanted to hear him say he had enjoyed it as much as she had.

She watched as he led Rachel out of the paddock on a leading rein. It looked to Cathleen like he was going to stay with them, and she now wished she had said she would ride too. She had to admit Tilly looked good on a horse. Cathleen had forgotten how her friend had ridden at some stables in Canada. She couldn't help but feel envious at Tilly's easiness in the saddle. Her eyes strayed to Rosie, she trotted with ease out of the paddock proving what she had told them was true, and by the looks of it, it was likely that she had ridden before she could walk. Both Hannah and Rachel were unable to ride alone and were on leading reins. Cathleen felt excluded as their chatter and giggles echoed across the field. She tired of watching them having fun at her expense, and wandered round the stables looking at the horses poking their heads over the stable doors. She bravely stroked their noses, talking to them, lost in self-pity. She jumped when she felt a pinch on her bottom. As she turned she came face to face with Michael, who said, "I've got them settled on the top field with Lucy, she'll look after them. Now to pick up where we left off the other week."

"Who's Lucy, Michael?"

He draped his arm round her shoulder leading her into one of the empty barns that held the feed. "Lucy works here, she's a stable hand." He changed the subject, "You look fantastic, Cathy. You've got a real sexy body."

Her conscience gave a little prick, "Michael, I'm engaged remember, and as your mother pointed out the other night, so will you be, come December."

"Don't be so stuffy, it doesn't suit you, Cathy Kay. A lot can happen between cup and lip."

The thought of Cathleen telling Ken she wasn't going through with the wedding was just being processed when Michael took her in his arms and kissed her long and hard. She melted into him as good sense left her."

Within minutes they were laying in the straw, her with her shirt pulled out of her jeans which with a bit of resistance from Cathleen, had been undone at the waist. When Michael put his hand down her lace knickers, she tried to slow his eagerness. "What's the matter, isn't this what we both want?"

She had dressed for this moment, and now it was happening she wasn't sure. Ken and Cathleen had indulged in some serious heavy petting, but this felt too fast. She was about to tell him she was still a virgin and wanted to stay that way, when a little voice at the door interrupted the moment with, "I want the toilet."

Cathleen jumped up, she turned her back on Rachel so she wouldn't witness her trying to tidy herself. In her haste, the buttons on her shirt were done up all skew whiff.

Rachel giggled, "You have straw stuck in your curls."

"Where are the toilets, Michael?" Cathleen brushed wildly at her hair tucking herself in as Michael pointed to the left. "Come on, Rachel, it's the next door along."

Cathleen was at a loss for what to say. *'Did a child like this understand?'*

She toyed with the idea of not saying anything, but was frightened that Rachel might blurt something inappropriate out of the blue. She knew she had to explain in some way. Cathleen laughed a little too loud, "Did you see me just then? I was laying in the straw, Rachel."

"I saw you kissing Michael." She joined in with the laughter, "I like kissing too."

"No, Rachel, we were not kissing, it just looked like it. I lost my necklace and was looking for it. I slipped and Michael fell on top of me. It looked funny didn't it?"

Rachel's face took on a look of defiance, "You were kissing him. I saw you." She covered her eyes up and said in a shy squeaky voice, "He was touching your private place too." Once Rachel had said this she giggled behind her hidden face.

Cathleen hated her. Her voice came out in slow threatening tones, "Now you listen to me, Rachel. You're not to ever say that to anyone, do you hear me?"

Rachel started to cry, she had picked up on Cathleen's anger. "I want Tilly, I don't like you."

Cathleen got down on her knees and held Rachel by her arms, fearful that she would run. She tried to lighten her voice, so desperate was she to get this child to promise silence, "Look,

Rachel, I'm sorry, really sorry. I didn't want to frighten you. You frightened me that was all." The child's tears subsided, Cathleen drew comfort that she seemed to listen. Whether Rachel knew how important this was, she couldn't be sure. "What you saw, Rachel, wasn't what you think. If you ever, ever say anything to anyone, you'll be called a liar. Do you understand what that is?"

Fear shone in Rachel's eyes making them look like saucers in her round face. She didn't seem able to find her voice, so shook her head up and down.

Cathleen was feeling a little more confident, she sensed she had this child's attention. "If people think you're a liar, Rachel, your new mummy will not want you, do you understand that?"

Tears filled Rachel's eyes as she nodded her head up and down again.

Cathleen softened her voice, "Now, do you remember you wanted to be my bridesmaid?" When Rachel said nothing, Cathleen prodded further, "Well, do you…eh?" She was relieved to see another nod of the head, "Well if you keep this a secret, a special secret just between you and me, I shall let you be my bridesmaid with Rosie and Hannah. You'd like that wouldn't you?"

Cathleen was pleased when Rachel threw her arms round her neck saying, "Can I wear a pretty dress too, one with puff sleeves?" It appeared that Rachel had forgotten just how hateful Cathleen had been only minutes before.

"You'll wear the same as Hannah and Rosie. You'll look lovely." Then feeling the need to instil her warning she said, "You're not to say anything about that little kiss with Michael though, you do understand…"

Cathleen didn't get to finish, Rachel said, "I don't care who you kiss. Can I go now? I want to tell Hannah I'm going to be a bridesmaid. Thank you Cathleen. Thank you, thank you. Can I kiss you?"

Cathleen let Rachel give her a sloppy kiss. In the process she tried to make it look like kisses were not important.

"People kiss all the time. Kiss, Kiss, Kiss." Cathleen kissed and blew raspberries in Rachel's neck making her squirm with ticklish laughter. She couldn't bring herself to remind Rachel about the fondling she had witnessed, so left it there hoping Rachel really had forgotten it all with the prospect of being a bridesmaid.

Holding Rachel's hand as if nothing untoward had happened, Cathleen managed to get herself together and walk back over the field to find the others.

Michael had disappeared. She was grateful for this, it felt like a small mercy. Rachel kept talking about the bridesmaid dress she was going to wear, the one with the puff sleeves.

As the girls came into view, Rachel jumped up and down shouting, "Guess what? I'm going to be a bridesmaid just like you two."

Tilly gave a quizzical look at this turn of events, saying, "Cathleen, have you had a change of heart?"

"Yes, I didn't realise until today what a cute little thing she is. The three of them do all get on well too, don't they?"

"Cathleen, that's really good of you. May will be chuffed to bits, and so will your mum."

*

Ken came down stairs to find Alf and his mother eating fish and chips out of the paper, watching television. Ken punched the air, "Did you watch the match? Wow! What a win for us, beating Germany."

Alf looked up, his mouth shone with grease, "Geoff Hurst was brilliant, wasn't he? What a match for the queen to witness too."

Ken wasn't worried about the queen, he was delighted for England. Another thing that had cheered his day, was he had managed to get Ed to watch the game at the Wheatsheaf. These days Ed shied away from drink. Ken had managed to convince him the atmosphere would be better watched in the pub.

Ken had bought the first round, and once there, Ed had shrieked and cheered with the rest of them. When Bobby Moore held up the World Cup for England, the whole pub had gone crazy.

Watching the game had taken Ken's mind off Cathleen. He hadn't liked the idea of her going down the stables, but she had been set on taking Hannah and the girls riding. Not wanting to look churlish he had given in graciously with the thought of being able to watch the match on her day off.

It was Cathleen's birthday tomorrow. Ken was taking her to Fontwell. There was a big country fete in the field.

His mum brought him back to the present, when she said, licking her fingers, "The chippy van came round tonight love, we didn't get you any. You usually go out of a Saturday night."

Ken leant over and kissed his mum's cheek, pinching a chip in the process, "That's fine, but they smell good."

Alf laughed, "They taste even better. You can have a bit of mine if you like?" Ken loved to see how happy his mother was these days. The memory of living with his step dad Harry, was now a distant nightmare.

"No ta, Alf, Cathleen and I are off to see Alfie at the cinema tonight. We'll get fish and chips after the film if she fancies."

"Have you thought anymore about where you'll live, love, after the wedding?" Ken knew his mother was hurt at Cathleen's rude outburst about not wanting to take over the tenancy of their home after the wedding, "No, mum, I'm thinking of a flat in Chichester. It'll be nearer my work too."

"What about Cathleen's work? She'll have to catch a bus."

"We'll see, mum. She's a bit touchy at the moment. I'm a bit worried about her."

"Oh, Ken, we're all like that before the wedding. We women get the wedding jitters. Marriage is a big step, you know."

"Okay, mum, you know best. I better get round there for her or I'll be starting off on the wrong foot tonight as well."

He could hear the two of them laughing as he closed the front door. He wondered what his mother really thought of his marriage. Cathleen rarely made a visit to his home. *'She's never eaten dinner here, ever. She always came up with a plausible excuse.'*

This detrimental thought of the young woman he loved, put him in a disgruntled mood. He parked his van outside her house and made his way to the back door, "Come in, Ken, Cathleen's just getting ready. They've had a wonderful time today. The best news is that Cathleen's decided Rachel can be a bridesmaid too. It'll be the three girls. Isn't that wonderful? I knew my Cathleen had a heart in there somewhere."

If Ken was surprised he hid it well. He did think it was a turn up for the books though. Breaking into his thoughts Cathleen appeared, looking ravishing, "Wow!" Cathleen looked fantastic, "What sort of day have you had?"

Cathleen draped her arms round his neck and kissed him full on the lips in view of her mother. "You know - so, so. Missed you though."

Ken welcomed this show of affection, unaware that it was fear and guilt that had instigated it. "I hear you've been building bridges with Rachel. That'll please a lot of people including Ed."

Ken didn't realise it, but her back had gone up as she thought, *Who cares about Ed bloody Barrett, she's not his real sister anyway.'* Instead she smiled, saying, "She's a real cutie, we had a wonderful day. Tilly's booked Rosie in again for next Saturday, she's a natural in the saddle, and I can tell you, Tilly's a good rider too."

"What were you like?"

"I just watched them all. Ridings not for me, but I loved the horses."

Ken felt foolish now. He had tormented himself all week with thoughts of the two young men from those stables who had tried their hardest to woo Cathleen away from him at the Newtown dances, years ago.

"Come on, let's go, Ken. They'll be a huge queue. It's Michael Caine."

Ken didn't realise how her stomach had turned at the sound of the name Michael on her lips. He followed her out of the house as she called, "Bye, mum, dad. Don't wait up."

Once Ken and Cathleen were on their way to the cinema, he had to ask the question, "Did you see either of those clowns from Jive, who came from down that way?"

He felt foolish as Cathleen laughed, "Ooh do we have the green eyed monster raising his ugly head?"

"I'm only asking. You know what they say, Cathleen, no jealousy, no love."

Once parked she leant over in her seat and gave him a long lingering kiss. "I love you Ken. I'll be married to you in three months' time, surely you don't worry about them anymore?"

The kiss had aroused other feelings. He groaned inwardly, "I ache to have you, Cathleen."

"We'll go somewhere quiet after the film. I know I've been a bit neglectful of you of late. It's a lot of organising, getting married. Can't you see the weight I've lost? Everyone's noticing it."

"You look gorgeous to me. Perfect. I pinch myself every day to make sure I'm not dreaming. I'm a lucky, lucky, man, Cathleen. You could've had the pick of the bunch."

"You're very eligible these days you know. What with your own business."

"Partners remember. Ed owns half." He liked the compliment, they were few and far between from Cathleen's lips, "But yes I've done alright really, even if I say so myself."

He fell sideways as she pushed him in the arm, "Steady on you won't get your head out the van in a minute."

They went into the film laughing and came out arm in arm. Ken found a secluded spot where they lay in the back of the van like old times, exploring each other's bodies. Ken knew the boundaries and had accepted that three months was not a long time to wait now, in the scheme of things.

He pulled up outside Cathleen's house a good hour after the film finished. "I love you very much, Cathleen, you do know that, don't you? When she leant over with closed eyes he added, "Thanks for a lovely evening. I feel like we're getting back on a better footing again, instead of rowing all the time."

He watched as she opened the front door with her key. He liked to think he had seen her home safely. He was unaware that sitting on the hall table was a message by the phone in her mother's hand writing, saying quite simply – *'A Michael phoned for you this evening.'*

*

The Rainbow

Chapter Five

New Beginnings

Agnes knew half the house belonged to her daughter June, Tilly's, mother. When June had left for Canada, Agnes had assured June, that when she died she would leave her the property. At the time June had been so excited to be reunited with Stanley, she had said, "Don't be daft, mum. This was your home with dad. I know I'll have it one day, but I don't want to think about that."

That is how it had been left. Agnes had remained in the house that both, June and Tilly had grown up in.

When June had got herself in the family way with a married Canadian soldier during the war, Agnes and June had found their way with a sewing business. It had proved very profitable. They had managed to get a mortgage when Tilly had been about eighteen months old.

Agnes held the phone to her ear listening to the phone ringing down the line. She waited with butterflies in her stomach. June could be a little hot- headed, and with all these miles between her and her daughter she didn't like bad feeling between them. Stanley answered, which made Agnes' heart sink, their relationship had never been easy. But she had been forced to admit, that when Stanley's wife died, and he had found out that he had fathered a child eighteen years ago, he had wanted June back in his life, as well as his daughter. June had left for Canada taking Tilly with her, it had broken Agnes' heart.

"Hello, Stanley. It's Agnes. How are you?

"Good, Agnes, Good. How's our Tilly. Is married life suiting her?"

Agnes didn't want to make small talk with Stanley. She hated the phone at the best of times, but calling Canada was expensive. Today she wanted the time to discuss business that needed careful handling.

"Stanley, is June around? I really need to speak to her."

Agnes could hear muffled voices echoing through their house and footsteps coming closer, "Hello, Mum, what's up? Tilly's okay isn't she?"

"Yes, love, Tilly's fine."

Agnes told her how her heart was failing, and that she was on medication now. She updated her with the news on Rosie, telling her Tilly would be sending her to a little primary school in a village called North Mundham, come September.

"Mum, what is this call really about? You wouldn't phone at this time of day to just pass niceties."

"June, I know you own half the house, but I was hoping you would agree to let me sell it, so Tilly, Ed and I can buy something nearer to Rosie's school. I can't manage the stairs so well these days and Tilly and Ed have agreed that we could buy something with a room on ground level."

"Couldn't you just get a smaller place, mum, and let Ed and Tilly make their own way? I'm sure they would prefer that."

"No, love, I've put all those options to them. Even offering to help them out financially. Ed is doing well here, June. He has his own business. I think the plans are we'll buy a bigger home, and Ed will

73

get a mortgage. I didn't want to offer the house without speaking to you."

"Mum, that's fine. You know in your heart I won't be coming back to England. My life is with Stanley, now. I would have loved it more if Tilly had stayed here with us, but I have learnt she has to make her own way."

"Are you saying you don't mind if I help them get started? I was going to give them the house as a deposit. It will be a wonderful start for them all."

"Mum, it's absolutely fine. I'm here with Stanley. I don't need anything else." June was still curious to hear news on the child that was now living with them, "How's this little girl settling in... Did you say her name is Rosie?"

"Yes, that's what Tilly named her. They're wonderful with her. You would think she was theirs. She's settled too. As I said, Tilly's given real thought to her first school. She's starting in September as a first year, but already Tilly's taught her to write her name, and she can now recognise the letters of the alphabet. I reckon she'll be a bright little thing given the chance."

"What about her mother though, mum, what happens when she wants her back?"

"Who knows, love? For now Tilly's very happy. I've learnt not to look too far down the road. If I'd known that one day your Stanley would call for you again, I'd have lived seventeen years in pieces."

"Oh mum, please don't say that."

"Sorry, love. I'm okay really. I'd love to think you'd came back for a visit though, before I curl my toes up."

This was not how Agnes wanted the phone call to end. It had gone so much better than she had thought, "June, love, I'm happy for you, honestly I am. Thank you so much for being so reasonable over the house. You'll not miss out, you'll get my savings and that's a tidy penny."

"Mum! I don't want to think about it. If Tilly needs it I'd rather she had it. After all she's looking after you."

Agnes didn't add, 'my thoughts literally.' She was so happy at June's generosity, that she brought the conversation to an end. She sent her love to them all, even Kevin, Tilly's half-brother who Agnes had never met.

*

Agnes smiled at Tilly's youthful display of excitement. It made her eyes sparkle. "We've seen the perfect house in Hunston, you'll love it, gran. It has a room downstairs that'll suit you fine. Save you climbing all these stairs."

Rosie was caught up in the excitement too. There was a play park opposite the house, and next door had two girls aged six and eight.

Agnes was looking forward to seeing the house that Tilly and Ed had set their hearts on. When she had voiced her concerns that North Mundham or Runcton would have been closer to the school, Tilly had pooh pooed the idea, saying, "This house is perfect, gran. Ed said he'll buy me a little car if needs be, and if not, Ed's put a seat for Rosie on the back of my bike, so I could cycle if I wanted.

"What about when it rains?"

"Gran, stop worrying! The next door neighbour says the children from the village all walk to school together, and if it's pouring with rain they catch the school bus that stops just steps away from the house." Tilly had paused briefly for breath, "Come on gran, smile, it's perfect, it has everything, including the stables up the road." Tilly had looked at Rosie, and the two had giggled, their love of horses had connected them further.

When Agnes got to see the house, she knew it was indeed perfect. Her room on the ground floor was large enough to take two arm chairs, her book case and a few other odds and ends of her furniture, as well as her double bed. It was as Tilly had raved, like a little bed sit without a kitchen.

*

Collyer Avenue

Brenda twisted her engagement ring on her finger, round and round worrying, unaware that Alf was watching her.

"For goodness sake, Brenda, what's the problem?"

"I don't know, Alf. I can't help feeling uneasy about the things Ken was saying last night."

"He's a big boy now, Bren, you can't sort out his tiffs."

Brenda fidgeted in the chair unable to sit still, "Alf it's not normal for them to be having these sort of arguments, surely?"

"Look, Cathleen's made it clear she doesn't want to live here after they're married. Ken's said he's happy to rent somewhere, you can't do anymore."

"It's not just the house, it's this trip away. I know Ken isn't happy about it. Fancy going to Blackpool for a long weekend with a friend from school, rather than be with your fiancé. I'm sorry, Alf, it doesn't feel right to me."

Alf rubbed his chin in thought, "I know what you're saying, Bren, but we're older and wiser. Times are changing, the youngsters want more these days."

"Yes, I know, and I hear you, and part of me understands that…" Brenda started twiddling her ring again in nervous angst, "Ken is so besotted with Cathleen, Alf." Brenda paused, looking for the right words, "I think I'm just so worried he's going to get hurt. I try to like the girl, and I do... Not that I see much of her. Oh, Alf, she has a way of making me feel beneath her."

"You can stop that now. You are as good as she is any day, better in my eyes. And your boy, Bren, has more than proved himself. Cathleen's a waitress for god's sake, there's nothing special in that, that's if we're looking to score points?"

Brenda didn't like this turn of attack, it was not what she had wanted, "Alf there's nothing wrong with being a waitress..." Alf interrupted her, "I know that, Brenda, but you need to remind yourself of it when you get these silly thoughts in your head. I'm tired of this now. Cathleen's going away for a weekend with a friend. Ken will have to deal with his insecurities, not you. They don't want this house, well that's no skin off our noses. We were only trying to help them. It wasn't Ken, Brenda, you know that. Let's leave it there, can we? I can't bear to see you this unsettled."

"Oh, Alf, I know you're right. It's just Ken and I..."

"Brenda, no more. Ken will make his way. Their wedding is a couple of months away, and then it'll be our turn. Let's put all your energy into that, please." Alf's voice softened, "Come on, come over here you old softie, Ken and Cathleen will be fine, you'll see."

*

Friday 26ᵗʰ August 1966 – Blackpool

Cathleen dressed with care. She had packed a small vanity case which carried everything she would need for a couple of nights away. Everyone believed when she finished her Friday shift she was meeting up with an old school friend, and staying in Blackpool for a long weekend.

When Ken had asked too many questions, there were rows, which ended with Cathleen having the last word, "For goodness sake, Ken, it's a little hen night. I don't intend to live in your pocket. We're in the 1960's."

When Ken had kissed her goodbye it hadn't dispelled the unsettled, bad feeling between them.

Cathleen stood looking at herself in the long dressing mirror. Her suitcase swore deceit at her feet, making her feel jittery. Nervous excitement made her green eyes shine. *'How am I going to get through today?'*

Michael was meeting her at Chichester bus station in his little MGB. It was a red, soft top sports car, her stomach did somersaults at the thought of getting a ride in it. Tilly and Ed were moving today, and she knew Ken was going to help. Everything had worked out well, there was no chance of him seeing her with Michael.

Cathleen broke three cups at work, had been on the toilet twice, and by the time her shift was over it felt like her stomach held a bag of kittens.

The day had dragged. The excitement and anticipation of her weekend ahead had taken her appetite, yet it didn't stop her empty stomach rumbling with hunger.

The bus was on time, which Cathleen was grateful for. She felt conspicuous standing with her overnight bag, and she was sure she looked as guilty as she felt. Once sat on the bus, making her way to meet Michael she felt easier.

Cathleen was prepared for what she knew would result in an active sexual weekend. Their first love making had been hurried, and unplanned with neither of them using contraception. Cathleen not

78

wanting to take any more chances, had broadened her shoulders, born the blushes, and asked at the Chemist for some contraceptive pessaries.

When the bus got held up at the railway gates just outside the station, Cathleen could see Michael's car, he was there already, waiting. She could visualise him, his hair neatly creamed back, sporting the latest fashion. He was tall, broad, and brown from working outdoors with the horses. Cathleen knew she loved him. This weekend she would tell him. She would get him to beg that she should marry him instead of Ken. What a life she would have, married to someone of means. Cathleen knew now, she had been foolish to set her sights at Ken. She had always said she would not let herself get tied down to soon. If her mother hadn't got pregnant again, causing such an upset, she knew she wouldn't have looked at Ken as a lifetime partner. The more she thought about it, the clearer it became. *I've been bulldozed into this forthcoming marriage, and with Michael's help I'll find the strength to escape it.'*

Michael threw Cathleen's case in the little boot, while she settled herself in the front seat. She did feel grand. She wished she had one of those white scarves that would fly round her head as the wind whipped in the open top car. Cathleen had seen this many times on films, and thought it looked so romantic.

The journey to Blackpool had no scarves, but the little car was filled with their laughter. Michael had one hand on the wheel and the other across Cathleen's shoulder. She knew this was what love felt like.

The boarding house wasn't as grand as Cathleen had hoped, but it looked clean, and was far enough away from prying eyes.

They checked in as Mr and Mrs Forrester, making Cathleen tingle with pride. When the young girl behind the desk gave them their key, Cathleen could feel her envy.

Once in the privacy of their room, Cathleen looked at the basic accommodation that didn't even have an en suite. There was a small wash basin in the corner next to the bed, "Michael! You can't swing a cat in here, where are we meant to bathe?"

"Ooh, little miss snobby, there's a bathroom on the landing. Come here, I wasn't planning to spend my day in the bath… unless of course you were joining me."

Cathleen felt foolish, she laughed as he took her in his arms and threw her on the bed saying, "I'm going to ravish you all weekend, you little beauty."

Cathleen thought of the pessaries in her case. She knew she should insert one, but so caught up in the moment of urgent passion, the good sense that had flashed across her mind flitted out just as quick.

The light was disappearing when they eventually ventured from their room. Down in the foyer there was now an older woman manning the reception desk. Michael spoke, "We're popping out for fish and chips, what time do we have to be back?"

The woman was small, and thin. She wore those half lens glasses, and looked over them with a sour expression, thin lips pursed. Cathleen could feel her disapproval. It was obvious she knew they were pretending to be married, and the Woolworths wedding ring she had bought wasn't fooling anyone. The woman's clipped reply left no doubt in Cathleen's mind that she could see right through them, "The doors are locked at eleven, breakfast is served at seven thirty till nine." She turned her back on them putting their key on the hook.

Embarrassment made Cathleen giggle, Michael broke the rude dismissal with, "That sounds great, see you soon. We didn't want to be out all night anyway."

Once outside laughter bubbled out of them like a shaken champagne bottle, "Wow, Cathy Kay, what an old battle axe."

"Oh Michael, she's scary, isn't she?"

"No, she's just jealous. Can you imagine anyone wanting to make love to her?"

This comment had them both in hysterics.

They bought fish and chips on the promenade. Cathleen felt she ought to offer to pay, after all, Michael was covering the cost of the boarding house. When he accepted she couldn't help but feel slightly disgruntled, *'Ken never lets me pay for anything.'*

The thought left as quickly as it surfaced, and the two of them walked along the prom, eating, talking and laughing. A happy atmosphere radiated from them both. This matched the organ music and happy screams that came from the funfair as people flew through the air on dare devil rides.

"I'd like to have had a skinny dip, Cathy Kay, but with a full moon and all this activity I think we'd get arrested."

This made Cathleen laugh all over again, "Michael, don't you ever think of anything else?"

"I can't get enough of you. I shall miss you when you marry that curly chap next month."

"It's not next month, Michael, it's not until October..."

Michael interrupted her, "What difference does it make? By the end of the year I'll be engaged, and you'll be married."

This is what Cathleen had hoped for, she could feel the sadness in Michael's voice. She wanted him to feel she was the best fun ever. She wanted him to want her over this Christine, "Come on, Michael let's get back to the room before that old witch locks us out."

They ran hand in hand to the boarding house. Cathleen's cheeks were flushed from the run, but the real glow inside her was the fact that Michael had made it obvious he didn't want her to marry Ken.

Tomorrow she would tell him she would end her engagement, but tonight she would keep him guessing, she enjoyed his need.

Once in the privacy of their room, Cathleen rummaged in her case for the pessaries and discreetly went to the bathroom on the landing. She knew she had to be careful. Michael had made it clear he wanted her to marry him, and not Ken, but she didn't want anyone saying, "He had to marry her."

Cathleen jumped as the door tapped, "Who is it? I'm in here…"

Relief flooded when she heard Michael's voice, "It's me, silly, let me in. I thought we could share a bath?"

Cathleen quickly put her pessaries away, she didn't want to look churlish. She had pushed three high into her womb, hoping to kill off the earlier activity. She unlocked the door and Michael entered in a dressing gown. Amongst the bubbles, the two of them started giggling.

There was another tap on the door, it was Michael who called out this time, "Yes? I'm in here."

As soon as Cathleen heard the voice on the other side of the door, she knew it was the sour puss from downstairs, "I hope you won't be long, other guests use this bathroom, so please make sure you wash it out."

Cathleen held her hand over her mouth, such was the urge to laugh out loud, Michael managed to say, "Of course, won't be long." And they both slid under the water, their laughter making the water bubble.

Once in their room Cathleen enjoyed the familiarity and closeness that loving so intimately had brought to their relationship.

If their headboard was annoying the holiday makers in the next room as it knocked against the wall, they didn't care, so lost were they in the moment. Cathleen's euphoria was shattered when

Michael knelt up and swore, "Fuck me, Cathy, have you got something?"

Cathleen opened her eyes to see the whole of Michael's penis and pubic hair covered in a white foam. She realised what it was immediately and her cheeks coloured with embarrassment. The pessary packet had not warned of such a scenario, but she thought, *'Perhaps three was too many.'* Cathleen found her voice as Michael frantically tried to wipe off the sticky substance. It looked like he thought she had given him some deadly disease, "For goodness sake, Michael, it's only a contraceptive cream. I guessed one of us ought to use something."

"Bloody hell, Cathy, this is not funny. What is this stuff? I thought you would've been on the pill. You could have got pregnant. How safe is this fanny foam?"

It was one accusation and question after another. Gone was the happy carefree laughter. Cathleen was now near to tears, "Earlier it sounded as though you would like me to finish with Ken so we could get married."

Michael was on his feet now, standing completely naked. He was trying to find his toiletries bag, "Are you completely insane? I couldn't marry you even if I wanted to. I'm marrying Christine, they own the stables at Petworth. It's all set for the spring next year."

He left the room with his soap and flannel, making Cathleen feel dirty. Tears pricked her eyes. *'What a fool I've been.'*

When Michael came back his mood was a little softer. He took Cathleen in his arms, "Sorry about my reaction, but it was a bit scary. It looked like I'd dipped him in a pint of Guinness."

The laughter had gone from Cathleen, she could see as clear as daylight that Michael was using her, "Take me home, Michael, you've spoilt everything."

"Oh, come on, Cathy Kay. It was a shock. You wouldn't have liked it if your fanny looked like a foam bath, now, would you?"

"I took it into my head to get those pessaries to avoid an unwanted accident. You've ridiculed me, Michael. If you dislike the idea of marrying me so much, perhaps you should have worn a Johnny."

Michael ignored her argument, "You've been kidding yourself, Cathy Kay, this was meant to be just a bit of fun for us both. You understand, surely? Before we settle down…"

"Shut up, Michael, how could you? I thought you loved me, I love you. I wanted to finish with Ken, and marry you instead. You've made a fool out of me."

Cathleen was pleased to see Michael had the decency to look sheepish, "I'm very fond of you, Cathy, but…"

"My name is Cathleen, no one calls me Cath, Cathy or silly bloody Cathy Kay. I want to go home now. I don't want to stay a moment longer."

"Come on, Cathy…"

"Cathleen, my name is Cathleen, Michael, and I want to go home."

"Look, steady on, we can't go now, I've paid for the weekend."

"You're not listening to me. Either you get dressed and take me home or I shall start screaming."

Michael was annoyed, this was not how he had imagined his dirty weekend to pan out, "You always were a spoilt little bitch, Joe and I used to say your friend Tilly was much more personable."

Cathleen started screaming at the top of her voice. Michael jumped on her, holding his hand over her mouth, "Shut up, you silly cow, I'll take you home. Just shut your mouth, this is crazy."

Anger seethed through Cathleen, which helped her hold back the tears that were waiting to be shed. She bit his hand causing him to

84

pull away. By the look on his face, Cathleen knew he wanted to be rid of her. They both packed in unfriendly silence, the laughter gone.

Michael pulled up outside Cathleen's house just as day was dawning. She didn't care who saw her, she was desperate to get to the security of her room where she could think about how foolish and cheap she had made herself. Without looking round or saying a word she got her own case out of the boot and made her way up the path to her front door. Michael's parting words were like a punch in her already sore stomach, "Don't come hanging round the stables anymore. I don't think it's a good idea."

Before she had the key in her front door he was gone.

*

26th August 1966 - The Move

The removal lorry arrived at nine.

Agnes was staying with May and Norman for the weekend so Tilly and Ed could get organised. May had offered to have Rosie as well, but she'd begged to go to the new house. Tilly hadn't had the heart to disappoint the child. Things were easing between the two families since Rosie's arrival. Rosie and Rachel still argued, but seemed to have found their way together.

It was a glorious day for the move, and Rosie made friends with her new neighbours. They were all about the same age.

Ed had taken the day off and Ken was coming over to help in the evening. He had said it would take his mind off the fact that Cathleen was away on some hen night with an old school friend.

Tilly felt sorry for Ken, he loved her so much, and both Ed and Tilly felt she led him a sorry dance at times.

*

Ken arrived at seven. "What's left to do? You're looking quite straight already."

Tilly looked out from the larder, "It's an optical illusion I can assure you."

"Where's Ed, Can I give him a hand?"

Tilly had already started putting away packets and tins, "Yes, there's a garage at the bottom of the garden, he's out there." Tilly put her head back round the door calling, "Hey, Ken, take this box with you please."

Making his way up the garden he felt low. Tilly and Ed seemed to fall on their feet every time. They seemed so happy with whatever life delivered. Of late Cathleen worried him. It wasn't just that she was spending so much time at the stables, it was something bigger, and he couldn't put his finger on it.

If he questioned her she became defensive, and aggressive. He had spoken with his mother the other night, so desperate was he to air his concerns over Cathleen's time spent at these stables. She had defended Cathleen, saying, "For goodness sake, Ken, the girl's allowed to have some free time away from you. You want her to have her own interests, surely?"

The horrible feeling of insecurity had settled in the pit of his stomach, and he couldn't shift it. Ken was sick of everyone saying, 'It's just pre wedding nerves.'

He put the box he was carrying down in what felt like the only space left. There was no sign of Ed. The garage was full, there were boxes, carpets and crates everywhere. He could see it wasn't stacked properly and thought about trying to organise some space when Ed's voice made him jump. "It's a bloody mess isn't it? We haven't stopped. Come on, come inside, I'll get us a beer."

Ken raised his eyes, "Really? Sounds good. You drinking again?"

"Nah, but I like a pale ale. Nothing too heavy."

They walked back up to the house, Ken pushed open the back door to find Tilly on her hands and knees with her head in a cupboard, "We're coming in for a beer, Ed says he's had enough."

Tilly sat back pushing her hair away with her forearm, "That sounds lovely, do me a Shandy." Taking off her gloves she asked, "When's Cathleen back?"

"Sunday night, she's away for the weekend."

Ken wanted to question Tilly on the stables, but he couldn't find the right words, and he couldn't trust that she wouldn't tell Cathleen. He tried another tactic, "Do you know this girl from school that she's gone with, Tilly?"

Before Tilly could answer Rosie burst into the kitchen, her cheeks were flushed with excitement and her grey eyes shone making them appear blue, "Tilly, Tilly! We saw a foal born, it was all wet. She's brown, brown all over. They're going to call her Mars bar."

They all looked rosy from the walk back. Ken wiped his hands on his trousers as Tilly introduced him to her new neighbours. He held out his hand, saying, "Pleased to meet you."

He was fascinated to see the excitement on all their faces.

"It was amazing, Tilly, you should have seen it. She was on her feet in minutes. Sorry we were longer than we said, but we couldn't miss that."

Tilly picked Rosie up and popped her on the draining-board. "We were just about to send out a search party for you weren't we, Ken?"

Ken ignored this show of family life, it made him feel sad. He went into the lounge to find Ed already downing the last of his beer.

*

When Cathleen had told her mother she had had a fall out with her friend and come home early, she was pleased her mother had not raised too many questions, or none that Cathleen couldn't find an answer for.

"Why don't you go over and see Tilly later? They moved yesterday you know."

"No, I'm going to give Ken a call. He'll be pleased I'm home early, he didn't want me to go. I wished I hadn't now."

Cathleen didn't think she had any more tears left, but from nowhere big drops trickled down her cheeks.

"Come on, love, it can't be that bad. Why don't you give the girl a ring and say you're sorry. What was all the fuss about anyway?"

"It was nothing, mum, I just wished I hadn't gone. It's caused so many rows between Ken and I, I've wasted my weekend off, and I'm shattered."

Tears fell, and sobs escaped as Cathleen let herself be cuddled by her mother. Her soft voice was comforting to Cathleen's shattered heart, "Shush now. Come on, love." Pam kissed the top of Cathleen's head, "Why don't you phone Ken, and tell him you're home, I'm sure he'll pop round after work. He finishes at lunchtime on a Saturday, doesn't he?"

Between sobs Cathleen managed to say sometimes. She didn't want to face Ken, not yet. She needed to sleep, yet she couldn't switch off, so wretched did she feel.

Cathleen let Ken know she was back, but asked him not to visit. She had claimed she was unwell and needed to get herself better for work on Monday. It had been left she would see him then.

When Monday arrived, Cathleen had got herself together, but was far from well. There were dark shadows under her eyes that seemed to have sunk in her pale face. Her hair had lost its bounce and she hadn't eaten since the fish and chip supper on Friday night.

There were comments from the two older ladies at work, which Cathleen shrugged off. When Daisy came in she made a joke, 'If that's what a girly weekend in Blackpool does for you, I'll give it a miss. You look bleeding awful, Cathleen. Are you ill?'

Cathleen had managed a weak smile, but had cast her eyes down. She was so ashamed of herself. She felt everyone could see what she had been up to.

Cathleen didn't know how she managed to get through the morning. At ten o'clock when Daisy said, "Come on, Cathleen, pick a cake, it's our tea break." She had just followed Daisy up empty handed.

Once seated, Daisy had come back carrying two cakes and two cups of tea. "Now listen here, Cathleen, what's going on?" When Cathleen put her head in her hands saying nothing, Daisy continued on a gentler note, "Come on spit it out, something's going on. You're going to be ill if you're not careful. You've got to start eating for a start. You're not on one of those stupid diets, are you?"

Cathleen couldn't speak, it was all too much. Her heart was broken, she felt filthy, and this kindness she didn't deserve. Tears poured down her face. Daisy moved from her seat so she could sit beside her friend. She draped her arm around Cathleen's shoulders, her voice sounded weary as she asked in a pleading voice, "What is wrong, Cathleen? Don't you want to marry Ken, is that it?"

Cathleen shook her head, saying between sobs, "No it's not that. I feel dreadful, that's all."

"Are you preggers?"

This caused a little laugh, she shook her head, "No, Daisy, no I'm not pregnant."

"Well come on then, eat this bun, they're your favourite. You have to start eating something, you're going to waste away."

Cathleen knew Daisy talked sense, but her appetite had at first waned in nervous excited energy, to completely diminishing with desperate depression.

"I'm going to ask to go home. I need some time. If I look as ill as you say, there shouldn't be too many questions."

When Cathleen got home there was no sign of her mum, nor Hannah. She made herself a milky coffee, thinking *'Daisy's right, I must start feeding this body of mine'*

*

Cathleen arrived at the health centre at nine o'clock. There were three ladies and an elderly gent in front of her. She sat with a magazine, but her mind wasn't on stories.

She was still thanking the lord every night that Ken was unaware of her shocking behaviour. She knew it was more than shocking, she had cheapened herself. Her only fear was Rachel, she had witnessed that stupid tumble in the stable. Cathleen only hoped the threat of people calling her a liar, and the promise of being her bridesmaid would keep the child's silence.

90

"Cathleen Hills?"

Cathleen looked up from the magazine to see Doctor Covax looking at her expectantly. She stood up quickly, dropping the magazine on the chair behind her and followed him through to his room.

She took the chair without instruction, and watched as he wrote the date on her card, "What can I do for you, Cathleen?"

"My mum wanted me to come. I've lost a lot of weight lately and feel…" Before she could finish tears filled her eyes.

This didn't escape the Doctor. He placed the pen down giving her his undivided attention. His voice was low and soft. "You're getting married soon, aren't you?"

Cathleen nodded, unable to speak as tears fell unashamedly down her cheeks.

"You're not on one of these fad diets, trying to follow this Twiggy fashion, are you?"

Again Cathleen shook her head, this time she managed, "I just feel horrible inside. Sad, it's impossible for me to eat. I've been trying to have milky drinks to build me up a bit."

"Do you want to get married, Cathleen?"

She took the tissue he offered, and nodded, "I think I do… yes I do… It's just that we're arguing all the time, and, it feels such a big step. Sometimes I just want to run away… Does that sound foolish?"

"No, Cathleen, it doesn't. Many young brides and grooms feel like that. We call it getting cold feet. If you don't think you're ready to marry then it's better to pull out now and face the music, than live a life of wishing you had found the strength to speak up. Marriage is forever, you know how it goes – till death do us part, and all."

"I do want to marry Ken, I know I do, now…but," Cathleen had the urge to tell the Doctor what a fool she had been, but it was all so shocking she couldn't risk seeing his kind sympathetic face look down at her with disgust. When Cathleen offered no more explanation, the Doctor took on a different tone, "Now, miss, you need to start eating, do you hear me? You just wouldn't understand the damage you can do to your young body when you go on these fad diets. Just think about what you ask of your body in a day, it needs nourishment, Cathleen."

Cathleen watched as he scrawled on the card some unreadable notes. He looked over his half- moon glasses, "I could give you something to help you sleep. Would that help?"

"No, no - talking to you has helped, thank you. I feel I've wasted your time really."

"No you haven't, and if you don't perk up you must come back, I can run a few blood tests."

Once Cathleen was out in the fresh air, she felt better. She made her mind up that what had happened was a moment of madness. She told herself how lucky she was that no one knew and she could continue with her marriage plans. *Tonight when Ken calls for me, we'll get back on a better footing. I shall try and put right the wrong I've done.*

*

Friday 2nd September

"Come on, Rosie, I've said we'll meet Cathleen on the bus. We have quite a walk to Mundham corner."

Tilly put the last of the crockery away, hung the tea towel over the cleared drainer and went in to Agnes, "Are you going to be alright, Gran? We'll be gone for the best part of the day. When we finish shopping we're going to the warehouse and cadging a lift home with Ed. It'll be a long day for you on your own." Agnes puffed out her bosom, "Go on with you, girl, I'll be perfectly fine."

"I've asked the neighbour to pop in about lunch time, is that alright?"

"Oh Tilly, love, I don't want her in from next door. I know you mean well, but I'll be fine. I lived on my own for two years when you were in Canada, remember."

"I know, gran, but you weren't ill then, were you?"

"Tilly, love, these days I'm a lot better, I can assure you of that."

Tilly kissed Agnes on the cheek, "I'm sorry to fuss, gran, I love you so much. I couldn't imagine life without you."

"Go, go on. I don't want to hear any more of this nonsense. You get that little one kitted out with a school uniform."

Tilly lunged forward as Rosie ran at her, calling, "I'm ready, look."

Both Tilly and Agnes laughed at Rosie's outfit. She stood wearing black wellingtons, red shorts and a yellow woollen jumper. Tilly took hold of Rosie's hand, "Okay, gran. I'm going to sort out this pickle, then we'll leave to catch the bus. We've got quite a walk."

Tilly caught sight of the bus, clutching hold of Rosie's hand, she ran. It was lucky for them that there was someone else waiting at the bus stop or they would have missed it.

Once on the bus, a little out of breath, Tilly asked Cathleen how she was feeling.

"Much better thanks. I'm going back to work tomorrow. I can't take another weekend off."

Rosie had gone to the back of the bus with Hannah, and the two of them were kneeling up, waving out of the back window.

"Ed said Ken's been really worried about you, Cathleen. I think he thought you were having second thoughts."

"I don't know, Tilly. It seems such a difficult time, we argue over the silliest things. I'm trying, though..."

Tilly, watched, as Cathleen seemed to hesitate, and then stop. "Is everything alright, Cathleen? You do want to marry him, don't you?"

"I do, yes. But it's easy to feel confused. Didn't you have feelings of doubt, Tilly?"

"No, Cathleen, I didn't. There was no time for doubts. Once I got home from Canada, plans just took off. Ours was only a quiet do though, not like yours is going to be."

"How could you have been so sure that Ed was the one? You've never had another boyfriend. What about if someone else takes your fancy?"

Tilly had a funny feeling creep over, "Is there something you're not telling me, Cathleen?"

"No, I just wondered, that's all. I had lots of boyfriends when I went dancing, but you, you seem to have spent your life loving Ed. What if, that's all?"

The bus pulled into the station, bringing the conversation to an end. Tilly felt there was a lot more to say on the subject. Tilly, also had a horrible feeling, that with a little bit of privacy and time, Cathleen would open up, and they would get to the bottom of Cathleen's dramatic weight loss."

Cathleen looked at her watch, "How much longer, Tilly? I'm getting hungry, I've been told I have to eat, remember."

It was twelve o'clock. Tilly had bought Rosie what she felt were sensible clothes for school. Two grey pinafore dresses, two white shirts, socks and two jumpers, one blue and one a deep red.

"Okay, Cathleen. I'll just get Rosie some shoes, then we'll get some lunch. Shall we buy some sandwiches, and take the girls to Priory Park? They can play on the swings."

Cathleen thought about the conversation on the bus. She had the urge to confide in Tilly. Tell her, her sordid little secret. She wanted to rid herself of this pent up guilt. All Cathleen's childhood she had felt better than her friend. She was scared of sharing her secret with Tilly for fear of losing the superiority she felt she had over her.

The park was fun, the girls ate their picnic, and played in the park.

When Cathleen probed Tilly on her life in Canada, she was amazed at Tilly's revelations that she had had a relationship with an older man. She had said that when things had got serious between them, and he had wanted to marry her, Tilly had known then that she had to come home to Ed.

Cathleen felt better. Just knowing her friend had fallen in love before, helped. Cathleen could now convince herself that she, too, had needed that last little fling to make sure she was doing the right thing in giving herself to Ken for life.

*

Tilly waited anxiously with the other mothers. Rosie had gone off this morning, without any tears, appearing happy and confident. This hadn't stopped Tilly worrying. She had been unable to settle all day. Her gran had said 'For goodness sake Tilly, Rosie will be fine,

95

you'll see.' Even her gran's wise words hadn't calmed Tilly, she had been on edge all day.

Tilly stood at the gate, passing the time of day with the other mothers, when she caught sight of Mr Wallsing approaching. He was a funny looking man, in his fifties. He had a shaved strip of hair that ran round his head, but the top was as bald as an egg. His arms swung at his sides, his posture was bent over making him look very determined. When he asked Tilly if he could have a quiet word once she had picked Rosie up, her heart quickened, *'What's she been up to?'*

No sooner had Mr Wallsing made it back down the path, the playground came alive. Doors swung open, and children poured out, running for the gate to see their mothers.

Tilly could see Rosie running with the others. The sides of hair had come free of its ponytail, and her long socks were down by her ankles, "Tilly, Tilly, guess what?" before Tilly could guess anything Rosie filled her in with her news, "I've been put up with the six year olds. The teacher said I would manage. I'm in with the kids of me own age."

Tilly hugged her, to her, not bothering to correct her slip of using good English, "You clever, clever girl. Your mum would be so proud of you, Rosie, I just know she would."

Taking hold of Rosie's hand, making her way to Mr Wallsing's office, she told her, "I've got to have a word with your head master, I'm sure it won't take long…"

"Tilly, can I walk with the others? You'll catch us up on your bike. They all walk together, there's loads of them."

Tilly made sure Rosie had caught up with her new friends, before she made her way back to Mr Wallsing.

She knocked on the door, and waited for a response. The door opened wide, Mr Wallsing stood smiling, "Come in, come in. Good afternoon, Mrs Barrett. I won't beat around the bush. I hear you have done a child care course, is that right?"

Tilly was slightly hesitant, "Yes… yes I have."

"Well, now we have your little one here, Rosie, isn't it?" Before Tilly could answer he warbled on, "You will undoubtedly be walking her to school in the mornings? I wondered if you would give some thought to being our Lollypop lady. You'll have to see the children across the road. It's an 8.30am start till 9.00am and be back here for 2:45pm, ready for the 3 o'clock home time. Would you be interested? You've been highly recommended."

Tilly didn't have to think about this, it sounded great. "Yes, I'd love it, thank you for thinking of me. It would be perfect."

With that said, Mr Wallsing took Tilly to the little school hut, and showed her, her, long white cloth coat and bright yellow and black lollypop, which she would walk out in the road with to stop the traffic. "There's a plastic white coat for you on rainy days, and winter."

Tilly took the form he gave her which laid out her working terms, hours and wages. Saying goodbye, she cocked her leg over her saddle and pedalled off to catch Rosie up.

Tilly reached the Forresters' stables before she caught sight of them. They had walked through the farm, which gave a short cut to their journey. Tilly stopped her bike, "Rosie, you were quick. Do you want to get on the back of the bike?" Ed had fitted a child's seat, which Rosie loved sitting in when they went to the stables.

"No thanks, Tilly, I wanna walk with me friends."

There were eight children, Tilly only recognised the two from next door.

"I'll see you at home, then. Don't dawdle. Straight home, please. Gran will be delighted with your news."

Tilly pedalled off to the sound of Rosie calling, "Don't tell granny A, Tilly, I want to."

"I won't, but hurry up." Tilly had her own news to tell gran. A job at the school, that couldn't be better. The hours, the holidays, it was tailor made.

*

Cathleen was woken by the sound of a tap on her bedroom door, and her mother's soft voice, "It's only me, love. I've got a cuppa for you."

It was Cathleen's Saturday off, and the house seemed unusually quiet, "What time is it, where is everyone, Mum?"

"You've had a lay in, it's gone ten. Your dad left early, he's pricing up a job in Chichester, and Hannah's playing next door with Rachel."

Cathleen pulled herself up to a sitting position. Pam put a cup of tea and two chocolate biscuits on her bedside cabinet. Cathleen dipped one in the tea, while her mum pulled back her curtains. With a mouth full of biscuit, she asked, "What's the weather doing? Ken said we're going to look at a flat this afternoon."

"A flat, where?"

Cathleen dipped her next biscuit in. She was feeling better, and her appetite was back. "Don't tell anyone yet, mum, it's all in the air, but Ken's thinking of starting out on his own, buying the shop in Hawthorn road on the corner of Mons Avenue. He's going to open it up as a greengrocers. Like Oldswells' on the Chichester road."

"That sounds ambitious. What about Ed, does he know?"

Cathleen didn't know why, but the mention of Ed's name always made her bristle, "No, mum. No one knows anything at the moment. Have you forgotten that Ken ran old Mr Oldswells business for him for two years without any help from Ed?"

"I know, love, I just thought, that was all. Ed and Ken are good friends, they seem to help each other."

Cathleen ignored her mother's observation, filling her in on the details, "It'll be perfect for us though, the flat's spacious with three bedrooms."

"It all sounds good, Cathleen." Pam gathered up the clothes that were thrown across Cathleen's chair asking, "Is this for the wash too?"

"Oh, yes, I'll need them next week. Here you are, mum, take my cup. I'll be down in a minute."

Cathleen threw back her covers. Before her feet could touch the carpet, Pam's parting words caused her heart to miss a beat, "I'm lighting a fire while the house is quiet, bring down your ladies bits, will you? So I can burn them."

Cathleen knew the ritual. Every month her mother would ask for her sanitary towels, so she could destroy them in the fire. A cold chill went down Cathleen's spine as it dawned on her that she hadn't used any this month. She tried hard to think when her period would have been due. Cathleen remembered that she had carried a sanitary towel in her bag, when she had gone to the fair on her birthday. She hadn't had a period then, but her low mood and tummy cramps had warned her it was on its way.

She used her birthday as an indication as to when her period should have arrived. The more she thought about it, the more she knew it had been around then. She counted the days in her diary, her monthly should have arrived on the 29th August. Cathleen had never had a regular twenty eight day cycle, but it had always been close, and never this late.

She turned back the pages, trying to pin point the day exactly, but it didn't matter how many times she counted or shuffled, she knew she was at least two weeks late. She ran her hands over her stomach, up to her breasts. *'I can't be pregnant. Oh, please don't let me be pregnant.'*

Her mind did cartwheels, causing it to jump from one thought to another. *'What can I give mum to burn this month? How can I say to Ken I'm pregnant when we haven't even slept together?'*

These thoughts sent her plummeting back down, this new worry caused her to feel sick. *'I can't start throwing up every morning, mum's no fool.'*

Cathleen heard the back door slam. She looked out of the window and saw her mother carrying the washing down the garden. Cathleen hurriedly pulled open her little cabinet, grabbed a few sanitary towels and ran down stairs. The last few of her mother's towels were burning in the grate. She threw a few of her unused ones in, mixing them round with the poker and went into the garden still in her dressing gown to stall her mother.

"Here you are, mum, I've sorted my bits out. Do you want a hand here?"

Cathleen, noted the horror on her mum's face as she took in her appearance. "For goodness sake, girl, you'll catch your death out here dressed like that. Go and get some clothes on."

It was three o'clock in the afternoon before Cathleen heard Ken's van pull up outside her house. She had been trying to calm her nerves all morning, but all to no avail. Her appetite had diminished again, and her mood was prickly, causing her to snap at her sister, Hannah.

*

Cathleen's stomach lurched when she opened the door to Ken, *'How could I have been so stupid?'* The Prospect of looking over the shop had given Ken an added sparkle. She called out goodbye to her mum, and when she climbed in to the van, she tried to smile when he said, "You alright, Cathleen?"

"Just excited, I can't believe it. We'll be home owners, with our own business below."

She leant into him, as he brushed the top of her head with one hand, while holding the steering wheel with the other. "Do you have any idea how much I love you?"

From nowhere, tears sprung. She tried to look out of the window and get herself together, but it was no use. The anguish of what she had done, the loss of Michael, who she had thought she had been in love with, and now finding herself in the family way with another man's child. It was all too much.

"What is it, Cathleen, what have I said?"

The little mini skirt she was wearing had ridden up, and her tears spilled down her cheeks unchecked on to her bare legs. She pulled a hanky from her handbag, "You haven't said anything, Ken. It's just me, I think, with the wedding I'm run down."

As they pulled up outside the shop, Cathleen was pleased there didn't seem to be anyone around yet. She knew she had to get herself together, and come up with a way out of this mess. All morning she had thought about abortions, and then reminded herself what had happened to her friend. She thought about visiting Michael and telling him, but the shame. How could she wed a man, who had to marry her? Cathleen wasn't sure Michael would even acknowledge the pregnancy as his responsibility. She realised all too late that she knew so little about him, and what she did know she didn't like anymore. The only positive option she had managed to come up with was to excite Ken and get him to take her before the wedding, and pass the baby off as his. Even Cathleen had the decency to know this was shocking, but nothing else would spring to mind. She had tried to think of someone she could confide in, but there was no one. *What would they think of me? What would I think of someone, if they were in this position?'*

Ken took her in his arms and she sobbed like she had never sobbed before. She'd thought her heart was breaking two weeks ago, but, that was nothing to the fear that had settled over her, with this new revelation. "Ken can we not look at this place today? I need to speak to you."

Making them both jump was a tap on the van window. Ken wound it down, while Cathleen avoided eye contact with the man. She couldn't bear to let anyone see her tears. It was the agent to show them the shop.

"Come on, Cathleen, let's just have a quick look, we don't have to finalise anything, then we'll get a coffee somewhere and we can sort this out."

She got out of the car, blew her nose and took hold of Ken's hand. Never had she loved him as much. She questioned her actions again, *'How could I have been so, so stupid?'*

The shop was perfect. It had been used as a bakery, so was laid out very well already. Upstairs, there was a new kitchen, with fitted work tops and a stainless steel sink. It all looked very modern to Cathleen. She loved it, but she had this black cloud hanging over her. There were three bedrooms, all were a good size, even the little box room. Cathleen found herself thinking, *'It would be perfect for the baby.'*

She didn't know if it was that thought that made her mind up or not, but as soon as she saw this place she knew she wanted to live here. *'I've got to get Ken to make love to me. We've got seven weeks until we get married. If all goes to plan, I'll tell him three weeks before I go down the aisle that we've been unlucky and I've got caught in the family way. I've just got to get him to take me… tonight.'*

Cathleen didn't give any thought for the security Ken gave her. She was so confident of his love that she took it for granted he would be delighted at the prospect of becoming a father. She not only knew he would stand by her, but that he wouldn't worry if anyone doubted their dates or not. She was brought out of her reverie, with Ken saying, "What do you think, it's perfect isn't it?"

If the man noticed her red eyes he made a good job of ignoring the fact. There were smiles on both men's faces when Cathleen said, "I love it, Ken, I couldn't think of anywhere better to start our married life."

She watched as hands got shaken on a silent agreement, excitement mingled with her anticipation of what lay ahead.

Once they were back outside, Ken took her by the arm, "What was all that about, before… you know… the chap came? Do you want to go somewhere now?"

She pulled at her skirt trying to hitch it down a bit, "No, we'll go somewhere quiet tonight, shall we? To celebrate?"

"Oh, you little minx, tease me some more no doubt."

The laughter that came from Cathleen's throat was too loud, and sounded false to her own ears, but Ken was oblivious to it. The kiss they shared held promises for the night ahead.

*

Cathleen dressed carefully. She wore a new mini dress that was pale cream in colour, and had pink and yellow daisies running along the hem. She rubbed her tanned legs with lotion, and slipped on lemon sandals.

She brushed her cheeks with blusher, and applied a lipstick shine to her lips, finishing off with a generous application of black mascara to her lashes. When she checked herself in the mirror she told herself, *'It's enough.'*

The sound of her mother's voice shouting up the stairs caused her to jump. "Cathleen, Tilly's here."

"Send her up, mum, I'm nearly ready."

Cathleen turned from the mirror as Tilly pushed open her bedroom door, saying. "Ooh! Look at you, dressed to kill."

"Do I look alright? Ken and I are going out. I want to look my best."

"You always look fantastic, Cathleen. You don't need me to tell you that. You make me feel like an old frump."

"Don't be daft, Tilly, you always look pretty. Blue eyes and blonde hair, you don't have to try. You never have."

Cathleen noticed the blush creep across Tilly's cheeks, "That's so nice of you, Cathleen, to say that about me. Do you know you've never given me a compliment, in all our friendship?"

"Of course I have, and if I haven't it's because I was probably jealous 'cause you've never had to try, all the boys liked you, and you didn't even realise it. Anyway I'm not giving you any more so stop fishing. What do you want, anyway?"

"Nothing really, Ed and Rosie are round May and Norman's. I thought I'd come round here and catch up with your news."

"Sorry, no can do. I'm out tonight with Ken, we need to spend more time together. This wedding has put a lot of strain on both of us."

"You've lost a lot of weight. I know we all want to look like Twiggy these days, but you can be too thin, you know."

Cathleen thought, '*Not for much longer.*' But said instead, "I've just lost all that puppy fat I had. It's alright for you, you've always been one of Pharaoh's thin ones."

Cathleen sprayed her neck and arms with Youth Dew, which caused Tilly to wave her hand in front of her nose, coughing.

*

Rosie had been told by May that Rachel was next door with the new neighbours, who Rachel, now called, Uncle George and Auntie Florrie.

Rosie couldn't get round there quick enough, but no sooner had she hopped over the fence, it happened. A darkness shrouded the excitement of playing with Rachel. Some horrible feeling swept over her, which brought a feeling of dread. Rosie heard voices coming from the shed. Her curiosity caused her to creep up to the window, but it was too high to see. She felt the warning as if it had been spoken, her heart hammered in her chest. Rosie didn't understand the fear, but it kept her rooted outside.

The sound of movement caused Rosie to take flight. She jumped back over the fence, faster than she had hopped over. She could not only hear her heart thumping, she could feel it. The problem was, she didn't know why.

Rosie nearly knocked the tray out of May's hand as she pushed open the back door.

"For goodness sake, Rosie, where's the fire? What are you doing, where's Rachel?

"I don't want to go round there. I like it here."

"You go round and play. Auntie Florrie would love to meet you. Uncle George makes all sorts of wonderful things in his shed, out of matchsticks."

"I don't want to go, I'm not going, and they – are - not my auntie or uncle."

Rosie, who was still on edge jumped as the back door opened. She was relieved to see it was Tilly, back from Cathleen's. "I don't want to go round next door, ever. I don't have to, do I?"

Rosie threw herself at Tilly's legs, causing her to laugh. "You are funny at times, Rosie, but no, not if you don't want to."

Rosie shut her eyes tight trying to see what she was so frightened of, but May's voice moaning on and on to Tilly, how children should do as they are told, stopped Rosie's concentration, and she could feel nothing, just unexplained fear.

It was a good half hour before Rachel came back babbling on like she tended to do. The two girls were shooed upstairs.

Rosie sat on Rachel's bed, there was a big teddy on Rachel's pillow. Rosie picked him up and fiddled with a ribbon that had been tied in a bow round the bear's neck. She could see Rachel was excited, she couldn't keep still. She chattered on and on about how wonderful she thought Uncle George was.

"You should see Uncle George's collection of models, Rosie. He has lots. I told him your mummy worked on a fair, and he's going to make you a round-a-bout."

This had Rosie's attention, "How?"

"He puts all these little matchsticks together and sticks them. You can come round next time."

There it was again, that feeling. Rosie didn't understand it, *What is this?*

Rosie wanted to warn Rachel something was wrong round there, but she couldn't. Not when she couldn't explain it herself, but it was at times like this she knew she was different. She could still remember when she had told Norman at his allotment that she could feel the earth's heartbeat, he had laughed at her. Rosie had felt it. She had laid her hands in the soil and spread out her tiny fingers, and she could feel life. She didn't know why, but something had told her to keep her thoughts secret. Rosie didn't want to appear strange, or frighten anyone.

These were early feelings, feelings she had inherited from her mother. She was too young to understand them, yet she knew to keep them to herself.

*

George wiped his hand over his tobacco stained moustache. His hair was greying but you could see it had been dark. It was still thick, and wavy. He was quite a distinguished looking older man.

He turned at the sound of a tap on the shed door, "Yes?"

It was his sister, Florrie, "Are you coming in, George? The news will be on in a minute, you know you don't like to miss it."

"Just tidying up a bit. The littlun came round, she's a real cutie she is, loveable too."

"George, please. You know what happened last time."

"Not out here, Florrie, this is a new start, remember."

He watched from the small shed window as Florrie went back indoors. George knew the scandal that they had fled from wasn't going to die. If his sister Florrie wasn't convinced of his innocence, there was no hope.

He put away the glue and stacked the matches in a box, before making his way indoors.

A mug of tea was waiting on the side. He washed his hands in hot soapy water, picking at the glue on his fingers. He took his tea into the sitting room, annoyed at his sister's concerns. "Florrie, every time I spend time with a child, I don't want you reminding me of the horror I went through in Liverpool. This is a new beginning for…"

"I know, George, it's just…"

"It's just, nothing. I was found not guilty. That isn't enough for you though, is it? I tell you, as I told everyone else, I never laid a hand on that child, only in affection. I was giving her the love she lacked at home, that was all. It was misunderstood, you heard the officer…"

George was interrupted by Florrie, "But…"

"No, Florrie. There are no buts. The officer said, get away from it all. Start again, put it behind you. Oh no, I can't, not with you and your suspicious mind. You…"

"I'm sorry, George, It's just they seem such nice people and I don't want to spoil anything. I like it here already…"

"I like it too. I like children, Florrie, like – children, that's all. If that little one wants to come round and watch old Uncle George make his models, I don't see any harm in it. Do you?

Before Florrie could pass comment, he told her there was a little girl next door to May as well, and that Rachel had a sort of adopted cousin.

"We are surrounded by children, Florrie, there will always be children. I don't want to spend my time here accused of being a misery. I love children, you know that. This is a new start. If you don't believe in my innocence I might just as well leave you here on your own, and make my own way."

He could see by her deflated shoulders that he had won the argument, this was also reflected in her voice, "I'm sorry, I know you love children, George. It was just so horrible, the talking, the hate mail, the defacing of our property. I couldn't go through all that again."

"There you go again with your doubt. I didn't do anything, I was innocent, I…"

"Alright, I'm sorry. I won't bring it up again."

He watched his sister fold up the towels that she had thrown over the chair backs and take them upstairs to the airing cupboard. He knew Florrie wouldn't mention it again for a while, but she knew, he could see it in her eyes.

*

Seven o'clock on the dot, Ken knocked on the Hills' door. Cathleen let her father answer it, and she heard him say, "Come in, Ken, Cathleen's ready."

She could tell by the way his eyes swept over her appearance that he liked what he saw. Cathleen wanted to be away, she didn't want to waste time passing niceties.

"Come on, Ken, where are we going?"

The front door slammed as Ken said, "Where the mood takes us. Do you fancy the cinema?"

She liked the idea, but tonight she needed somewhere quiet, just the two of them. "Shall we just go for a drive, Ken? I fancy having some, us time."

Once they were both sat in the van, he said, "How about Goodwood? It's a nice evening, we could do a little walk if you like." Cathleen squeezed his knee, "Sounds good to me, I'm not dressed for walking though."

Ken parked the van at the top of the trundle. There was no one around, and once the hand brake was on, and the engine off, Cathleen wasted no time. She leant over and kissed him, teasing his bottom lip with her tongue. His response was instant. Within minutes they had climbed into the back of the van, lying on an old picnic blanket. The two of them continued to explore each other's bodies lost in the moment.

"I missed you, Cathleen, it was like you weren't with me anymore?"

Between kisses, she said, "I've been so overwhelmed with this wedding, it got me down for a while, but I'm better now."

The kisses and fondles took over, and the conversation dried up, and Cathleen used her new knowledge on seduction to lead the way. She wriggled in the right direction so Ken could ease her dress off, "You're beautiful. Do you know that?"

As his kisses traced up the length of her body, she knew it was going to happen. Ken was going to make love to her. It had proved easier than even she could imagine. The pair of them lay naked, the nights were drawing in, but it was still light. Cathleen lay back and closed her eyes. Ken eased himself on top of her. It wasn't the most comfortable position, laying on a blanket in the back of a van, but she knew this was her only chance.

"You're my world, Cathleen, do you know that? I couldn't imagine my life without you."

Guilt pricked, she opened her eyes to witness, not the lust she had seen a few weeks ago in Michael's eyes, but Ken's liquid brown eyes clouded with passion.

"Are you sure you want this to happen, Cathleen? I know you wanted to wait until the wedding."

She didn't know if it was his concern for her feelings, or his claim of loving her so completely. Whatever it was she couldn't be sure, she only knew she couldn't go through with this.

She tried to sit up, "I'm sorry, Ken, so sorry."

He moved off her, putting his arm across her bare stomach, but Cathleen pushed him off, she wanted to get dressed. "Please, Ken, I have to talk to you."

They both got dressed in silence, and climbed into the front of the van. The moment of undiluted passion had passed, a heavy feeling of anticipation hung in the air. "What is it, Cathleen, does it have anything to do with the tears earlier today?" I thought you liked the shop, and the idea to live above. Did I get that wrong?"

She now looked decent. She pulled her hand through her hair and slipped her feet back into her sandals. "Can we go to Bognor? I need to be near my home, with what I have to say to you."

Cathleen, could see Ken was worried. The frown across his face made him look old. "Why do we have to go Bognor? Just tell me now. Here."

She shook her head, tears started to fall again.

"I can't, Ken. Please just do as I ask. Take me somewhere near my home."

Cathleen watched Ken drag his hand through his own hair, she knew she had unnerved him. The silence in the van was deafening. Neither of them spoke on the way back to Bognor.

He parked his van outside the pier. "Will this do?" The worry that was etched across his face made Cathleen's heart ache. Tears shone in her eyes as she found her voice.

"I'm so frightened to say this to you, Ken. You're going to hate me, I know you will."

He tried to resist her accusation, but Cathleen put her hand on his knee, "Please let me speak, Ken. Before I lose my nerve."

111

She could see he was becoming desperate, "You do want to marry me, still, don't you? ...Cathleen?"

She ignored his question, "I've thought and thought about who I could tell this to, yet there is no one, it has to be you. The problem I have, is, I just don't know how to begin." She repeated her biggest fear, "You're going to hate me, Ken. I know you will."

"Cathleen, I could never hate you, ever. I've loved you for as long as I can remember. I still love you. I love you more than life itself. Does that help?"

She couldn't answer, her confession seemed jammed in her throat. Ken looked exasperated. "Whatever it is that's worrying you, we'll sort together. In seven weeks we'll be married. I'll be your husband, Cathleen. You have to be able to talk to me."

She took a deep breath and said it quickly, not how she wanted to, but she blurted out that she had been unfaithful to him, a moment of madness.

Ken paled, "Unfaithful, with who?"

Before she could answer he put two and two together, "It was that clown from the stables, wasn't it?"

When Cathleen sat with her head in her hands, sobbing into them. Ken hit the steering wheel with his fist, "I knew it! I knew something funny was going on at those stables."

"Don't, Ken, you don't know nothing."

"Are you saying you don't want to marry me? Are you in love with him, is that what all this is about?"

She shook her head in denial, sobs made it difficult for her to speak, "I want to marry you, Ken, I've been so foolish. I want to marry you more than anything in this world, it's just..."

"How could you do this to me, how could you fall for that twerp? I love you, really love you. Was that not enough?"

She watched as he pulled at his own wild curls, "I've never been good enough for you, have I?"

Words failed Cathleen, as she watched hurt replace the anger. Ken seemed to spit at her, "That's it, isn't it? He had more to offer you. Go on, say it, you think he's better than me. Wake up, missy, I'm telling you now, he's not better, just richer, but what I have I've worked for, worked bloody hard."

"No, Ken! Stop it. You're a lot too good for me. I know that now. If I could turn the clock back I would, but it's too late."

Ken got out of the van. Cathleen opened her door and pulled at his shirt sleeve, "Wait, Ken, please."

"I need a drink, Cathleen. You can come. We need to sort this mess out."

Once they were seated in The Pig and Whistle, he bought a large Whiskey for himself, and a pineapple juice for Cathleen.

She watched as he downed his drink in one, "What are your plans then? Does lover boy want you to call off the wedding so you can go out with him?"

Cathleen started to cry again, "No, Ken, it's not like that. It was a stupid fling. I wished I'd never set eyes on him again, I…"

Cathleen recognised hope flicker in his eyes. She leant forward so she could hear Ken's slow whisper, "Are you telling me it's over, completely over?"

Cathleen nodded. As she thought, *'If only it was that easy.'*

Ken reached over for her hand, his voice had lost its hushed tones. "I'm hurt, Cathleen, bloody hurt. How could you do that to me… to us?"

She couldn't answer, tears poured down her cheeks, unchecked.

"Are you really sure it's over, Cathleen?"

She nodded again, still unable to speak.

Do you love me? I need you to be honest. I need you to be sure now. I need to know if you really want me, like I want you."

Her shoulders shook as the crying took over. People in the pub were starting to look across at them.

"Come on, Cathleen, you've told me now. We'll work it out, somehow. You have to be sure though, sure that you still want to marry me as much as I want to marry you."

"Ken, it's more than that. I'm pregnant. I'm carrying Michael's child."

Cathleen jumped as Ken pushed the table away, his glass smashed on the floor. He stood up, the colour had gone from his face. She could see he had seen through her plans, and worked out her motivation. The quiet time Cathleen had wanted with just the two of them on the trundle, all became clear. She wasn't prepared for his onslaught, "You little bitch, you whore. That's what you are. You were hoping to palm that bastard's child off on me. That was it, wasn't it?"

The whole pub went quiet, heads turned in their direction. The landlord approached their table, but before he could speak, Ken pushed past him. "Don't waste your breath, I'm leaving."

Cathleen watched as Ken walked away without a backward glance.

*

Ken sat in his van, he had been sick, and his head had started to pound. His feet shook on the pedals, his hands felt wet and clammy on the steering wheel.

His whole body was shaking. He knew what he had to do. He turned the key in the ignition, and headed for Hunston.

He pulled into the Forresters drive, which was lit up making him feel conspicuous.

His stomach was like a tight ball, apprehension made him feel nervous, he kept telling himself, *'I have to do this.'*

The door opened before he knocked. Ken had a clear view of the kitchen. A large table sat in the middle of the room with fitted work tops that ran along the side of one wall. A tall gentleman stood, blocking any further view, "Can I help you?"

Ken couldn't believe how normal his voice sounded, "Yes, I've come to speak to Michael, we're old friends."

"Do come in?"

"No thanks, I'll wait here."

A young woman with dark straight hair came into the kitchen. She grabbed a glass from the draining board, and started to fill it with water.

Ken watched as the gentleman turned to her saying, "Christine, can you tell Michael …" he stopped, turned, and looked at Ken, "Who, shall we say is calling?"

Before Ken could answer, Michael came into the kitchen, "There you are, Chrissie, I wondered where you went."

Nerves left Ken, the sight of him made his blood run cold. A sheet of red fell before his eyes as he pushed his way into the kitchen and punched Michael clean in the side of his head.

"You bastard, how…" Ken didn't get chance to finish, Michael retaliated, punching Ken full in the face. His lip split, and he recognised the taste of salty blood. The adrenalin was so great, Ken felt no pain, and the screams that echoed round the kitchen from

Christine seemed to give justice to his motive. The gentleman who Ken guessed was Michael's father, was behaving like a pestering fly. He kept trying to grab Ken between punches. Fists continued to flay, and punches found their mark. Michael was taller, fitter, and heavier, but anger gave Ken an added strength.

When Ken found himself pinned back by the older gent, the anger disappeared, and fear took its place. He witnessed the chaos he had caused. Not just the furniture that lay knocked over on the stone floor, but there was an older lady huddled in the doorway cuddling Christine. They were both crying, but the older woman found her voice and screeched, "Phone the police, he's mad. Who does he think he is?"

It felt to Ken like his nose was broken. His lip felt twice its size, and he could not only taste blood, he could feel it. Speaking was difficult for him, but he found a voice, "Yes, call the police. Let's let the whole world know he's got my girlfriend pregnant, and tried to pass it off as mine."

The scream that came from the girl called Christine was piercing. Ken turned and left. He could hear the woman saying, "Don't listen to him, Christine, you know that can't be true. He must be mad. That's what he is, mad."

Ken sat in his van listening to the raised voices that seemed to echo down the drive. His temper had left him, allowing the pain to find his nerves. His hand was swollen and throbbed. The lit drive meant he could see his face in the rear view mirror, he was unrecognisable. Ken sat, head bent, nursing his hand, crying. Sobs took over. How long he sat like that he had no idea. A tap on his driver's side window caused him to look up. It was Michael's dad. "Are you alright, sonny?"

Ken couldn't answer. His face felt like it wasn't connected properly. His lips felt like rubber, only they hurt. Ken had no choice but to sit and listen. "I don't know what your girlfriend's told you, sonny."

Ken flinched at the accusation that Cathleen was being made to look a liar. Pain, caused him to sit quiet, and the man continued, seeming to understand he was on difficult ground. "Steady on. I'm not saying Michael's not guilty, he has a habit of playing the field, he's known for it here at the stables, but I'm telling you, young man, if your young lady says she's pregnant, I can assure you it isn't Michael's."

Ken dabbed at his swollen eyes with his shirt sleeve, they were painful. His right eye had already closed. When Ken didn't answer, he continued. "Michael had an accident as a small boy, it left him sterile. We put his play boy behaviour down to this. You've come here this evening, and not only hurt my wife, you've destroyed his fiancé. You've every right to be angry, every right. I'm not saying you're mistaken either. I'm sure our Michael has been playing around with your young lady, if she says so. But I'm telling you sonny, if she's got herself in the family way, it isn't his."

This news was like another punch in his stomach. *'Cathleen must have just fancied pinning it on Michael because of their money. But who else has she been playing around with.'* It was all too much for Ken. He didn't know where he hurt most.

He couldn't answer if he wanted to. The conversation was brought to an end with, "You get yourself home, and don't darken our doorstep again. You're lucky the police weren't called." Ken watched the gent turn and make his way back to the mayhem, that he had caused them all.

Ken wound up his window and drove slowly home.

*

Cathleen put her key in the door. She had never, ever, before, felt so wretched. She knew she would have to face her parents. It was too early for them to be in bed, and the sound of the television wafting

117

up the hall told her she was right. The only good thing, was, that Hannah would be asleep by now.

Cathleen went through to the lounge, she didn't have to say a word, just one look at her, had her parents leaping up, from concern. "Whatever's happened, love, where's Ken?"

Hal, looked at the door expectantly, but Cathleen had closed it on purpose, not wanting to wake Hannah with raised voices.

"We've had a row. There's to be no wedding…"

She didn't get to finish, Hal's temper was up. "Did he let you walk home on your own?"

Cathleen nodded, finding she wasn't brave enough to give an explanation. This fuelled Hal's anger.

"Anything could have happened to you, what was he thinking? Why didn't you phone? I'd have come and got you, don't you ever…"

Cathleen couldn't take this show of love, and affection. Tears poured down her cheeks, unchecked. It was Pam who spoke next, "Now, now, love, nothing's as bad as all that. Tomorrow when you've both slept on it, you'll see. Ken will be round here with his tail between his legs…"

Pam didn't get to finish. Hal had his shoes on. "I'll give him tomorrow, tail between his legs, he'll have more than that by the time I've finished with him." Hal looked at Cathleen, saying, "You get yourself off to bed, love…"

Cathleen watched in horror as her parents started arguing.

"No, Hal, don't go round there upsetting Brenda. It'll sort."

"I don't often swear Pam, but bloody sort. I'll give him sort. Letting our girl walk home on her own at this time of night. I think we need an explanation, don't you?"

118

"Mum, dad, I've been sat at the pier. I didn't know what to do. Ken left me about nine, it wasn't dark then. I've been thinking, that's all. Please don't go round dad."

"I don't care what you've been doing. He had a duty to see you safely home. What's got into him? You, you get yourself up to bed, there's my girl."

Cathleen was dumbfounded. Her dad was already getting his keys off the hook in the kitchen. She didn't have the courage to tell him, herself, so perhaps it would be easier if Ken said it for her. Knowing Ken, he would make it sound a bit better. Fear took over as she thought, *'How could it sound better? I've behaved like a tramp.'* Fresh tears spilled from her eyes as she thought of all her dad's anger and disappointment transferring from Ken to her. Cathleen knew it wouldn't just be her parents she would have to face, she would be the laughing stock of the village.

Once they were alone, Pam put her arm across Cathleen's shoulder, "Come on love, you heard your dad. He'll sort all this out. Don't you worry about his temper either, he'll calm down. It gave us a shock seeing you so distressed, and then finding out you'd walked home on your own. What was Ken thinking, Cathleen, honestly? He must have known we would be none too pleased."

Cathleen didn't know where her courage came from, but with her dad out of the way she blurted out her predicament. The truth behind the row.

Cathleen lay upstairs in bed, her mother's words still echoed in her brain, "Oh my god, girl, how could you Cathleen, how could you?" The horror, and disgust on her face had sworn at her accusingly.

Cathleen hadn't been able to answer, she had fled to her room. She didn't want to be around when her dad came back.

Cathleen was still awake when her father's van pulled up outside. She could feel her heart pounding in her chest. Fear caused her to tuck her head under her covers, hoping she could shield herself from what was coming. She thought hopefully, *'Perhaps Ken hasn't said anything.'*

This hopeful thought didn't last two minutes as her father seemed to crash into the house, "Where is she, where is that little slut?"

Pam's voice rose to Cathleen's defence, "Don't you talk like that in this house, ever, Hal...?"

"You don't know half, love. That little bag of nothing, up there, has gone and..."

"I know, Hal, I know. She told me. I'm as shocked as you, but..."

"But! Are you kidding? But! But! I'll tell you but. I've been round there, the kid is broken, broken Pam. Not just broken hearted, he's broken to pieces. He's been round to those stables, got into a fight, and if looks is anything to go by, he's come off worse. His face is smashed, and his soul is shattered. He's sat at home crying like a baby. Then there's her, her up there, swanning in here crying. What was it she said? 'I've been sitting at the pier'. Well, I tell you, Pam, I wished she'd bloody jumped off. The shame she's going to bring to this family. I..."

"Shut up, Hal, Shut up. Yes, it's awful, but it's happened. You'll wake Hannah, do you want that?"

"It's not all, Pam, it's not all. She tried to push herself on Ken tonight. Did she tell you that? Oh no, she hadn't given herself to the man she was planning to marry, kept him waiting. But tonight she thought she would. Tried to get him to make love to her, up at the trundle, so she could pin it on him. Did she tell you that? I suppose we must thank the lord for some sort of decency that switched on in that filthy little brain of hers. She at least had the guts to tell him

120

she'd got herself pregnant, with this Michael from the stables. Ken's been round there tonight. I tell you Pam, he got a hiding of a lifetime. Ken's at home now, sitting with Brenda and Alf, worrying that he's split up this Michael's engagement…"

Pam tried to intervene, but Hal was determined to have his say, "No, Pam. Wait for this next bit. Oh yes, it gets better, because by all accounts, this Michael can't have kids, this Michael's infertile. So who else has she been opening her legs to, I…"

"Stop it, Hal, I tell you stop it. Tomorrow when we've slept on it, and all cooled down, we'll discuss it calmly and get to the bottom of it…"

"Oh no, Pam. Oh no. Tomorrow, she up there packs her bags and goes. I'm not having her living under my roof, not now. Pregnant with someone she can't even name. Gutter, that's where she belongs, the gutter."

"She's our daughter, and she…"

"She's no daughter of mine, Pam. As of tonight she's out, do you hear me? She goes tomorrow, she can go to your sisters."

"I can't send our trouble over there, be reasonable Hal. It'll calm down, you'll see. I'm as shocked as you are, but this anger will get us nowhere."

"You haven't seen that young kid's face. Smashed it is, smashed. As if he hadn't enough to contend with as a boy, and now her, her upstairs. She's a slut, nothing more and…"

Cathleen was huddled under her bed clothes trying to fathom out these new revelations, '*How can this be, what are they trying to do? They must want it to look like I've been sleeping with lots of blokes so they can wriggle out of their responsibility. Oh god, I've been such a fool.*'

None of her thoughts could muffle the sound of the slap that hit Hal's face, which had caused him to stop his tirade in mid-sentence.

Never, in all her years had she ever heard her parents argue like this, and never ever anything physical. She slid out of bed, and made her way downstairs on tiptoe.

She entered the living room, wearing only a nightie. She didn't have a clue what she would say, but the sight that met her eyes, not only kept her quiet, but had her rooted to the spot. Cathleen's parents were crying. They clung together as one. It looked as if they were trying to hold each other up. Cathleen had only ever seen grief like this once before. It had been at her grandmother's funeral, years ago.

So lost were her parents in the horror she had caused that she turned, unnoticed, and went back upstairs. She climbed back into bed feeling like the world hated her. Her life had come to an end. For the first time ever, Cathleen wished she could go to sleep and not wake up.

*

The Rainbow

Chapter Six

Disappointments

Tilly's heart was heavy. She was cross with Ed, and asked herself over and over, what was he thinking?

Rosie couldn't sit still. "Do you think mummy will let me go back with her, Tilly?"

Tilly forced a smile, "Well, we'll have to see. Don't get your hopes up, she might not be there."

"Ed says it's a big fair. I know she'll be there, Tilly. You'll come too…Won't you? We can show her me letters."

Tilly's heart felt like it was breaking. Sloe Fair came to Chichester every year in October, and Ed had seen the poster advertising it. Without thinking, he had told Rosie they would take her to see if they could find her mummy. Tilly didn't know what she would do if Rhana wanted Rosie back.

She had a horrible feeling she was about to lose the child that had become as precious as her own flesh and blood. Trying to move the conversation away from fairs, Tilly said, "Enough of what might be. Now off to bed, go and say your goodnights to gran, we have an early horse ride tomorrow."

Rosie punched her arm in the air, leaping off the chair, "Oh yes! No Sunday school."

"Come on, missy, you used to love Sunday school." "I don't like the teacher. She's bossy. I'd rather go riding."

Agnes went through to the main lounge, and read Rosie a bedtime story. She had a hot chocolate with them all, but could sense the atmosphere was not happy.

Once Rosie was in bed Agnes scuttled off to the safety of her room. It was like her own little bedsit, and she loved the privacy it provided. There was tension between Tilly and Ed, and she wanted to be out of the way.

So much had changed since her granddaughter's wedding four months ago.

Agnes had embraced the surprise of becoming a great-grandmother, to a now, six year old. Tonight, she didn't want to get caught up in an argument that was about to take place. She understood Ed's reasons for wanting to find the girl's mother, he was trying to do what he thought was right. It wasn't that easy now, though. Even she felt it would be a sorry day to see the child go, but what worried her more was Tilly. Tilly would be heartbroken.

Agnes turned up her television as raised voices filtered through the walls.

*

Tilly, hadn't been up for going to the stables this morning, and wanting Rosie out of the way, had let her next door neighbour take her with her own two girls. Rosie had skipped off quite happy, seeming unaware of the tension that seemed to hang in the house like a smog. Tilly was still annoyed with Ed, which meant Sunday was spent with an awkward silence. She couldn't get him to see Rosie was better off staying with them. His, argument had been, they had a duty to try and reunite Rosie with her mother. He had understood it, that it was only a temporary arrangement and that they were to look for the rainbow on the tent at any fairs that came their way.

Tilly felt low, she couldn't even face going over to Ed's parents for their usual Sunday tea. These visits had become a habit, since Rosie's arrival, and Tilly braced herself for some flak at cancelling at such short notice. She was more than surprised when May accepted the decline, saying, 'George and Florrie are coming round. It would have been nice though, if we could have all got to know each other a little better.'

Tilly was well aware that May knew, Rosie had taken a real dislike of the couple next door. Nothing any of them said helped the situation.

The telephone rang just after six. She went into the hall to answer it, but Ed had got there first. She stood in the doorway listening, "No problem. Yes. No, I understand. Get yourself sorted." He replaced the receiver and caught sight of Tilly standing, watching him, he reached out for her. He put his arms around her waist, and she leant into him asking, "What's all that about?"

"Ken's ill, he sounds awful. Seems he needs the week off. Alf's offered to lend a hand, but I said I'll manage."

"That was silly, it would help just having him to answer the phone, put up orders…" Ed interrupted, "No, I'll manage. I'd have to go over and get him. It's easier just to get on with it, honestly…" he hesitated, then said, "I'm sorry about Rosie, Tilly. It just came out. I saw the poster advertising the fair, and thought about her mum."

Tilly couldn't say anything, she was choked with emotion. "Come on, Tilly, she probably won't even be there. You never know if things were as horrible as you say, this Rhana will want us to keep Rosie, if only for her own safety."

Tilly's shoulders shook as tears fell down her cheeks, "I can't bear to think what will happen if we lose her, Ed. She's part of me now."

Tilly was folded into Ed's big arms, where he said over and over, "I'm so sorry, Tilly, so sorry."

*

Christine Hardy

Michael was three months older than Christine. Both were born in 1943. Michael was as blonde as she was dark. The friendship between the two families led to a connection between the two children. It was a friendship that remained, even when her parents moved away to Petworth.

Christine had loved Michael for as long as she could remember. He had kissed her when she was fourteen. A proper kiss, where he had teased her with his tongue. It was at a hop night. He'd skipped her over to the window which had shielded them from the crowd. The laughter between them had died with his expression. Michael had tipped his head down, and their eyes had become transfixed, his had sparkled like sunshine on a clear blue lake. She could still remember it. The tingles that spread over her body had made her knees buckle. She'd fallen in love.

Michael had a lovely way about him. He was fun, confident, and excellent with the horses. He was well liked at the stables. The youngsters adored him, following him around like soppy, puppy dogs, and those that were teenagers loved him. Christine, was confident in herself and their long friendship, to know he was hers. She would laugh off his flirty behaviour, seeing it as harmless fun.

Things changed in a big way, Christmas 1958. Michael had been bought a motor cycle. He rode the thing full speed round and round the stables, and when he turned sixteen a few weeks later he thought he was proficient. His licence had come through with his birthday cards, and his test was set for the end of March. It didn't happen, as that February, Michael went down with Mumps. It had been a bad case from the start, which developed into orchitis, an inflammation of the scrotum. He was too ill to take his test, and it had had to be postponed until the summer.

When Michael recovered, the news that he would never father a child had hit him hard, Christine too. But she was young and in love and children didn't enter her thoughts at sixteen, but it was here that their relationship had changed.

Michael appeared just as besotted with her, but she noticed he was always out to prove he was still attractive to the opposite sex. He had started going dancing at some club in Bognor with his friend Joe. Christine had an idea he was flirting there, but he seemed just as keen to see her, and she loved him so completely she put such thoughts to the back of her mind.

When one Saturday, Christine had turned up at the stables early to surprise him, she'd more than done that. She had caught Michael kissing one of the girls in the barn. Both of them had lain practically naked in the straw. The girl had burst into tears and fled behind the hay store trying to make herself decent, and he had chased after Christine, doing his trousers up as he ran. He had managed to convince her it was just a bit of harmless fun, and that he only loved her.

When she had cried to her parents, her father had come to Michael's defence saying, "It's the illness, give him time. He needs to feel a man, Christine. You wouldn't understand."

So she had given him time. And time, and time again, he had let her down.

Christine was brought out of thought when she heard the phone ringing, her mother answered. The conversation filtered up the stairs. She knew it was the Forresters, probably Michael's mother hoping to put things right. Christine tensed as she heard her name being called, "Christine... Christine?" There was a pause, but she lay still not wanting to move. Her mother's voice rose, and it sounded exasperated, "Christine, its Michael, he wants to speak to you." When she gave no answer, she heard her mother say, "Sorry, Michael, she must have gone out, probably for an early ride on Belle. I'll tell her you've called, she'll get back to you."

Anger stirred, *'Why is no one upset at the accusations? It's obvious there's some truth in it.'*

Her mother's footsteps could be heard coming up the stairs, her door opened, "You should be ashamed of yourself. The boy only wants to speak to you. He wants to put things right. What sort of a marriage are you to have if you shut down like this on every little tiff."

Tears threatened at the unfairness of her parent's loyalties, "Go away mum, please. I need time, even if you don't. Michael has been accused of getting some girl pregnant, doesn't that tell you anything?"

She could see her mother was out of her depth, but it didn't stop her line of attack, "How long have you known Michael, Christine? You should know by now he's a good catch. This young girl is just trying her luck. He must be worth fighting for, surely?"

"Mum, just say the doctors are wrong, and just maybe, he has got someone pregnant. What then? Will he still be your golden boy? I was there remember. I saw the heart ache on the other fella's face. I tell you, there's some truth in this, even if you don't want to believe it." Her bedroom door closed, she heard her mum muttering as she went down the stairs. Christine felt saddened by her parents, *'Why can't they support me? Most parents would be telling their children to throw the towel in while they still have the chance. What is it with them?'*

*

Michael sat with Merry Bess, she was due to foal at any time. Her behaviour showed it was imminent.

He stroked her back, moving round to face her. Her eyes were bright, and seemed to stare into his as if to ask, what was this pain

128

all about? She started to paw at the ground, becoming more restless with each contraction. Michael blew on her face, and stroked her nose, talking to her in soft tones, "There girl, steady on. Steady on."

When, fifty minutes later, a white foal lay in the straw with Merry Bess licking her clean, tears fell down Michael's face. It was still bruised, but not painful now.

He was confused, he had asked himself over and over *'What was Cathleen doing? Why would she make out she was having my baby?'* He wished he hadn't put on that ridiculous façade about worrying she might get pregnant. *'Why hadn't I just come clean, told her I fired blanks. It would have saved that horrendous scenario with that sticky foam.'* Hope stirred in him as he wondered if she really was having his baby. *'Could it be mine?'* He thought of all the times he had made love to Christine, and all the other girls who had relented to his charms, there had been too many to count, but none of them claimed he had fathered a child. He wiped his eyes, telling himself to stop fooling himself. He let his thoughts drift back to Cathleen. He liked her. He remembered their early friendship at the Newtown dance classes, she was a good mover. He liked her spirit too. She was like him in a way.

The foal was on its feet now, and feeding. He filled up the hay bag encouraging Merry Bess to stand still, but he could see she didn't need coaxing, she was already showing signs of being a good mother.

Michael blew his nose, he knew he ought to leave mother and baby to bond on their own now, but he felt safe shut in here. He didn't want any questions, he had enough of his own he couldn't answer.

His mother wasn't talking to him, his father was disappointed, Michael could see it in his face, but Christine, what was he going to do about her? Then there was her parents.

It didn't matter how many times Michael tortured himself with these problems, it always came back to Cathleen. *'Cathleen's pregnant, or is she? Who else has she been sleeping with? Her fella was pretty sure it wasn't his, so whose is it?'* Michael thought back to Blackpool, and wondered if she was already pregnant then, *'Was she just trying to pin it on me?'*

There were no answers. There was no way of talking to Cathleen. He thought about their last hours together. How she had screamed at him to take her home. He knew his parting words had been cruel, but he had, had no choice. He had, had to shake her loose, she had started talking about marriage and finishing with her fiancé. Michael wondered if perhaps Ken couldn't have children either, that is how he was so sure it wasn't his.

Michael made his way over the paddock, telling himself he had to stop worrying about Cathleen, she was not his concern. He was kidding himself to think it might be his baby, he had been up to Harley Street, he knew for sure. Christine had to be his only concern now. He wondered if she would ever be able to forgive him, and he questioned if he really wanted her to.

He looked up as Lucy called out to him. She wasn't wearing a riding hat and her short brown hair had been swept to one side, making her look boyish.

"Open the gate, Michael."

He waited while she went through on horseback, three riders followed, having finished their lesson. He called out to Lucy, "Merry Bess has had her foal, it's a colt, white. Beautiful he is."

The news had the horses put into a trot at the thought of the new arrival. They all wanted to get a peek at it.

Lucy left Michael to shut the gate. He stood and watched them dismount and walk their horses towards the paddock.

He shouted across at them, "Don't crowd her, one at a time."

Lucy wanted a word with him. There was a problem with one of the windows on her caravan. His left cheek was a yellow colour, causing her to side-track, "Your face looks better, I hope the other bloke came off worse?"

"Not now, Luce, I'm not in the mood."

"I've heard all about it, Michael. Christine will come round, you'll see. She's forgiven you before, she will again."

It was no secret at the stables that Michael was a playboy. Lucy kept her distance, she wasn't quite yet eighteen, and had her own plans for her destiny.

"This is different, Luce, I'm getting accused of fathering a child."

Her hazel eyes stared right at him, accusingly. He had never noticed them before, or her for that matter, and found the green flecks in them fascinating. To Michael, Lucy was just someone who lived and worked at the stables. He could feel her disapproval when she asked, "Are you guilty as charged?"

Michael faltered, his old ego flickered, but as if she had bewitched him, he found himself being honest. "I can't have kids, Lucy. Me! Being accused of getting her up the duffer is a joke really. I've had a hiding for nothing, and lost Christine in the bargain."

"Having kids is no big deal. Anyone can have them, it's the looking after them that's important."

Michael was taken aback by the vehemence in her voice. "You know what they say, we always want what we can't have." He was surprised when Lucy came out with, "It's that curly girl that was here a few weeks ago, isn't it? The red head."

Michael nodded, "Yes, Cathleen's her name. I knew her years ago. It was just a bit of fun. I don't know how this lot has exploded. I think I've blown it with Christine, I don't know who'll want me now."

Michael winced as Lucy ruffled his hair, "You'll marry, Michael, even if you get dumped by Christine. While you're at it, adopt a kid, lots of kids. Lots of needy kids."

He watched as she ran off to coo over the new foal. He was left, staring after her, speechless, wondering where all that had come from.

*

Lucy Elliott

The rain lashed against the caravan. Lucy tried to wedge the window closed, but it didn't work, it needed a new catch. She knew she should have mentioned it to Michael earlier, but the moment was lost in his own self-pity.

'What an idiot he is, playing around like he does, and now what? It looks like he might just lose Christine this time.'

The water was low in the canister, she didn't fancy going over to the farm tap to fill it. She would have to make do. She rinsed her plate and cup out, put a little water in the kettle for her morning drink, and rinsed her face and brushed her teeth with the last drop.

Michael came to mind again. *'Why had I told him Christine would forgive him? What do I know? I've never had a boyfriend in my life.'* Lucy knew she, herself, would never be able to forgive such a betrayal, *'Surely Christine will have enough about her this time. He's been caught at least three times with girls, and that's just in the last twenty months that I've been here. Surely she'll think, enough is enough. Or will she?'*

Tiredness swept over her, it had been a long day. She worked hard at the stables, with little to show for it. The job had appealed to Lucy because it came with accommodation, but it had meant her wages were low. She wanted to use the toilet before she settled down for the night. There were bathroom facilities at the stables, but for Lucy it meant a good walk across the field. *I'm not traipsing over there for the loo in this weather.'* She squatted behind the caravan with a rain-mac shielding her head.

Once in bed Lucy's thoughts turned to Michael again. She had taken this job three days after her sixteenth birthday. She had liked the way Michael was so sure of himself, so able. It had been the first time Lucy had ever let her reserve slip. She had always promised herself she would not complicate her life, with men. When a few weeks into the job Michael had been caught in the hay barn with one of the stable hands, she knew she had made the right decision. He was the same as the rest. Ruled by one thing, the thing that dangles in his trousers. She had felt great pity for Christine, who seemed so right for him. It was common knowledge they had grown up together, and the long childhood friendship reflected this. It was a shame he had no morals, no values or thought for Christine's loyalty, or respect for her emotionally. It was always all about him.

She soon learnt that with a little encouragement you could be Michael's next conquest. By all accounts, you had to understand he was spoken for, and it would be just a bit of fun to him.

'Well, he's lost his way this time, and it looks like Christine has come to her senses.'

Lucy pulled the covers up to her chin, the autumn was fast approaching, and at night it could be felt. She thought about the way he'd looked at her earlier, then chastised herself for it. *'Who would look at me? My hair's cut so short I could be a boy, there's more meat on a chicken's lip, and I'm knee high to a grasshopper.'*

Lucy was only 5'3, she was as thin as a poker, but it suited her tiny face, and so did her very short brown hair. Her lips were naturally on the red side, giving her a pale complexion. What really was appealing about Lucy was that she had no idea she was naturally attractive, it suited her to be thought of as plain. She had her own plans for life and going down a road that held risks of being cheated on was not on her agenda.

*

Monday 19th September.

Cathleen struggled to eat her breakfast, the thought of facing people today, outside the security of her home, was scary. Things were a bit easier with her dad, he was at least speaking to her again, just. The big trial was going to be today, it was her first day back at work.

Last week she couldn't face going out, and managed to get signed off. Ed's visit had been a surprise. She thought about the things he had said, and felt warm towards him.

Cathleen had disliked Ed for so long that she couldn't remember why. *'Was it what he did to Tilly? Probably not. It was more to do with Ken, he was always in Ed's shadow. It was Ed this, Ed said that.'* She got sick of it. So it had been a surprise when her mum had called up on Friday night saying that Ed was downstairs, wanting to see her.

Cathleen had tried to put on an air of, 'I don't care what you think.' But tears fell. Ed had put his arms around her and rocked her like a baby, talking to her softly. Some of it she couldn't remember, but she remembered the words that rang true.

"We're not unalike you and I Cathleen. We had parents that thought we walked on water. It's good in so many ways, but it makes falling more difficult. I've made dreadful, life changing decisions, that I could beat myself up for every day, but we can't turn the clock back. There comes a time when we have to go forward, and it's how we do that that counts. Look at me. I thought I'd never be able to show my face again in this town, but what happened is like a distant memory now. I remember though, and I shall never forgive myself. So I try my hardest to make it up to Tilly, always. I love her, you see, and I believe you love Ken."

134

Cathleen, wasn't so sure she loved Ken, but asked herself, *'How can I get him back? He would never trust me. Every time he looked at this baby he would be reminded. It couldn't work.'* Her tears at breakfast, had her mother saying, 'Take one day at a time, tongues will wag, but soon enough there'll be someone else to talk about.'

She walked into Lesley's café and it felt like all eyes were on her. There was a silence. Cathleen didn't know how she did it, but she said, "Morning all. Stop gaping, I'm back now, with double trouble."

Daisy laughed out loud, "Welcome back, Cathleen. I missed you. Are you feeling better?"

The two of them made their way upstairs to the cloakroom. Cathleen hung up her coat, Daisy passed her, her, apron, "Honestly, Cathleen, you have more nerve than a fox in a hen house."

"It's all bravado. I feel scared, scared stiff."

Cathleen was grateful for Daisy's friendship, but was surprised when she said, "You won't be the first to go up the aisle with a little one under the dress, and you won't be the last."

Cathleen didn't have the nerve or the energy to tell Daisy the baby wasn't Ken's. She knew she owed her an explanation, but couldn't find the words, so said. "I'm sure it'll all come out in the wash, as my mum always says."

*

Ed called out to Ken as he recounted the boxes of bananas. "How many times are you going to go over them? I've watched you count them three times now."

135

Ken looked up, his face a beautiful array of colours, "I'm just checking, I need three boxes for The Royal Norfolk tomorrow."

Ed moved over to Ken so he didn't have to shout. "Look mate, why don't you go and speak to her? You know you want to."

"How can I? After what she did, I'd be the laughing stock of the village."

"I don't really want to get involved, Ken. But I went to see Cathleen, and she's sorry, really sorry..."

Ken's brown eyes flashed bright in anger. "Of course she's sorry. Bloody hell, Ed, she's got herself up the spout and no one's accepting the responsibility. She thought she could pin it on me."

"No she didn't, Ken. She told you, remember. I know it's awful, but she made a mistake."

Ken was rattled now, he didn't like this show of loyalty to Cathleen. "What's got into you, how would you feel if it was Tilly?"

"I don't know, Ken, but I feel sorry for her. I know what it feels like to think the world hates you. My own parents couldn't even look at me. Even you turned your back on me."

Ken's cheeks turned red at Ed's accusation, "No I didn't. It was just you wouldn't come to work. I had to bring in a wage, I didn't live in clover like you, you know. Harry would have kicked me out if I didn't earn my keep."

Ed thought of Harry, and how he had suffered himself at the hands of Ken's step dad. "I know that, Ken, but you called me a coward for not standing by Tilly. You said you would have married her and sod the gossips. I remember, Ken."

The conversation was bringing painful memories back for Ed, memories he wanted to bury. Tilly had nearly lost her life with that back street abortion he had arranged. "Look, Ken, I don't want to interfere. It's just I know you love Cathleen, and I know she loves

136

you. Yes she's pregnant, so what if it isn't yours. This chappie from the stables isn't exactly trying to claim his rights to it, is he? You could marry Cathleen and take the kid on."

Ken's anger had cooled, and he now looked at Ed like he was mad. "You are joking, surely?"

"No, I'm not actually. We have Rosie, and we love her like she's our own. You have the chance to have this kiddie as yours, we are about to lose ours."

Ken looked puzzled at this news. Forgetting his own woes, he questioned, "Why, how come?"

"I saw some silly blooming poster advertising Sloe Fair. I pointed it out to Rosie, and said that we would try and find her mum. Don't ask me what I was thinking, but now she wants to go home. Tilly's scared stiff that Rosie's mother will be there, and will want her back. It's a right mess, Ken. Tilly's only just started speaking to me again. She's worried though, I can tell, and so am I."

Ken could see the worry on Ed's face, and realised he wasn't the only one with problems, "I thought you had legal guardianship."

"We do, Ken. But if her mum wants her back, and it's likely that she will, we'll have to give her over. You should see Rosie, she's that excited it's painful. So you see, Ken, you have a chance to still have the woman you love, raise a child as yours and have no fear that someone will come and claim it."

Ken was softening, Ed could tell. "I don't think I could stand it, it's alright for you, Ed, your family have always been held in high esteem. I've always been, the smelly kid from Collyers. I just don't want to be laughed at, or have people pitying me."

"I do pity you, Ken, because you love Cathleen, you always have. I genuinely believe she loves you. What she was thinking of, I don't know, but you won't either if you're too proud to speak to her... How would you feel if this bloke from Hunston goes round there

137

and claims her, what then? I can tell you that'll have people pitying you."

Ed knew he had said enough, Ken looked close to tears, "Look, mate, it's up to you. I just don't want you to throw away a chance of happiness. Cathleen's learnt a hard lesson, you will probably have a better life with her now than you would have done if this hadn't happened."

Ken started counting the boxes again, "Just leave it, Ed. I know you mean well, but I need time."

"Time waits for no one, Ken, I wish I could turn the clock back. I'm not threatening, but I tell you one thing, if you don't claim this babe, I shall. I'll put the pressure on Cathleen to give it to us. Especially if we lose Rosie."

Ed moved away to the office area. He hadn't really thought about adopting Cathleen's baby, but now he had said it, it appealed."

*

Cathleen got home just after six. The town had been quiet, so they had shut up the shop a little early.

She changed out of her overalls and dressed with care. Ken wanted to see her. He had left a message with her mum to say could she go round this evening?

She didn't have tea with her parents. The thought of seeing Ken again had her stomach doing somersaults. She guessed he wanted to sort out the wedding plans and the return of all the gifts. It still made her nervous, the thought of seeing him. He hadn't said he would pick her up, so she decided to walk, sure he would give her a lift home. She corrected these thoughts, telling herself that things had changed, and Ken would not be so amenable. She would take her cycle, and ride there and back. It wouldn't take long.

When Ken invited Cathleen in she was pleased to see they were alone. She wasn't ready to face his mother yet. Ken placed two cups of tea on the kitchen table, she noticed the cups didn't match the saucers. There was a time when this would have caused her to feel contempt for his home, today it made her feel even more ashamed.

"Ken, I don't know what to say, sorry, doesn't seem enough, and yet I need you to know, I – am - sorry, really sorry. Not because I got caught out, but because I've hurt you. I know we can't go back…" Tears threatened, causing her to falter, "What I'm trying to say is, I've been a silly fool, a typical spoilt little brat fool. I've no one to blame but me, and my sorry is said from the heart."

She could see Ken's hand shaking as he held his cup, the silence was deafening. Cathleen had the urge to reach out and touch him, she wanted to comfort him. "You won't believe me Ken, but I love you, not just because of the predicament I'm in. I don't know what I was thinking, and I've had a lot of reflecting. I know I'm selfish, I've been spoilt all my life and it's made me foolish. Ed came to see me, did you know?"

When Ken didn't respond, Cathleen kept talking, "Ed was kind to me he seemed to understand. I've spent so many years resenting him, even when he went in that loony bin, I still didn't like him. Yet when my world crumbled it was Ed who came. Not Tilly, not my best friend, she hasn't been near, god knows what she thinks of me."

Ken's voice was accusing, "What is there to understand? You fancied someone else, and you slept with him, a weekend away. Why, Cathleen, Why?"

The tears that had threatened to fall earlier, fell, "I don't know, hungry for adventure. One last fling. I don't know…" This wasn't enough for Ken, he wanted to know who else she had been with. "There was never anyone else, I promise. It was only Michael."

She wouldn't let Ken interrupt, she was annoyed at the unfair accusation, she raised her voice, "Quiet, let me finish. I know what you're thinking. It's all nonsense, all this rubbish about him not being able to get anyone pregnant, its lies. We argued, and fell out over contraception. He was horrified when I said I wasn't on the pill, well if he couldn't have kids why would he have made such a fuss? I tell you, Ken, they're just trying to wriggle out of it so his precious wedding can take place next year. Well I don't care what they say, it suits me fine, because I wouldn't want him near my baby if he paid me in diamonds."

"Cathleen, you're lying. Why? You've nothing to lose now. I spoke to Michael's father, he was sincere. I could tell."

It was all too much, Cathleen lost her temper, spitting as the words spewed out of her mouth, "You're going to believe them over me. How long have you known me, Ken? I'm telling you I'm pregnant, there was only Michael. What I'd planned at the trundle for you was dreadful. I admit it, I was hoping to tell you in a few weeks the baby was yours. I can't be more honest. It was going to be my way out. Only, I couldn't go through with it. When I looked into your eyes and saw the love there I knew it was impossible. I knew then how foolish I'd been and how much I loved you. It's all too little, too late, I know. I'm here now to tell you I'm sorry, really sorry." She took a deep breath trying to cool her anger, "I know we have to sort things out. We've got to tell our family and friends there'll be no wedding…"

Ken stopped Cathleen midsentence, "What will you do, Cathleen?"

"I don't know, if I'm honest. Mum's being great, dad's coming round a bit. I'll manage, people do. Look at Tilly's mum, and that was years ago…"

"I still want to marry you, Cathleen, if you still want me, that is."

"What did you say?"

140

"I love you, Cathleen. I wish I didn't at times, but I do. I still want to marry you."

"You can't do, Ken. What about the baby? Every time you look at him or her it will remind you of what I did."

"I don't know how it will be, what I do know is, I don't want to live without you in my life. This baby is you, and I will love it because of that."

She couldn't believe what she was hearing, she sat still shocked into silence.

"I'm waiting for an answer. Do you still want me, Cathleen?"

Tears fell again down her face, "Ken, I didn't dare dream of this moment. I never ever in a million years thought even you could be this generous."

"I love you, Cathleen, I can't remember a time when I haven't…"

"Stop, Ken, I love you, honest I do. From today I don't want to be called Cathleen, I want to be plain old Cath. I don't want airs anymore."

"Don't be daft, you'll always be Cathleen. You are humbled now, but I know you, give you a few weeks and you'll be on your high horse again. Don't ever change, Cathleen, I love you just the way you are."

Ken took her in his arms. Amongst tears, she felt safe again. She looked at the clock, "I've got to go, I rode my bike here, and it's getting dark."

"I'll run you back, we can tell your mum and dad our news. That will please them."

Cathleen voiced the awful thought that sprang to mind at the mention of parents. "What about your mum, Ken? She must hate me."

"I'm sure like everyone, she's shocked. After all it was pretty · shocking. Mum will want me to be happy, and if loving you is the only way then she'll be pleased for us."

"I know I said I wouldn't live in this house Ken, but I will, I'll live anywhere with you."

Ken brushed the top of her head, "I've already put a deposit down on the shop at Hawthorn road. I've spoken to Ed, he's fine about it. He even joked he would deliver to us." Ken noticed Cathleen's concerned, pained expression, "What's up, aren't you pleased? I thought you loved the idea of the shop."

"I'm fine, Ken, I'm just pinching myself to make sure I'm not dreaming. It's all too good to be true."

*

Agnes looked up from her magazine as Tilly tapped the door, "Hello, love, what brings you in here at this hour?"

Tilly flopped in the chair opposite saying, "Rosie's found a rook. It must have fallen out of the tree, the big old oak on the bank, just outside. Ed's busy making it some kind of cage. Rosie's set her heart on keeping it."

She could sense there was more to Tilly's visit, "What's up, love? You don't seem yourself lately."

"Oh, gran, I'm so frightened to speak my fears in case they come true."

Agnes reached out and touched Tilly's shoulder, "You know what they say, a trouble shared and all that."

"I know, Gran… It's all this talk of finding Rosie's mum next month. I've a horrible feeling she's going to be in her rainbow tent."

"Don't be daft, girl. Do you know how many travelling fairs there are? Hundreds. What makes you think her mother will be at this one?"

Agnes' heart went out to her granddaughter as she watched her lean forward and put her head in her hands, she sounded defeated, "I've got a funny feeling, that's all. Having Rosie given to us like that was just too good to be true." Agnes didn't respond, the silence encouraged Tilly to continue, "I'm worried about lots of things. I'm having the most horrible thoughts, and my feelings for Ed have changed."

Agnes could tell Tilly wanted to confide and unburden herself, but was finding it difficult. She reached out and took Tilly's hand trying to coax the anxiety out of her.

"Gran, I feel Ed forced me into that abortion. I can't stop thinking if he'd offered to marry me back then we would have twins now, our twins. No one could have taken them…"

Agnes had to interrupt Tilly, she felt this was an unfair accusation, and not healthy. "Tilly, I don't think Ed forced you. If I remember right, you both saw it as a way out. Ed…"

"No, gran, I wanted him to marry me. I begged and begged him at the time. No! It was his idea. I was young, and he was so full of his job, he saw it as the only way. I didn't want to do it, he just convinced me it was the right thing to do, for both of us. When he didn't offer to stand by me I didn't have any other options open."

Agnes didn't like this train of thought, "Tilly these thoughts are destructive. This has come about because of Rosie and your fear of losing her. Now you listen to me, young lady, Ed knows he made a mistake, he doesn't need punishing anymore. He punished himself, you know that. You have to let this go. Now I bet if you mentioned your fears to him about losing Rosie, he would say he wished he'd never seen the poster advertising the fair…" Agnes faltered, she wanted to say they wouldn't lose Rosie, and that her mother

143

wouldn't be there, but what if she was? So she played safe choosing her words carefully, "Look, Tilly, you have to stop worrying about what ifs, we should only cross bridges if we have to."

"What though, gran, what will I do if I do lose her? Will I end up hating Ed? I'm frightened, that's all. I feel so unhappy. It's awful, all Rosie talks about these days is when she sees her mummy she's going to tell her how she can read and write. I just know Rosie wants to go back to her old life. I thought she would see how lucky she was to be with us, and the opportunities we've opened up for her."

Agnes got out of the chair and put the magazine she had been reading in the rack. "I'm going to put the kettle on now. Do you want a cuppa?" Tilly nodded and got up to join her. Agnes said, "Rosie is – very - lucky. You've both given her a good start. If her mother's there, Tilly, you'll have to be brave. The child will want to go home, it's only natural. Rosie'll miss you though, given time. But surely you want her to be reunited with her mum? It's the right thing…" Agnes paused, but when Tilly said nothing she tried to reassure her the best she could, "And you never know, Rosie's mother might not be in a position to take the child back. Now that would make a difference too, wouldn't it?"

Once they were in the main part of the house Agnes could see Rosie and Ed at the bottom of the garden. Both heads were bent over the crate - like cage that had been made for the bird. "Look at them, Tilly, don't be too hard on Ed, if she goes he'll miss her too, and he'll have to cope with his guilt."

"I know, gran, I know all that. It goes round and round my head. I think all this ghastly business with Cathleen has got to me too. Her getting pregnant has uneased me. How could she do that to Ken? And the latest is he's taking the baby on as his. Ed couldn't take me on, and I was carrying his child. Why does everything always go her way? It was like that when we were kids, she always came out smelling of roses, not me. Everything about me always felt wrong and dirty."

Agnes was unused to making drinks these days and the water slopped on the side. Tilly had taken on the role of running the house. She broke into Tilly's tirade as she placed two mugs of tea on the table, "Nothing about you has ever been dirty. You've been one of the most wonderful things in my life, but these thoughts you're having are unhealthy, love. You need to talk to Ed, tell him how you're feeling without blaming. As to Cathleen, she'll have a whole lot of flak to swallow with this scandal. You wouldn't want to be in her shoes, Tilly, I'll tell you."

"I don't believe you, Gran, you wait and see. Everyone will accept her predicament because everything always goes her way. I know I'm being hateful but I can't help it."

Agnes' face looked pained at what she was hearing.

"Gran don't look at me like that. I don't like myself at the moment either. I'm having really bad thoughts about Ed, and I hate Cathleen, and I think…"

Agnes couldn't stand anymore, "Stop it, Tilly. Stop! I don't hate you, I could never hate you. I don't care what you think about Cathleen, but I tell you this, everyone is shocked at her, not just shocked but horrified. I wouldn't want to change places with her, and I can assure you neither would you. Contrary to what you think, she's going to be talk of the village for quite a while, and not good talk. Gossip, the gossip that sticks…"

"No, gran, no it doesn't. Look at me and Ed. No one says or thinks anything. We're the ones left with the result of our mistake. No one cares anymore. If we had had our twins we would be a family now, living here. No one would bat an eye lid. You only have to look at Rosie, we have her, no one keeps saying, 'Why doesn't she call you mummy?' people get used to things, gran."

145

Rosie pushed open the back door, "Granny A you should see my bird. I'm going to call him Rookie."

Agnes rose from her seat to show an interest, but Tilly's exit upstairs didn't go unnoticed, Agnes could see she was crying.

*

Tilly woke with the daylight. She looked at the bedside clock it was now eight o'clock. Ed had left at three this morning for the market, and she had lain awake worrying, which felt like forever. She must have drifted off to sleep because now she was running late. She called out as she ran to the bathroom, "Come on, Rosie, we've overslept."

When she got no answer she peeked in the child's room to rouse her, the bed was empty. Her school uniform was gone from the hanger, and her pyjamas were thrown on her unmade bed.

Tilly made her way downstairs, stopping at the hall window. There was Rosie with a bowl of what looked like weetabix, feeding the bird off a spoon.

She called from the back door, "Rosie come on in. Have you had your breakfast?"

The child was ready for school, it was just her hair that needed tying up. "No, but Rookie has. He was waiting for me, he opens his beak like this…"

Tilly watched, amused as she demonstrated the bird's hunger. "What are you going to have, missy? There's some bacon left over, do you want a sandwich?"

"No thanks, I'll just have cornflakes."

Tilly poured a few in a bowl, and left her eating them while she hurried upstairs to get ready herself. She would have to leave shortly or she would be late for the school crossing.

Once Tilly had brushed Rosie's hair, and tied it up in pigtails, they were ready to leave. The child climbed into the seat on the back of Tilly's bike saying she wanted to be dropped off at the newsagents where she hoped to meet her friends and walk with them across the fields.

"I'll drop you off if they're there, if not you'll have to come with me. We're later today."

When they reached the top of Hunston hill, Tilly caught sight of the children making their way to school. She pulled over, letting Rosie climb out of the bike seat to join her friends. "Don't dawdle. I'll be waiting to see you across the road." As she cycled off with an empty seat behind her, her heart felt heavy, *'How will I cope if she goes for good?'*

*

After seeing Rachel off on the bus, May started to tackle the washing up. Florrie and George had been round for Sunday tea. It was becoming a regular habit, especially since Ed and Tilly had moved to Hunston.

Florrie and George could play bridge, this news had pleased May. Since Agnes moved, and Brenda settled with Alf, their Bridge nights had ceased. Hearing Florrie and George could play would mean they could start their card nights again.

As she put the last of the bowls away, she thought how lucky she was to have such good neighbours. They had both taken to Rachel, and George was smitten with her, and she him. She felt it was a lucky day when her last neighbours moved out and the Coffins moved in.

Feeling in a good mood she picked up the phone and dialled Tilly's number. Agnes answered, May could tell she had hurried for the phone as she sounded out of breath.

"Hello, Agnes, its May here, how are things?"

"Good, and with you?"

"Lovely. We have bridge partners again, George and Florrie play. It's a shame you are so far away now."

There was disappointment in Agnes' voice when she said, "That's alright. My eyes are not what they were, May. Have you seen Ed lately?"

May sensed trouble. When Agnes filled her in with the prospect of Rosie returning to her mother and the funfair, May felt her temper rise. "I told you, Agnes, I knew this would happen. It'll be tears all round. If she blames my Ed it'll be disastrous, he can't take it. Ed's still fragile."

When Agnes changed the subject, asking after Cathleen, May relished the idea of filling her in with the details. She didn't realise Agnes had deliberately diverted the conversation to neutral ground.

"Oh you would never guess, Agnes, it seems like Ken's going to marry her, take on the baby as well. We're all supposed to think it's his, but there are whispers…"

Agnes interrupted, "I was asking how they're coping as a family. I've got a daughter and a granddaughter, and it leaves you living in a glass house."

May was flummoxed. "I wasn't meaning… I was just saying, that's all. At least your June knew the …" She didn't get to finish, Agnes changed the subject again.

148

"Ed tells us your new neighbours have taken a shine to young Rachel."

"Yes, they love her. George spends hours in his shed making things, yet he's so patient with her, Agnes. All Rachel talks about these days is Auntie Florrie and Uncle George."

"I've yet to meet them. Shame our Sunday tea visits have ceased. I miss your sponges."

May glowed with the praise, and saw her chance to bring the conversation back to Rosie. "Yes I miss you all too. I don't want to say too much, especially if she's going back, but I blame her a bit for our absence. Did Tilly tell you how rude Rosie was to George?"

When Agnes remained quiet on the other end of the line, May guessed she had heard all about it. Going into defending mode May said. "I know you've taken to her, Agnes, and she's a cute little thing in some ways, but she needs discipline, and Tilly and Ed haven't got it in them. When I was young we had to respect our elders not insult them. You should have heard her, Agnes…"

"May I'm not being awkward. I have trouble hearing on the phone. I'll get Tilly to call you, but please don't say anything to upset her, Tilly's fragile at the moment."

May stared at the phone as it signalled the dialling tone. Agnes had hung up. *Tilly, fragile. Oh that family! They always stick together. At least when that gypsy girl goes it'll be one less problem.'*

May's good mood disappeared with the phone call.

*

George sat in his shed cutting the heads off the matchsticks. Looking at his watch he thought, *'the youngun' will be home soon.'* He knew she would like to stick this next lot on. No sooner had he had the thought than his shed door flew open. "Uncle George I've been really quick. Can we do the gluing like you said?"

149

"Yes, you come in. Lock the door like I showed you. We don't want mummy seeing our surprise, do we?"

Rachel moved her chair over to the door and pushed the bolt across. George wiped his hand down his beard, "Come and give old Uncle George one of your kisses." He lifted her onto his knee and her tongue touched his lips, "That's like a little snake bite."

Rachel giggled, "Uncle George you're funny. Shall we do it again?"

Noses bumped as they played the little kissing game. George's voice became serious, "Now my little angel this won't get the sticking done, will it? You sit this way, on my lap…" He turned her round so she could work at the table, and adjusted her so her legs were astride his own. He held the tops of her bare thighs, exciting himself with the feel of soft warm flesh. They were making a house, it was to be for May. George had said it could be a surprise present for Christmas. While Rachel concentrated on sticking the matchsticks on the roof, George stroked her inner thigh.

Rachel giggled, "It tickles."

"You concentrate on the gluing, there's a good girl. You're doing an excellent job."

He licked his upper lip, and asked himself if he dare. *'Be patient, Georgy boy, don't hurry her.'*

"Oops, sit still my little angel, Uncle George can't hold you if you wriggle."

George licked his upper lip again, he wanted to wipe his beard which was a habit of his, but he didn't want to move his hands from their position.

A voice from the garden broke the spell. May was calling Rachel for dinner. The latch on the door went several times. George had already jumped up, "Hang on, hang on, I'm coming." George's heart lurched, he didn't open the door immediately, but called

150

through the locked door, "May can you give us a minute. Couldn't you go in to Florrie? This is top secret stuff in here."

"I haven't got time today, George. Hurry up, her dinner's on the table."

George could tell May was disgruntled. This is not what he wanted. He needed to keep her sweet. He slid open the bolt and opened the door. He caught sight of her head disappearing, she was back in her own garden. Turning to Rachel he whispered, "You did tell mummy we were making a surprise for her, and she mustn't see, didn't you?"

Rachel giggled, "I did. I said it was our secret. I won't tell her."

"There's my little angel. This'll be our special secret."

Rachel thought this a fun game, but was already hurrying over the little fence calling, "I got to go now."

George stood watching at the door. May was just coming out again. Her annoyance was reflected in the way she spoke to Rachel, "Come on, you know we're going out this evening."

George was pleased to hear Rachel say, "Mummy, we're making a surprise, no one must see. Not until it's finished. It's a secret."

Satisfied, his nerves settled. The thrill of getting caught added to his excitement. George went back into his shed. He locked the door, pulled down the blind, and took out his hanky.

*

May didn't know where the week had gone. It was Friday already. She had made some cheese scones and rock cakes for supper as George and Florrie were coming round for a game of Bridge this evening.

151

Rachel broke into May's preparations asking, "I want to go round to Uncle George. We've got work to do."

"Oh no, not tonight missy, you've been round there every night this week. You'll be making a nuisance of yourself at this rate."

Rachel started to cry, "Uncle George likes me to go, he says I have to, or he'll be upset and cry."

"Don't be so ridiculous, Rachel. It's naughty to tell falsehoods. You'll get a pimple on your tongue."

Before May could stop her she fled from the house, jumped over the fence and ran to the shed, banging on the door. "Uncle George, let me in."

May was already over the fence by the time he got the door opened. He picked Rachel up, saying, "What's all this?"

Rachel clung round George's neck. "I wanted to come round. Mummy said I couldn't. I told her you would be upset and cry. I don't want you to cry, Uncle George, you're my friend."

May noticed his laugh sounded too loud. He looked uncomfortable. There was a red flush that crept across his cheeks as he told her not to be silly. He prised her off his neck and put her on the ground. Rachel didn't like this. When things didn't go her way she had the most terrible, childish temper. She stamped her feet, tears fell, and her accusations were shouted, "You're telling lies, Uncle George. You said I had to come round. He did mummy, tell him if he lies he'll get a pimple on his tongue."

The commotion in the garden brought Florrie out, "What is going on? It sounds like World War Three's broke out."

May couldn't put her finger on it, but there was something here she didn't like. Something didn't fit. Trying to bring calm to a tense situation, she said, "It's alright, Florrie, I was coming to say I've got the most terrible headache, and need to cancel the Bridge tonight.

Rachel wanted to help George again, but I've said no. She's throwing one of her paddies."

May was aware George had disappeared back to his shed, leaving the three of them in the garden. Rachel was still stamping and screaming. May knew she would take some calming down. Her tantrums were few and far between, but when they erupted she was difficult to handle.

Florrie spoke to her, hoping to win her round, "What's all this noise for? You can help Uncle George tomorrow. Mummy isn't very well, she'll need her big girl to help her."

"Uncle George tells lies, I don't want to help him."

May could see Florrie was upset, but she had questions of her own to ask. "Don't worry, Florrie, she'll calm down once I get her indoors. Sorry about this evening, another time."

May grabbed hold of Rachel harder than she should, and dragged her indoors by her arm. She was still kicking and screaming. Once May had closed her door she raised her voice in warning. "Pack this in, Rachel. Come on! Mummy's got a headache."

May managed to pick her up and sit with her in the armchair. "Come on now, come on." As she rocked her, whispering over and over in her ear, Rachel's rigid body sagged, and she gave way to tears.

"What was all that about? Calling Uncle George a liar. You've upset Auntie Florrie. You have to learn if I say no, I mean no. You mustn't start calling people liars."

Rachel sniffed, the tears had subsided. "He did say I had to go every day. He did. He said he would cry if I didn't. He said he wouldn't be my friend."

May tried to hide her concern. She knew Rachel was well able to tell lies to get what she wanted, or to wriggle out of things, but May had never seen her as righteous as this. "Alright, we'll say Uncle George is very naughty. You told him he would get a pimple on his tongue, let's hope it's a great big one."

May was pleased to see Rachel giggle. "We'll box up the cakes and scones, and perhaps we'll go over to see Ed and Tilly tonight. Would you like that?"

May waited for a response. Rachel's eyes shone a watery green, and her little round face was still flushed from her temper tantrum, "You said you had a headache. Is that a lie too?"

May was always amazed at the child's perception at times. "It's not a real lie, it's what you call a white lie. It's what we tell when we don't want to hurt anyone's feelings. When you said Uncle George was lying Rachel, I believed you. The trouble is, now I know Uncle George tells lies I don't want to play card games with him. So it was easier to make an excuse rather than hurt Auntie Florrie, do you understand?"

Rachel said she did, but her attention had turned to finding a Tupperware box for the cakes. "I shall see Rosie, we can play in the park."

May watched Rachel put the cakes in two tins, and her mind wandered to her own childhood.

May had had an Aunt and Uncle who had no children, and she and her brother, Billy, used to go and stay with them in the school holidays. Uncle Ganga, as she called him, was always good fun. He seemed to like May more than Billy. He liked her to brush his hair and sit on his lap. He would tell Billy he was too big, or boys don't sit on men's knees. It had been accepted, and it had been obvious that she was Uncle Ganga's favourite. May had relished in the attention. Her own mother had always favoured Billy over her. So, to have someone love and dote on her, had been special.

What troubled May now is the memory of when her Aunt had taken Billy to the shops, May had stayed behind with her Uncle Ganga. He had sat her on his lap and bounced her up and down saying it was a horse ride. May had giggled at first, but after a while she had got frightened. She hadn't liked it, and when she had said stop, Uncle Ganga hadn't listened. He had seemed to lose himself in the game, while she was bounced and rubbed up and down on his lap. This had made May feel uncomfortable, but she had never said a word to anyone. It wasn't until many years later that she had fully understood what Uncle Ganga had been up to.

Rachel's excitable chatter brought her out of her reverie, she peeked her head round the lounge door to see her playing with her dolly. May was tempted to ask her if Uncle George ever makes her feel nervous, but she didn't know how? With this thought in mind she told herself she would speak to Norman. She thought of Rosie, the child had taken a dislike to George on first sight. Could she see something? May was in a turmoil, and the headache she had feigned had become a reality.

Leaving Rachel playing she dialled Ed's phone number. Tilly answered.

"Hello, Tilly, we're at a loose end tonight, we thought we might pop over. I haven't seen your gran for weeks." May held her breath, hoping for an acceptance.

Tilly's voice sounded sincere, "May, we're at the village hall this evening. It's a Harvest Supper dance. Rosie's excited to go, and has been looking forward to it all week."

May was desperate to get over there now, she didn't know why, but she didn't want to stay here. "Can't we come over and sit with your Gran, as I said I haven't seen her in a long while."

"May, gran's coming too." Tilly must have sensed May's need for a visit, kindness had her saying "You can come if you like. Rachel will love it. We have to take something for the table, Gran's made a loaf, and I'm in the middle of making cheese pastries…"

She didn't let Tilly finish, "That would be wonderful. I've already made a batch of scones and cakes. Tilly, thank you, love, you're a life saver. I've had an afternoon of it with Rachel…" May was going to tell Tilly about George but she interrupted her.

"May, Rachel can spend the weekend here with us if she likes, It'll give you a break. Tonight we're at the Harvest Supper, and tomorrow we're pony trekking to Dell Quay with The Forresters. She'll love that."

May thought about the trouble with Cathleen that happened there, but good sense kept her quiet. "Thank you, Tilly, I shall look forward to seeing you all this evening. What time?"

"It starts at seven, I'll let gran know. I've got to go, May, the cheese pastries need taking out of the oven. See you later. Bye."

May put the receiver down, thinking, *'how could I have let next door take precedence over my Sunday family teas?'*

*

Tilly walked the girls to the stables. Despite the three years between them, these days Rachel and Rosie got on well. When they turned into the paddock Tilly caught sight of Lucy, who was saddling up the ponies, "Hello, Luce, we've an extra, that's not a problem is it?" Lucy looked across at Rachel and Rosie. They were hanging over the stable door where the new foal was. They were both on tiptoe. "More the merrier. Rachel does well, doesn't she?"

Tilly knew what Lucy meant, what with her being Down syndrome. "Rachel has private education, and lots of time put into her development. As awkward as my Mother - in-law can be she's done wonders with her."

156

Lucy pulled on her riding hat, "She's really cute. I love her. Michael was good with her too."

"Oh, don't mention that name. Is he here today?"

Lucy slipped the leading reins over, and led the first two ponies out, "No, Michael's in Ireland, some horse trading fair. You know Christine's finished with him?"

Tilly swung herself up on the gate, "I'm not surprised. Can you believe it, Ken's forgiven Cathleen. I can't bear to speak to her at the moment. She still says the baby's Michael's, she won't budge."

"It can't be, Tilly, honest. I think Michael would love it to be, but there's no way."

"Well she's a bigger tramp than we give her credit for."

Lucy pulled open the gate causing Tilly to jump down, "I don't think there's any credit in it. Do you?"

Tilly followed her, "No, but Cathleen's always had her own way, always. Poor Christine. How is she?"

"To be honest I think it's the best thing that could have happened to her. He has used her for so long. They were childhood friends, this relationship was expected rather than developed."

Tilly fell forward as Rosie ran at her from behind, and Rachel took hold of Tilly's hand. "Come on, girls, ponies are ready."

Tilly liked Lucy, she worked long, hard hours, managing some big beasts, yet she was a gentle girl. Her hair made her look boyish, but she was naturally cute. Her patience with Rachel was admirable. Tilly had so many questions to ask on the Cathleen and Michael front, and was intending to bring the conversation back to them again. Tilly wondered if Lucy had a soft spot for Michael herself, but the chance to speak again didn't arise. Rosie was a natural in the saddle, but Rachel needed close supervision, and had to be led.

"Kick him gently in his sides, Rachel, there's a good girl."

Tilly had hold of the leading rein while she rode in front on a frisky horse. It didn't want to follow the others, and seemed to resent having a pony following on a rope draped over its back. Rachel spoke out in a sulky voice when she realised they were dragging behind. "I want Michael to lead me. You make my horse slow."

"Come on, Rachel, Michael isn't here. Shall I call Lucy? She might be able to chivvy him on."

"Mummy's cross with Michael, I hear her telling daddy."

Tilly smiled, she was well aware of how May would love this gossip on Cathleen. She didn't comment, as she couldn't trust what Rachel would repeat, or how it would be interpreted.

"I don't like Cathleen, she shouts at me."

Tilly was shocked at this revelation, "I'm sure she doesn't shout at you, Rachel. Perhaps she's sometimes frightened you'll hurt yourself, and she gets concerned."

"No, Tilly. I saw her with Michael, they were kissing. She shouted at me... like this."

Rachel's voice rose in a scream making Tilly's horse jump sideways. "Steady, steady. Rachel, don't!"

"She did, Tilly, she said everyone kisses. It doesn't mean anything, Uncle George kisses me too. We kiss every day before we work on our sticking."

Tilly felt goose-pimples go up her arms. This sounded horrible. She wondered how she could probe without saying too much. She chose to keep the conversation with Cathleen.

"Why didn't you tell on Cathleen, Rachel?"

"She said it was a secret, and if I didn't tell I could be a bridesmaid, and wear puff sleeves like Rosie."

158

Tilly's heart hardened even more towards her best friend. "When anyone tells you things are a secret, Rachel, it normally means it's wrong. Do you understand?"

"Uncle George and me have a secret."

Tilly felt sick. "You should never have secrets from your Mummy. Mummies have to know everything to keep us safe."

"No, Tilly. Uncle George is making Mummy a gift for Christmas, I can't tell her. It will ruin her surprise."

Relief flooded over Tilly. She knew Rachel was an affectionate little thing, and guessed George was bombarded with Rachel's sloppy kisses the minute she saw him. The same kisses Rosie hated when she first met her.

Tilly's thoughts went back to her friend. *What a bitch, she only let Rachel be bridesmaid for fear of what she might tell. Cathleen Hills, you deserve all you get."* Tilly thought about Ken getting a hiding from Michael, which in turn led to Christine's broken engagement, and then this baby Cathleen's carrying, and the fact that no one seems to know whose it is. Tilly's heart hardened, *'How could Ed have gone round there and offered her support? If we lose Rosie next month, the only thing I shall be pleased about is not having to watch Rosie follow Cathleen up the aisle.'* Tilly toyed with the idea of telling May why Cathleen had a sudden change of heart on the bridesmaid front. Only, not even Tilly could bring herself to be that vindictive. She told herself that as of today, Lucy seemed a much nicer friend to have.

*

May put two mugs of tea on the tray, buttered the toast, and smeared her homemade plum jam over the top. She couldn't remember the last time her and Norman had had breakfast in bed like this. Certainly not since they took Rachel on. This brought her thoughts back to George next door, and the nagging worry it had caused. May had thought about sharing it with Norman, but was

159

frightened he would say, 'It's just your nasty mind.' She was known for being outspoken. She thought about her Uncle Ganga again, *'Could I confide in Norm about that?'* The thought of it made May cringe. *'What would he think?'* May had kept that secret close to her chest since she was about ten years old, she was too old to start sharing it now. Just remembering it made her feel dirty. *'No, I will have to sort this out myself. I will talk to Florrie.'* As she carried the tray loaded up with breakfast, she couldn't help wishing she hadn't got so friendly with them.

"Here we go, love, my homemade jam too."

"This is heaven, May. Come on, settle back beside me. I've kept your side warm."

May slipped off her dressing gown, slid in beside Norman, and found herself hedging round her worries. "Norman, didn't you enjoy the harvest supper Friday? It was lovely to see the girls dancing together like that, wasn't it?"

Norman pulled himself up, reaching for his tea, "Yes, it was a good evening. I was looking forward to a game of Bridge though. I'm still not sure why our plans changed."

"Oh Rachel threw a paddy, I already had a bit of a headache, and that sort of finished the idea of an evening of cards."

"Are they coming in for tea this afternoon? We could play this evening."

May's reply was too quick, and a little too loud, "No, Norman. We have to pick Rachel up this evening. Tilly's invited us over for tea. I'm looking forward to it. I think we've been a bit foolish putting the neighbours before our family. How long has it been since we had tea at Tilly and Ed's?"

"Oh I can't remember, and I really don't care. I'll go where ever you want. I didn't think our not going to Tilly and Ed's had anything to do with our neighbours, I just thought you'd taken a dislike to Rosie."

"Nonsense, it's that child that's got the opinions. She hated George before she even met him."

When the subject moved to Rosie's dislike of the man, May felt able to air her concerns, "Norman, do you think it possible that Rosie can see things we can't?"

Norman brushed the crumbs off the bedspread causing May to shout about not wanting crumbs in the bed. Norman swung his legs over the side, "I need the loo, but on the Rosie front, it sounds like she'll be leaving them soon. I can see trouble then, and I'm no psychic."

May watched Norman go to the bathroom. He had aged, he moved slower, and his back took a while to straighten. *We're not getting any younger. Perhaps taking Rachel on was a bit ambitious for a couple of oldies like us.'*

May watered the pot plant and was putting it back on the lounge window sill when she caught sight of Florrie in the garden. May didn't want to confront her, so she pushed open the window and called out, "Florrie, alright?"

Florrie stepped over the fence. May's heart sank, she didn't want to invite her in, nor get into deep conversation. "Florrie, have to take a rain check on tea this afternoon, Rachel's been at Ed's all weekend, we are picking her up, and have been invited there."

May could see the disappointment on her face, but was relieved when Florrie smiled, saying she understood.

"Sorry, Florrie, that's my phone ringing."

Whether Florrie could hear there was no phone ringing or not, May didn't care. She didn't want to get caught up in explanations, she wanted to do a little probing of her own first.

*

When May and Norman arrived at Park View they could hear the excited squeals coming from the garden. The girls were feeding Rosie's bird.

Norman went in, in front of May. Hearing his greeting made her envious. He was always so relaxed with Tilly, "Hello, love, how have the horrors been?"

Tilly laughed, "They're as good as gold, Norman. They're up the garden. Go and see."

May pushed forward. "I'll go, Tilly. How was the horse riding?"

"Fine, May, Rachel loves the horses. It has been a good weekend, she is welcome anytime."

May ignored this invite, saying, "I'll go out there and see this bird."

Watching from the door, she could hear Rosie telling Rachel to hold the sugar tongs still so Rookie could take the food off. Rachel was squealing, frightened he would peck her fingers. It was a good sight for a troubled mind, and May chastised herself for her earlier thoughts of wondering if she was too old to give this lovable child a home. Rachel spotted May, she dropped the sugar tongs and ran full pelt at her.

"Mummy, I've been riding, and we had a tea party with Rosie's dolls. Tilly laid a blanket on Rosie's bedroom floor, we had her teddies and dollies all join us. Can we do that, mummy, can we?"

162

May hugged Rachel back, stroking her hair which Tilly had put in plaits, she said, "Yes I'm sure we can? Perhaps Rosie would like to come and stay at ours one weekend?"

Rachel jumped up and down, "Yes, Rosie, say you will, please."

Rosie looked up from feeding Rookie, "I'm going home soon, Auntie May. Didn't you know?"

Rachel ran indoors claiming she needed the toilet. May knelt down with Rosie asking if she could have a go at feeding the bird. May was as frightened of its beak as Rachel was, but she told herself, needs must.

"Rosie, so you're going home then. What about here, isn't this your home now?"

"No, Auntie May, my home's with me mummy. If we can find her, I wanna go. Ed says it right."

"It is right, darling, it is right. I expect she has missed you. We will miss you too."

"But you don't like me, really like me. I knows you don't."

Rosie's dreadful English jarred May, but she ignored it trying to keep the conversation going. "Of course I like you, Rosie. I've just been worried about this, that's all."

Rosie was all ears, her grey eyes looked witch like as they stared at May looking for answers. May hadn't realised before what a pretty child she was. "Auntie May, what do you mean, this?"

May sat back on her ankles putting the sugar tongs down. The bird started hopping up and down trying to peck them. Rosie picked them up and started spooning food into its mouth as if she was its mother.

"You love animals don't you, Rosie?" When Rosie ignored her, engrossed in the feeding, May continued.

163

"I have tried not to love you the way Granny A has, because I didn't want to feel sad when you went back to your mummy. That's what I mean by, all this. You're still very young, and you won't understand. But look at that bird you're feeding. He thinks you're its mummy, you're doing a good job of looking after it. How would you feel if in the morning a big rook was waiting by the cage to take it back to its nest? You would feel very sad, wouldn't you?"

When Rosie still stared at May, saying nothing, she felt inclined to ask, "Do you understand what I'm trying to say, Rosie?"

"Auntie May, I know Tilly will be sad. I'll be crying too. But I wants to see me mummy. I don't belong here. I misses the fair, and me Uncle Jimmy."

"I know, and I understand. I think you're like your mummy, I think you sense things like she does. You sense things about Rachel's Uncle George don't you?"

Rosie was quiet. "You can tell me, Rosie. I need to know if you're going away. I need you to tell me what you feel, or I won't be able to protect Rachel."

Rosie sat stroking the rook's head not saying a word. May questioned whether the child was too young to understand what she was asking, or whether it was the right thing to have done. The rook hopped on Rosie's outstretched hand, it pecked at her jumper. May was just going to brush the top of Rosie's head and leave her to her antics when she spoke. May had to lean in closer so as to hear.

"I don't know about your Uncle George. I knows something. It makes me heart beat fast. I feel real scared when I go near that garden."

May felt bewitched, "What does that mean, Rosie? Is Uncle George a bad man?"

"Sometimes I see things, then when it happens I think I must have dreamed it. I feel things. I told Uncle Norman I could feel the heartbeat in the dirt. He laughed at me. I don't like it, Auntie May."

"You have a gift, Rosie. You have the same gift as your mummy. Could you please try hard to see what it is about our Uncle George that I need to worry about?"

Tilly broke the spell, "Come on, you two, tea's ready. I didn't know you liked birds, May."

May got to her knees ignoring Tilly's observation, "We're coming. Rosie's doing a fantastic job being mummy to this creature, that's for sure."

May was amazed Rosie never said a word about their conversation. Tea was a jolly affair.

When it was time to go May gave heartfelt thanks for having Rachel, and when she said good bye to Rosie, she got down and hugged her. If any of the others thought this show of affection strange, nothing was said. May could feel the child's breath on the side of her face. Then her mouth found May's ear, and Rosie whispered, 'He's a bad man.'

*

Monday 3rd October 1966

Geoffrey Covax looked at his list, Cathleen Hills. His heart sank. He'd known this family personally for about six years. Pam had worked in their home as a mother's help when his wife had had the twins. Hal had worked on the doctor's home to make room for his large family. They had shared Christmas' in each other's houses, and now this. What a disgrace the girl has shamed them with.

He turned Cathleen's card over, and lost himself in thought. *'A month ago she'd come in here with what looked like the symptoms of depression.*

I'd thought with the wedding looming she was getting cold feet. I'd never in a million years thought this was the reason. To be having a little one on the way a few weeks before the wedding was one thing, but to be carrying another man's child…'

A knock at his door brought him out of his reverie, "Yes?"

"Are you ready, Doctor? There is quite a queue forming."

"Yes, yes, send in Cathleen Hills please."

As she entered he pointed to the chair for her to sit. He found it difficult to speak, and focused for a few seconds writing on her card. When he looked up he was pleased to see she looked suitably embarrassed. "What can I do for you, Cathleen?" He wasn't going to make this visit easy for her.

"I've not had a period since the beginning of August, or thereabout."

"Is it possible that you are pregnant?" He waited, staring at her over his half-moon reading glasses. He could feel her uncomfortableness.

She had the decency to look down at her lap, she twisted her fingers in her lap, "Yes, I have been in a sexual relationship."

Geoffrey thought about the state of Ken's face and broken heart, when only a couple of weeks ago he had come to him. He didn't want to let Cathleen off the hook that easy. "Is the father standing by you?"

"Yes… no… well, I'm marrying Ken in October."

"So the father is standing by you, you are getting married in October, it isn't too drastic then, is it?"

Cathleen started to cry. "The baby isn't Ken's. You must have heard?"

Geoffrey sat quietly, he turned his attention to writing down a few notes on her medical card. When Cathleen spoke next Geoffrey felt perhaps he should have kept his own feelings out of it.

"I know you know. Ken told me he had been to see you. I feel dreadful enough with the gossip all around me, without coming here to be judged. My work have just found out about my predicament, at first they thought it was Ken's, now all I get is whisper, whisper. What is it with…"

Geoffrey interrupted her, becoming professional. "Come now. I was just making sure. Sometimes I hear things that are not as they appear. Let's start again, shall we?"

He gave her a tissue, and she blew her nose, getting herself together.

"Now you say your last period was August?"

Cathleen nodded, she couldn't speak.

"Have you had any morning sickness?"

Cathleen shook her head in answer.

Geoffrey stood up, "Okay. I'll need a urine sample, but let's have a look at you first. If you go behind the curtain and remove your underclothes I'll give you an examination, I should be able to tell you roughly how far you're gone."

Geoffrey washed his hands in the basin, while Cathleen got dressed.

"I can't feel anything to suggest you are having a baby, Cathleen. I think we need to look at what has been happening over these last few weeks…"

Cathleen didn't let Geoffrey finish, "You told my mum she wasn't pregnant and nine months later she had Hannah, you…"

"Yes, I know that, Cathleen, but I think with what you have been putting your body through, with the not eating, the worry of all this trouble, your body has gone on strike, so to speak. Once you settle down things will go back to normal."

Geoffrey watched relief spread over Cathleen's face as she said. "Are you sure?"

"I can't be a hundred percent certain, until we do further tests. I would bet that in a few weeks you will find things return to normal with a healthy diet."

This was a huge weight off Cathleen's shoulders. "When will I know for sure?"

"One step at a time. I will send this off to the lab. You come back and see me next week, and I will be able to confirm what I feel I already know."

As the door closed behind her Geoffrey sighed. *'God, forbid any of mine bring home trouble like that.'*

He got out of his chair, opened his door and called, "Mrs Jenkins."

*

Pam was relieved to hear Cathleen's news, but she couldn't help remembering her own false diagnosis. Pam sighed at the memory of how Cathleen had spoilt those early days of Hannah's imminent arrival. She couldn't help thinking, *'Perhaps Hal is right. Cathleen's been too spoilt by far.'* She took a tray into the lounge to find Cathleen sprawled on the sofa, reading a magazine. "Come on, put your feet down. Let me sit with you."

Cathleen swung her legs round, "Can't you sit over there? I'm worn out."

Pam put the strainer in the cup and started pouring the tea, "Now, if Geoffrey had said you were having a baby I would have had sympathy for you. The early weeks of pregnancy are exhausting, but you're not, so we need to start looking at our original plans for the big day.

Cathleen jumped up off the sofa, "Not now, mum. I might go and see Tilly. I can tell her the good news. She hasn't been near me since she heard I might be pregnant. I know she can't have kids, so she was probably jealous."

Pam was appalled at Cathleen's judgement of Tilly's distance. "Don't you think it possible that she was upset at how you hurt Ken?"

"Here you go, I'm never going to live this down, am I? It's all been a mistake, I want to start again, put it behind me."

Pam was determined not to bow down to Cathleen's temper, "You might want to, but Tilly might not be so quick to forgive and forget. Your behaviour was shocking, Cathleen, shocking. There will be people in the village too that will have long memories."

"So! I didn't hurt her, or any of them, did I? Tilly is meant to be my best friend. I went to see her when she had that abortion, and…"

Pam looked at her daughter standing in front of her, defiance flashing in her eyes, her cheeks had taken on that tell-tale red stain, and for the first time Pam felt feelings of dislike towards her. "Cathleen, I think you're forgetting, Tilly has been Ken's friend for a long time now. They worked together for many years in her garden, she would have become very fond of him."

Cathleen wasn't bowing down, she was quick to defend herself, "So has Ed, yet he came to see me. Told me we all make mistakes. Funny how he understands, but my family don't. No, they just point the finger, they have to keep jabbing. I…"

"Go, Cathleen. Go and see Tilly. I hope you're right, and she welcomes you with open arms. Perhaps it's as you say, just us, and we've got it all wrong. Yes, what you did was just a silly mistake.

169

Your behaviour led to Ken getting a hiding of a life time. It left you thinking you were carrying another man's child." Cathleen went to butt in, "No, Cathleen, you hear me out. This Michael's fiancé has broken off her engagement, and not forgetting the shame you have brought to our good name…"

Pam had never seen Cathleen rear up so vehemently, "That's it, isn't it. It's all about you, you and your silly…"

Pam slapped Cathleen hard. It shocked them both into silence. Cathleen stood holding the side of her face, and Pam slumped back in the chair horrified at the thought that she had been pushed to such violence. Only a few weeks ago she had slapped her husband. It was again over Cathleen, and what she called a silly mistake. Pam's voice sounded tired, she didn't apologise, "Get out of my sight, Cathleen. I've nothing more to say to you at the moment.

When Pam heard the front door slam shut she felt relief that Cathleen had gone. *Where did all that come from? We should have been sitting here relieved there is no baby on the way, and been able to sit and sort out the wedding plans that are looming fast.*' Pam wondered how they would put this right. She had never hit either of her children, ever. Pam reached for the tea, her hands were shaking so much she couldn't hold the cup. *'Oh Cathleen, you'll be the death of me.'*

*

Cathleen didn't go to Tillys'. Her mother had made her unsure of the reception she would get. *'Would Tilly take Ken's side over me? We've been friends for, forever.'*

Cathleen told herself she didn't care. She would go to the warehouse and tell Ken the good news. She caught the bus on Chichester road, enjoying the appreciative look the bus driver gave her as she boarded the bus.

She sat behind a woman who had a baby on her lap, and a toddler who was sitting next to her with a sticky lolly in its mouth. The baby was being rocked, by what looked like its mother. She was trying to calm the crying.

Cathleen sat watching, thinking, *'Urgh! That could have been me in a couple of years. What a thought.'* She was glad when the bus stopped for her at the bottom of Quarry Lane. She giggled at the driver, who gave her a saucy wink as she hopped off the bus.

Ed was out on deliveries, it was just Ken at the warehouse, boxing up orders. He looked up, a smile spread across his face, "Hello, Cathleen, to what do I owe this honour?"

"I thought you ought to know, Michael's dad was telling the truth, there's to be no baby."

Ken dropped the box and came over to Cathleen. He put his arms around her, "Are you okay?"

"Mum went ballistic at me." Cathleen gave way to tears, "She slapped me, you should have heard her, Ken. You would have thought I was the worst person in the world."

"Sometimes, Cathleen, people manage to hold themselves together while things look bad, and then when the pressure's off they collapse."

"Well, I wish she'd collapsed out of my sight, that's all I can say. She was horrid to me, spiteful."

Cathleen nestled into Ken's shoulder. It felt safe and familiar, "It was as if she was cross that I wasn't pregnant. Do you know, she even hinted that Tilly wouldn't want to see me?"

"Hush now, it's as I say, relief that it's all over. We can go back to planning our future now. Like it should be, on our own first. You never know, Cathleen, we might have our own sound of tiny feet before next year's out."

Cathleen shuddered. The thought of that woman on the bus made it all the more unappealing. "Let's have some time on our own, Ken, just the two of us. I think what with what happened, we need to start again."

"You are pleased there's no baby, aren't you?"

"Of course I am, Ken. This is the best news. You've been wonderful to me. I want you to know, you've been a better support than my family. Between mum and dad, they've made me feel like a tramp."

Cathleen noticed Ken didn't say, 'of course you're not' nor did he offer any support against her parents' verbal attacks, he just said, "You're right, let's start again. I'd got used to the idea, Cathleen, of a little one. I would have accepted it, you do know that, don't you?"

Cathleen ignored the question, she was tired of the subject. She was pleased to be able to unburden herself. Cathleen felt better, until she said "Is it okay if I phone Tilly? I want to check she's in. I'm going to see her and tell her my news. She'll be pleased."

Ken shuffled his feet, making out he was busy again with the boxes. He avoided eye contact. "I would give Tilly a bit of time, Cathleen."

"Why? What have I done to her?"

"It's what you did to me, Cathleen." He didn't want to tell her how disgusted Tilly was, yet he didn't know how to let Cathleen down without hurting her feelings. "You know how loyal Tilly is…"

Cathleen butted in, "I've been her friend longer than I've been yours."

"It's a bit like Ed said, you and him are alike, well so are Tilly and I. We both had a struggle in childhood, nothing came easy to us."

Cathleen felt her anger rising again, "Well, if you're so alike, perhaps you should have married her. Then…"

Ken grabbed at Cathleen's arm frightened she might flee, "Stop it, Cathleen. I just wanted you to understand, there's a reason Tilly's kept her distance. Let her come to you."

"I won't lose any sleep over her, Ken. I've made new friends. Daisy understands. I don't get this grief at work. They're my true friends."

Cathleen knew she had won this argument. She walked out of the warehouse without a good bye to Ken. Her back was up, she was annoyed. She walked to the bus stop, and while she waited the fifteen minutes for it to arrive she thought, *'everyone was kinder when I thought I was pregnant, now I'm not they're all venting their anger out on me. Why, what's the point?'*

The bus came round the corner, it was the same driver who had winked at her earlier. She had no intention of smiling or giggling at him now. She was in no mood for fraternising with anyone. It dawned on her that she had to go home and face her mum. This wasn't a good thought.

*

Ed came up behind Tilly, putting his arms around her waist. "You'll never guess what, Tilly?"

She pulled off the bright yellow washing up gloves, and wriggled round to face him. "What?"

"Cathleen's not preggers. All that trouble she caused, and it was a false alarm."

Tilly looked bored, "Why does that not surprise me?"

173

Ed pushed Tilly's hair back out of her eyes, "Come on, this isn't like you, Tilly. It's a huge relief for Ken. Be pleased for him, if nothing else."

Tilly pulled out of Ed's embrace, she picked up the tea towel and started wiping up the saucepans. "I am pleased for him. If he's got any sense he'll finish with her now. Let her find some other mug to kick down."

Ed watched the stiff way she held her shoulders, and the punishing way she was drying the saucepans. "Tilly, what is it, what's eating at you?"

"I've made up my mind not to go to their wedding. I cannot watch her waltz up the aisle, full of false promises. I think I'd be sick."

"Don't be daft, Tilly. Rosie's going to be a bridesmaid, she would be so disappointed."

Tilly turned round so she could face Ed, the drying up put on hold for the moment, "No, Ed. Rosie will be gone on the twenty first, or have you forgotten that already?"

Ed tried to take Tilly in his arms again, but she held him at arm's length, "Leave it, Ed, I'm not blaming you. I just want you to take on board that I'm finished with Cathleen…" She didn't get to finish, Ed lost his patience, "Tilly, she made a mistake. I can't believe you're being like this. She's been your best friend for years. You two used to drive me mad with your giggling. What she's done doesn't affect you, it's… "

"Oh, shut up, Ed. She's a bitch, a real bitch. Do you know, Rachel wasn't originally allowed to be her bridesmaid, do you know why? Because Cathleen said she would ruin the photos. You might well gape, I wouldn't have believed it if I hadn't heard it with my own ears. Do you know why she changed her mind?" When Ed stood dumbfounded at this outburst Tilly continued, "Well, let me fill you in. Rachel caught Cathleen and Michael kissing in the stable. She was so frightened Rachel would tell, Cathleen said she could be her bridesmaid, just to keep her quiet. This is your precious friend, the one you say is so like you, and the one you went round to, to offer friendship. I tell you Ed, the more I think about what she's done, the more I hate her. There you are, I've said it. I hate her, Ed. I think she's a selfish, spoilt, bitch."

Ed paled. "Tilly, that's a dreadful thing to say. Cathleen couldn't..." Ed didn't get to finish, "What part are you having trouble swallowing, Ed? Because it's all true. Why would I lie to you? Ask Rachel if you don't believe me. That's if she'll tell you. I think she was upset that she'd let it slip to me. I bet Cathleen frightened the kiddie into silence."

"Does mum know, Tilly?"

"I doubt it. Though she might remember when she first asked if Rachel could be a bridesmaid. Pam had given her the brush off because she already knew Cathleen didn't want Rachel under any circumstances."

Ed plonked himself down on the kitchen stool, the one placed at the sink for Rosie to stand on. "Tilly I'd no idea. I'm sickened. If what you say is true, I really wish I hadn't offered a hand of friendship. I only did it because I knew what it felt like to think the whole world hates you."

Tilly picked up the tea towel, and started the drying up again. "It wouldn't matter if the whole world did hate her, Ed. Cathleen's in love with herself. Anyway, I've made up my mind. I'm not going to the wedding, and that's final."

"Tilly, what about if Rosie doesn't go home? Say her mum isn't there on the twenty first. She'll want to be a bridesmaid. God, Tilly, she's been going on and on about it for weeks."

Ed watched Tilly falter, "I don't know, Ed. I only know that I'm not going, neither is gran, and if I have to, I will tell Rosie the reason she can't be her bridesmaid."

Ed looked horrified, "Tilly! You can't do that."

She moved Ed off the stool so she could put the saucepans away. "I can. I can tell the truth. Rosie has enough about her, at six, to know that that's horrid. You'll see? And I tell you if you told your mum what Cathleen said about not wanting Rachel, she wouldn't let her be bridesmaid either. That would jolly well suit me down to the ground."

Ed had never known Tilly be so nasty about anyone. He hoped there wasn't more behind it. Perhaps he didn't know Cathleen at all. *'I shouldn't have talked Ken into giving her a chance, convincing him he still loved her.'*

Ed was cross with himself, sickened at what Tilly had just revealed. He told himself, *'I must learn to worry about what goes on in my own four walls, and keep my nose out of other people's business.'* Tilly's stiff posture told him he had rocky waters of his own to deal with.

*

Wednesday October 12th 1966

Rosie hurried her breakfast down, threw her bowl in the soapy water making a splash. This caused Tilly to grumble, "Slow down, for goodness sake. You've got me soaked."

Rosie had the decency to look sheepish. Tilly was always on edge at the moment. Rosie seemed to understand it had something to do with the fact that she would be leaving them all soon. She had heard the arguments between Tilly and Ed. Agnes had tried to explain, but it didn't help Rosie, there was that horrible feeling in her stomach that reminded her of being in a running race, waiting for the off.

"I'm sorry, Tilly. I have to feed Rookie before I go to school."

Rosie grabbed a slice of bread, tore it up in a bowl, and tipped some milk over it. She grabbed the sugar tongs, which she now claimed as hers for the bird, and ran out of the house.

The scream that echoed down the garden had Tilly running to Rosie. "Whatever's the matter?"

"Rookies' gone, Tilly, he's got out." Somehow the bird had managed to get through the bars. Rosie fell over the crate and wept. She was aware that Tilly had come to kneel down beside her.

Through tears, Rosie said, "Someone must have let him out."

Tilly stroked Rosie's hair, trying to reassure her, "No one let him out. It was time for him to fly. He could've got out of those bars anytime if he'd wanted to..."

"Where will he go? Who'll feed him?"

Rosie was pulled on to Tilly's lap, "Rookie's a wild creature. You couldn't keep him in this old crate forever. It would be cruel. He'll hunt for his own food now, he'll fly with his own kind. You might see him soaring in the sky."

Rosie wiped her eyes and looked around, there was no sign of him. "Is that why you're sad, Tilly? Because I want to go home to me mum."

Rosie felt Tilly rest her head against her own, "Yes, Rosie, yes. That's why I'm sad. Like you wanted to keep Rookie forever, I wanted to keep you."

"I'm not a wild creature, am I?"

Rosie was pleased to hear Tilly laugh, and say, "No, darling, you're not, though some might not agree with me. Your mother will be delighted to see you, just like Rookie's will be, if he finds his way back. You must..."

"Tilly, me mum might not want me. I might not be able to go back, then I'd stay a bit longer, would that make you happy."

"Rosie, you can stay as long as you want, but you don't belong here. You want to go home, I understand that, but it doesn't make it any easier. I love you, Rosie, just like you loved Rookie."

Rosie turned to face her, she put her little arms around Tilly's neck and squeezed. "I love you too, Tilly, I really do."

Tilly's tears dripped down the collar of Rosie's school shirt, "Don't cry Tilly, I'll come back, I promise."

"Come on, this won't get the children across the road now, will it?"

Rosie took hold of Tilly's hand and they made their way indoors.

"I'll ride on the back of the bike with you today, Tilly. I don't want to walk with the others."

"Go on in and clean your teeth, say goodbye to gran, and I'll get the bike out."

Within minutes Rosie was back, her satchel over her shoulder. "I told Granny A about Rookie. She said the same as you, she…"

Rosie didn't get to finish, Rookie flew down from the shed roof trying to land on Rosie's head. The laughter that rang round the garden was a joy to be heard, "Look, Tilly, he's back." Rosie held out her arm and he rested on it, squawking at her in the process. "I think he's come back for his breakfast."

Tilly lifted Rosie into the bike seat, which caused Rookie to fly in the air. "Not now. You've got to go to school, and I've got to see the children over the road. I'll give him something when I get home."

Rookie flew back down, perching himself on Rosie's bent back. "He's mine, Tilly, really mine."

178

"He certainly is, Rosie. He's chosen to come back when he was free to fly. Yes, Rosie, he's yours."

The bird flew with them all the way to North Mundham, coming down to rest on Rosie when it got the chance. The bike wobbled as she fidgeted in the little seat, "Come on, Rookie, come on."

*

Florrie hadn't seen May to speak to for nearly a week. They had called out to each other, but there was a silence in the friendship that had gone eerily quiet, and didn't sit well with Florrie.

"George, I'm going round to see May this morning, see if I can't put my finger on what is eating at her. What do you think?"

When George just mumbled into his newspaper, Florrie kept talking, as if to herself, "It's strange how she was so full of Bridge nights, and our Sunday teas round there, and now, nothing. I don't like it, George, no, I don't like it at all."

George peered over his paper, "Stop worrying. How do you think I feel? I haven't seen that little one in a while either. We've been making a surprise for May, but it's all on hold. You know how I like to see projects through. Perhaps she's fickle, women are."

"Thank you, George. I'm a woman too, remember."

Florrie noticed he had ignored her. She knew he was missing Rachel's visits. George loved children, he always had. She wondered, *'If Daphne had lived, and George had married her, maybe they would have had their own little family by now.'* She chastised herself, *'No good worrying about what if's'* Florrie thought back to the trouble that had caused them to leave their hometown in Liverpool. It had been horrific, one she wanted to forget. But at times like this it came back to haunt her. She sat back and let the memory float over her like a persistent nightmare.

There had been a little girl living on the green in the next road. She must have been seven or eight at the time. I'd gone out shopping, it was market day. The child had knocked at the door asking if George had any shopping he wanted doing, He'd invited her in.

If the child were to be believed, he had made up some silly game that resulted in the girl having to take her knickers off, and then he had refused to give them back. God knows what else happened, but George had claimed he was innocent and denied it all. The girl was known to have come from a rough home, which I'm sure helped George's case. Her story was doubted. The police had told us to put the incident behind us, but there were people in the village who couldn't let them live it down. Rumours like that stick. We had woken three weeks after the event to find the word 'Dirty Perverts' sprayed on our front door. It hadn't just been that though, it was the whispers when I called in at our local shop, the looks too. I felt every one of them. The crunch had come when I'd missed my bus home from the town and ended up having to catch the one full of the school children.

Florrie shivered as she remembered the song they had sang. "Georgie Porgie puddeny pie, likes the girls when they're only knee high." There had been a barrage of insulting innuendoes from little Tommy Tucker which they changed to George Sucker. The filth that came out of their mouths had astonished Florrie as well as horrified and disgusted her. The trouble was she wasn't a hundred percent sure that it wasn't founded. He had been a very curious brother in that department, and she could remember incidents of their own childhood, especially when their cousin used to come and stay. The answer to this problem had been to leave Liverpool and move to Bognor.

Why did our neighbours have to have a little girl? Surely George wouldn't be foolish to stir trouble here. Would he?'

George put his paper down, reached for his coffee and gave a slurp. This caused Florrie to come back to the present. "Yes, George! I shall go and have it out with May today. I'm sure she's avoiding me."

"Leave her be, she'll send the little one round when she wants a moments peace. She's too old to cope with a child like that, they both are."

This angered Florrie, she didn't know why, but her reply was sharp, "Don't be so ridiculous, George. Rachel is a dream to look after. Warm, funny and affectionate. I would rather she didn't come round here if I'm honest."

George got out of his chair. He seemed to move in slow motion, which made Florrie's heartbeat quicken. He put his hand round her neck and applied pressure with his thumb on her Adams apple. This had Florrie wide eyed, trying desperately to swallow. "You would rather she didn't come round here, if you're honest. If, you're honest, you would rather she didn't come into my shed, say it, go on, say it."

Florrie couldn't say anything, George's grip had tightened. "You couldn't let it drop, could you? No, you had to keep on reminding me of that incident. You heard the policeman, 'put it behind you, both of you' that is what he said, Florrie, he told you I was innocent, but no, in your head I was guilty. I…"

Florrie managed to break free, "For goodness sake, George, you nearly choked me. What has got into you? I was just asking about May, and wondering why the stony silence. Are you mad, George?"

"I'm sick of you going on all the time. You don't have to say it, Florrie, I can see it in your eyes. You think I was guilty back then, and you think I'm up to no good in my shed with that little one next door. Go on, say it, shame the devil and be honest with me."

"No, George, I don't. I think you're foolish to put yourself in a position where it could be thought, that's all."

"People will always think, Florrie. If you go round there, to her next door, you'll put doubt in her mind too. Is that what you want?"

Florrie rubbed her neck, he had frightened her with that show of aggression. This was something she hadn't seen before, she asked herself, *'Is he too concerned about the child's absence, and the implications of it?'*

"George! I was just going to go round and check all is well. Don't you want to play Bridge of an evening again? It used to be one of your favourites, along with Chess." When he didn't answer, and flopped himself down in his comfy chair, Florrie could see the fight had gone out of him. "I'm sorry, George, if it felt accusing, you know how I worry. I wanted us all to get along, George, that's all."

Florrie didn't make it round to May's, and Rachel didn't visit either. *'Perhaps I'll invite the Barretts round here for Sunday tea, even though it is their turn?'*

*

The Rainbow

Chapter Seven

Monday 17th October 1966

Cathleen woke to a heavy feeling in her stomach, and a dull ache in her back. She knew her period had arrived. *'I'm not pregnant then, that's one thing I'm now sure of.'*

Cathleen still hadn't heard from Tilly. Ken had been tactful, but she knew her friend had turned her back on her. Cathleen tried to convince herself she didn't care, but she did. Tilly had chased their friendship all their childhood, and it felt like Tilly didn't need her anymore. This hurt Cathleen more than she dared to admit. She went into the bathroom to sort herself out, cursing her curse that had caused so much trouble. *'Why did you have to come so late?'*

This was typical of Cathleen, always looking for something or someone to blame for her upsets, rather than looking at herself.

She could hear the rattling of crockery, and guessed it was her mum clearing away the breakfast things. Cathleen pushed open Hannah's bedroom door, her bed was empty and unmade. Wrapped in her dressing gown, a dull ache in her stomach, she made her way downstairs. Hannah was kneeling on the floor, which was covered with bricks. "Morning, Hannah, that looks fun, what are you building?"

Her sister looked up, her hair was not brushed, and she, too, was still in her dressing gown. "I'm making a castle for my Sindy, she is going to be a princess…"

Cathleen didn't comment, she smiled and went into the kitchen, not listening to Hannah's unfinished story. Her mother was at the sink washing a few woolies by hand. "Morning, mum. I've come on, I'm definitely not pregnant."

Pam dropped the washing in the bowl, dried her hands on a towel, and reached out for Cathleen, "Love, that's a relief. Things are really getting back to normal now, aren't they?"

Cathleen pulled away from her mum, she didn't like the smell of laundry soap on her red, cold hands. "I don't know, mum, I feel restless. Do you know Tilly hates me?" She..."

Cathleen didn't get to finish, Pam interrupted her, "Tilly, she couldn't hate anyone. She was probably a little shocked, like us all. I warned you earlier how fond she was of Ken. I honestly believe now you are not having a baby things will improve between you. It could have been a little bit of jealousy mixed in as well. You must have heard that Rosie's going to the fair on Friday, she's hoping to find her mother and return to a travelling life. That'll break Tilly's heart."

Cathleen had had no idea of this, why hadn't she heard. "Ken didn't say. When did all this come about?"

"It's been in the wind for a while, you've had a lot going on in your own life, Cathleen. You probably shut your ears to it."

Her old temper rose, "Why does everyone try and make me out to be selfish? I would have phoned Tilly. That would have given me a good excuse to..."

"There you go again, why do you always need an excuse? Pick up the phone and take what's coming to you. Go and see the girl, tell her how sorry you are for hurting her friend, tell her anything, Cathleen, but stop trying to look for excuses to blame others for your comedowns."

Cathleen's temper had heightened, more so with her hormones so ripe with her monthly arriving, "I hate it here. I hate my job these days, I feel like they are all pointing the finger. Daisy is the only one who speaks to me, really speaks. My best friend has turned her back on me, and do you know what, mum, I feel you and dad don't like me much…"

"Shut up, Cathleen, Hannah's only in the other room. Just get out of my sight, you have the clever knack of upsetting everything and everyone. Of course we love you, if we didn't, you wouldn't still be living under our roof, what with the trouble you've caused of late."

Cathleen stormed out of the room, not looking at Hannah as she passed through the lounge, her feet made exaggerated stomps up the stairs, saying to herself, *'Well I hate you, I hate you all.'*

*

Friday 21st October – Sloe Fair

Rosie woke early, she could hardly contain herself. A big brown case was filled with her clothes, and Agnes had given her, her old carpet bag which she had filled with books and some exercises given to her by the school that she could do, so as to continue her education while travelling. Tilly had made her promise she would attend school whenever she got the chance. All this went over Rosie's head, the joy at the prospect of seeing her mother again overrode any of the losses she would occur.

Despite the 'sixth sense' Rosie had inherited from her mother, her youth meant that she didn't really comprehend the sadness her leaving would do to those around her who loved her. She was in mid-air doing a jump on her bed when Tilly opened her door, "What is all this noise, Rosie? I thought you were coming through the ceiling."

"I'm going home today, Tilly, I'm going home to me mum."

"Well, school's first, young lady. You also have a bird waiting to greet you at the bottom of the garden, cawing his head off. So I suggest you get yourself ready and deal with first things first."

Rosie bounced on the bed three more times before she attempted to get dressed.

Downstairs, Tilly tried to control the shake in her hands. She didn't know why she was so angry at the child. She told herself over and over, of course she would want to go home to her mum. It was only natural. It was the ache and hole in their lives she was going to leave behind that Tilly couldn't bear to think about.

The phone ringing brought her out of thought. As soon as she picked it up and heard Cathleen's voice she wished she had let it ring.

"No, Cathleen, I'm busy today." Tilly couldn't believe the nerve of her, *'How could she just phone up when we haven't had any contact for over a month, and think I would want to see her?'*

"I'm not pregnant, Tilly. My curse showed today, I'm really not."

Tilly's voice was sarcastic, "I thought we already knew that, Cathleen."

"Why are you being like this, Tilly, It didn't affect you, did it? I was the one who was shamed, not you. I'm the one who…"

"Cathleen, you really don't get it, do you? Take a good look at yourself in the mirror, a real good look and ask yourself, do I like what I see, really see. As to me seeing you today the answer is no, I'm not in the mood. I'm about to lose someone from my life who I love with all my heart, and it feels like its breaking. Do you care? No. What do I get from you? My curse has showed, well, yippee! Let's all be happy for Cathleen…"

The phone went dead. Tilly stood looking at it for a few moments, listening to the whirr of the dialling tone, but the heavy feeling in her heart outweighed any feelings of guilt that she ought to have felt at attacking her old friend in such a manner.

"I love you, Granny A, I really do. Thank you for everything. When I'm this way I'll come and see you all, I promise."

Agnes' old heart felt like it was about to stop, she stood glassy - eyed and watched the child lugging the carpet bag into the front seat of the van. Ed slid the case in the back.

She watched her granddaughter slide in beside Rosie and the three of them set off for Sloe Fair. Once the van was out of sight she was able to let her façade go and give way to tears. She knew she had seen the last of the child, Sloe Fair is one of the biggest travelling fairs to visit, she felt Rosie's mother was be bound to be there.

Ed parked up the van, and the three of them got out. Rosie seemed unaware of the heavy atmosphere, and if she was she ignored it, so great was her anticipation of seeing her mother again.

"No, Rosie, leave the stuff in the van. We need to find your mum first, and see if she can take you back. Now you must calm down, it is a big place, we don't want to lose you."

The throb of the music could be heard from where they stood. Rosie threw her arms open, relishing it. She had been born to the sound of this music.

No sooner had they entered the gate, there in the distance a bright coloured streamer could be seen. The flying wisps of canvas shouted out to them, "It's the rainbow, Tilly, look, it's me mum."

Rosie pulled free of Tilly's hand, despite how firm she was being held, and ran as fast as her little legs could take her.

"Jesus wept, Ed, get her."

Rosie was already screaming by the time Ed managed to get through the crowds to the tent. She threw herself in his arms when

187

he pulled aside the flap of the tent. "Me mum's gone, Ed, she's not here anymore. She's gone home, home to her people."

Between sobs, she told him "Me, Uncle Jimmy's gone too. There's no one for me here, I'll never find her now."

Tilly had joined the sorry scene, and seeing there was no Rhana brought a tingle of hope that spread through her veins, which she knew was selfish. She stood rooted to the spot watching the distraught child in Ed's arms trying to be consoled.

"Give her to me, Ed, come on, Rosie, come on, love, we'll sort it out."

Tilly recognised the lady from the goldfish stall. She was now dressed in the same long flowing skirt that Rhana had worn.

"Don't cry now, Rainbow, yer mum wanted yer, honest she did, she walked the area for nearly a week trying to find yer, honest. But we ad to move on, we couldn't wait."

Tilly hated to hear Rosie being called Rainbow, but was forced to listen to it being repeated over and over.

Ed spoke, his voice was husk. "Tilly, take Rosie and get her a toffee apple…"

"I don't want a toffee apple, I want me mum. I wants Uncle Jimmy."

The lady wearing the burgundy skirt and bright yellow scarf, who Rosie kept referring to as Auntie Audrey, said, "Now you do as yous told, these good people will look after yer. Your mummy told you, didn't she, stay with em, it's safer."

"No, I want me mummy, I want Uncle Jimmy."

There was nothing for it, Tilly had to sit cradling Rosie on her knee with Ed at her side, while this Audrey filled them all in.

First Audrey put the sign up to indicate the tent was closed. "This is very inconvenient, yer shouldn't have brought 'er 'ere like this, it ain't right. I can sees you've done a good job with 'er, yous best be keeping her. "

"I want me mummy, I do. She said to look for the rainbow…"

"Alright, alright, I'm just saying that's all."

Rosie's tears were heart wrenching for Tilly, but she couldn't help feeling relieved she would be going home with the child. She rocked her on her knee, trying to settle her. Audrey told them, Rhana would be in the Lake District for the Apple Fair in the coming spring.

"All 'er lot gather there. Take 'er, she'll find her mum, you can be sure."

Rosie looked into Tilly's eyes, pleading silently to hear her say she would take her. Tilly stroked Rosie's head, "Of course we'll go. We'll all go, gran and all."

"No we won't Tilly, Gran won't, but we'll go."

Tilly read this statement wrong, she thought Rosie wanted it to be her and Ed. With a more settled Rosie on her knee she said, "Come on, let's go and have some fun on the round-a-bouts. I first met you on a round-a-bout. Do you remember? Ed tried to help you down, and later I tried to give you a teddy."

Rosie giggled, "I do, and me Uncle Jimmy came, didn't he?"

"Yes he did, he frightened me a bit." Tilly tickled Rosie and the two of them left Ed and Audrey alone.

Once Tilly had gone Audrey spoke in different tones, "She's better off with you and the lady, yer can surely see that. What are yer doing bringing 'er 'ere now? I can sees yer wants her."

189

"Of course we want her, we love her. It isn't as easy as that, Rosie loves her mum. When we saw the poster it was an obvious thing to do. Rhana's last words to my wife were 'look for the rainbow'."

"yer won't want to send 'er back to 'er lot, wait till yer sees 'em. They're nasty buggers. We 'ad real trouble that day I can tell yer. When yer left and took the littlun, the father was lying down knocked out cold. Jimmy did it, he hit 'im with a crowbar. He 'ad to or Rhana would be dead now. That night when we was all packed up to leave, they all came back. Trouble, that's what it was, real trouble. I'd never seen anything like it. It made news, you must 'av 'eard?"

"I think we did, but didn't take any notice, it seemed to die down. What with us having Rosie, we kept quiet too."

"Well that was wise, I can tell yer. Jimmy killed the littlun's father, it was either him or Jimmy and Jimmy got the lucky strike."

"Is that why they fled?"

"No, police were called, Jimmy was taken to hospital. We had to go on. It was our time to move. Rhana stayed, she was 'oping to find the child. Jimmy would have been charged with murder, only he's as silly as a baby now. They hit him so bad he doesn't know what day it is. Rhana looks after him. With her father killed at the hands of that lot, and now the littlun's father killed by Jimmy, she could go home, but she'll be wanting Rainbow, she loved that kiddie, I can tell you."

Ed was confused, half of him felt like they should keep Rosie forever, and yet his heart went out to the woman who had lost her daughter amongst so much violence.

"Look, yer changed the littlun's name, she's better off with the likes of yer. Surely yer can see that? Yer just as well keep 'er, she'll settle, she's young."

"We'd love to keep her, but she has to want to stay. You don't know what she's like, she'll go on now about going to the Apple Fair to find her mum. I know her. Maybe Rhana will want her to stay with us. Who knows? But thanks for filling me in."

Ed left the tent to look for Tilly. *'God how I wished I'd never mentioned this bloody fair. What sort of life will Rosie have if she goes back with that lot?'*

*

Rosie threw herself into Agnes' arms.

"I'm back Granny A, me mum has left. She's gone back with her real family. She wants me though, I'm to go to the Apple Fair in the spring, that's right, aint it, Tilly?"

Tilly laughed at the acceptance and excitement, "Yes, Rosie, that's right. Now, young lady, we must work on your language. You know it isn't, aint, and we don't say me mum. Do we?"

Rosie promptly said, "I know it's my mum, and I know I should say, isn't, it's just when I speak fast it comes out like that. Does it matter, really matter, Tilly? Everyone knows what I'm saying."

"It will make a world of difference in later life, darling. If you went for a job, say, in a restaurant, and there were two of you wanting the job, and one of you said, 'I aint working on the weekends' and the other one said, 'I'm unable to work on the weekends.' Who do you think might stand the better chance of getting the job?"

Rosie laughed, "I'll try, Tilly, I will."

"Well just think how proud your mum will be when we find her in the spring, and you are speaking beautifully, she will be so proud of you, and knowing your letters too."

Rosie did a little skip, "Oh, Tilly, I can't wait. Will you be happier for me this time?"

"I'll try, Rosie, I will try. It will give me a bit longer to prepare myself, but you must try with your speech too."

Rosie put out her little hand, "It's a deal."

Tilly shook the child's hand, laughing, "Where did a saying like that come from?"

"We says it all…" The look from Tilly held any further conversation, as Rosie started again, "We say it all the time at school, Tilly."

"Go on up to bed now. I'll be up in a minute to tuck you in. It's late."

Tilly was pleased when Ed said, "You stay and fill your gran in on the night's events, and I'll sort Rosie out. Come on curly, let's get you to bed."

Tilly's heart warmed as she heard the parting squeals, "I'm not curly." And the hurried footsteps, as they ran up the stairs after each other.

*

It was one week before Cathleen's wedding, and she had handed her notice in at Lesley's, knowing that was the easy part of her plans. Tonight was going to be difficult, as tonight she would tell Ken.

Applying for the waitressing job in Bournemouth had been done on impulse. She had been browsing through The Lady magazine while in the dentist waiting room, when she saw the job advertised. It was as if the page fell open for her.

These past few weeks had forced Cathleen to take a good look at herself. Tilly, her best friend, had turned her back on her. She was the one person Cathleen thought she could have depended on for support. May had stormed into their house saying that Rachel wouldn't be being her bridesmaid, lucky for Cathleen she hadn't given a reason. Tilly had sent a card, through Ken, saying it was unfortunate, but she felt unable to attend his wedding, the wording of it had offended and hurt Cathleen, she had expected it to have included herself. She had tried to put this down to the fact that Rosie was going back to her mother, but as that scenario didn't manifest, she had expected a change of heart, and couldn't understand fully, why she was being shunned.

It seemed to Cathleen that her only real friend was Daisy at the café. There were some there that were being judgemental. They didn't say anything but Cathleen could feel it.

Seeing the job had given her a way out. She had applied for it on impulse, because it included accommodation. The position was temporary, for four months, which was to cover Christmas and the New Year. Cathleen had torn out the advert and written off that night. This morning she had received a letter offering her the position. No interview, just a reference needed from the café. She knew that wouldn't be a problem, she had worked there now for nearly four years, and worked hard.

Cathleen could see Daisy was dying to ask questions, she kept trying to whisper, but the café was busy and there was no time to stand around. She would fill her in with the details on their break.

At ten thirty the two of them climbed the stairs, each carrying a doughnut and a cup of tea.

Daisy pulled out her chair causing it to scrape along the tiled flooring, "What's going on? Why are you quitting?"

"I've got another job, Daisy. Waitressing at a hotel in Bournemouth. It's called the Three Chimneys."

Daisy was so shocked she sat holding her doughnut with her mouth wide open as if catching flies.

"There, now you know. I haven't told anyone yet, only you, so keep it quiet, please."

Daisy put her cake back on the plate, licking the sugar off her fingers, "What about the wedding?"

"There isn't going to be a wedding, I've decided it's not what I want."

Cathleen could see Daisy was flabbergasted and tried to defend herself, not wanting to lose what felt like her only friend. "It doesn't feel right anymore, Daisy. Ken loves me, I know, but I don't know how I feel anymore. Please stop looking like that, surely even you must think if I loved Ken, really loved him, how could I have gone off with another bloke, like I did?"

Daisy now had a mouthful of her cake, and licking her lips pushing the cake to the side of her cheeks, she said, "Cathleen, you'll destroy him, you can't do this. What about all the presents you have received, the wedding dress, the invites…?"

"Don't! Please. I have made up my mind. I won't be the first person to end my engagement, and I won't be the last. Surely you can see, Daisy? Just think about it, what would it be like if I married him and then realised it was a mistake? No, I've been over and over this, it is kinder to set him free now."

"The thing is, Cathleen, he doesn't' want to be set free."

Cathleen pushed her cake across to her friend, her own appetite had vanished with Daisy's tea and doughnut "Ken will get over it, I know he will. I only wish now I'd never agreed to marry him when he offered his olive branch." Sensing her friend's disapproval she added, "I know I sound a bitch, Daisy, but it's for the best. I have to get away. Please say you understand, you are my one and only friend now, and I don't want to lose you too."

"Go on with you, you're being a bit melodramatic, but I'll tell you one thing, Cathleen, I wouldn't want to trade places with you, not for all the tea downstairs nor cakes for that matter, having to spill that one is going to cause more than a stir. It's a good job you are getting away, girl, that's all I can say. When do you go?"

"Fourth of November. I'll write to you, Daisy, you could come and visit for a weekend if you like. When I find my feet of course."

Excitement mingled with nerves bubbled in Cathleen's chest, she couldn't wait to go. Telling Ken was going to be difficult, she had already acknowledged that, but she kept telling herself it was for the best, best for everyone.

Chapter Eight

November - 1966

Pam stood with her husband Hal and Hannah at the coach park and waved Cathleen off. There were no tears, just a quick hug. The thought that crossed Pam's mind as she watched her daughter board the coach was one of relief. She couldn't rid herself of the shame she felt her daughter had brought to their doorstep these past few months. *Now this, jilting Ken a week before the wedding, all the plans, the explanations, all left for me to cancel while she swans off on a new venture. What did we do to deserve this?'*

Pam was brought out of thought as Hal put his arm round her saying, "Come on, love, let's go home."

She took hold of Hannah's hand and pulled her towards Hal's work van. Hannah held up her free arm, waving as the coach disappeared out of sight. She was the only one calling, "Bye, Cathleen, bye." Neither, Hal or Pam said anything. The only sound on the way home was Hannah singing, 'This old man, he played one…' The silence between themselves felt like electricity.

Pam was relieved when they pulled up outside their home, and heard Hal say, "I can't stop, love, I must get going. I want to put this job to bed before Christmas."

"Yes, yes, Hal, you go, I'll see you later."

Once indoors, Hannah asked to go round to May's to play with Rachel, she scowled as Pam told her, "She's at school, maybe later."

"Can I go and make matchsticks with Mr Coffin?"

"Not today, Hannah, go and play in the other room, mummy will be in in a minute." Feeling guilty at her bad mood, she added, "Once I've had a coffee, we'll go and feed the ducks"

As Hannah disappeared, Pam leant against the kitchen sink. There were still no tears, she felt empty. Her body felt like it had been through a war. She hurt for her husband, Hal, he was heartbroken. Cathleen had been the apple of his eye since the day he had first held her in his arms.

The milk boiled over on the stove, this caused her to swear. She poured the milk she had salvaged from the pan into her mug, topping it up with boiled water from the kettle. When she went through to the lounge Hannah was sitting on the floor playing with her Tiny Tears dolly, oblivious of the heartache that surrounded her.

"Mummy are we going to feed the ducks now?"

"In a minute, let me have this cuppa, then I'll get some bread."

Pam knew they still had to visit Ken's mum, Brenda, there were things to discuss. *'Poor Bren, what must she think of us all?'*

It was cold out, winter had arrived. "Go and get your gloves, Hannah."

Once outside, the biting wind seemed more noticeable to Pam than it had done earlier. *'Saying goodbye to Cathleen must have numbed every nerve in my body.'*

They hadn't got far when they met May. Pam thought by the look of her she had been to the hairdressers. "Morning, May, hair looks nice."

Before May could answer Hannah asked if she could play with Rachel later. Her reply was terse, "Not today, Hannah, Rachel has homework these days."

Pam couldn't bear it. She recalled how supportive she had been to May when her own son, Ed, had brought trouble to their doorstep. She found herself saying, "May! You of all people should understand we cannot be held responsible for the decisions our children make."

May appeared to falter before finding her voice, "Pam, I don't know what you made of our refusal to let Rachel be Cathleen's bridesmaid, but do you know the background of it?"

"May, does it matter now? I'm more concerned about the huge job of cancelling, and the bills we're about to incur."

Pam knew she was going to have to hear May's gripes whether she wanted to or not. Pam braced herself as May spat out, "I'm sure you are, but we're hurt. Did you know she only wanted Rachel as a bridesmaid to keep her quiet because she'd caught her and her fancy fella in the stables? She bribed her, Pam, bribed her. What does that tell you about your precious daughter?"

"Oh, May, I can only apologise, but as saddened as I am to hear this, nothing Cathleen does surprises me anymore. I have yet to face Brenda, and then there's Ken. Shamed, we are, shamed. I'm sorry, May. I hope you felt some justification when you told her Rachel wouldn't be being her bridesmaid. I know it hurt her."

"Nothing hurts her, Pam, she is a law unto herself. I'm sorry to say that to you too, but it's true."

"May please, let's not fall out now, not after all these years of being neighbours. Cathleen's gone, gone today. Did you know that?"

Pam watched May relax, "Yes I heard. Might be a good thing. I just hope Ken survives, poor lad. Ed says he's heartbroken."

"I know, Cathleen doesn't do things by halves, does she?"

Before anyone could say anything else on the matter of broken hearts, and weddings, Hannah, who was swinging on a little post spotted George coming up the road, she ran full pelt at him. Both May and Pam watched in silence as George swung her round. George took hold of Hannah's hand and walked towards them. "Morning, Ladies, it's a cold one, isn't it?"

Pam lifted Hannah onto her hip, "Yes it is, we're off to feed the ducks, they'll be hungry." George complimented May on her hairdo, but she ignored him, this caused an uncomfortable moment. Pam filled the silence with a cheery, "Hannah was hoping to come round and help you with your matchstick project later. Will you be in?"

George wiped his beard with his gloved hand, "I will that, I will. Lovely, I shall be waiting."

Once George was out of earshot, Pam asked. "Are you alright, May, is there a problem with you and George?"

"Not really, but there's something odd about him, Pam. I can't put my finger on it."

This caused laughter, "May you are funny. Him and Florrie were the best thing since sliced bread a few weeks ago, what's changed?"

May's serious face gave a reprieve from the worry that Pam was experiencing over Cathleen, "Are you serious, May?"

"Yes, Pam. I'm sorry to say it, but I think there's something a bit dodgy about him, do you know what I mean?"

"Dodgy! Dodgy in what way?"

"Oh I don't know, I just feel it. I wouldn't let Hannah go round if I were you."

Hannah was wriggling to get down, she had caught sight of something pretty stuck in a hedge. "Rachel goes round to them, doesn't she?"

"Not any more, I got suspicious. I don't want to go into it, Pam, but watch him, that's all."

May said she had to be going. Pam moved over to inspect the brightly coloured ribbon Hannah had pulled from the hedge, thinking *what did she mean, dodgy?*

As Hannah threw bread in for the ducks, Pam found herself lost in thought. Cathleen was forgotten for the moment, and her head was filled with George and May.

*

Cathleen put the last of her clothes in the tallboy that stood next to her bed. She felt disgruntled and kept telling herself over and over, *'It doesn't matter this is a new start for me.'*

She thought back to the advert in The Lady magazine, 'Catering assistant needed to cover Christmas and New Year for busy Hotel in Bournemouth...' there had been more written, but Cathleen had honed in on the word, hotel, The Three Chimneys. It had sounded very grand, yet here she was in what could only be described as a boarding house. Cathleen thought back to when she had got off the coach, and there standing waiting to meet her was a tall thin man who looked like a stick insect with long flat black hair. He was dressed in a bright red t-shirt, flared white jeans and a long turquoise shirt which was undone and seemed to float down past his bottom. He looked to Cathleen like an aged hippy. This look was topped off with a pair of those black and white trendy boot plimsolls. He had been friendly, his smile was wide which showed big square horse like teeth, he had greeted her with an outstretched hand, "Great to meet you in person, Cathleen. Welcome to Bournemouth."

He had chatted away on the return journey, but she was only half listening. She wondered where this odd man fitted in in such a luxurious setting.

When they had pulled up outside what could only be called a boarding house, Cathleen had had to bite the inside of her mouth for fear of speaking her mind.

"Here we are, home at last." He had spread his arms out wide in a gracious manner, "The Three Chimneys."

She had wanted to say, is this it? But held her tongue as she looked up at what looked like three odd shaped pot plant holders on top of the roof.

She hadn't wanted to go in the little green gate that led to a green door. It all looked very plain, her own front door at home was grander.

She had no choice but to go forward, no one wanted her back home. Whatever lay ahead was her only option. There were more disappointments inside, for one there were no other waitresses, just her and Simon the aged hippy who had picked her up, and his wife, Jackie, Jackie Robes. Cathleen closed the door to the room she was told was to be hers, and sat on the bed, tears threatened.

A tap at the door startled her, "Yes?"

"It's only me, can I come in?"

Jackie stood in the doorway, filling it with her big frame; she was solid looking. Cathleen thought this was down to a good corset, but what fascinated her more was the beehive hairstyle, it made her look larger than ever. She, like her husband, wore baggy, bright coloured clothing. Cathleen didn't invite her in, but said, "I was just on my way down."

Jackie gave her a wide smile, her red lipstick had smudged on her top teeth which caused Cathleen to rub her tongue under her own top lip. "Cathleen, let me give you the guided tour."

Jackie told her there were five guest rooms, but only two were occupied at the moment. There was a businessman who would check out in the morning, and an elderly lady who was here for another week. The season was over, but the hotel was fully booked for the Christmas period and New Year. Cathleen wanted to inform her this was not a hotel, but kept her mouth shut.

She had imagined herself walking up wide steps with a butler waiting at the top. Perhaps a rotating door like the ones she had seen in films. None of it met her expectations, there were no marble halls, or glitzy dance floors here. Tears were not far away as she followed Jackie down the first flight of steps.

"Cathleen this is what we call the top floor. There are three bedrooms on this level. All rooms have showers," She pushed open a cream door that had a plaque screwed into the wood work. Painted on the plaque was a lady wearing a shower cap, sitting in an old fashioned tin bath, "This is the shared bathroom, you will use this too. It's important that you clean it when you finish, as it's for the use of the guests as well."

Cathleen peeked in, it was a large room with pale blue lino covering the floor. It had a blue coloured suite, a shade or two darker than the floor. The bath stood in the middle of the room with a ledge all the way round which gave the appearance of a step. The words were out of Cathleen's mouth on impulse, "Oh I like this. You have to climb into it."

Jackie pulled the door to, and pushed a button on a fake wooden door panel, "This is the lift, it doesn't go up to our floor, but there are only nine steps for us to climb, I think we can manage that don't you?"

Cathleen noticed the lipstick smile again, she wasn't sure if Jackie was trying to be funny or just friendly, either way she smiled back, giving a light chuckle to cover either scenario.

"This is the ground floor. This is where our guests are at the moment. These are the best two rooms in the house, both with full en-suite bathrooms."

As Cathleen found herself escorted round the place, she had to admit it was deceiving from the outside, it was actually very spacious and she told Jackie so. "What will I do all day if there are only two guests?"

"Cathleen, this room here with bay windows is a café, it's open all year round to the general public. It isn't as busy out of season, but it's probably a bit like the café you worked in. In the summer we are heaving with customers, but come the winter it just ticks over."

"What about when the hotel is busy and your guests want a coffee and there's nowhere to sit?"

"You'll do well here, Cathleen. Common sense, hard work and good manners is all that's needed. I can see you qualify for all."

Cathleen glowed with the praise as she followed Jackie through to the bar, "This is the guest area, and in reply to your earlier question, this is also reserved for our guests to enjoy our café menu should they wish it." When Cathleen browsed the room saying nothing, Jackie continued to chatter, "Our guests tend not to use the café, they normally go out for the day, and come back of an evening."

The more Cathleen saw, the more she warmed to the place. It wasn't what she had expected, there were to be no friendships here, unless you counted Jackie and Simon, who had to be at least forty.

Last but not least, she was shown the dance hall. Cathleen gasped at the parquet floor, it covered the whole area. At the back of the room was a plinth where she was told the band played. She listened as Jackie filled her in, "We hold a dance every month. It's a ticket affair and we put on a buffet. It's a popular event all year round."

Up until now Cathleen had said very little, "Jackie, is there a possibility that you could keep me on after New Year, if I work hard and prove my worth that is?"

"You bet there is. Now you go and sit in the bar and I'll get Simon to serve us … tea or coffee?"

"Tea would be lovely. Thank you."

Cathleen sat taking in her surroundings. She made up her mind she wouldn't go home, her parents could come here for a holiday if they wanted to see her. This is where she would make her life. She reminded herself that no one back in Bognor would miss her. Everyone she cared about hated her. She would start her life again. A new chapter. As she sat thinking how she would change, turn over a new leaf, she made the decision to use the Basildonbond writing pad her mother had given her to write home every week. She would keep them up to date with her news, but she wouldn't go home. *Yes, that's what I'll do. They'll miss me first.'*

Cathleen sensed the cups rattling on the tray, she looked up as Simon appeared "There we go, Jack will be with you in a mo."

It was all very friendly and relaxed. She was left alone again with her thoughts until Jackie returned and flopped in the chair opposite her. She picked up the cigarettes that were on the tea tray, and slid one into a fancy holder, this reminded Cathleen of Audrey Hepburn. When Jackie held the packet out to her, Cathleen took one without thinking. She wasn't a smoker and had only had a puff years ago at a jive night, she hadn't liked it back then but she told herself, this is the new me. She leant forward to catch the flame of Jackie's gold lighter. She dragged slowly not wanting to cough all over the place, she leant back in the seat holding the cigarette in the tip of her two fingers feeling very grown up.

Cathleen declined the biscuits and enjoyed the heady feeling the cigarette seemed to bring about.

"What time do you serve dinner?"

Jackie put her cup down on the saucer, "Don't you worry about dinner, Cathleen. You enjoy the weekend to look around and settle in. Monday morning at seven I shall expect to see you in the kitchen ready to serve breakfast, does that sound fair?"

"Jackie?" Cathleen hesitated, "I would really like to get started, find my feet and learn the ropes. I don't know a single soul in Bournemouth. I would rather be working and learning than twiddling my fingers doing nothing."

Jackie patted Cathleen's knee, "Bless you. If you're sure, you can start by learning the reception. I'll help Simon in the kitchen. You can hold the fort at the front desk. That'll be a huge help, as you'll see."

Cathleen looked puzzled, "Why? You said there are only two guests in at the moment."

Cathleen was relieved, when Jackie smiled the red lipstick had disappeared on her teeth. "You wait and see. As soon we start serving dinner that blessed phone won't stop ringing."

Cathleen jumped up, "Well in that case I'll go upstairs to my room and put something on more suitable." She took the stairs two at a time pleased to hear Jackie say to her husband, "We've hit the jackpot there, love."

Cathleen smiled to herself, thinking, *This is a good start, it feels nice to be liked again.'*

*

George had heard Rachel arrive home over an hour ago, he knew she wouldn't be round now. He looked at his watch, he asked himself, *'Where's that Hannah?'* His annoyance was aimed at May, as he guessed she had put her pennyworth of poison in. He tidied away his work bench and went indoors, his mood had not improved.

"There you are, George, I was just coming for you." Noticing his sour look, she added, "What's eating at you then?"

"Nothing really. It's just that I was expecting Hannah to be round this afternoon. I bumped into Pam and her littlun' this morning, they were off to feed the ducks. May was with them, ignored me she did, bloody ignored me. What have I done to her I ask you?"

"Don't be so sensitive, George. I'm sure she hasn't got anything to do with the child's absence. Children change their minds like the weather. I expect something better cropped up."

George stroked his beard, then twisted his hands together. He felt frustrated and irritable, "What have you said to her next door?"

Florrie sensed George's mood, "Nothing, George. It was probably all that business with you locking the shed door, or Rachel's tantrums. You'll find she'll probably be back round within a week or two."

"There you go, locking the door, locking the door. You love to make it sound sordid, don't you?"

"I don't want to fight, George. I'm looking for answers for you."

George thought about the power he had felt when a few weeks ago he had grabbed Florrie by the throat. It had excited him so much that he had relieved himself that night while thinking of her frightened starry eyed look."

He sat down throwing his weight in the chair, causing it to hit the wall. Florrie's voice rose a notch, "Steady, George, you'll mark the paint work."

"Make me a cuppa, please. I need a drink." As the kettle started to whistle George felt better, he had made a decision.

*

Cathleen had enjoyed her first evening of manning the desk. She had booked three couples in for New Year, and taken six bookings for the bonfire night tomorrow evening. She had marvelled at how confident she had been at handling the telephone bookings and queries.

Once the two guests had retired to bed she sat with Simon and Jackie in the bar enjoying her second cigarette of the day with a glass of sherry. She told them about the bookings she had taken, showing them the book. Simon told her all about the firework evening tomorrow and as the sherry relaxed them they sat chatting like old friends. When Jackie pulled off her Beehive hair style to reveal greying hair rolled up in a hair net, Cathleen couldn't stop her horrified gasp. Jackie laughed out loud "Sorry to shock you, love, but this is boiling under here. I can't wait to get it off of an evening. I look awful don't I? We aren't all blessed with red curls."

Cathleen looked at Simon, half expecting him to reveal a different hair style under his hippy long locks, she was thankful that he didn't, she had got used to the look, and wanted things to stay as they seemed. Not knowing what to say to this woman who was nowhere near as glamorous as she'd first thought. Watching her sitting in a hair net, drinking sherry and smoking, she looked quite common. Cathleen stubbed out her cigarette and excused herself, saying, that what with the journey it had been a long day.

*

"There you are. I was worried sick, Ken. Where have you been?"

Ken looked at his watch, "It's only nine, mum. Is there a problem?"

Brenda didn't have to say a word, Ken knew it was because Cathleen had left today, and she had been worried about his state of mind. "Mum I'm okay, honest. I wish things could have been different but I'll get there. You just worry about your own day coming up."

207

Ken didn't stay in the lounge, but went straight upstairs calling out goodnight to Alf as he went through. He had a quick wash and laid on his bed in his underwear. Every time he replayed Cathleen's rejection the blood seemed to rush to his ears, making him feel light headed. He had asked himself over and over, *'How could she?'* Ken knew she had made him look a fool. He could imagine everyone saying what a Charlie he was. The insecurities that he had had when he was a small boy living in this house with his abusive step father seemed to fill the room. He could feel and hear his heart beating. He felt scared. *'Oh, Cathleen, why, why would you do this to me? One week before the wedding too.'*

He replayed that fateful evening when she had told him that she wanted her freedom. They had sat opposite each other in the Wimpy Bar enjoying Cola Sundaes. There had been no warning, just her in her usual way blurting out, "I can't go through with this, Ken." He hadn't understood at first and wondered what she was talking about. It was when she had said, "The wedding, Ken, I can't marry you."

He rolled himself up in a tight ball as his stomach tightened at the memory. He could hear the sound of blood rushing in his ears again, and his heart seemed to hammer in his chest. He groaned aloud as he recalled his realisation of what she was implying. He hadn't been able to speak to her, he now understood what it was to be struck dumb. Cathleen had said, "I'm sorry, Ken, really sorry. I know you'll hate me for a while, but you'll thank me one day. I know this is right for us…" Ken hadn't been able to listen to anymore. He had pushed his chair away from the table trying to distance himself from her. Cathleen had tried to reach out to him but he had flinched as if her hands were burning torches. His chair had screeched as it slid back on the floor. He hadn't looked at her again, he had turned and walked out, leaving her with their half-drunk Cola Sundaes and the bill.

Ken wiped at his eyes with his arm, he was crying again. He swung his legs round and pulled open his top drawer where he knew he would find a hanky. He thought about how he had laid on this bed holding the cuff links his mother had given him years ago for Christmas. They had been his father's and his father's before him, he couldn't help smiling as he remembered how he believed they had special powers to rescue him from all sorts of dilemmas. He was a man now, and he knew that time was what would heal his heart. He lay back and let his plans fill his troubled mind. He told himself he would never love again. He would live life worrying about just him. He had lost the shop in Hawthorn road and had told Ed he would remain with him at the warehouse. Ed had looked not only pleased but relieved. He had also told his mum he would take over the tenancy of this house when she married Alf in December. The big plan that filled his thoughts and lifted his wounded spirits, was that when his mother and Alf left for the Lake District he was going to get a dog. He fancied a Jack Russell. It could sit in the van and go to work with him, keep him company. The more he thought about it the better he felt. He remembered Ed's family getting a dog when his brother had died, it had seemed to help them all. '*Yes, I shall get a dog.*'

Although these thoughts helped, nothing could rid him of the sickening feeling in the pit of his stomach that just would not shift. When he slipped into sleep, he didn't dream of the Jack Russel he was planning to get, he dreamt of Cathleen, Cathleen and him together, happy.

*

The mantle clock struck ten. Florrie gave a yawn and stretched in her chair before she picked up her cup and saucer. She asked George for his mug which he had left on the floor by his chair. She rinsed them in cold water and left them on the side to drain.

Florrie had a routine at bedtime which was typical of her old maid behaviour. She rinsed out her tights and hung them over a towel, leaving them on the bath to dry. She washed herself down and rubbed Pond's Cold Cream on her face. She put a lanolin cream on her hands, then slipped on her little cotton gloves. Her floral nightgown came down to her ankles and tied at the neck with a little lace ribbon. She brushed out her hair and rolled it round her fingers making little curls, then clipped them in place with Kirby grips. She finished off by covering her head with a net that held everything together.

She hung over the banister and called down the stairs, "Night, George."

She turned on her bedside light and settled down to reading. It was a good book by Agatha Christie, called Murder in the Calais Coach. So engrossed was she in her book that she jumped when George opened her bedroom door, "Jesus, George, you made me jump. What do you want?"

George never entered her bedroom, and on the rare occasion that she might be needed, he would knock.

He stood filling the doorway, just looking at her. Her nerves were heightened with the thriller she was reading. When she got no answer from him she repeated herself, "What is it, what do you want?"

When he still remained silent, Florrie's earlier jittery nerves were replaced with fear. She tried to tell herself to calm down, this was George, her brother.

"George, are you sick?"

Florrie grabbed at her bed clothes holding them up to her chin as he approached her bed. "For goodness sake, George, you're frightening me, what is wrong with you?"

He sat on the side of her bed, and started to stroke her arm. She brushed him away like an unwanted fly, "Get off! What has come over you?"

Florrie didn't like this at all, she remembered his show of violence a few weeks ago and knew she was no match for his strength. Not knowing quite how to handle the situation she tried to distract him. She held up her novel, "I'm reading this book, it's by Agatha Christie, George. It's good. You'll like it, I'm sure."

When he didn't answer, she added in a voice that exposed her fear, "I've nearly finished it, I'll probably be able to give it to you tomorrow if I get on with it."

She felt his hand untie the ribbon at her throat. "George, for heaven's sake, what do you think you're doing?" She held her hand over his, trying to stop further movement, but he had forced his way in the now open neck line. Florrie had never had a sexual relationship and his hand on her body felt intrusive, and uncomfortable. His other hand came round and covered her mouth. She felt the weight of him pushing her back on her pillow. Florrie was horrified as he straddled her bed and his dressing gown opened to reveal his naked body, which showed obvious signs of arousal. She tried to bite his hand as she kicked at the covers. It was no use, he was too heavy. He pulled out a handkerchief and forced it into her mouth to muffle her protest. This caused Florrie to retch as the salty taste of mucus reached her taste buds. George became determined. When he forced his hand up her nightie she managed to spit out the hanky and let out a scream that echoed round the walls. For a split second Florrie was pleased to see George halted in his attack, but the reprieve was short as she found herself forced under her pillow which was held down so she couldn't breathe, let alone scream. Florrie kicked best she could with the weight of George upon her. The bedclothes stilled as the fight went out of her.

*

George had been awake early. He didn't touch Florrie's bedroom door as he walked past. His first job was to put a note in the milk bottle which read, No *milk until further notice.*

The milk man came whistling up the path as George was just placing the bottles on the step. George removed the note and said, "Morning, no milk today. We're going away. Please don't leave any more until further notice."

George backed back, shutting the door, ignoring the question, "Are you off on your holidays?"

George sat at the kitchen table and made a list of all the things he had to do today. He sat mumbling to himself as he went through his tasks, *'The papers need cancelling. Florrie's ordered coal, but I can't do anything about that now.'* He looked around him, everywhere was tidy. Florrie always washed up before she went to bed. He plumped up the cushions in the front room and straightened the chair backs. He scanned the room and was satisfied with his efforts. He went back upstairs and took out a bottle of Aspirin. Shaking four little white tablets into his hand he went back downstairs and washed them down with a large glass of water. He looked on the calendar to see if there was anything written on there. November fifth seemed to swear at him. He knew his neighbours were off to Hunston with the littlun' for a firework night. He smiled to himself as he thought how funny it was that even though he had been made to feel like an outcast, he still heard all their news. It was obvious to George that May still liked Florrie, but he sensed she had taken a dislike to him. What he couldn't understand was why? He cast his mind back to that Friday when the littlun' had thrown a tantrum, and told himself, *'that's when it had all started.'*

George lifted the seal on the envelope and took out the letter he had spent most of the night writing. He reread it again even though he knew it off by heart now. This time he licked the seal and folded it over, sticking a stamp in the corner.

He put on his hat and coat. He knew by his brief conversation with the milkman that it was a cold morning. He looked at himself in the mirror telling himself, he looked the same. He wound his scarf round his neck and pulled on his gloves.

He walked to Chichester road and posted his letter. He went into the chemist on the corner and bought another bottle of Aspirin. There were only a few left at home. His next stop was the grocers, he bought himself some cheese, a blue vein and a strong cheddar, then went next door to the green grocer where he bought one rosy apple. He cancelled the paper in the Newsagents, when the woman raised an eyebrow, George said, "I'm getting a bit weighty, I think the walk down of a morning will do me good." He patted his stomach in the process, which caused a laugh from them both.

He was back indoors before ten thirty and took a few more pills that he had bought at the chemist. The sound of the littlun' next door filtered through the wall. He wanted to see her, they still hadn't finished their matchstick model for May. The thought crossed his mind to go out there on his own to finish it, but it was freezing in the shed. George shivered, the house felt cold. Florrie would have lit the fire by now and the house would be warm and welcoming. He wanted to listen to the football match this afternoon on the radio. They had a television, but George still preferred the comfort of listening to the voices wafting out from the radio. When the clock struck midday he took out the bottle of painkillers again and took a few more, this time he swigged them down with a large port. Fireworks could be heard popping off, '*Bit early,*' he told himself. '*In my day it was an evening event, with a bonfire and hot soup if you were lucky.*'

He chastised himself. He didn't want to reminisce on days gone by, especially not his childhood, not now.

George went into the kitchen, he put the cheeses on a plate with a hunk of bread from the larder. The apple rolled on the floor, George bent to pick it up but it seemed to move around on the floor as if avoiding capture.

The news came on the radio, he hurried through to the warmth of the lounge, only to find the fire was still unlit. His lunch sat on the table untouched. He flopped in the chair and poured himself a larger than normal glass of port. An uneasy feeling settled in his stomach, causing him to gulp it down in one. The cheese came to mind, it had looked tempting, but he didn't think he would be able to eat it, not now. He hoped the port would quell his nerves, he had everything planned and didn't want to lose heart.

When the clock chimed out, he woke with a start. He was cold, nerves flickered in his stomach. What had seemed like such a good idea in the early hours of the morning was proving harder for him as the day went on. George opened the aspirins, swallowed another few and washed them down with the last of the port. The sound of fireworks had silenced but George was unaware, he was now in a drug induced coma.

George's arms felt heavy, they hung down by the side of the chair, he tried to lift them, but couldn't. He seemed to be looking down at himself from a height, *'I'm floating?'* He could see the uneaten cheese in the kitchen, he tried to throw it away but it wouldn't go in the bin. It was enormous. Wrapping it in newspaper, an enormous parcel appeared. The paper changed colour and a bright red package sparkled at him. He could see himself stood in the garden by the dustbin. A voice echoed across the lawn.

"Hello, George, it's a cold one."

It was May, he wanted to speak to her but the words floated around his head and he couldn't pronounce them. He started laughing. Rachel was there now, she had started laughing too.

"George?" May's voice sounded high and lyrical, "Are you alright?"

George watched as Rachel stood naked spinning round and round in the garden. When she stopped she had grown breasts. George stopped laughing, he turned to go indoors, May's laughter whirled round his head. The house was tidy, the tea-towel was hung over the oven door just how Florrie always left it.

He cast his eyes over the rooms, everything seemed in order. There was no sound, everywhere was quiet.

The clock started chiming, there were clocks everywhere now. George looked frantically at his watch trying to read the face, *'Does it say three?'* He couldn't be sure, *'Perhaps it says four.'* His dressing gown was on the bed ready, he tried to put it on for warmth but his arms wouldn't go in the sleeves. He wanted to be found lying beside his sister. *'I must be with Florrie.'*

The clock struck seven, fireworks lit up the night sky, but George heard nothing.

*

"Look, Rachel." Tilly pointed in the air "Ahh! It's beautiful isn't it?" Fireworks flew in the sky popping and banging, sprinkling the night sky with colour.

Rachel was jumping up and down holding onto May's hand. Rosie was sitting on Norman's shoulders. Ed and Ken were in their element lighting the fireworks.

The cold seemed to filter through Tilly's clothes despite the warmth of the bonfire, "May, I'm going in to check on Gran. I'll get the food going too."

"I'll come." She paused, and added, "To give you a hand. Norman, here, take Rachel's hand. Keep hold of her, I don't want her too near the fire."

Tilly knew Agnes would be fine, but went through to her room just the same, "Alright, Gran?" Agnes had her feet up on a stool watching TV. Tilly knew she was not interested in the fireworks.

"I'm fine, love. Everything alright out there?"

"Yes, the girls love it. Mind you, so do Ed and Ken for that matter. It's good to see him here, I had a feeling he wouldn't come."

The kettle started whistling from the kitchen. "May's put the kettle on, do you want a cuppa?"

"I'll come through, love. Catch up on the news from Bognor."

Tilly laughed, "Things will be dead now Cathleen's gone, but don't let Ken hear me say that." She pulled out a kitchen chair "There you go, gran, sit there. You sit too, May, I can manage the food."

Tilly put sixteen sausages under the grill, she turned the baked potatoes and turned on the stove to warm the soup through. "Can you two butter the bread while you're sitting there?"

The conversation found its way to the saga of Cathleen. May voiced her concerns, "She's caused such worry and heartache to Pam, Tilly. I haven't said much but she has aged over these past few weeks, even Norman said so."

Tilly smiled inwardly, she found it funny how May always used Norman's feelings for back up to any of her arguments or tales. Whenever she said anything detrimental, she would always say, "Didn't she Norm?" or "You saw it, didn't you Norm?" Norman would say in a resigned way, "Yes, May, no, May, she did, May." Tilly was sure he just said those words on auto pilot, always being the peacemaker.

The door flew open and the girls burst through the door, runny red noses and rosy cheeks. Tilly bellowed "Take your wellies off, both of you."

The girls ran upstairs to the toilet, both giggling.

Tilly moved over to the table and took a place mat away, she had hoped Lucy would join them but she had had to stay at the stables because it was Bonfire Night. Tilly had insisted that Michael should take charge, but Lucy had said he was away. Rumours were flying round that Christine was going to give him another chance. Tilly and Lucy agreed that she must be mad.

Once everyone was sat at the table, the conversation flitted to Brenda and Alf and their planned December wedding. Ken didn't seem to mind talking about it despite his own ditched big day. Silence lay heavy at the table when Rachel said, "Ken, now you're not getting married can't we all be bridesmaid to your mum?" The uncomfortable atmosphere was lifted when Ken smiled and assured her, "I don't see why not, Rachel. I'll speak to mum, it's a shame not to see you all in your pretty dresses."

Tilly could have got out of her chair and kissed him. Her heart warmed as she watched Rosie wriggle in her chair, "Yes! Well done, Rachel. That'll be great."

"Sit your bottom down, Rosie, I'm going to bring the supper through."

Tilly came back wearing oven gloves, she was carrying a large platter laden with jacket potatoes. She put the plate on the table with the sausages and went back for the baked beans. "Tuck in, everyone, eat it while it's hot."

Ed tinkled the side of his glass with his fork, "Before we eat I want to make a toast."

Tilly picked up her glass and smiled when he said, "To family."

May as usual spoiled the moment. "We're not all family."

Tilly reached over for a sausage, "Yes we are, May. We're the family we've chosen."

She smiled a smug look of satisfaction when Norman followed suit, raising his glass, saying, "Hear, hear. To family - I'll drink to that."

Tilly noticed the sour look settle on May's face. Not wanting to spoil the evening, she filled the silent moment "What about your neighbours, May? You haven't mentioned them of late."

Tilly omitted to say that a few weeks ago it was all they heard. Norman answered for his wife, causing her to grimace a bit more. "May's got a bee in her bonnet that George is a bit odd."

The silence was replaced with laughter filling the dining room. The look Rosie gave May went unnoticed.

*

May left Norman downstairs while she tackled getting Rachel to bed. "No story tonight, it's too late."

"I want a story, a small one."

"Not tonight, Rachel, you can have the light on for ten minutes and read to yourself."

May closed the bedroom door on her, "Lights out in ten minutes. I shall call up, do you hear me?"

Ignoring Rachel's childish protests she went downstairs to tackle Norman. She was still annoyed at him for making her feel foolish in front of the others earlier.

"There you are, May, I've made you a cuppa. Come on, sit down, love."

A little of May's anger subsided with the thoughtful gesture, "Norm, you made me feel foolish earlier..." May hesitated, "You know... mentioning George like that. I didn't know what to say."

"Don't be so silly, May. I was just jesting. Everyone knows what you're like."

"There you go again, what's that meant to mean?"

Norman picked up his own mug of tea, "Nothing, May. It's true though, the poor man's been excluded because you've taken a dislike to him, blaming him for one of Rachel's tantrums."

May's cheeks took on that tell-tale flush which gave warning of her rising temper. Her hands shook as she reached for her cup, "Is that what you think? You're so wrong, Norman. I liked them a lot, I wanted to like them. I wanted to take up our Bridge nights again." She paused briefly, not knowing how to explain herself. She knew she couldn't say Rosie had warned her off him, he really would think she was mad. So she said in tones that belied her feelings, "Norman, it's a woman's intuition. I know you think I'm wrong but you know…" She hesitated again, "Norman, you hear things about men, you know?" She waited, hoping he would get her meaning, but was flustered when he just stared at her with a gormless blank expression on his face. May lost her patience with him, her anger replaced with frustration, "Oh for goodness sake, Norman, stop acting so thick. Men who like children, you know, men who never marry. Do I have to spell it out? Dirty old buggers that get a thrill out of little…"

"Shut up, May! That's despicable. You really are a vicious woman at times. I like them, I like them both. Like you I was looking forward to Bridge again, but you…"

May jumped to her own defence after Norman's onslaught had silenced her, "Don't you tell me to shut up, you shut up. I know what I felt and I sensed something wrong… Okay?" When Norman took on a sulky expression May continued, "You can call it a woman's intuition or you can call it vicious, I really don't care. I'm looking after our daughter, Norman…"

May stopped her tirade as Rachel's little voice was heard, "Why are you angry with daddy, mummy?"

May was relieved not to have to answer. Norman got out of his chair, "Come on, sweet pea, up to bed. Daddy will tuck you in."

Norman cast a glance in May's direction, his next words made her feel sick, "Or do you think I have an ulterior motive?"

219

May was lost for words at his insinuation, so concentrated on Rachel's tears.

"Stop that silly noise, Rachel. Mummy and Daddy have had a little tiff, just like you do sometimes with Rosie. Now let Daddy take you back upstairs and tuck you in. I expect he'll read you a little story, seeing as he has so much to say for himself." May could hear Rachel's sobs catching in her throat as she was taken up to bed. She knew her reprimand was unnecessarily harsh and was annoyed how the argument had unfolded. Instead of Norman apologising, May had angered him further. *'Perhaps that little gypsy girl has bewitched me, and poisoned my mind.'*

May took the cups into the kitchen. She could hear Norman's voice floating down the stairs, he was reading, 'Cheeky Monkey finds a Pop Gun'. It was one of Rachel's favourites, and May knew that it would settle her down. She draped a tea towel over the draining board and made her way up to Rachel's room and pushed open the door. She wanted to make her peace with the child, "Can mummy listen too?"

Norman put his finger to his lips and shushed May. Rachel was already asleep.

Norman got carefully off the side of the bed and May closed the door behind them, "I've locked up, Norm. I'm sorry, but…"

Norman interrupted her, "Where did all that come from?"

May wanted the bad feeling sorted, she felt foolish and unsure of her accusations, "I don't know. Perhaps as you say I've let my imagination run away with me, but you embarrassed me tonight, Norman, your comments were uncalled for."

"May, it was a joke, l didn't expect you to take offence or I would have kept my mouth shut." Norman paused and May guessed he wanted to say something, "Please say it, Norm, say what's on your mind."

"May… I know you mean well… and that you're looking out for Rachel, but you can't go round accusing people of things, especially those sort of things. Surely even you know that?"

May didn't want this row to start all over again, so chose her words carefully, "I haven't accused anyone of anything. I just felt something. I don't know, perhaps I have been being silly, but it felt real at the time."

She was relieved when Norman said they were to say no more about it and he didn't want to fall out with her over neighbours.

*

May took the joint out of the oven and poured the juices into a jug which was half full of vegetable water. "Rachel, go and wash your hands for dinner, there's a good girl."

May could hear Norman putting his bike away in the shed. She opened the kitchen door, "Did you bring a cabbage?"

"I did, love, and some carrots and swede. The allotment has done well this year."

May took the wicker basket off him, she took it indoors and within minutes, had stripped the cabbage of its outer leaves and had it cooking in the pan.

Norman kissed May's cheek as he went through to wash. Rachel was already sitting at the table, she loved her food. May heard Norman speak to her as he walked through the lounge.

"Rachel, come and help mummy please."

May had plated up the food, and gave Rachel her own lunch to carry through. May followed, carrying the gravy jug. Norman was now sitting at the table, waiting. "Smells good, love, I've been thinking about this all morning. It's freezing out there."

May placed the gravy in the middle of the table, "Rachel wait until we've got our dinners, we eat together."

The conversation round the table found its way to the neighbours, "Did you see Florrie this morning, May?" May finished her mouthful of food, giving herself time to think before she answered, "I tried, Norman, but there was no answer. The radio's on in there, but there's no sign of anyone."

Norman scraped his knife round his plate causing May to glare at him, it didn't deter him from licking it clean. Norman wiped his chin with his sleeve, saying, "I saw old whistler at the allotment, he said they were going away and did I know where and for how long?"

The milkman was known as whistler because you could hear his whistling before the bottles rattled on the step. Whistler kept a plot on the allotment alongside Norman's. May was all ears, "Really. Did he say where?"

Norman was as vague as Whistler had been, and relayed how when he went to deliver the milk Saturday, Mr Coffin was putting a note in the milk bottle to cancel their delivery.

"They couldn't have gone away, Norman. I peeked in the kitchen window and there's cheese plated up. I swear that radio was blaring out too."

"Cheese, May! Since when has anyone had cheese for Sunday lunch? You must've been mistaken."

May was relieved Norman hadn't accused her of being nosy. While she had been peeping in the window of her neighbour's home she had felt very conspicuous. "I was not mistaken, Norm, and if they've gone away Florrie would've left that house spick and span, of that I'm sure."

May put her own knife and fork together on her empty plate, "I'll try again later. We'll go round, Rachel, we'll go together; Uncle George would like that, wouldn't he?"

"You don't like him, mummy."

May was harassed now, "Of course I like him, don't talk such rubbish."

"I heard you shouting at daddy, you said…"

May stood up, and grabbed the plates, "Rachel - people say all sorts of silly things in anger, I didn't mean it. Once we have washed up, we'll go round together and I don't want to hear another word from you about it." When Norman gave a sign with his hand to May to calm down she felt like exploding. *I'll never get involved with neighbours like this again. They're more trouble than they're worth.*

By the evening both May and Norman had tried to get an answer from next door. They had come to the conclusion that Whistler must be right, and they had gone away. May had pointed out the plated uneaten cheese to Norman, who had said what a shame it was if they had gone away and left a good blue to go to waste like that. Rachel had tried to get in the shed, but it was all locked up. Although it was affirmed that their neighbours were definitely not in, May felt something didn't feel right.

*

Chapter Nine

Prospects

The week flew by, it was Friday already and May and Norman were going to parents evening at Little Acorns, the private school they had chosen to send Rachel to, to give her the very best start they could.

"Rachel, will you hurry up, we have to get you to Tilly's and then drive to Arundel by six."

"I want to take the pink case."

"No, Rachel, I have your things down here already. You are only staying one night, stop being silly."

Norman tooted outside to let them know he was waiting. May held up Rachel's coat as the child slipped her arms through. "I hope you are a lot less trouble for Mrs Waters than you are for me at times."

Rachel giggled as she ran out into the dark, pulling at the car door handle. May ordered the dog into his basket and slammed the front door shut.

Despite May's panic, they arrived at Little Acorns twenty minutes before their appointment. They looked round the classroom, viewing the children's work on the walls. Memories flooded May's mind as she recalled Parents evening for her boys. Ed had always been such a disappointment back then, but Luke, Luke had always shone.

"Look, Norman, that's Rachel's work again."

It was obvious to them both by the time they were called in that Rachel was doing well.

Mrs Waters stood and shook hands, telling them to take a seat. May sat up straight with her handbag on her lap. Her legs were uncrossed and her knees were held tight together in a prim fashion as she waited to hear how Rachel was progressing. Norman held a handkerchief to his mouth clearing his throat in a cough. Before either of them could ask any questions Mrs Waters was speaking, "Mr and Mrs Barrett, Rachel is a dream child in school. How do you find her at home?"

May let go of the breath she hadn't realised she was holding. Her heart seemed to swell with pride. "She has her moments, but in general, yes, she's a good girl."

Mrs Waters knew Rachel was an adopted child and wanted to clarify a few things in her own mind before she discussed her plans.

"I don't know how much you understand about Down- Syndrome children?" She waited for some sort of confirmation, but both May and Norman just sat waiting to see where this conversation was going. "Rachel has a very good understanding of her letters and number work. I am urging you to consider sending her to the Four Oaks from here. It's our sister boarding school, not all children get this very privileged opportunity, but I feel Rachel is the ideal candidate for a place. I believe she could achieve a good level of education with the prospect of being able to manage independent living in the future. Is this something you had thought of?"

May crossed her legs, moving her bag on to the floor, "She's nine years old, surely we're not thinking about independent living at this stage?"

Norman interrupted, "May, let Mrs Waters explain. Are you sure Rachel could cope?"

The teacher smiled at Norman, leaning back in her chair. "I do. I really do. She's sat some level three tests." Mrs Waters pulled out some sheets, showing them both. The page was full of ticks. "Rachel got 78%, it's an exceptional mark."

May leant forward, taking the papers, "When did she sit these? She didn't say she had been doing tests."

"Mrs Barrett, we wouldn't tell a student they were sitting any sort of test, it causes unnecessary angst. These were done in class as an exercise. The average score from her class were between 48% and 60%, Rachel was the only student here to achieve a mark in the 70's. I've had a meeting with the head, and we feel Rachel should be given a place at The Four Oaks, should you wish it."

May reached for Norman's hand, he squeezed it and smiled, saying, "I speak for us both, I'm sure, when I say this. We're happy for Rachel to have this chance of private education and delighted that she's doing so well, but…"

May interrupted, "When would she leave here?"

Mrs Waters was ready with her answers, "Rachel will be ten next year. She would start the new September term there."

May looked at Norman. There was a worried expression on his face, "What is it, Norman. What's worrying you?"

"We'll talk when we get home, May."

Mrs Waters looked at them both, "Is it the money?"

Norman was glad this was mentioned, he'd guessed it would come at a cost. He couldn't help feel relieved it was being brought up here, May wouldn't lose her temper in front of Mrs Waters, nor become too defensive. "Would the fees be a lot higher than these?"

"As a boarder, yes. You would pay quarterly, eight hundred and fifty pounds at the start of the four terms. The full cost of the year would be three thousand four hundred pounds." This was considerably more than they were paying now. "If you wanted, Rachel could come home for weekends, but the school is situated in Kent, so you would have a lot of travelling to consider. The choice would be yours."

It was May who spoke, Norman had paled. "Would that make a lot of difference to the fees if we took her home at weekends?"

"Marginally, but not much. You need to take into account that her full board will ease the outgoings in your own home…"

Mrs Waters sensed that May and Norman were no longer listening, she closed the meeting with, "You have a lot to talk and think about. If you have no further questions I must see my next appointment."

They stood and shook hands with Mrs Waters. They thanked her for her encouragement and were warmed by the genuine belief she seemed to have in their adopted daughter.

Once in the car May reminded Norman of April Springs. It had been a special school that had been for a while Rachel's destiny. She had hated it there. "No, May, that wasn't a school that was going to be Rachel's home. We saved her from that by adopting her. This is a chance for Rachel, a chance for her to grow, to grow into an independent woman. We won't always be here, what then?"

"I know, Norman. What about her? I can't see her wanting to board, she loves going to stay with Tilly and Ed."

"Things are changing there, May. When Rosie leaves next year they won't want Rachel. Life for them will take a different direction. What worries me is the money. It's enormous. We didn't ever put our hands in our pockets for our lad's education."

"With Luke we didn't have to, and Ed, he didn't have the interest. We would have done though, Norm, if a teacher had said it was necessary."

Norman changed gear, "Are you saying now, that you want Rachel to be given this chance?"

"No, no I'm not saying anything. I'm dead proud of her though. I know, like you, it's a huge amount of money, money we don't have,

Norman. I hate to think of her going away too, she's still very young."

"May, whatever we do, we do for Rachel. The truth of the matter is, even if we both decide it's best for her to go, I don't think we can sensibly afford to send her. Do you?"

May couldn't help but feel relieved. The thought of losing Rachel had caused an unease to settle in her stomach. She was delighted and proud at the progress Rachel had made at Little Acorns, her exam results had made the money spent on it worth every penny. "Seventy eight percent, Norman, that's good isn't it?"

*

May and Norman had discussed the prospect of Rachel's new school and as much as they would have liked to send her, the fees were just too high.

It hadn't stopped May rising early, telling Norman she was going over to Tilly's on the bus. It had been met with resistance, but May had gotten her own way.

As she sat on the bus watching for Mundham corner, excitement bubbled inside of her. She couldn't wait to tell Tilly how well Rachel was doing.

It was cold to hang about on Mundham corner waiting for the connecting bus, but she didn't fancy the long walk down to Hunston. She shuffled her feet trying to keep warm. If the weather had been better she might have gone along to the stables and watched Rachel riding. She knew that was where they would be until twelve. *'Perhaps I should have phoned Tilly and said I'd be early.'*

Before May could give this anymore thought the bus came along, and within minutes she was getting off and crossing the road to Tilly and Ed's.

It felt like ages before the door was answered, and it wasn't Tilly but Agnes who stood in the hallway smiling. She looked genuinely pleased to see her, early or not, "Hello, May, are the girls running late or are you early?"

"It's me, I'm early. I didn't want to wait for Norman. You know what he's like, he gets at that allotment and you don't see him till two, sometimes three."

"No bother, come in, you look frozen. I'll put the kettle on and we can take it through to my bit."

May didn't like the thought of going into Agnes's bit, as she called it. It reminded her that the old lady was living with her son. May was sure if she was alone there would be no way this offer of kindness would reach out to her. Feeling disgruntled that her plans were ruined, as she was hoping to brag to Tilly about Rachel's achievement, her tone came out sharper than she intended, "Where's Tilly? I thought she would be here."

Agnes lit the gas, moving the kettle over the flame, "No, May, she normally stays up there with Rosie, if Rachel wasn't there she would have ridden too."

"What's the attraction, I wonder?" No sooner the words were out of May's mouth she knew she had made an error. Agnes was a mild tempered woman, but she loved her family. May braced herself for the onslaught.

"I don't know what you mean there, May? What I do know is, Tilly loves the horses, she loves your boy too - so do I for that matter. I also know that Tilly will be at the stables, riding or watching the girls ride. The only person she likes there is Lucy, Lucy is a lovely young girl who adores your Rachel. Does that answer your question?" May had the decency to look embarrassed, "I'm sorry, Agnes. That was uncalled for. I think I was just so looking forward to telling her my good news that disappointment made me judgmental."

"There is no need to judge my Tilly, May. Tilly's as good as gold. I thought the way she helps you out with Rachel would have thawed you a bit."

Anger rose in May, she didn't like being made to feel in the wrong, but she managed to hold her tongue.

"I said I'm sorry, Agnes, and you're right Tilly and Ed are wonderful with Rachel."

If Agnes noticed that May had added Ed to the praise she showed no signs of it. May decided to unload all her gloating pride on Agnes at how well Rachel was doing at school. The only comment Agnes made was how expensive education comes when it's private.

Norman arrived with Tilly and the girls, he had picked them up by the shops making their way home.

Rachel was always pleased to see May, and ran to her like she hadn't seen her for weeks. "Mummy, I rode a new horse called Durberry, not a pony, was it, Tilly? It was a horse." Tilly laughed, agreeing with Rachel, which caused May to feel envious at Tilly's youthful relaxed attitude to life.

May told them all over lunch how well Rachel had done at school. Tilly was the first to praise Rachel's efforts, "You must be very proud of her, May, and you, Norman?"

When the girls left the table and went out to play, May continued to brag about the private boarding school. She hadn't wanted to speak of it in front of Rachel, as she knew that on Norman's wage they would not be able to fund such a venture.

When Tilly said The Four Oaks sounded very posh, May lost the joy in it all. The realisation of bragging about it had hit hard. It now felt like a slap in the face. Rachel was being given the chance to go to a special school, but they couldn't afford to send her. May sat quiet and chastised herself. *Why was I so set on getting over here to gloat about our failings? I should have stayed at home.*

230

Knight's Solicitors, Paradise Street, Liverpool

Monday 14ᵗʰ November 1966

Jack Knight got to his office early. He had been away for the past week skiing, and he was pleased to see his post all sorted in the in-tray for his attention.

The unopened blue envelope marked Private and Confidential in big bold letters made him curious, but he wanted a coffee first.

Within minutes Jack was back, stirring three heaped spoons of sugar into his oversized mug. His leather chair twisted as he sat. It was one of those seats that swivelled round like a round-a-bout. Jack liked the sensation of spinning when he had clinched a deal or finished work on a Friday. He enjoyed the view of the street from his window too. One of Jack's favourite pastimes was people watching, he could amuse himself like that for hours.

Jack dipped a biscuit in his coffee, popping it in his mouth, whole, so he could open the mysterious letter.

Reaching for his coffee, he tried to comprehend what he was reading. He lit a cigarette, leaning back in his chair he took a long drag. He read the letter again, took another long drag on the cigarette, and leaving it in the ashtray, he went to find George Coffin's file. Sitting back at his desk with the letter out in front of him, he studied the neat hand writing which seemed to blur under his scrutiny.

The Hollies,
Pevensey Road,
Bognor Regis,
West Sussex.

Friday 4ᵗʰ November 1966

231

Dear Mr Knight

When you receive this letter I shall already have left this world. My sister Florence Coffin has suffered a heart attack and I know I can no longer go on without her.

In my will, filed with your firm, you will see that I stated quite clearly that if I should die before my sister, Florence, she was to inherit all my estate, this is no longer applicable. I should like Rachel Barrett of Hard Acre Cottage, Pevensey Road Bognor Regis West Sussex to be my sole beneficiary.

Neither Florence nor I have any family, and I hope I can rely on you to make sure this last wish is carried out for me.

Yours Sincerely

George Coffin

Jack picked up the phone and dialled nine, nine, nine. He could have done without this today.

*

May couldn't believe it when she saw police cars draw up next door. She was just about to go out and say George and Florrie were away when she heard their front door forced open. May lay back against the wall covering her mouth with her hand, *'Dear God, what's going on there?'*

She stood behind the net curtain fascinated at the comings and goings. Curiosity was killing her, she needed the toilet, but was so frightened of missing something she jiggled to and fro, craning her neck. When the doctor's car pulled up and Geoffrey got out, May thought her legs would give way. She had stood glued to the window for over twenty minutes and hadn't seen anything of any importance, but she knew something was wrong round there. She thought about the cheese left out that Norman had mocked her about, and a cold unease settled over her.

The school bus dropped Rachel off at three thirty, giving May the perfect excuse to go out the front.

There were three police cars now, but the doctor had gone. *'Surely Florrie isn't in there?'* May dismissed this thought, only to have another one fly through her troubled mind pricking her conscience, *'No, I would have heard her moving around. I don't like the look of this though.'*

Rachel sat watching her programmes, oblivious of the drama next door, while May stayed close behind the curtain, straining her neck to see if she could spot anything worth seeing. When a funeral car crept up the road she nearly collapsed.

*

May flew to the door before Norman could turn the handle, the dog picked up on the excitement and started barking, leaping up at her. "Shut up, Prince, get in your bed." Before Norman could take his coat off May was at him, "My God, Norm, the police have been here all day. It looks like Florrie and George are dead. Dead, Norman. The funeral directors were here, the doctor too. I'm going round to Pam later, she'll know something, she's thick with the doctor, and his wife. I haven't been…"

"Keep your voice down, you'll frighten Rachel."

"Norman, I've been…"

She was stopped midsentence with Norman trying to calm her, "I know, May, I know. It's been on the radio."

"What, when? I missed that. I've been glued I have, glued to that bloody window trying to make it out. What happened, what's been said?"

Norman pulled off his coat and hung it on the peg, "Nothing really, May. You're right though, they are dead. The radio said the police are looking into the suspicious death of a couple believed to be brother and sister in Bognor Regis."

"Suspicious, Jesus, Norm, lock the door."

"Don't be daft, woman, it's…" Rachel appeared "Daddy, We've been making Christmas puddings at school."

May watched as her husband picked up the child and carried her through to the lounge. So many questions needed answering. She switched on the radio, hoping to hear for herself any updates of next door. Murder, next door. Fear started to replace curiosity.

*

The next day May sent Rachel off to school, and through Pam had found out that the assumption was Florrie had suffered a heart attack and George had taken an overdose. May had many emotions to deal with, she was upset they had all fallen out, it felt very foolish now. She was angry at Rosie, she shouldn't have let the child bewitch her into thinking bad thoughts about her neighbours, and relief that she could rest easy again and stop worrying about keeping the back door locked. At least this small news made her feel more settled.

Norman brought home the Bognor Post that evening. There was a bit in there about the deaths of their neighbours, but it didn't say anything that either of them didn't now already know.

May had struggled to settle Rachel to bed. The news that Uncle George and Auntie Florrie had died and gone to heaven had caused lots of questions. Rachel wanted to know where heaven was. Could they come back if they didn't like it and could they visit? Under any other circumstances this would have made May smile at her innocence, but she had all sorts of guilt attached to the sudden death of her neighbours. The real angst that lay heavy on May was Norman. She knew he was disappointed at her accusations, and she asked herself over and over, *'What was I thinking to get such disgusting thoughts in my head? Yes, it was that Gypsy child's fault, she ignited the doubts what with her refusing to visit them, telling me he was a bad man. The sooner she goes the better.'*

May wished she could share her thoughts with Norman, if only to put a little understanding between them, but she knew he would think badly of her. She was so angry with herself. She asked herself over and over, how she could have thought such things about someone? Someone she hardly knew.

*

Wednesday 16th November

The phone ringing caused May to jump and run indoors. There was a large black car parked outside of next door, and May had missed who had gone in. She knew there was someone in there as the door to George's shed was open. May had been in and out of the garden twice to hang washing which she knew wouldn't dry. The weather was too cold and damp.

Picking up the phone her voice was impatient, she was so frightened if she moved from the window she would miss something. "Yes?"

"Hello, May, are you alright?"

"Tilly, yes, yes I'm okay. What do you want?"

May could sense Tilly's hesitance, and found herself apologising "I'm sorry, Tilly, you must have heard about our neighbours?" When Tilly said she had and asked if she knew anymore, May felt happy to tell her how there was someone round there now and that she was trying to see who it was.

"I won't keep you, May, It's just its Lucy's birthday today, and we're having a little surprise party tea for her."

"What, tonight? This was short notice for May, and midweek she liked to keep Rachel in a routine.

"Yes, May. Lucy doesn't seem to have family, so I wanted to do something for her, Ken's coming with Brenda and Alf. They're picking up Hannah too. Rachel would love it here with them all. I shouldn't tell you this as it's a surprise, but Brenda and Alf..."

May cut Tilly off midsentence, "Oh! Hang on a minute, I think they're leaving." May moved across to the window, pulling the wire of the phone till it was out stretched. "It's no good, Tilly, I've got to go. I'll call you back later."

No sooner had May placed the phone down, she was knocking it off the receiver in her hurry to answer the front door.

Two men in suits stood on the doorstep, "Mrs Barret, Detective Jupitus and my colleague Sergeant Wilkins." ID was flashed at May and they asked if they could come in.

May pulled the door open wide as a silent invite. Nerves had her offering tea.

She returned to the lounge carrying a tray laden with her best china tea service and a plate of homemade biscuits. Once she was seated the Detective started asking questions, "Mrs Barrett, how well did you know your neighbours?"

She tried to steady the noticeable hand shake as she poured the tea. "Do you take milk and sugar?" When they both said yes, May answered his question.

"We were friends." Guilt made May falter, she didn't have to worry, the silence was broken with another question.

"Friends? Did you know anything about them before they moved here?"

236

The cup rattled on the saucer as May passed it to the Detective. She told them to help themselves to biscuits. "No, I didn't know them before. They said they came from Liverpool."

The sergeant sat writing in his note-book, and the Detective seemed to ignore her answer, asking, "What did you make of George?"

"He seemed kind, he liked our daughter, Rachel. He took a real interest in her. They were making a model for me out of matchsticks, Rachel would go round there of an evening and help him."

Everything she said seemed to be written down. He stopped writing and reached for his tea, speaking for the first time on the subject, "How old is your daughter, Rachel?"

"Rachel's nine, she's special." When the Sergeant looked at her for a better understanding, May enlightened them both with her condition. The sergeant started writing again while the Detective took up the questions, "Were you comfortable with George spending time with your little girl?"

Goose-pimples spread up May's arms. She wasn't sure whether she should be honest about her fears. *What good would it do now?* Norman had already told her about her vicious accusations, so May turned the question back on him. "Why do you ask such a thing?"

"We're doing an inquiry, we need to know as many facts as we can get. We're trying to build a picture here."

"I understood it was straightforward, Florrie died of a heart attack and George took his own life. What picture is needed?"

"Mrs Barrett, we are not dealing with a suicide here, we are dealing with a murder inquiry."

May's hand flew to her face, "Oh dear God, surely not."

The policeman hadn't expected this response and leant over and placed a hand on hers. "I'm sorry, I didn't mean to shock you like that. Were they very good friends of yours?"

May ignored the question again, saying, "Are you sure? Murder."

"Yes the autopsy has revealed that some suspicious acts have taken place."

May thought she was going to be sick. She stood at the horror of what she was hearing. "Oh dear God, I need my husband. Please can you get him home for me?" May told them Norman worked at Lec, several calls were made, and May sat quiet, her mind worked overtime.

There was another knock on the front door, causing Prince to start up barking. May couldn't even find a voice to shut him up, she sat unable to move. The Detective answered it. Voices could be heard in the hall, and when they came into the lounge he was accompanied by a policewoman. She introduced herself to May, while the Sergeant and the Detective asked if they could have a look in Rachel's bedroom. May still felt like her legs had gone to lead, so pointed at the stairs, "It's the first door on the left at the top of the landing. Her name is on it."

May was frightened, "I need my husband here."

Relief flooded May's being as Norman's presence filled the room. He knelt down beside May, "What is it, love, what's happened?"

"Didn't they tell you? George is being accused of murder."

The police woman interrupted May, "This is an inquiry, Mrs Barrett. We don't know for sure yet what happened. We are still investigating." Norman turned as the Detective came back into the room, "Mr Barrett, I asked your wife how she found the couple next door, she was unable to help, can you?"

Norman cleared his throat, moved away from May's side, and stood up. "Florrie and George were our neighbours, we got quite friendly with them. My wife took a dislike to George over an incident…" Before Norman could speak any further the Detective stopped him, "Incident, what incident?"

May found her voice, frightened how she might be viewed. "It sounds silly now, but it was over our daughter, Rachel. She threw a temper because I said she couldn't go round one evening, we were going out, you see. Rachel, being the way she is, isn't always easy to pacify and became hysterical. George came out to see what the commotion was all about…"May paused as she tried to recall the incident, "George seemed defensive when Rachel said something about him, I can't remember exactly what it was, but she said he told lies. That was it, lies. George had disappeared into his shed, it just felt wrong to me. I distanced myself from both of them after this, both George and Florrie." May looked across at Norman, who was still standing. His pale face made her feel justified for her earlier thoughts and accusations. Norman seemed to be shuffling his feet as if the floor was hot. The Detective followed May's gaze and looked at Norman, "Mr Barrett, what did you make of this disagreement with your wife and neighbour?"

Norman had the decency to look uncomfortable, but May's back went up at Norman's description of her. "My wife often sees the bad in people before the good, so I was afraid she was misjudging him. She accused him of some terrible things that made me feel uncomfortable. I felt she was being cruel, yes that is what I thought. Now I feel foolish."

"Mr Barrett, can you enlighten us on what you felt was cruel about your wife's accusations? The accusations that you referred to as cruel?"

Tears fell down May's face, "Dear God, don't let him have touched my daughter, not like that. Not Rachel, she's so innocent, so loving…"

"Mrs Barrett, it seems to me that you had come to a conclusion that could quite well have protected your little girl from harm's way."

"No, she was always round there, it was weeks before I noticed anything. Oh God, Norm, you don't think, do you?"

"May, we don't know anything for sure, and unless you want to ask her that is how it will stay. What I do know is, Rachel is still the same little girl she was yesterday. Our little girl."

The Detective interrupted Norman, "I don't want to cause unnecessary alarm, I just wanted to get a picture of the type of neighbours you thought they were. You have helped, thank you. Is there anyone else you know of that could help with these enquiries, anyone else they befriended?"

Norman spoke for them, "No, they hadn't been here long. We seemed to be their only visitors, as far as I could see."

When the police left, May took the tray out into the kitchen to wash up. Norman came out into the kitchen, put his arms around May's waist and said "I'm so sorry, May, really sorry."

"Do you know what frightens me more, Norman?" When he raised his eyes in question, she said, "Rosie. That little girl warned me. She did, Norman, she told me, 'He was a bad man'. God, Norm, do you think she's bewitched?"

Norman's laugh told May he thought she was being silly again, but May was spooked. She couldn't help thinking. *'I'll be glad when she's gone, that I will.'*

*

When Rachel got home at three thirty, May's nerves had calmed. She wanted to question Rachel on Uncle George and their time spent in the shed, but didn't know how to start the conversation without sounding accusing. Instead she asked her about her day and if she felt like going to Tilly's for a little tea party with Hannah and Rosie. It was a silly question, as Rachel loved going over to Hunston. "Homework first, young lady. Let me see what you've got to do."

There was a page of five times tables to fill out, and a picture to colour of different fruits. "Go upstairs and get your colours, and I will set you up at the dining table. Think about the fruits and their colours before you fill it in."

May phoned Tilly and said she would be there. She filled her in on the news of next door, but didn't mention her underlying fear of what George might have been up to with Rachel. May couldn't rid herself of the guilt. She couldn't help feeling she was somewhat to blame, *'Perhaps I should have kept a closer eye on her.'*

Norman came home a little later due to the fact he had spent the latter part of the morning and early afternoon comforting May. Ken had picked up Hannah at five o'clock, and May had seen that Brenda and Alf were in the car too.

When Norman got home May and Rachel were ready. "Hurry up and change, Norm, Ken picked Hannah up ages ago."

"Seems funny to me, a party mid-week. I would rather have stayed in, love."

"I know, me too. Tilly seemed keen for us to go though. I thought after the day we had had it would be good for us too."

Norman went upstairs to change, agreeing with May. Rachel called after him, "Hurry, daddy, I want to go to the party."

While Norman had a quick wash and change of clothes, May looked at Rachel's homework. The tables were all correct, and the fruits were all coloured in. May looked at the bananas, "Rachel, bananas are yellow, what have you done here?"

"Mine are green because you always buy them that colour so they last longer."

Norman came in at that moment and had obviously caught the tail end of the conversation, "That told you, May. I think that's a clever answer, Rachel. Come on, let's go."

Prince was ordered to his bed, Norman locked the door behind them as Rachel clambered into the back of the car, full of excited chatter.

*

Tilly opened the door, waving them in as if she was calling traffic through. Excitement could be felt through her wide smile and dancing feet which looked like she was jogging on the spot. "Quick, quick, come on in, Lucy isn't here yet; she thinks it is just a small tea with Gran, Ed and I." When May scanned the room for Ed, Tilly said, "Ed's just gone to pick her up, he'll be back in a mo."

Everyone was sat at the table when Lucy walked in, "Happy Birthday, Lucy." Glasses filled with fizzy drink were clinked and held up in the air, excitable giggles came from the three little girls, who were kneeling on their chairs.

Lucy stood, tears welled in her eyes, "Oh, Tilly, thank you so much. Thank you, everyone."

The table was laden with sandwiches, homemade cheese biscuits, two different types of pie and cheeses. A cake that was topped with thick green icing, it was meant to represent a field, and Rosie had stuck her plastic horses from her farm set on the top, which looked a little ridiculous as their feet were lost in the sticky icing. Lucy didn't seem to care, her smile told them all that she loved it. "I've never had a proper birthday in my whole life. I shall remember this day till the day I die. Thank you, Tilly, Ed, all of you."

No one pressed to ask why she hadn't had a birthday party, but sympathy for the young girl could be felt around the table. Tilly noticed even May seemed to have warmed to Lucy.

When the girls had eaten their jelly and ice-cream, Brenda tapped the side of her glass to get everyone's attention, "As you know, Alf and I are to be married next month, well, we're in need of some bridesmaids. Do you know any little girls that might like to walk behind me?" Before Brenda could explain it wouldn't be in a church, Rachel jumped up on her chair shouting "Yes, I said so, didn't I, Ken?"

The laughter drowned out May's reprimand instructing Rachel to sit down.

The girls went up to Rosie's room while Tilly and Agnes made tea, sliced up the cake and took slices in with the tea tray. "There we go, everyone, Brenda you've made their day, you have."

No one mentioned Ken's aborted wedding, and the cake and tea was eaten in a happy atmosphere, with May and Brenda reminiscing about their Friday Bridge nights, which seemed like years ago now. There was laughter as May said, "We all knew Alf had set his sights at you, Bren, you didn't fool any of us, did she, Agnes?"

Brenda blushed like a teenager, "They were good days…" She halted, remembering the circumstances and the pain for May and Norman at that time, and added, "In some ways, that is."

Tilly felt excluded from this reminiscing as she had been miles away in Canada, and she knew the time they were talking about was when Ed was ill, living at that retreat in a silent world. She changed the subject, bringing the evening to a close for the oldies, "I don't want to chuck you all out, but Rosie has school tomorrow, and I will never get her to bed with the girls here."

Tilly was relieved when May said, "Norm, we can take Brenda and Alf home with Hannah, can't we, unless you'd rather wait for Ken, that is?"

"No, no that would be lovely, May. Will you get us all in?"

When Ken piped up saying he was happy to take them all home, Tilly squashed that train of thought, "Ken, I want to play Monopoly later, once I get Rosie to bed. I can't have Lucy remembering her eighteenth birthday as a glorified child's tea party."

Everyone took the hint, and at eight o'clock the washing up had been done, Agnes was settled back in her little room with hot cocoa, and Rosie was asleep upstairs.

Tilly got out the Monopoly board and laid it on the table where only an hour ago it had been laden with food. Lucy bought everything she landed on, and the money wedged under her side of the board had them all laughing at what a tycoon she was. There was more laughter when Lucy told them, "If only life were this easy."

The game was over by ten thirty. Lucy had won hands down. She had hotels on Mayfair and Park Lane, she'd managed to buy up all the stations and even made Old Kent road work for her. It had been a fun, relaxed evening, until Ed said, "Can you pop Lucy back to the stables, Ken, seeing as you're passing?"

There was an awkward silence. Lucy broke it with, "No worries, I like to walk."

Tilly breathed a sigh of relief when this comment seemed to bring Ken back to life, "No you won't. Of course I can. It is pitch black out there, and freezing."

Lucy left, carrying a huge piece of cake wrapped in greaseproof paper as well as cheese biscuits and pie. She ran down the steps to meet Ken, who was standing by his car holding the passenger door open. She laughed, calling over her shoulder, "Oops I'm keeping the chauffeur waiting, but I'm set for lunch tomorrow. Thank you so much, both of you. It was wonderful."

Once in the car an awkward silence hung like dense fog, Lucy couldn't bear it. She didn't want anything to spoil this wonderful day. "That was awfully good of Tilly, don't you think?" she sighed relief as her simple conversation brought Ken to life, "Tilly is a good sort. She always was."

"Have you known her long?"

"All my life. We went to the same school. In the early days of our vegetable business it was held in Tilly's garden, did you know that?" Lucy shook her head "Really, how come?"

"It's a long story, Lucy, but Tilly used to help us even back then. In fact she was on the scene before I was." Lucy was intrigued, "So it was Ed's business first?"

Ken was tired, the stables were looming, and he wasn't in the mood for long explanations. He felt it wasn't really his place either to be gossiping about Ed and Tilly's sorry history. "Speak to Tilly, I'm sure she'll tell you."

Lucy felt embarrassed, "Oh I wasn't being nosey…" deciding to be completely honest she added, "I just couldn't stand the awkward silence in the car."

When Ken pulled up outside the stables he had a quick flash back of remembering when he had sat outside here with his face smashed up. "Lucy, I'm sorry. You're a real nice girl, but I'm just not interested like that." Before Lucy could interrupt he said "Please let me finish." He turned off the ignition, twisting round so he could look at her, "I just had a feeling Tilly was up to a bit of match making. You know the sorry tale of Cathleen and I and what a prat I've been. I'm not ready for any sort of relationship…" Lucy reached out and touched Ken's arm, stopping his explanations,

245

"Ken, I'm the perfect friend for you then. I made up my mind years ago I was never going to marry anyone. Like you, I don't want to go into it all, but the fact that I've reached eighteen and never had a birthday party… and might I add never been kissed, says something. You're safe with me, Ken. Friends?"

Ken laughed, holding out his hand, "Friends. I could do with a friend at the moment too."

"You have Tilly and Ed, they love you."

"I know, but they love each other, I have always been the gooseberry, always."

Lucy released her hand, "Friends it is then."

Ken found himself smiling as she hopped out of the car carrying her goodies Tilly had sent her off with like they were the crown jewels. *'She's a nice kid, I wonder what's made her so determined to stay single?'*

He didn't know why, but as he made his way home he felt better than he had in months. He started whistling Bing Crosby's White Christmas.

*

May took the large brown envelope Rachel had brought home from school and left it on the table while she sent Rachel up to get changed.

When Rachel came down carrying her school clothes for the washing basket, May was sat staring at the letter, which was now spread out on the table. "What is it, mummy, does it say I'm good?"

"No, darling, it's giving us some choices for your next school."

"I like my school, I don't want to go anywhere."

May folded the letter up with its forms and changed the subject. "Come on, let's get you a drink and a biscuit, Blue Peter will be on in a minute."

"Can I go to Tilly's tomorrow, riding?"

"No, not tomorrow. You have been there already this week, and you stayed over last weekend. Perhaps…"

Rachel stood up, her cheeks flushed red as her temper rose. She stamped her feet, "I want to go riding, I…"

"The only place you're going, madam, is up to your room until you can behave properly."

Rachel's tears followed the outburst. May wasn't alarmed, she was used to these temper tantrums. By Friday Rachel was always tired, and this week, what with the party at Tilly's it was no surprise to May that Rachel was struggling. Picking her up she sat her on her knee, "You're getting too big to carry. Come on now. Mummy was going to say perhaps Rosie would like to come here to play this weekend?"

Rachel sniffed, the heat had gone out of her anger. "I like to go there best. I like the horses. There's nothing to do here."

May sat the child on the chair and switched on the television for Blue Peter, "You have lots of lovely toys to play with here, that's a silly thing to say. I reckon Rosie would love to come."

"No she wouldn't." Rachel's anger was surfacing again, "They have the play park, the horses, Granny A's special room and Rosie's bedroom is big, bigger than mine. I want to go there."

May was at a loss for words. It did seem much more fun for Rachel at Tilly and Ed's, but she didn't feel she could keep asking if Rachel could go over. This weekend she would invite them all over for Sunday lunch, and perhaps Norman could take the girls to the allotment, May knew Rosie liked it there. The Blue Peter theme

247

tune started up and May crept out of the lounge, this programme gave her twenty five minutes peace. Leaving Rachel sat in front of the TV, she started peeling the vegetables for dinner.

Norman came home at six, and was surprised to see that May had Rachel bathed and ready for bed. "What's all this then?"

May explained how tired Rachel was and that an early night was in order.

It wasn't until eight o'clock that May got Rachel settled. She had left Norman reading the letter and forms for The Four Oaks School. When she took a tray of tea into the lounge to join him he had folded it back up and put it in the envelope. "Norman, what do you think, can she go?"

Norman pushed the envelope to the edge of the little table, making room for his tea, "I'd love her to go, May, but be reasonable, we don't have the money. Sending her to Little Acorns is stretching our budget."

"I just feel, Norm… you know, we won't always be here, and I really would like to think she could live independently - if possible."

Norman picked up the envelope and turned it over tapping it on his other hand, "May if we had the money you would be worrying about sending her away. I know you, love, it's because you can't send her you want to all the more."

May didn't like this, Norman had a way of making her out to be fickle, "That's unfair, Norm. I want what's best for her. I feel she's worked for this place and should be given a chance. I wouldn't choose for her to go to a boarding school, but I would do what I believed was for the best. As long as I knew Rachel was happy there, I would settle. Surely you believe that?"

Norman put the envelope down, he sighed heavily, "I think, May, the truth of it is, I feel I've let the kiddie down not being able to fund this school, so…"

May stopped Norman mid flow, with his honesty, came compassion, "Don't, Norm, you work very hard for us as a family, you always have. One thing you've never done is let us down. Rachel can stay at Little Acorns until next September, and then when she has to leave we'll try and get her in that special school at Chichester. We've given her a good start, and it has proved that with the right teaching she's very capable and able to learn."

"Do you mean that, May?"

"I do, Norm, I do. I can help her here expand on her learning. You'll see, she'll be fine. How many nine year olds do you know that can make Rock Cakes and Raisin and Cherry Buns?"

"I love you, May, I don't often tell you that these days, but it's at times like this I realise what a lucky man I am."

May felt warm with the praise. She picked up the cups and took the envelope over to the side board.

"There's a good play on tonight, Cathy come home. I've got a bar of Fruit and Nut in the fridge, we'll stoke up the fire and sit together on the sofa and watch it."

"Sounds good to me, love. Are we at Ed's on Sunday?"

May sat on the sofa, patting the cushion beside her with one hand, holding a bar of chocolate in the other, "I'm going to invite Ed and his lot for Sunday lunch, all of them, Agnes as well. Come on, come over here and sit with me, the play starts in five minutes."

*

Bournemouth – Monday 21ˢᵗ November

Cathleen sat at the table glad the breakfasts were finished and the last of their guests had left the dining room. They had had their end of the month dance, and the hotel had been full since Friday. Every time she said hotel it jarred. She couldn't think of this oversized house as a hotel, but she had settled here, and was enjoying being liked again. No one had written from her home town, not even her mum. Every week that passed with no contact, Cathleen told herself, *'It's early days'*. She had sent a postcard to Daisy, but as yet had had no answer. *'Perhaps there was no one back home who missed her?'* This hurt Cathleen more than she cared to admit.

Simon placed a breakfast tray down in front of her with tea, toast and marmalade, saying, "Is Jackie coming through?"

Cathleen was brought back to the present. Looking up she stubbed out her cigarette in the ash tray, "I don't know. She had a coffee earlier at the reception, but she might come through if everyone has checked out. Shall I go and ask her?"

"No, you sit there, love, I'll go."

Within minutes Jackie plopped down heavily, making the table rock, "For you, darling." Jackie held out an envelope, Cathleen recognised her mum's neat hand writing. "Oh…Thank you."

Cathleen couldn't hide the pleasure the little envelope had brought. But when Jackie asked "Are you going to open it?"

Cathleen turned it over, "No, it's from my mum and dad. I'll read it later." With that said she folded it up and pushed it down in her apron pocket. "Have we no guests here now?"

"No, they're all gone. Until Wednesday that is."

Cathleen had an uneasy feeling in her stomach, she didn't like it when the house was empty "Jackie, there will be enough work for me after Christmas, won't there?"

"Yes, darling, now don't you worry your pretty head about that. These past weeks you have more than proved yourself. You'll be a godsend come the spring."

Cathleen lit another cigarette, "I'll have this with you and then I shall go up and strip the beds and clean through."

"Lovely, darling. I'll come with you, you can hoover and dust and I'll do the bathrooms"

Cathleen was glad of the offer of help, cleaning was not one of her favourite jobs, but she was so determined to be seen as indispensable she did anything asked of her these days, and with a smile.

It was lunch time before Cathleen got the chance to shut herself in her room. She took out the envelope that had been making her feel jittery since she had received it. She sat on the side of her bed and opened the seal.

Dear Cathleen,

Just a few lines to let you know I got your letters and was pleased to hear you had settled in your new job.

I know you said you were not planning to return to Bognor for fear of people's long memories, but already there is gossip here to replace yours.

You must remember May and Norman's neighbours, George and Florrie Coffin? Well they are both dead. It seems George murdered his sister and then did himself in. Everyone is talking about it, so I can assure you what you did is paling into the distance.

Anger rose in Cathleen's throat, she stopped reading and gave way to thought, *'What I did! She just doesn't get it. I don't give a hoot what anyone thinks of me, but I thought my family would have stuck by me.'* She was annoyed as tears stung her eyes blurring the words before her.

There is a bit of good news, Brenda and Alf have asked the girls to be their bridesmaids, that event is coming round now, it's on the 9th December, I was moved that they included Hannah in the invite, but as your dad says, what happened had nothing to do with Hannah or us for that matter. Brenda is a good sort, Cathleen. It would be a thoughtful touch if you could send a card for their special day.

I don't have anything else to say, Cathleen, but wanted to write as I appreciate your letters.

Keep in touch, and yes we just might visit you in the summer, we will have to see what your dad is doing.

Love mum X

Cathleen looked at the letter till it went out of focus. It felt cold, *There wasn't one mention of missing me, nothing from dad, or Hannah. What was all that baloney about George and Florrie? As if I would care.* Cathleen gave way to disappointed tears. *'She only wrote to me because she felt she had to.'*

Jackie tapped on Cathleen's door, "Are you ready, darling? We've got all day to shop, Simon's going to man the desk for us." When there was no answer, she guessed Cathleen was down in one of the bathrooms having a shower. Jackie went to her own room to change. She looked at herself in the mirror and was critical at the lines that had appeared around her mouth and eyes. *'Where have the years gone? I'll be forty next year. What a thought, forty.'* She pulled off her wig wincing at her appearance, she gave her face a good rub with a cleanser then rubbed moisturiser round her eyes and top lip, trying to smooth out the tell-tale lines of her heavy smoking habit. Once she had applied her makeup, finishing with a liberal smear of scarlet red lipstick, she combed out her wig and sprayed it with hairspray, trying to keep its height. Looking at her watch, she stood in front of the long mirror giving herself the once over, pleased with her efforts she made her way to Cathleen's room. When she tapped on the door again and still got no answer she made her way down to the reception where Simon was sitting reading the newspaper, "Is Cathleen down yet?"

Simon raised his eyes, shaking his head, "Haven't seen her, she went upstairs before you, didn't she?" Giving Jackie his attention, he picked his cigarette out of the ash tray and took a long drag, blowing out the smoke slowly, "Make a cuppa, love. She'll be down in a minute. You know what the youngsters are like, they take forever to get ready."

Within minutes Jackie was back with a tray of tea, "Simon, you don't think her delay has anything to do with that letter, do you?"

"What do you mean?"

Jackie felt uneasy, "I don't know. I thought it was funny that she has written several letters to her home town and this is the first one she's received back. You'd think her family would be keeping in touch, wouldn't you?"

Stubbing out his cigarette he reached for his tea, "Don't look for problems, go up there, Jacks, I expect she had her music blaring in her ears with headphones on."

Without answering she took the stairs again. She pressed her ear to the door, feeling foolish as she heard movement coming on the other side of the door. She knocked again, calling "Come on, darling, the day's slipping away."

Jackie couldn't ignore Cathleen's red swollen eyes that shone at her when she opened the door, "Oh my darling, what's happened?" Guessing it was the letter.

This sudden show of concern had Cathleen crying all over again, Jackie moved her back into the room and sat her on the bed, "Do you want to talk about it?"

Cathleen fell to pieces, great sobs racked from her. Jackie's heart went out to the girl as she cradled her in her arms waiting for the crying to subside. Her mind worked overtime, wondering what could have caused such distress. "Come on, Cathleen, I'm all ears."

253

"You wouldn't understand."

Jackie stroked the wet hair from Cathleen's cheek, tucking it behind her ear, saying "Try me, darling."

"My...I" Cathleen didn't know where to start.

Jackie moved off the bed and pulled the chair across the room so she could sit in front of Cathleen. She took hold of the girl's hands and said, "Come on, you know what they say, a problem shared and all that..."

"It's the letter. It's from my mum and dad... But it's not from my dad, she didn't even put his name on it..."

"And..." Jackie waited. "Cathleen?"

"Oh, Jackie, if I tell you you'll hate me, you will send me away and not let me stay after Christmas, after all..."

"Stop this at once. What you have done back home isn't going to change how either Simon or I feel about you, unless you have robbed or murdered someone... You haven't done that, have you?"

Jackie was relieved to see Cathleen smile, "No, but the way my mum and dad carry on you would think I had."

Jackie straightened up in the chair, letting go of Cathleen's hands so she could listen in comfort.

"I was due to get married in October just gone, but I... got cold feet? Well, not cold feet exactly, but I took a fancy to someone else..."

Jackie was not a good listener, and before Cathleen could explain fully she jumped in with "Oh you are not the first to get cold feet and you won't be the last. Where's this fella you took a shine to?"

"It isn't as simple as that, Jackie, we were both engaged to other people but..."

"I think, darling, you are worrying over nothing. Did your mum like this fiancé of yours, is that it?"

"They did, do… But it is more complicated than that, I…"

"Now you listen to me, I think you've been very brave. To end your engagement because you realised you were not in love takes a lot of courage. The young man will thank you one day. Promise. Your mum and dad will come round too, I expect they live in a little gossipy village and are the butt of everyone's conversation at the moment. Time heals, and if your mum is a little cold at the moment she'll warm up, you're her daughter after all. I would love to have had a daughter like you, I really would."

Jackie had no idea what she would have heard from Cathleen if she had sat and listened, but from where she was sitting it all seemed straight forward. "Come on, Cathleen, we'll have a bit of lunch before we go, and we'll cheer ourselves up with a bit of Christmas shopping. We'll pick something nice for your mum and dad and send it to them, you keep writing, you'll see, things will improve. You've got a sister too, haven't you?" When Cathleen nodded, Jackie added, "Well, send her something, it might help to win her round as well."

Cathleen stood inching her way round Jackie, who was still sat in the chair, "Hannah isn't the problem, she's only four. She doesn't fully understand." Jackie didn't realise it but Cathleen's thoughts were, 'and neither do you.'

"Jackie… Thank you. I feel much better. If you give me a few minutes I'll touch up my make up and be down in a minute."

Jackie took the hint and pushed the chair back under the window. "There's a girl, don't you worry."

*

That night Cathleen read the letter again. Her hurt turned to anger, she made up her mind that she wouldn't write again. She would send a card to Brenda and Alf on their wedding, just so her mum would know she had received this cold letter, but she would make them grovel to her. After all, even though Jackie and Simon didn't know the whole story, they knew enough and believed in her. Simon had given her a cuddle this evening, telling her, "You're a long time married girl, you have to get it right."

She didn't care anymore that this hotel was nothing more than a boarding house, she loved the people in it. She told herself over and over that leaving Bognor was the right thing to have done.

*

December 1st 1966

Pam looked at Hannah's toy box, toys lay round the bottom of it where there was no room inside. The lid wouldn't close. *'It's no good, Christmas is round the corner, where's all this stuff going to go?'*

Pam made her way down the shed to get a box, she would clear it while Hannah was at Play school.

"Morning, May. What are you doing?" May was bent over Prince in the most unladylike fashion. "Pam give us a hand, I've got to catch a urine sample from this silly dog, but he won't squat, he keeps cocking his leg and it's spilling out the side.

Pam forgot her own troubles for the moment as she climbed over the little fence, "How much do you need?" It was easier with two and it wasn't long before they had enough urine in the bowl, "I need enough for the vet to test. Prince hasn't stopped drinking, and I mean drinking. The vet reckons he has diabetes. Funny, I thought it was only adults that got these troubles." May shooed the dog indoors, pleased she had the sample, "Thanks, Pam. Do you fancy a cuppa?"

Pam didn't often get invited into May's house and she had a lot on her mind at present and felt it might be good to rid herself of it if she got the chance. She was aware if May invited her in, she must have something to brag about. Pam chastised herself for her ill thoughts, saying instead, "Give me a minute, May, I'm just going up to Hal's shed to get a box. Christmas is round the corner and we've enough toys indoors to open a shop of our own."

"Give them to that family that live near Brenda, they have nothing. Have you seen them? Snotty nosed little buggers with their arses hanging out their trousers. Poor little sods."

Pam couldn't help smiling. May gave herself such airs, yet she spoke worse at times than the lot she was referring to. "I was going to donate them to Hannah's little play school, but that sounds a better idea."

Pam made her way to the shed, aware of May moaning at the dog for not going in earlier. She found a big wooden chest in the shed lined with newspaper. It was a bit big to give to the family May was talking about, but it was a good size if she was going to sort out Hannah's room. Pam dragged it down the garden and left it at the back door.

May called "Come in, it's unlocked"

The tea was made and waiting on the tray. "That's a pretty cosy, May. Did you make it?"

"Yes, now you sit down and warm yourself. You look freezing."

Pam listened to May telling her how well Rachel had done at school and the place she had been offered at Four Oaks, but that they couldn't afford to send the child there. When May went on to say how much it was already costing to send Rachel to Little Acorns, Pam stifled a yawn. May stopped midsentence, "Sorry, Pam, am I going on a bit? It's just I've had this on my mind, but it's silly really. If we had the money to send her to this boarding school we would be worrying about sending her away. Kids, Pam, eh? It never stops, there's always something."

May lifted the plate, offering Pam a biscuit, "It's good about the girls being bridesmaid to Brenda though. Who would have thought…"

Pam wondered if she would ever get a chance to air her own worries, when May leapt to her feet, scolding at the dog who was scratching at the door, dying to be let out, "This is the problem with him, Pam, he drinks so much he can't hold his water. Norm was up and down last night, fluffing the covers, making me cold as he got in and out of bed."

Once May was sat down again, Pam managed to steer the conversation away from Rachel, "Have you heard any more about next door?"

"No, that was shocking though, wasn't it? Murder, Murder on our own doorstep."

Pam put her cup down, "When you told me he could be a bit weird I wasn't wholly convinced, But I'm grateful to you, May, grateful."

"I didn't mean weird like that though, Pam, I meant… Oh it doesn't matter now, does it? Still I expect you're pleased of the distraction, it's stopped everyone focusing on your Cathleen."

Pam was pleased to see May flush and splutter at what she had just said, "Oh forgive me, Pam, I didn't mean…"

"It's alright, May. I wrote to Cathleen last week and told her as much, but somehow I think she has taken it the wrong way. She has written home once a week every week since she went, and I answer one of her letters and everything stops. I am taking it I must have written something to upset her."

"The postman hasn't been yet, he might bring something today."

"I don't think so. My letter didn't say a lot. I told her about your neighbours, I even tried to joke that it was taking the gossip away from her. I told her about Brenda's wedding and the girls being bridesmaid…"

May interrupted her. Cathleen was not her favourite person. She still hadn't forgiven her for the disgusting treatment she had given to Rachel "There doesn't sound anything wrong in your letter to me, Pam. I expect she's busy doing her own thing."

Pam saw her chance, "The letter I sent wasn't a good idea, May. Hal was against me writing. He has this thing that Cathleen needs to reflect a bit. I don't think he can forgive her for the shame…That's the word, shame. I think he feels she has dirtied our name."

"Pam, don't. You're beating yourself up. Do you remember when I came round to you over my Ed?" Pam remained silent, she was so near to tears, "Pam, Cathleen will be fine. She isn't ill, she hasn't run off pregnant. She's working, and it sounds like she has a good roof over her head and you say she is settled. From where I'm sitting it won't do her any harm to know that she hurt a lot of people back here and has caused you both a lot of angst. She's a big girl, Pam, she'll get over it."

Tears fell down Pam's cheeks unchecked, "Shall I write again? I could write nicer things, say we missed her, that we send our love. Enclose a picture perhaps? One that Hannah has drawn. The more I think about it I wish I hadn't written. It's Hal's fault, he was so against me writing. So when I did get round to it I had Hal's disapproval going through my mind, which caused me to sound cold. I wanted to say we miss you, and that we love you, but I didn't, and I just know she has taken umbrage. You don't know what she can be like, she…"

May poured another cup of tea, "Oh yes I do. I still remember her outburst when you were having Hannah, do you remember that?"

Pam managed a weak smile, "What a trial she's been at times. It's our own fault, we spoilt her. We wanted her to have all the things we didn't have, and being an only child for so long didn't help either."

May handed Pam the tea, "Come on, get this down you, you'll feel better." The sound of the front door had May on her feet. "Hang on, Pam, I'll be back in a tick."

Pam sank back in the chair, it was good to talk. Nothing had been solved, but somehow she felt better. May came back carrying a large brown envelope, causing Pam to ask. "Was that the postman?"

"Yes, I've got something from Liverpool, Liverpool? I don't know anyone from there. It must be about Rachel's school. It has been one brochure after another, and if it's not brochures its forms or letters. Honestly, Pam, it's ridiculous. I'll have to sit down and write, making it very clear that we just can't afford it."

Pam finished her tea and stood, "Thanks for being an ear to my problems, May. You've helped enormously. Hopefully I'll go back in and there'll be a letter from Cathleen, and then I'll feel even better."

*

May didn't give another thought as to whether Pam had a letter waiting indoors for her or not. May sat with the big brown envelope that she had torn open on her lap. She reread the letter with shaking hands, unable to take in its contents.

The bold letters across the top stating Knight's Solicitors stared at her accusingly. The Reference letters and numbers looked so official, but it was the RE: The Deceased Walter George Coffin that made her blood pound in her head.

What can it possibly mean? We'll be in touch when they have more information. Rachel being the sole beneficiary to his will, how can this be? How can this…' May's eyes swept over the top of the letter as she read

260

Jack Knight. *'How can he possibly know anything about our, Rachel or her condition? But he must or he wouldn't be talking about trust funds.'*

Questions she couldn't answer kept whirling round her head. The clock on the mantle chimed out eleven o'clock. *'It'll be ages till Norm comes home.'*

With this thought May slid the letter back in its envelope and left it on the sideboard. It didn't stop the anticipation of what it all meant, and the word trust fund kept niggling at the back of her mind, *'There must be a considerable amount of money if he's talking trust fund, surely?'*

May was tempted to phone Tilly, but good sense stopped her, *'What can I tell her? The letter doesn't say a lot. No, this was to be a waiting game.'*

Prince scratching at the mat had May rushing for the back door, "Out, out you go."

*

Friday 9th December 1966

The Wedding

Tilly, Ed and Agnes arrived at May's just before ten o'clock with an excited Rosie. Hannah was already there, and the hairdresser May had organised was plaiting flowers in between the strands of her hair. Rachel had gone first and already looked lovely. May was still in her dressing gown, looking flustered. Her hair was still in curlers which showed under the brown coloured net. "Come on, come in. Can I leave you in charge for a moment, Tilly? I really need to go up and get ready."

"Yes, shall I get Rachel dressed while Hannah is in the chair?"

May wasn't listening, she hadn't waited for an answer. Her question had been an order, and one, she took for granted would be obeyed.

When Hannah jumped down from the chair Rosie wriggled up into the seat, "Can I have mine done the same, Tilly?"

"You can, but your flowers are pink."

The girls had floral dresses and their hair was to be adorned in flowers of pink, lemon and white.

May entered the room wearing a navy blue suit with a little pillar box hat, she was pleased to see Tilly had the girls dressed and waiting. "Oh, Tilly, they look lovely. Thank you."

The toot of the car outside had Tilly ushering the three girls out to the front, Ken was waiting with the back door open of a hired Ford Cortina which had white ribbons tied on the sides for the occasion.

Tilly called out to Brenda, who was waving from the passenger seat. "You look lovely, Brenda, lovely."

Agnes, Tilly and May stood waving the girls off who were now giggling in the back of the car. May's voice suddenly bellowed into the street as she shouted "Don't kneel up, Rachel, sit like the others."

It was a quick ceremony. A few photos were taken, but there were doubts as to what they would turn out like. Most were taken on Tilly's Box Brownie camera. Brenda had chosen a red suit with a green trim, which was very topical for the year, but the girls behind clashed in their pink and lemon floral dresses, which had been chosen for Cathleen and Ken's grand affair. Ed had bought Tilly the camera, and she snapped away trying to gather as many memories of Rosie as she could. It felt to Tilly like the child's departure was rolling here on motorised skates.

The reception was a simple buffet, which was laid on for them at The Old Oak pub. Ken had organised and paid for it as a wedding present.

Pam had worried unnecessarily that the day would feel awkward, Brenda and Alf seemed delighted to have them as part of their celebration. Brenda even asked how Cathleen had settled in, in Bournemouth, and added, "Don't be too hard on Cathleen, better she changes her mind before the wedding than after, when there might have been children." Pam felt humbled, and leant forward to kiss Brenda on the cheek telling her she was a good woman and that Alf was a lucky man.

When Ken stood and clinked his glass for quiet, Pam couldn't help thinking what a fine young man he had turned out to be. She reached over and squeezed Hal's hand, but his gaze was fixed ahead. She knew he was struggling in his own way with his own thoughts. Feeling tearful, Pam momentarily cast her eyes down and fiddled with her wedding ring. When Ken cleared his throat ready to speak, good manners had her looking up and paying attention, "We've always been a small family, and the people that are important to mum are here today. Firstly, I want to thank you all for coming, I also want to thank the bridesmaids for doing a fantastic job…" The claps filled the small room, halting his speech momentarily, "Mum looks pretty grand too…" More claps and a few giggles, Ken swallowed hard. "My mum deserves happiness, life hasn't always been easy for her, but I don't want to think about that today and I'm sure she doesn't, but I want to say how happy Alf has made her and welcome him into our family, albeit small. Before I read the cards from well-wishers let's raise our glasses to Mr and Mrs Davies. Ken leant over and took an envelope from behind the table, "Oh, there are only two cards…" Ken looked at his mother, who nodded, He laughed, saying "I said the important people are here." He opened the first envelope and glanced over the writing, "To dear Brenda and Alf with very good wishes from Hetty and Len. Wishing you a fantastic day, and we're looking forward to you living in our neck of the woods, where we can all resume our Bridge nights over a glass or two." This caused another murmur of giggles, but silence fell when Ken said. "And this one's from … Cathleen." Pam wondered if the atmosphere was as thick as she felt it to be. What was obvious, was the shake in Ken's voice as he read, "To

Brenda and Alf, have a lovely day and I wish you the best wishes for your future from Cathleen Hills."

Brenda was the first to clap, which eased the uncomfortable moment. Pam lost herself in her own private thoughts. *'So she got my letter after all. I bet this was her way of telling me.'* Pam was pleased when Hal said "That's the first decent thing she's done in a long time."

"Hal, please."

The wedding was over by five o'clock, which Pam was grateful for as Hannah's excitable behaviour told how tired she was. "Say good bye, Hannah, and thank Mrs Davies for having you as bridesmaid." Brenda laughed "Don't be daft, the pleasure was all mine." She leant forward and kissed both Hal and Pam on the cheek "Thank you for coming, and please thank Cathleen for her lovely card when you next speak to her."

If Brenda noticed the uneasy silence between Hal and Pam, they were pleased she ignored it.

Pam was pleased to be home. It had been a long day, and despite Brenda and Alf's open friendliness it had at times felt awkward, which Pam found stressful and tiring.

"I'll put the kettle on, Hal, you can light a fire it's freezing in here."

When Pam took the tea through, Hal was sat watching television, waiting for the news to come on. Hannah was playing quite happily behind the sofa with her dolls, "It's nearly Christmas, Hal. We haven't heard from Cathleen for weeks now..."

"It's your own fault, I told you not to write to her, she needed to stew a bit first, let her see what she's done to us."

Pam felt sick, "It isn't about us, Hal, it's Ken who should be sore, Ken and Brenda, but look at them, they're getting on with life. I don't want to lose Cathleen over a decision she made…"

"Decision, Pam, bloody decision. She behaved like a…"

"Please don't, Hal, Hannah's playing there behind you."

Hal reached for his tea. His voice sounded tired, "Pam, do what you want. Phone her if you're worried. I've given up caring."

"No you haven't, or you wouldn't say that. You love Cathleen, you always have."

"Of course I do, but I don't love what she's done, but… " Hal paused as if searching for the right words "I can see this is eating at you, and as I love you, Pam, for you, I will go along with what you decide to do, but only for you."

She got up and went over and kissed his cheek, "Thanks, love, thanks. I shall send her a few photos to prompt a response in a Christmas card, and then if we hear nothing we'll phone on Christmas day, at the hotel… that would be okay, wouldn't it?"

"Of course, Pam, under normal circumstances we would be phoning her every week."

*

Cathleen took the key from the visitor, smiling she hung it on the board. "It's cold this morning, but the sun's shining. Are you off to the Christmas market?"

The phone ringing halted any further conversation, "Good Morning, The Three Chimneys, how can I help you?" Cathleen knew this spiel off by heart now.

"Hello, love." Pam recognised Cathleen's voice, and hearing it brought with it a longing to put this bad feeling behind them. When Cathleen didn't answer, Pam filled the silence, "I wanted to thank you for the wedding card you sent to Brenda and Alf. They were moved by it, love, moved."

Cathleen's tone and words were like a knife in Pam's heart. "You told me to do it…"

Pam didn't let Cathleen finish, "Love, I haven't phoned to fight. I miss your letters, I miss you…"

"Oh, you do, do you? I didn't read one word of missing me in your letter. No just…"

"Cathleen, it's been difficult, it's hard for us, please try and understand. Of course I miss you, we all do. The house is empty without you. Hannah goes on all the time about when are you coming home…"

Pam was relieved to hear the fight had gone from Cathleen's voice, but her words were unwavering, "I told you I'm not coming home, ever. Jackie and Simon are keeping me on. I'm not wanted in Bognor now, I'm happy here. You're welcome to come and see me, but I'm not coming home."

Pam kept the conversation friction free, "We will, your father is already saying perhaps we'll come for a week next summer."

"Did he, mum, did he really?"

Pam sighed as she spoke, "Yes, love, he did."

Cathleen's shoulders sagged, she was pleased her mother couldn't see the tears well up in her eyes or her feeling of relief. People milling around the desk had her saying, "I'll write, mum, I will. Thanks for phoning, bye."

Pam heard the wobble in Cathleen's voice, and she knew the first step had been made to rebuilding a better relationship between them all.

*

266

Ken waved his mum and Alf off, "I'll be up for Christmas, Mum. You never know, I might not be alone."

Brenda hung out of the lorry window raising her eyebrows, "Does this have anything to do with a certain little lady from those stables I wonder?"

Ken laughed, he felt happier than he had in months, "Don't go looking into anything like that, we're friends, that's all."

"Yes, I believe you, that's what we used to say, isn't it Alf."

Alf was now climbing into the removal lorry that was taking them up to the Lake District, "That's enough matchmaking. Leave the boy alone. See you Christmas, son, with or without a friend. You're always welcome, you know that."

Alf called everyone son; but Ken liked it, it was good to feel part of this family his mum had now created.

Ken closed the front door and looked around the rooms. They looked empty. His mum had left a few bits for him to tide him over, but he had been adamant that he would do up the old place and furnish it out. It would never be as grand as the shop he was hoping to buy with Cathleen, but he would make this old place comfortable and fill it with better memories.

He took a mug down and made himself a coffee. *'I'll drink this and then go over to Hunston and see if Lucy wants to come to the pictures with me tonight.'*

*

Ed tooted his van at Tilly and pulled up at the side of the curb. "Where are you going?"

"I've just posted the reels of film off for developing, and now I'm going to pick Rosie up from the stables, then I'll be home."

"I'll give you a lift, come on get in."

Tilly pulled open the van door, "You finished for the day then?"

"Yes, Ken and I did most of the deliveries early due to the wedding. It's gonna get busy though, what with Christmas round the corner."

Ed was pleased Tilly seemed happier these days. The thought of losing Rosie had put a huge strain on their relationship. He tried hard to push it to the back of his mind but he knew next June, Rosie would be going. He hated himself for thinking it, but he really wished he had never set eyes on that fairground.

Ken's car caused Tilly to nudge Ed, "Ooh, look who's here already. I think our Ken's smitten, don't you?"

Ed smiled, "Who knows? He certainly deserves a bit of happiness, doesn't he?"

Tilly felt a bit uneasy, "I'm not too sure that romance is on Lucy's mind, but she seems happy to go about with him. Something might develop."

"What's the story on that kid anyway?"

Tilly pulled open the van door, "I'm not wholly sure? She's a dark horse. I do know she isn't one for romance though."

"She's not one of those lady lovers, is she?"

Ed loved the sound of Tilly's laughter, it was rare these days, "No she's not. I reckon she's been hurt, like Ken maybe."

"Really, she's only a kid. She couldn't have had a relationship, surely."

Tilly clipped Ed's ear, messing with his hair, "What about us? I loved you from the age of twelve, don't you remember?"

Ed put his arm round her waist, "Do you still love me, Tilly, really love me like you did back then?"

He felt warmed as she leant into him, "I always love you Ed. Things are just a bit difficult for me. You know… the thought of losing Rosie."

Ed kissed the top of her head, "You know, I've been thinking, Tilly. We could adopt, Geoffrey said he could get us a six week old baby to adopt, you'd like that, wouldn't you?"

"I would, of course I would. It's just Rosie came into our lives like it was meant to be, and I love her, really love her. I want to keep her. Can you understand that?"

"Tilly, Tilly, I've been riding Mr Benny." Rosie's excitement ceased any further discussion. Ed was upset, he felt like they were making a positive headway in their fractured relationship.

Ken climbed over the fence, calling out to them. "How did it go, Ed? You're finished early."

"Yes, it was a doddle. We did the bulk of it on Thursday. Monday will be busy mind." Tilly and Rosie had made their way to the van and were already sitting inside sheltering from the winter's chill. "What brings you to the stables, Ken, or dare I ask?"

"Lucy's coming to the cinema with me tonight, wanna come?"

"What and play gooseberry, not likely." Ed laughed as Ken said, "Friends, Ed, just friends. I'm done with women. Still, I've got the house to myself now, mum and Alf left this morning. I'll be going to the Lakes for Christmas, that'll still be ok, won't it?"

Ed held on to Ken's car door, "Yeah, no probs, dad said he'd help out and Tilly says Jimmy's home from university."

"Bloody hell, Ed, it seems like years ago he helped us out, doesn't it? What was he, thirteen?"

"Yeah, about that, but I want to keep in with the Covaxs' as I'm thinking Geoffrey might be able to help us get a little babe of our own in the New Year."

"You don't have to find jobs for his kids for him to help you out, Geoffrey loves Tilly; you know he does."

Ed pushed the door shut, "Ken everyone loves Tilly." As Ed strode over to the van, he made up his mind that in the New Year he would speak with Geoffrey and see how they go about adopting a baby.

*

May sat breaking up a puzzle she had done with Rachel, while Norman had his head in the Newspaper.

"We haven't heard anything from this solicitor yet, what do you think?"

Norman put down the paper, "I said not to think about it, May, I can't imagine it's worth getting excited about. You haven't said anything to anyone, have you?"

"No I haven't. Stop being bossy. I was just wondering, that's all."

Norman folded up his paper, and knelt down at the hearth throwing another log on the fire, "They rented next door, May. He didn't have a car, so what assets are there to leave to Rachel, do you think?"

May slid the Puzzle box under her chair to save her getting up, "Well it sounded important…"

Before she could finish Norman interrupted, "For goodness sake, May, it's probably a standard letter. Don't go bragging to anyone or we'll end up with egg on our faces."

"I wasn't going to brag actually, I'm allowed to wonder though, surely. If it's a good amount we could send her to…"

"Stop it, May, you're kidding yourself. You've heard that saying, chicken and eggs."

May pulled her knitting out from the magazine rack. The way she attacked the wool told Norman she was annoyed with his negativity. "Ed was here earlier. Says he's taking young Jimmy on again over the New Year." Norman grunted, but didn't show any real interest. "He also says Ken's taking that young girl out again tonight, pictures. I reckon there's something blossoming there." Norman ignored the gossip, "Love, get me a brandy, I'm cold on the inside as well as out, tonight. I just can't get warm."

May got up taking the Puzzle out from under her chair, and put it away in the sideboard. She poured Norman his drink, "You don't need any excuse for a brandy, who do you think you're kidding? You didn't say anything about Ken and that girl from the stables, what do you think?"

Holding his hand out for his drink, he said, "I don't think anything, May. Good luck to him is all I say, he could do with a bit of it from the rum deal he's had with her next door."

"That's what I say, can you imagine how…"

"No, May, No! Don't even think about running their daughter down. We have had our own fair share of trouble on this doorstep, and Pam was a good friend, don't you forget that."

May was really annoyed now, she wound the wool round her fingers and wriggled in her seat, showing her disgruntled mood, "Good God, Norm, is a woman not allowed to have an opinion these days?"

Norman decided to ignore the bait, he didn't want to get into a full blown battle. He felt he was getting too old for it these days. "Sorry, love, I'm a bit tired. I hear what you're saying, can we just say what will be will be, eh?"

The heat went out of the conversation as her knitting needles clicked away.

*

"That was so funny, Ken." Lucy couldn't remember ever laughing like she had tonight. Ken had taken her to see 'You're a Big Boy Now', and the overbearing mother, the snoopy neighbour and the rooster had all been too much for Lucy, she had laughed so much she wanted the film to stop for a minute so she could catch her breath. Ken looked at her smiling face, "You're a real joy to take out, do' ya know that?"

Lucy pushed him in the arm, "Why, because I laugh like a child?"

"No, you're just so uncomplicated. It's more than a joy, honest. Since Cathleen…" Lucy noticed the hesitation, "You and Cathleen had a lot of pressure on you, what with the wedding, and all that nonsense she got herself caught up in. I expect she's already wishing she hadn't been so hasty in leaving now." When Ken remained silent, Lucy reminded him of the funny scenes in the film, and before long they were back at the carpark laughing together again. Ken fished his keys out of his pocket and opened the car door for her. "Do you fancy coming back to mine for a coffee before I take you home? You can see where I live… and on my own."

Lucy liked the idea of seeing his home, after spending nine years in an orphanage seeing inside people's houses and how they lived fascinated her. "I'd like that, Ken, but I can't be too late, we have a lot of organising for the Christmas ride at the weekend, and I have to be up earlier than normal."

"But it's Sunday tomorrow."

"It doesn't work like that when you work with animals. They need feeding every day, people come for their riding lessons, and they need mucking out. Should I go on?"

Ken pulled up outside his house, "I know, but you're always working."

"I don't mind, before you befriended me it kept me busy. I didn't know anyone, so it was easy just to work. I need the money."

Ken held the front door open with one arm, while he stretched out the other, saying, "Dah, dah. What do you think?"

"It's a bit bare, but I like it. It's homely, but cold."

"I'd light a fire if I thought you were staying longer."

Lucy moved into the lounge, she took in the tired looking sofa with its worn appearance, and warmed to Ken even more, "This looks really comfortable, I like it. You were lucky being brought up here."

The kettle whistled, and while Ken stirred the coffees he said on a sarcastic laugh, "You think so, do you? You don't know half."

"Why? You had a family who loved you, and now your mums married Alf, she's left you the house. I would have given anything to have that when…"

"She hasn't given it to me, I still have to pay the rent, and when I was a kid my dad died in an accident and she had to take in a lodger, she ended up marrying him. He was an absolute bastard to me, and her. I haven't been lucky."

Lucy fell silent, causing Ken to reach out and touch her shoulder, "I'm sorry. I didn't mean to explode like that. I just think what with Cathleen leaving me like that, making me feel worthless and foolish, you saying I've been lucky, raised some feelings I've tried to bury."

"No, Ken, I'm sorry. Whenever I see people with family I automatically think they're lucky. I have no one, no one to call my family now. I'm totally alone." When Ken asked her why and where her family was, Lucy faltered, "I could tell you, but I'm frightened it will put you off me. I like going around with you and I don't want to lose your friendship…"

"Nothing will put me off you, silly, I could tell you some real horror stories about me, I once nearly killed my stepdad…"

"You didn't, tell me you didn't." Lucy stared, eyes wide, waiting for reassurance, "I did. It was fear. He, Harry was his name, he came at me, in here, at this table. It was Christmas, Mum had been making a sandwich for him, and when she took it in to him he blew up in one of his rages like he was prone to do. When I heard he was coming out here to get to me, I was so frightened I grabbed the knife, just as a deterrent, but once I'd threatened him with it I couldn't put it down or I swear he would have beaten me to death. He was chasing me round this table." Ken patted it, accentuating the moment, "Chasing me, he was, in a menacing way, and when he laid his hands on the table like this, leering at me, telling me what he would do to me when he caught hold of me, I stabbed him in the hand, he spread them out like this…" Lucy interrupted, horrified at this tale, "Ken that's awful, what about your mum?"

"Mum's face was black and blue from the beating she had suffered the night before, so you see nothing about your childhood could compare to that, surely?"

Lucy looked at the honesty that shone in Ken's brown eyes, and she found her voice. She had locked these memories up for so many years she thought she would never voice them.

"My mum was a drug addict." She looked up, expecting some sort of shock or dislike to show on Ken's face, but all she saw was kindness which seemed to shine making his brown eyes look liquid. He waited for her to continue. "I didn't know my dad, but we used to have men callers, I don't have to explain why, do I? Mum had a baby, she called him Robert. I called him Bobby, and I loved him, really loved him. He used to cry all the time, and mum's men friends used to hate him, one in particular. Mum used to put drink in Bobby's bottle to shut him up. I don't have to go into it all do I? I'm sure you're getting the picture. I was six, and already the kids at school used to pick on me, Loopy Lucy they called me, one boy in particular, Raymond Droys was his name, he used to spit at me. That doesn't matter anymore, just that it made me feel worthless and dirty, do you understand?" Ken reached out and took her hand but said nothing. When Lucy took up her story her voice betrayed her emotion, "Bobby died before he was three months old, and

Mum was found shortly after in a field, she had taken an overdose. I don't think it had anything to do with Bobby, because she didn't seem to like him much either. I lived for a while with my Nana, it was only weeks, not months, when she said she couldn't cope with me, so I went into an orphanage and there I stayed until I was fifteen. I got a job at a stables and it led to me coming here a year later."

Ken's voice was soft and the concern was still reflected in his eyes, "What happened to your Nana, is she still alive?"

"She died when I was about seven, I think, but she never came to see me, or write to me."

"Lucy, that's so sad, I'm so sorry. Is that why you say you don't like men?"

"I don't say I don't like men, I hate men. I don't want to go into it, but sometimes mum's gentlemen friends paid more if…" Lucy couldn't say it, the words stuck in her throat, so she shut the conversation down with, "Look, I've just made up my mind they're all the same, some look nicer than others, but they're all after one thing, they all let you down in the end. Look at poor Christine, and now she's giving Michael another chance, how many times does he have to kick her before…"

"You can't say that, Lucy, I can honestly say I never looked at another girl. Cathleen was the love of my life, I would have laid down and died for her…"

Lucy knew what he was saying was true, "I know, Ken, you and Ed are the first men I've met that have raised my faith in mankind. What Cathleen did to you was terrible, and when you were going to marry her thinking she was having someone else's child…"

Lucy stopped, seeing the colour drain from his face, "Sorry, Ken, I didn't want to…"

"No, it's alright. We're alike you and I, more than you realise. I put up with so much from Cathleen because I thought she was better than me, I thought I was lucky to have her. All my school life I'd been known as smelly Ken from Collyers. To have Cathleen walk out with me was something special. She, who had always been the catch of the school, made me feel like I'd achieved something. It took me a long time to learn, but the truth of it was - she wasn't better than me, she was just lucky enough to be born into a family where they had more money than we did. I used to wonder how it would have been if my real dad hadn't been killed, but it didn't help any."

"We're like kindred spirits you and I, Ken. I'm glad I've shared that with you. I feel better somehow, do you?"

"I do, Lucy, I like that, kindred spirits."

"Come on, you must get me home or I won't be up in time in the morning, and I can't afford to get the sack."

As Ken drove Lucy back to Hunston they sat in comfortable silence, each with their own private thoughts.

*

Tilly and Rosie scrambled in the back of the van while Agnes sat in the front with Ed. They hadn't been to Sunday tea at May's for weeks, and Tilly had iced a Swiss Roll with chocolate, sprinkled it with icing sugar and stuck a robin in it. Rosie sat in the back carrying it like it was the crown jewels.

"Tilly, can Rachel come to the Christmas ride next week with us?"

Rosie was so excited about the event. There would be dancing in the evening and hot food served in the marquees which were going up on the Saturday.

"She can come if Auntie May says so, Rosie, but you must remember you were invited there this weekend, and you said no. It isn't fair to just expect Rachel to come to ours."

Rosie moved the cake tin off her lap and knelt up, "I like to go riding on Saturdays, you know I do. Anyway, Rookie doesn't like it when I'm not around in the mornings. He looks for me, you know he does."

Tilly had the urge to say 'what will Rookie do when you go next year?' But she managed to hold her tongue. She knew it did no good to try and make the child feel guilty. Ed told her over and over it was only natural for Rosie to want to go home. The pain this thought brought to Tilly was becoming more and more unbearable with the passing weeks.

Ed helped Agnes out of the van, then held the chair forward so Tilly and Rosie could climb out. Ed gave Rosie the chocolate log, "Here you go, Rosie, take that in to Auntie May."

Ed went up the garden to find his dad, while Tilly sat in the lounge with May and Agnes, who chatted about Brenda's wedding, television programmes and knitting patterns. When the conversation got around to Pam next door, Tilly couldn't help being interested to hear how Cathleen was faring. When May said Cathleen seemed to be punishing Pam for her response to her letters, Tilly's heart hardened even more towards her old school pal. *'She doesn't learn.'*

The girls could be heard clattering around upstairs, which caused May to shout, "Quiet up there, you two, you'll come through the ceiling at this rate." Tilly raised her eyes at her Gran, who smiled.

A waft of cold air came in as Ed pushed open the door, followed by his dad, "Its bloody freezing out there." If May noticed the bad language she ignored it. "Come on, both of you, wash your hands and get at the table."

Tilly shouted up for the girls to come down. The table was laden with food. May did a plentiful spread, she was a good cook too.

When May poured the tea, Rachel said "Have you told them, mummy, about my new school?"

Tilly noticed the flush creep across May's face, and the look she gave Norman. "It's not your new school, Rachel, but yes, I've said how hard you've worked and that you've been offered a place, but it isn't good to boast."

Tilly, who had said precious little this visit, raised the question, "Are you not sending her, May?"

"No, we can't afford it, and that is the end of it really. There is a good school in Chichester, we'll look at that when we have to."

"Yes, I've heard that school is good, Saint Anthony's, isn't it?"

"Yes, yes. We don't have to think about it yet. She can have another two years at Little Acorns if we don't move her to Four Oaks."

Tilly changed the subject before Rosie was brought up and her looming departure. Tilly couldn't bear to think of May gloating that she was right all along, and that there would be pain from this set up. "There is a Christmas dance next Saturday at the stables. Rosie will ride in the morning and we'll all go to the dance in the evening. Do you want Rachel to come with us?"

Rachel was up, kneeling on her chair, "Yes, yes, please say I can go, mummy?"

"We'll see how you behave. Now sit back down on that chair before you fall off it." Rachel protested, which was quietened by Norman, "You heard mummy. That's – not - good behaviour, now finish up that cake, and you two can both get down and play nicely upstairs again."

Once the girls were out of earshot, Tilly said, "I need to know if she's coming, May, as it's a ticket affair."

"Yes, she can go. My life wouldn't be worth living if I said no. How much is the ticket."

"A shilling, but Rosie will ride in the morning as usual. Rachel can come over on the Friday and ride too if she likes. You can come to us for dinner on the Sunday and pick her up."

"Oh that sounds lovely, if you're sure?"

Ed spoke up laughing, "She wouldn't say so if she wasn't, would she?"

May flushed, "I know, I was just being polite. Tilly does a lot for Rachel, and I'm grateful." May looked at Tilly, who felt embarrassed at this unusual praise from her mother in law, "You do know that, don't you, Tilly? It's a real help when you have her over like you do. When Rosie goes home, I'll be happy for you to share…"

The compliment was over shadowed. Tilly shut the conversation down, unable to confront the fact that this time next year Rosie would be long gone from their lives. "Ed'll pick Rachel up next Friday, then. Rosie breaks up on the Wednesday for Christmas, when does Rachel's school close?"

"Not till the Friday. They don't go back until the third week of January, though."

The awkward moment passed with the change of subject, Tilly stood up, saying "Come on, let's get this washing up done, and then we best make our way home, Ed, Rosie's got school tomorrow, and so does Rachel."

The Rainbow

Chapter Ten

Revelations

Michael swung his legs out of bed, it was so cold he could see his breath billowing out in front of him. He pulled on his clothes before he washed, trying to get warm. The sound of his mother's voice calling up the stairs told him he should already be outside getting ready for the Christmas Party tonight. He skipped washing, grabbing a piece of toast that had been buttered up and left on the kitchen table. "Michael, you will need something inside you, it's freezing out there."

Michael ignored his mother, closing the door behind him, ramming the toast in his mouth in one. "Mooring oocy." Lucy looked up to see Michael, his cheeks bulging like a hamster, "It's rude to speak with your mouth full, Michael, didn't..."

Finding he now had room to push the food to one side, "It's not full, there's a bit of room left. What time's the marquee coming, do you know?"

"Your dad said it should be here by now, but with the roads icy I suppose it is taking longer. How did your engagement go last week?

Michael gave Lucy a sideways look, wondering if she was being sarcastic. Her face looked innocent of accusation, "You know... it was fine. Just the family. It's a bit awkward with them what with all that business."

"Well, I hope you have learnt your lesson. I can't believe you'll get another chance if you mess up again."

Michael felt the old irritation return, "Let it drop, Lucy, I don't owe you any explanations."

"Ohee touchy! I was just saying, that's all."

"Well I can do without it, thank you. I hear you're going out with that curly chap Cathleen ditched, is it true?"

He saw the embarrassed flush rise over Lucy's face, "No we are not going out, well not like that. His name's Ken, by the way…" Lucy turned her back on Michael and walked away. He didn't hear her parting words "And he's worth six of you."

Christine pulled up in her little bright green sports car, and Michael went across to meet her, "Morning Chrissie, the marquee hasn't arrived yet, it's gone ten now."

"The roads are awful, I came along at twenty miles an hour, so perhaps they are crawling along too."

Michael kissed Christine on the side of her mouth, he wished he could feel passion for her, but they had been friends for so long she was like a comfy pair of wellies. "Lucy's taken a couple of kids out on a ride this morning. They've gone to Dell Quay. You've just missed them, you could probably catch them up if you want. Shandy is free and would like the exercise?"

"No, ta, I rode this morning, early. I'll go and help your mum with the catering. What are the plans for tonight?"

We have a band playing, arriving at seven, and I think on the food front it's just Jacket potatoes, sausages and hot soup, nothing fancy."

Michael walked towards the house with Christine, who had linked arms with him, "I'll come in with you and have a coffee. I didn't stop for breakfast this morning."

The sound of the lorry reversing into the drive had Michael gulping down the last of his mug's contents, and heading for the door, hopping as he put his boots on. "Whoa, over here." Michael raised his arms directing the lorry over to the side of the stables. "Here, back up… back, back, steady, turn to the left." Once the lorry was parked as near as it could get to the spot, the driver jumped out of the front cab, "Sorry I'm late. There was an accident on the road, everything came to a stand-still."

Michael was transfixed, he stood and stared at the man before him. Thick brown hair waved over one eye, hiding it from view. He held out his hand to Michael, who still hadn't found his voice, "Me name's David. Where's this marquee going, here?"

Michael had the urge to move the hair away from his face so he could see him clearly, but forced himself to hold his hand out, introducing himself, "Michael, Michael Forrester." Remembering David's question, he said, "Yes, here's fine. I'll need some help though."

The old feelings that Michael thought he had buried when he left his old boys boarding school had stirred with the connection of hands, making him want what he knew he couldn't have. He followed David round the back of the lorry, watching him stretch up and unlock the door. Everything about his movements excited Michael.

*

In the kitchen, Christine chatted at ease with Michael's mother, while they prepared the vegetables. "I don't want to see another potato for as long as I live." Christine, laughed, "We've peeled enough carrots to feed an army."

Their talk was centred round the evening's event, Christmas, and the planned wedding that would take place next spring. "I'll go and check out the marquee and see if they want a hot drink, it's absolutely freezing out there today."

"Wait, Christine, take these carrot tops for the ponies, they'll eat them."

Christine carried a bowl full of vegetable peelings and chunky ends out to the paddock. She could see the marquee was unfolded, but it lay on the ground not yet up. She threw the carrots over the fence, and stroked one of the ponies. It nuzzled her hand. "There you go, boy, where's everyone, eh?"

Tucking her hands in her pockets, she made her way over to the stables, looking for Michael. "Hello, anyone around?" When there was no answer she guessed they were still getting bits from the lorry.

Christine stood on the rear bumper and pulled open the back door, and was met with the sight of some man bent over Michael moving rhythmically. She couldn't see Michael's face, but the sight of his trousers round his ankles brought bile to her throat, she retched, holding her hand over her mouth. She fled, sickened by what she had just witnessed. She could hear Michael calling her name, but she kept running. She wrenched open her car door, turned the key and put her foot, full down on the throttle. The tyres screeched, leaving black tyre marks, as she pulled out of the parking slot. The car was unable to cope with this sudden speed and skidded on the surface. She hit the side of the fence, but didn't bother to stop to check for damage. Her foot remained hard down as she headed for the road, blinded by tears.

*

Screams could be heard as the car appeared from nowhere. Lucy was thrown from her saddle as Rachel's horse reared up, putting two feet through the screen of the car. The other horses coming back from their ride started sidestepping as if in dance. Rosie's horse reared up, but she managed to stay in the saddle as it took off at a gallop into the riding school. Lucy lay on the drive, conscious that Rachel's body was not moving. She couldn't move to help her, the pain in her leg was excruciating.

Michael was first on the scene. He fell to his knees, terrified at the carnage sprawled out in front of him. He could hear footsteps running down the drive. It was his mother. When she took in the crumpled figures and the lifeless body in the car she physically wobbled, "Phone an ambulance, mum." When she didn't move but stood staring, Michael raised his voice, "Mum, go on inside and phone for an ambulance."

He crawled across to Lucy, she was conscious, "Lucy, are you …?"
"Rachel, Michael. See to Rachel."

He moved across to the child, who was lying at a twisted angle, not moving. His hands shook at the sight, not daring to touch her broken body. His eyes strayed to the car, he could see Christine, but her face was unrecognisable, she had taken a complete hit with the horse's hooves. Without any warning, Michael was sick. This was all his fault. The full impact of what had taken place and the reason behind it was all down to him. Christine was dead, and the loss was already painful. He knew he had never loved her like she deserved, but she had been his best friend for as long as he could remember. Tears were falling down his face, and to the crowd that had gathered it looked like he was the distraught fiancé. He pushed his father away as he tried to comfort him, and started running, where? He had no idea, but he ran across the fields towards North Mundham, he wanted to be as far away from this ugly sight as he could get.

*

Rosie sat between Agnes' legs, "What time will they be back, Granny A?"

"I don't know, love. They'll be home when Rachel's settled."

Rosie twiddled her fingers, thinking. She wanted to confide in her Granny A but was frightened. She thought about the things she felt and could sometimes see, yet she hadn't seen this coming.

"Granny A, what happens if Rachel doesn't wake up, and doesn't get better?" She felt Agnes' hand stroke her hair, "She will, love, you'll see. Rachel's a little fighter."

Tears fell down Rosie's cheeks, "I feel funny in my tummy. It makes me feel scared."

"Come on now, stop these silly notions. Tilly and Ed will be home soon. It's no good worrying and getting all het up when we don't know what is going on, now, is there?"

"Can I sleep here with you, Granny A? Just tonight, I could sleep on your sofa, I will be ever so good, please?" "Of course, go and get your things."

Rosie couldn't get through to the house quick enough, "Bring your toothbrush as well, there's a good girl."

Rosie lay asleep on top of Agnes' bed, cuddling a teddy that had belonged to Tilly when she was a child. She stirred as Agnes pulled the eiderdown from under her and covered her small frame with it.

*

Tilly sat at the hospital watching the nurses trot backwards and forwards. They smiled at her, but seemed unaware of the mental turmoil she was going through. Without looking up, she recognised Ed's footsteps. "It's over, Tilly, there's nothing else they can do." The reality of what Ed was saying, didn't make sense. Tilly stood, "Good, can I see her?"

Ed's face was grey, "You don't understand, Rachel's died. There's nothing more to be done."

Tilly flopped back in the chair, her legs unable to hold her up. She put her head in her hands and said to no one "Oh no, oh no... please God no."

Ed sat beside her, cradling her in his arms as she gave way to sobs. That is how Norman found them. He touched Ed's shoulder, "Take Tilly home, lad. There's nothing more to be done here now. You've a little one of your own to see to. Go on, both of you."

Tilly stood up, and putting her arms round Norman, said, "I'm so sorry, so, so, sorry."

Tilly's stomach lurched as she saw a Nurse approaching with May. The poor girl was trying to hold on to May's arm, but she shrugged her off. As they got closer, Tilly could see May's face was pale, but there were two bright red spots on each cheek. Tilly moved out of Norman's hold and braced herself for the accusations and onslaught that she felt sure would be coming. May's voice sounded hollow, "Come on, Norman, no good can be done now. I don't want to hang around here all night." Tilly moved over to May and touched her shoulder, "I'm so sorry. I don't know what to say." The tremor in Tilly's voice was present.

Tilly thought her heart would stop when May turned and looked at her with bright eyes that shone with unshed tears, "Stop that now. You're not to blame, that crazy flibberjibbet is, but she can't be held to account, she's gone with Rachel. Go home, go on, both of you." Tilly exhaled deeply as if a balloon had been let down, "May, but..."

"Take her home, Ed, go on, there is no good to come of staying here - thinking why?"

Tilly watched as Ed leant forward and hugged his mum and then turning to Norman, shook his hand. Norman pulled him into him, hugging him, "Goodnight, go on now, do as your mum says, there's a good lad."

Once Tilly was sat in the van she reached over and squeezed Ed's knee, "Your mum's in shock, you know that, don't you? She wouldn't be behaving like that if she wasn't. I'm worried for her, Ed, what will she do?"

"There's nothing we can do, Tilly, it'll probably hit her tomorrow."

"Your poor mum. First Luke and now Rachel."

"Don't, Tilly, please?"

Tilly knew to talk of Ed's brother caused him to shut down, but she couldn't help feeling that with Rachel's death, it will bring about a painful reminder of when they lost their son eight years ago.

*

Despite Lucy staying with Tilly and Ed, Christmas had been a sombre affair.

Ken hadn't gone as planned to the Lake District to see his mother, but had stayed behind so he could run the business, while Ed helped May and Norman sort out Rachel's funeral.

Lucy entered the kitchen on crutches, "Can I do anything, Tilly?"

"Sit down and I'll make you some toast."

"Where's Rosie?" Lucy fell heavily into the kitchen chair, asking, "Next door with Agnes?"

Tilly popped two slices of bread under the grill, "Yes, she seems to like it round there at the moment. I think she's taken Rachel's death quite hard."

Lucy started buttering the toast Tilly had put in front of her and smeared it with strawberry jam. "It was good of Ed's mum, you know, to send all Rachel's presents over for her, wasn't it?"

Tilly sat at the table with a mug of tea. She had eaten with Ed earlier. "I'm worried about May, Lucy. I expected to get the blame for not looking after Rachel properly, or worse still, having her point the finger at me, saying, trouble always follows you, but no, she has been nothing but pleasant."

"Perhaps she's still in shock, or maybe she knows it really is not your fault and the person responsible died along with Rachel."

Tilly took a swig of tea, "It's silly, isn't it? I can't help feeling guilty even though common sense tells me I'm not to blame."

Lucy jumped to her friend's defence, "Don't be daft. How could you possibly be to blame? I was the one in charge of the group, and I was the one leading her too. If anyone needs a finger pointing at them, it's me."

"No one's to blame, Lucy. Not even Christine, she wouldn't have done it on purpose. I wonder what ever got into her though. Do you think she caught Michael with another girl?"

"If she did, I don't know who with? There wasn't anyone."

Tilly stood, clearing the table, "Something must have upset her. Still I'll be glad when tomorrow comes and we can get the funeral over."

Lucy struggled to her feet, reaching for her crutches, "I feel like I've ruined everyone's plans."

"No, you haven't, I've enjoyed having you. Tilly filled the washing bowl with water before saying, "You could have stayed with Ken, you know. He was dead keen to have you."

"Yes I know. It was good of him to stay and help Ed out. He says there's a lot of them coming down from the Lakes for the funeral, why?"

"I wouldn't think it's a lot. Rachel was looked after by a woman who now lives in the Lake District. I believe she was her guardian. She used to have a home not far from here, in Selsey. I should imagine Rachel's death will have a huge impact on her."

"How come May and Norman got her?"

Tilly's answer was vague. Lucy said the obvious, "Christmas must have been awful for Ed's parents, having this funeral hanging above their heads."

"Yes, yes it must have been. I did invite them to us but May declined."

*

Friday 29th December 1966

The Funeral

There were many tears at Rachel's untimely departure. The vicar had tried to instil the great joy they should all feel at having known her. May and Norman had led the congregation outside, where eight years ago they had sprinkled the ashes of their son Luke. She was buried, facing views of open farm land.

It was followed by a well-set out tea in the village hall. Everyone helped with the preparation and the clearing.

*

January 1967

Tilly and Ed had seen the New Year in with Lucy and Ken, but there had been no real jollity. Rachel's death still seemed fresh in all their minds.

It wasn't until Thursday, Ed's birthday, that Tilly made up her mind they had to put the funeral behind them. Not just for her sake, but the atmosphere over the house was pulling Rosie down.

Tilly had booked a table at a little restaurant that had recently opened in Sidlesham. Lucy had said she would babysit Rosie while they went out. "Well, I hope there isn't a crisis, what with you on one leg."

Lucy had laughed, "You go out and enjoy yourself, Tilly, it'll do you good, both of you."

Tilly put on her coat, it was nearly four o'clock and she wanted Rosie in before dark, "Do you know, it was a year ago that I came home from Canada, so much has happened in a year."

"You met me for one. Good, for me, but I'm not so sure if it is likewise?"

Tilly smiled wistfully, her mind had gone back to those carefree days when she had first come home to find Ed working in her back garden. The joy of being held in his arms again, the hurried wedding plans, and how happy they had been, both so content just to be in each other's company, and then Rosie. It had all changed with Rosie. Tilly realised Lucy was looking for confirmation that she was happy to have her for a friend. "You are funny, Luce, you are the best friend I've ever had."

"What about Cathleen? Ken says you had been friends all your lives."

"It was always on Cathleen's terms. I didn't mind that really, I always thought I was lucky to have her as a friend, after all I had been 'that girl' for so many years I thought she was better than me."

"Oh, Tilly, you sound like Ken."

"Yes, poor Ken. I think what she did to him, was what opened my eyes to her. I wonder sometimes if I'll ever speak to her again, ever."

"She just lost her way for a while, I think. I don't know her like you, but it must be horrible to leave your home town like she did and know that no one is sorry."

Tilly ignored Lucy's understanding of Cathleen's shocking behaviour, looking at her watch she tied a scarf round her neck "I've got to go and find my little monkey, I expect she's up on the green. If you think you can manage, put the kettle on and call Gran through, she likes a cuppa around this time."

*

Ed sat opposite Tilly, the candle flickered in the dimly lit room where they were tucked in a corner on a table for two. The evening was quiet, with only one other couple eating.

They had had their starter, and while waiting for the main course Ed couldn't contain himself any longer, "Tilly, I've been dying to tell you this, but what with the accident, the funeral, and Lucy staying, there hasn't been a right time. Tilly's colour heightened in anticipation of what Ed was about to deliver. He reached over and took her hand, "Before Christmas, and the accident Tilly, I went to see the doctor…" Before Ed could finish Tilly's face dropped, "Are you ill?"

Laughing, Ed dropped back in his chair letting go of Tilly's hand. The moment passed as the waitress brought their main meals to the table.

"Don't stop, Ed, what is it, why did you go to the doctor?"

"Not our doctor, your doctor, your friend Geoffrey, Geoffrey Covax. I asked him if he could find us a baby, a new baby. Ours, Tilly, to keep." Tilly tried to speak, "No, Tilly, let me finish. I've felt terrible ever since I told Rosie we would find her mum. But it's what's right, she will want to go home, we are not her parents."

"We can give Rosie a better home than ever Rhana can. She can read now and…"

"It doesn't matter, Tilly, what we can give her, she wants her mum, her real mum. You can't blame her for that, but we have a chance, a real chance here, to have our own child. Say you'll visit, please?"

Tilly leant forward and clasped Ed's hand, causing a great relief to wash over him, "Of course I'll visit. I can't wait…"

"Tilly, can I just say this, just once and then put it to bed?" Tilly raised her eyes, "I'm sorry for what I made you do two years ago, really sorry."

"Stop it Ed, you didn't make me…"

"I did Tilly, I let you down. I didn't offer you the support you deserved. I still hate myself for it, but we have to let it go. Move on. If we don't Tilly it'll destroy us."

Ed watched Tilly blush, "I have of late been thinking horrible thoughts Ed. Not because I don't love you, it's just I love Rosie now too, like she's ours. It felt to me like you wanted to be rid of her."

"No, Tilly, No. I love Rosie too, just like you do, but of late, if I'm honest, with the way you have been, I've wished we never set eyes on her. Things have changed between us since her arrival. We didn't get any 'us' time, we married and met Rosie."

He watched as two big tears rolled down Tilly's cheeks, "If I hadn't had that abortion we wouldn't have had any 'us' time as you call it. I should imagine, less. I love you Ed, I've always loved you, for as long as I can remember. We've had a childhood together." Tilly blew her nose and looked at Ed with tears shining in her eyes, "I want to go to this place, I can't wait to go, Ed, and pick a baby. It feels like Christmas all over again. Oh, Ed, what shall we get?"

Ed leant over and brushed her cheek with his thumb, "I like the idea of a boy, what about you?"

"I don't care, Ed, I really don't care." Excitement shone from the pair of them, "We'll go on Sunday, Tilly, it's in Surrey, we'll make a day of it."

Saturday 7th January 1967

May took down the letter from the fireplace. She knew it word perfect. It read that Mr and Mrs Barrett were invited to Knight's Solicitors in Liverpool to discuss the late Mr Coffin's estate.

Norman had phoned the Solicitors on the Wednesday, the day the letter had arrived, and explained about Rachel's accident and their loss. May was struggling with the knowledge that, as Rachel's next of kin, they have become the beneficiaries.

The sound of a knock on the back door had May putting the letter back while calling out, "Come in, door's open." Prince wagged his tail, but didn't get out of his basket. As Tilly walked past she patted his head. "Hello, May, what's up with Prince? He didn't even bark."

"Tilly. Oh, it's good to see you." Realising Tilly was looking puzzled at Prince's behaviour, added, "No, he's not himself. The vet says he has diabetes, but I think he is missing something. He doesn't even want to go for his walks now."

Tilly sat at the kitchen table while May put the kettle on the stove, "What brings you over my way?"

When Tilly informed her that Rosie had gone to the stables, adding, "Lucy is walking without sticks now, she had to go and get a few things from her caravan. Rosie, after a lot of nagging, got to go too. I expect she'll end up having a ride."

May tried to hide her feelings at the mention of the stables, but Tilly noticed the sudden loss of colour in her cheeks, "May, I'm sorry, I didn't want to hurt you or remind you of…"

"Don't be a goof ball, life goes on."

May didn't realise, but it was this attitude, that had brought about Tilly's visit. There had been many tears at the funeral, but May appeared to have got herself together and seemed to be taking Rachel's death in her stride.

"May, I don't know where to start, but Ed's worried about you, we both…"

"Worried about me, whatever for?"

"You know, losing Rachel like you did. You seem to be coping well, a bit too well…"

May become annoyed, "Oh, I see. I can't win. If I fall to pieces I'd have you all round fussing, and yet I hold myself together, trying to move on, you…"

"Please don't, May. I want to help…If I can. You're doing wonderfully, everyone says so. It's just you must grieve, it's normal…"

May's hands were visibly shaking, she tried to disguise it, but she could see Tilly had noticed. "I, I don't know where to begin…" When May stopped, unable to find the words, Tilly said nothing, but picked up her tea, letting the silence hang like fog in the room. May sat with her head bent over her tea cup, staring at its contents. When she spoke, it was as if she was talking to the cup, "We took Rachel on because Ed had taken a real shine to her. It was reciprocated. I took to the kiddie too, Norman wasn't so keen at first. He liked her, but didn't want her, not like I did. Did you know that, Tilly?"

Tilly nodded, but said nothing, "She nearly drowned, you know."

Tilly sat very still, holding her cup on its saucer, frightened to move for fear of halting this heartfelt speech. "It doesn't matter now, but that was what made Ed find his voice. He spoke to her, called her name. It was that that turned Norman's head, and instead of Rachel having to go to some institution in London we took her on. I loved her, Tilly, oh I loved her, but it wasn't always easy. The big problem…"

If May was surprised when Tilly reached out and steadied her shaky hand she showed no signs of it. "This business with George Coffin.

294

I'm worried I let her down... Well, not so much let her down, I shouldn't have let her go round there. I'm questioning that I did it because it got her out from under my feet. I feel we...not we, I, I, didn't look after her properly."

Tilly jumped to her defence, "May, that's not so, you were wonderful with her. Rachel loved going round to George and Florrie's. She was making you a Christmas present round there, did you know?"

"Yes, I knew. But did you know, George was...misbehaving with her?"

May watched Tilly's chin drop in horror, and tried to back track, "I shouldn't say that as I don't know for sure, but he was accused of interfering with some little girl in Liverpool, they came here to escape the abusive hate there. I can feel it, I know in my heart that he was up to no good. So you see, Tilly, as much as I miss her and of course, I wish she was still here, it's a sort of relief in some ways."

May faltered, "That sounds horrible, I know. I'm sorry, Tilly, but that knowledge brought a worry of having to keep my eyes on her all the time. Rachel was very affectionate, which made her more vulnerable, do you understand what I'm saying?"

May didn't wait for Tilly to say one way or another, "What I'm trying to explain is, Norm and I are not getting any younger, and I'd started to worry at what would happen to her when we were gone. Rachel wouldn't have grown up, not like Ed did. She would have stayed our little girl forever. Do I sound horrible?"

"No, May, no you don't. I can sympathise with you. I just don't know what to say."

"There isn't anything to say, but perhaps you will understand that I am grieving, but I also can't help feeling that a huge weight has been lifted off my shoulders."

May told Tilly about the letter from the solicitor, and the money that George had left to Rachel.

"I don't want it. We would have used it to send Rachel to The Four Oaks, and Norman want's to donate it to her school, Little Acorns. She did so well there."

"Why don't you have a holiday, May? You deserve it. You both do. It's all the rage to go abroad, you could be the first to fly, go on, May. We might even come with you. I could speak to Ed."

"No, we don't want it. I lay awake last night thinking we should give it to the new school, the one we couldn't afford to send her to, The Four Oaks, but the more I think about it I feel I'd like to give it to the institution that Rachel was going to go to before we said she could live with us. It was in London, Alice Springs."

"Why, May, why do you feel you can't keep it for yourselves? Norman will be retiring in a few years, it will be a little nest egg."

"It wouldn't be a little nest egg. It's a great deal of money, Tilly. It seems George had a property in Liverpool. They fled from there, leaving it to be sold while they rented here. This solicitor was setting up a trust fund for Rachel."

"I wouldn't do anything hastily, May. Think on it for a while. You have had a big shock in more ways than one."

May looked across at Tilly, the girl she had been so quick to despise at every turn, yet she had sat and listened, really listened, and somehow it had eased her pain. "I know, Tilly, but I do know I don't want to give it to The Four Oaks. Children like Rachel have to have money to go there. I would rather donate it to the children that need help, help because there is no one to love them, look out for them. If Norman and I hadn't adopted Rachel, that is where she would have ended up. She would be alive, but I don't believe she would have been happy. She had hated it there on her trial weekend."

"I understand, May, I do, and I think you're handling everything admirably."

May stood, gathering up the cups and putting them on the tray, "Enough now of me, how was your meal out with Ed?"

Tilly raised her eyes questioningly, "Do you know?"

May couldn't contain the smile that spread across her face, "I do, Tilly. You're going tomorrow, aren't you?"

"We are. Come with us, May. We'll all go, gran as well. We'll go as a family."

For the first time ever, May hugged Tilly before she left, and as Tilly started up Ed's van, May found she felt better than she had in a long time.

*

Tilly stood with Ed on the steps of the big grey building. She knocked the red door with one hand and squeezed Ed's with the other. He gave her a smile, but it didn't stop the butterflies that fluttered in her stomach. There was an engraving in the brick work which read, The Hawthorns. Tilly thought it a grand name for such an ugly building.

May and Norman stood behind, holding Rosie's hand. Agnes had decided to stay at home with Lucy. The door opened, and a large woman with big blue, Bette Davis eyes smiled at them, "Yes, can I help you?"

The excitement was too much for Tilly, and her voice froze in her throat, it was Ed who introduced himself, "Mr Barrett, Ed. Ed and Tilly Barrett. We've come to look at adopting a baby, Geoffrey sent us… I mean Mr Covax."

The door was extended wide, allowing them all to traipse in, Tilly came to the rescue "It was Doctor Covax who referred us. He said there's a six week old baby boy that's up for adoption. He thinks we'll be ideal…"

Ignoring Tilly's hurried explanation, "Come on through. Matron will be able to help. She'll have all the necessary information."

There was a strong smell of disinfectant in the hall, and their heels echoed round the high ceilings on the red stone floors.

Tilly whispered to Ed, "Doesn't feel very warm, does it?" Rosie had skipped ahead, enjoying the sound of her shoes on the tiles. "May, can you get Rosie, please…"

A door on the left opened, and a thin woman stood wearing a grey and white striped dress. Her grey hair was short. The lady who'd escorted them made the introduction, "Ah, Mr and Mrs Barrett, yes, I've been expecting you. Welcome." She held out her hand to Ed first, despite her crooked teeth the smile lit up her face softening the starchy first impression. "Now, I have some questions to go over with you first." Looking at Rosie, she asked, "Who do we have here…?"

Tilly reached over and took Rosie's hand from May, "This is Rosie, we are her guardians, but she's hoping to go home in the summer."

Tilly was pleased there were no further questions, her attention had turned to May, "So do we have grandma and grandad here?"

Tilly watched May stutter, "No, no… What with the child being temporary we are Auntie and Uncle to Rosie."

Matron got down on one knee so she could look Rosie in the eyes. Her voice was an excited whisper, "Now would you like to go with your Auntie and Uncle to our play room while I speak with Mummy and Daddy?"

"No, we are Tilly and Ed to Rosie, like my mother in law said, we knew this was to be a temporary arrangement."

Without showing any sign of judgement she rang a bell on her desk. Within seconds the lady that had opened the door appeared, "Can you take Rosie with her Aunt and Uncle to the play room, please? I need to speak with Mr and Mrs Barrett and get the necessary forms filled in."

The questions took over an hour, Tilly couldn't help wondering how Rosie was faring. It was nearly lunch-time, and her own stomach was feeling empty. With the questions over there were forms to fill in. "I know this must feel like an inquisition to you both, but I can assure you it is necessary."

"I'm just a bit worried about Rosie, she'll be getting hungry."

"Don't worry about your family, they'll be served a light lunch in the visitors room. Would you like a bite to eat, or are you ready to go to the nursery?"

Tilly forgot her own rumbly tummy and squeezed Ed's hand. "We'd like to see the baby, please." Following Matron they traipsed down the hall following her like ducklings. Excitement shone in Tilly's blue eyes, making it look like a light had been switched on. She felt like skipping, but controlled herself. "Is that all there is to it, will we be able to take him?"

Matron gave a half-hearted laugh, "One step at a time, let's see what you think of him, and then I have to follow procedure. All in good time, I can assure you it will happen."

When they entered the nursery Tilly and Ed were told to wait on the seats just inside the door. This room had the same high ceilings like the halls and it felt cold. Tilly felt Ed's hand rest on her knee and she clasped it. There were six cots and three wicker baskets placed on tables. Tilly watched as Matron spoke to one of the women, and together they walked over to the far window. "Look, Ed. That must be him." Matron walked confidently across to them, carrying a baby wrapped in an off white blanket, "Here he is, he was born on the twenty sixth November, he was six weeks old yesterday. Tilly stood, letting go of Ed's hand, and pulled down the blanket to look at the little face, "He's perfect, Ed, look at him." With the blanket pulled away from his head a mop of dark hair sprung up like grass, he had an olive tint to his skin, and the sudden coldness had him opening his eyes. They were green, just like Ed's. "Oh, Ed, he's beautiful, look at his eyes, they look like yours… Ed?"

Tilly tore her eyes away from this perfect bundle to look at Ed for a reaction, and tears were falling down his face, "Ed, are you okay? Don't you like him?"

"I love him Tilly," he fished out his handkerchief and wiped his face, "I love him Tilly, I love him already." Tilly looked at the Matron, "Can I hold him, please?" The baby was placed in her arms, and she found tears falling down her own face, "Can we take him home today, please? We want him, we know we do."

"Slow down. As much as I would like to be able to hand him over to you both, it isn't that easy. There are still a few boxes that need ticking, and they will have to be passed by…" Matron paused, looking at them for answers. When they remained silent she said, "Doctor Covax. Yes, that's the doctor acting for you, isn't it?"

They seemed not to hear the question. Ed had his arm across Tilly's shoulder, and the two of them stood staring down at the bundle that Tilly held cradled in her arms, "I'm going to call him Peter, do you like that, Ed? Peter, it's perfect for a perfect baby. Oh, Ed, he's ours, isn't he wonderful." When they realised that Matron was waiting for confirmation on the Doctor front, Tilly relaxed, "Yes, Doctor Covax. Please sort it out with him. When do you think he'll be ours?"

"It could be as early as next Saturday, how does that sound?"

The smiles from both Ed and Tilly answered any questions. "Come on now, you two, we need to fill out the last of these forms and track your family down for you."

Tilly felt a stab of guilt. She had forgotten all about Rosie, May and Norman. "Oh can we show them, Peter, Please?"

"Yes, but all in good time, first things first."

"Can I bring him with us now?"

Matron straightened her back, her voice firm "No, he will have to stay here for now. Come along, give him to me. We'll come back later."

She reached out and took the baby from Tilly, calling to the woman at the far end of the room, "Come and get baby, we are finished here now."

Matron asked one of the ladies to find Mary. Within minutes they recognised the large lady who had opened the door to them on their arrival. "Mary, take Mr and Mrs Barrett to the day centre so they can catch up with their family."

Tilly took hold of Ed's hand again, and they looked at each other and smiled. Tilly couldn't think of a time when she had been happier, "Isn't he perfect, Ed?"

Ed nodded and squeezed her hand. When two doors were pushed open Tilly spotted May and Rosie sitting on big cushions doing floor puzzles with a circle of children. Tilly left Ed with his dad, who was sitting reading some kind of magazine, and went over to May. "Hello, what a lovely picture this makes."

Rosie was up on her feet at the arrival of Tilly, calling "Tilly, Tilly, this is Angus, isn't he lovely. Can he come and live with us too?"

Clutching hold of Rosie's little tartan skirt was a boy no more than three or four. His hair was blonde with a pretty cow lick at the front. "Yes, he's lovely, but we can't have everybody, darling, our little boy is in the nursery. Come on, we're going to see him now, all together."

"No, I want Angus. Please, Tilly, I've told him."

Tilly looked at May, hoping for some words of encouragement, and felt crestfallen when she said, "He's a cutie, Tilly. He seems to have taken a shine to Rosie too."

Tilly ignored May. She took hold of the little boy's hand who was called Angus, thinking *what a name*

"Come on now, let's go over to the Meccano. You can build something with your friends…"

"No, Tilly, I told him we could take him with us."

"Well, you shouldn't have, Rosie. We have our own little baby up the corridor, this little boy belongs here."

She felt a hand on her shoulder. It was Mary, the lady who had led them down here. "Don't trouble yourself, dear. These things happen all the time. Angus will forget all about you once you have gone. Take your family to the nursery, you'll see."

Tilly gave her what she hoped was a silent thank you, "Come on, Rosie, let's go and meet Peter. Then we'll see, eh?"

Her heart lurched as Rosie let go of Angus's hand, saying, "We'll be back in a minute, promise."

May eased herself up off the cushions. Rosie went to her and took hold of her hand. Tilly couldn't believe it when she heard Rosie say, "You'll speak to her, won't you, Auntie May? You said we'd take him, you did." She was more amazed to hear May say, "She will, love, give her time, Rosie. She took you on, didn't she?"

The two of them left Tilly and walked towards Ed and Norman, making her feel excluded.

The chatter amongst them while they stood in a circle waiting for the okay to visit the nursery was about Angus. Ed had laughed out loud, "We'll have to change his name for a start, Angus! What sort of name is that?" Tilly felt she had to be heard, "No, Ed, we can't take two children, it'll be hard work with the baby."

Ed laid his arm across her shoulders, "Dad says he's a lovely lad, why don't we stay open minded?"

"We can't, Ed, we might lose Peter. I want the baby."

"We might be able to have two, it would save us the journey back next year. Surely we wouldn't have only had one child, would we?"

"No, but..." Tilly couldn't believe how this was unfolding. It seemed the whole Barrett family had made a decision without her, and yet it was a decision that would affect her the most. Tilly felt May putting her opinion forward was one thing, but to hear Norman say, "Don't dismiss it, girl, meet him properly, he's a good little lad, I can feel it. You'll love him, you'll see."

With Tilly's joy of her new baby squashed a little, they all stood together laughing and talking. Rosie was still holding May's hand, jumping up and down beside her. The excitement seemed to radiate from them all.

Tilly peeped in the door of the nursery to see what the wait was for, it opened and Matron stood filling the view, "Come on, in you come."

Norman, May and Rosie sat on the chairs at the side of the wall while Tilly and Ed moved over to the wicker basket, the one that held Peter. Once he was placed in Tilly's arms she walked him over to May,

"Peter, May. Isn't he perfect?"

"Can I see? Let me see." Rosie was on tiptoe now, trying to pull at Tilly's arms. For the first time ever she felt annoyed with the child, "Stop it, Rosie, you'll hurt him. Let Auntie May have a look first." She knew she'd been too harsh, but was still cross at her behaviour in the day centre. Rosie's eyes filled with tears, this caused Tilly to feel instantly sorry, "Come on now, I didn't mean to upset you. You have to realise he isn't ours yet and you can't go pulling at him, he's only tiny, look."

Rosie stroked his tiny face with her finger, "Oh, Tilly, he's lovely. Can we have them both?"

Tilly ignored Rosie's persistence, she was fascinated at both May and Norman's expressions as they stared at baby Peter. They looked smitten with him already, it was the dark hair and green eyes that so resembled Ed's that did it. She heard Norman say, "You'd think it was our lad as a baby, wouldn't you?"

No one had realised Matron had left the room, so caught up were they with the baby. When she pushed open the nursery door, "With the help from your doctor, I've managed to tick the last boxes and fill in the forms, and doctor Covax assures me that there is not a single reason why you can't take baby home today if you wish to do so."

Tilly felt herself tingle all over. Ed's face looked like it would split, his smile was so wide, "Oh, we'd love to take him, but on thinking, it would be better for us to get prepared."

"I've still got the boys cots, Tilly, you could use them?"

"No, no thank you, May. I want to get things fresh. You do understand?"

Tilly was relieved to see she hadn't offended her, "Of course, that's sensible really. I can help though, you only have to ask."

Tilly, who was overcome with love and thankfulness, shocked them all with "We can take Angus, now, the little boy in the day room, if that's alright?"

Rosie leapt up in the air, "Yes, yes, oh, Tilly, thank you, thank you."

"Calm down, calm down, there's a good girl." Tilly looked across at Matron who looked puzzled, "Rosie's fallen in love with a little boy in the day centre, Angus?"

"Angus is always looking to be taken home, don't you let the little monkey pressure you."

"I think what my husband say's is true, it will save coming back next year. The question is, can we adopt two boys?"

Matron laughed, "With Doctor Covax's reference you could adopt sixty children."

When everyone had had a last hold of baby Peter, Tilly kissed his downy dark hair and placed him back in the wicker basket.

"I think I need to have a good look at this Angus who's wormed his way into all your affections."

Tilly tipped the bricks out, onto the table, and within minutes Angus was sitting with her. "And how old are you, little man?"

"I'm four, I am. I'm four… I really am."

Tilly raised her eyes in question at the girl watching on in uniform. "He's three, but nearly four. Angus thinks when he's four he'll be all grown up. Once he isn't a baby, a family will think he's easier to manage and will want …"

"Well, Angus, I don't care how old you are. I want you because you're you. You'll be a brother for Rosie and Peter."

The atmosphere changed when Rosie said, "Not me, Tilly, I'm going home, I'm going home to me mum." The brief silence was filled with Tilly saying, "It doesn't matter where you go, Rosie, you'll always be my girl. Come on, let's go and tell Matron we're taking Angus home and we'll be back on Saturday to get Peter."

*

The Forresters - January 9th 1967

Michael tried to change Lucy's mind, "Don't leave, Lucy, you can have the time off for your leg to heal. We need you…"

"Look, I'm sorry, Michael, the caravan's freezing. It was alright in the summertime, but I've been offered a better job and the chance to rent a room in a house. It'll save me walking up the field for a pee in the night, or crouching down at the side of the van. You wouldn't like it, would you? No, my minds made up."

Michael looked desperate, "Is it to do with the accident? It wasn't my fault, I…"

"Michael, no one blames you, only you. It's as you say, an accident. I'm leaving as I have a better offer."

Michael knew Lucy probably didn't blame him for the accident, his mother had even come to the conclusion that Christine was driving recklessly under dangerous conditions. After all there were no ladies present for him to have been flirting with.

It was only Michael's father that gave him the occasional odd looks. *'Does he know, has he guessed?'*

A few days after the accident, Michael found himself in the stable with his dad and for one horrible second Michael had thought he was going to say something to him, but he hadn't and the moment passed.

Christine's parents have said very little, he suspected that they blamed him, he didn't care he blamed himself. He knew it was his fault. It was also the first Christmas and New Year that the two families had not shared the festivities together.

He had hoped to move away, have a fresh start. Where, he hadn't yet decided, but with Lucy leaving he was never going to get away.

Christine's death was horrible. Michael found himself drinking more and more to numb the pain and shame. *What would have happened to me if Christine hadn't died and had spilled the beans? Being caught with the girls was one thing, but a man!'* Michael let the shame wash over him. He hated himself, he wanted to be different, but it didn't matter how much he tried, it was always there. He thought about Christine, they had grown up together and the love he felt for her was a friendship. He missed her, but he couldn't help but be relieved that she had gone. Taken his secret to the grave. He hated himself for these thoughts, telling himself *'I should have just finished with her, said I didn't love her like she deserved. She would have gone with that.'*

Michael was brought out of his reverie when he caught sight of Ken. *'Curly Shirley, so that's it is it?'*

The last time Michael had encountered him, it was in a fight over Cathleen. How he hated Ken for his normality. Michael remembered the jive classes, how he had watched Ken move Cathleen round the floor, his hips wriggling in time to the music, with such style. Michael ran his hands over his head, licking his top lip, *'How I wanted him, even then.'* Now here he was, taking Lucy from them. He felt compelled to go over, "So you're behind Lucy leaving."

Ken shrugged his shoulders, Michael could sense he wasn't bothered by him, "I'm not behind anything. She's big enough to make her own mind up. Now out of the way, I've got a lot to shift here. In fact you could give a hand if you're at a loose end. Do something decent."

Michael's guilt made him flinch, but he ignored him, watching, as Ken helped Lucy lug boxes and cases.

He let himself ogle what he couldn't have, and dream. How he wanted Ken. This want had gone on for so long it had caused a deep hate that had taken root inside him.

Michael had been able to sense his own kind, and he knew there was not an ounce in Ken that was even close to being homosexual. Seeing Lucy struggling, Michael called out, "Give that to me, Lucy." he took the case she was trying to slide down the van steps, and walked it down to the gate, "Here you go, curly. Stay there, I'll bring it all down for you." Ken ignored the jibe, and the two of them strode back up the field side by side in silence. When everything was packed in the van Michael hugged Lucy to him. "Don't be a stranger, you're welcome to ride anytime. Come with Tilly and her little one." The mention of Tilly, reminded him of Rachel, "How are the Barretts? It was a sad day and I'm sorry."

"It wasn't your fault, Michael, it was an accident."

'If you only knew, oh God, if you only knew.'

Guilt swamped over him as he watched Ken pull out of the drive, *'Perhaps her leaving is for the best. It closes down another door.'* Michael went indoors and poured himself a Scotch, not caring that his father sat in the same room, saying nothing but giving a distinct look of disapproval.

*

The Rainbow

Chapter Eleven – Bournemouth

Cathleen watched the back of Laurence Jackson as he waited by the lift. He had checked in for three nights, so would be here for tomorrow's end of the month dance. It was the first time a man had turned her head since Michael Forrester, but the gold band on his left finger had not been missed as he signed his name and reached for his small red and black suitcase. Cathleen had offered to show him to his room, but he had declined, saying he knew his way round.

So lost was she in daydreams, watching the back of Laurence's dark head which had the start of silver showing in streaks that when Jackie squealed out "Laurie, Laurie, hello. How lovely to see you darling. Did you have a good Christmas, how's your little family?"

"Whoa there, yes all good, and you, how's Simon?" He twitched his head over towards Cathleen, "I see you've employed a red headed beauty on the desk, since when?" Cathleen tingled with pride which increased with Jackie's praise. "That's Cathleen, she's our godsend."

The lift doors opened and the two of them disappeared, leaving Cathleen lost in thought, *'Now that's what I call delicious.'*

Cathleen was still drooling when the front door opened and an older couple stood struggling with a case on the steps. Cathleen left the desk and held the door open wide, "Let me help you. Leave it on the steps, I'll pull it in."

"Thank you, love, but I'll manage if you hold the door, oops, no, like that." Laurence Jackson was forgotten for now. When the postman brought in the mail he gave Cathleen a cheeky wink, saying, "One for you from Bognor Regis again." Without looking at the handwriting she stuffed it in her pocket, "Thanks, hang on, here's the post." Cathleen knew the letter was from her mother. Ever since they had cleared up their differences Pam had written every week. When her letters came they were newsy and full of love. Cathleen couldn't believe how much was happening back home, daily life at Bognor was like a saga in a magazine these days, making her own life seem dull in comparison. Rachel Barrett had died before Christmas, Cathleen had never taken to the child, but even she had the good grace to know that was shocking. Hearing Christine was dead too, now that had stirred a different kind of emotion in Cathleen, she thought how things might have been if it could have only happened a little earlier. She instantly felt remorseful, reminding herself how much happier she was these days.

Jackie had asked that Cathleen not use the phone for personal calls, she wanted it kept free for business. So between mother and daughter they had decided it was easier to keep in touch through post, unless urgent. Cathleen did make an effort to use the phone box on the sea front at least once a month so she could speak with her little sister, Hannah.

Her good friend Daisy, who had been her confidante in her time of need, didn't bother with her either. This had hurt at first, but time had healed, Cathleen wasn't one to brood on what was, she was enjoying her new found freedom, and being liked again for who she was.

Friday saw an influx of people checking in and out, and it was four in the afternoon before she managed a break. Cathleen sat and lit up a cigarette, breathing in deeply, she was about to open the letter from her mother when Jackie plonked herself down, "Is that coffee still hot?"

"Yes, Simon's just brought it over."

"Pour me one, darling."

Cathleen obliged, saying, "Everyone's checked in. Who's that American chappie?" Jackie smiled, "He's married, Cathleen, children too. There are plenty of fish in the sea for you, darling, don't go down that road."

"He still looks rather delicious."

The two of them roared with laughter, "You say the funniest things at times, girl. What are we to do with you?"

Cathleen changed the subject, "I've got a letter here from my mum, "It's all happening in Bognor I can tell you. When I lived there the only scandal was what I caused." Jackie laughed again. "What does she say this time, has the milkman ran off with the next door neighbour?"

"God no! Mrs Barrett. You wouldn't believe what an old battle axe she is. Although when my mum went into labour with Hannah it was quite serious, and she sat with me all night..."

"There you go, there's good in us all. I'll leave you with your letter, love. Remember what I said about Laurie, out of bounds. You don't want to get hurt again, now, do you?" Cathleen liked Jackie, she watched her move over to the bar with her coffee to talk to Simon.

Cathleen leaned back in the chair taking a long slow drag on her cigarette, then opened the letter.

Dear Cathleen,

It was lovely to speak with you at Christmas, and I'm glad you liked the bits I sent over. Hannah loves her colouring book and parades around in the dressing up shoes. You always seemed to know what she would like best. The slippers you sent fit me perfectly and your dad was tickled pink with his book. Thank you love.

The highlight of my news is that Tilly and Ed have adopted two little boys, one is only a babe in arms, May says they've called him Peter. The toddler, wait for it, he's called Angus. By all accounts Ed wanted to change his name but Tilly said 'No' so Angus it is. They still have Rosie but if everything goes to plan she

311

will leave for the Lake District in June, they are taking her to some fair where the gypsies all gather. I thought that would cause trouble for them, but now they've adopted the boys I am sure Rosie's departure won't be quite as painful.

May and Norman have bought a new car, a brand new one, and it is an estate. Their house is on the market and they are planning to move to Selsey. There are some bungalows being built on a new estate and May and Norman have decided they need a fresh start. I can't help feeling sad at that, they've been our neighbours for over twenty years. Still things change. I think they must have come into some money when Rachel died. Your father reckons Rachel must have had some kind of trust. It all makes sense now, the private school they sent her to. Still May has coped well with the loss of the little one, better than I imagined. I'm sure having these two grandchildren arrive has helped. She catches the early bus over to Hunston most days so she can help out. Things do appear to be a lot better between Tilly and May these days, so that has to be a good thing, don't you think? I don't know if you have managed to heal the rift between you and Tilly, but it might be a nice touch to send a congratulations card? (Only if you want to. I'm not saying you should.) It is just such a shame you were friends for so many years, and I always had a soft spot for Tilly, life was never easy for her.

I don't know if I mentioned the young girl, Lucy, she worked at the stables? She broke her leg in the accident and Tilly let her stay at theirs until she could walk properly. Well it seems she has left the riding school and is working for Ed and Ken. She is in the office taking the orders and doing the accounts. I only tell you this as I don't know who you hear from, from back home, but she has moved in with Ken as his lodger? What with the babies at Tilly's there wasn't room for her. May said the girl had been sharing with Agnes for a while, but what with her plaster coming off she has moved in with Ken. You know how May likes to gossip, she indicated they had been friends for a while now, and tapped the side of her nose. I am sure if there is a romance blooming, you will be pleased for him, Cathleen, and as I say, I'm only telling you this so you don't hear it from another source.

Hannah has started a bible class at the Manor House, the old Sunday school but has been demolished. She loves it, Cathleen, unlike you who I had to

312

practically drag there of a Sunday morning. When I think of those days love,
you could be such a trial at times, but what I wouldn't give to have them back.

I shall sign off now as I have the veggies to peel, and I want to catch the
postman. I look forward to hearing from you.

With lots of all our love, Mum, Dad and Hannah X

Cathleen tried to shift the heavy feeling that had settled in the pit of
her stomach, but the thought of Ken moving a girl into his home
made her feel low. Her mood failed to lift when Laurence came into
the dining area and smiled at her, saying, "It must be my lucky
night, having the best looking lady here, waiting on my table."

Cathleen had had her hair restyled very short when she had arrived
at the hotel three months ago. It had grown a good two inches in
length, and the natural curl her hair had, clung to her youthful face
like Ivy. She didn't realise just what a pretty picture she made. She
smiled back at Laurence, aware he looked appealing in his open
necked shirt. She placed a water jug on the table and got a whiff of
his aftershave. She had never smelt it before, but guessed it was
expensive. Everything about Laurence, Cathleen thought, looked
classy.

Simon plated up ten starters. Gammon pie with the egg running
through the middle. It was what Cathleen had come to recognise as
the usual dish to start the Friday night meal with. Their menus were
as predictable as a roast on Sunday.

Once dinner had been served Jackie came through to help with the
coffees. Many of the guests left their tables and moved to the
lounge to sit by the open fire in the comfy chairs. It was here that
Cathleen could see Laurence talking to a couple who had also
checked in today. He sat forward with his elbows resting on his
knees. He looked relaxed and confident in his surroundings, and by
the expression on his face his companions were amusing him.
Cathleen placed the tray on the table. "Coffee for four, is there
anything else you need?"

It was at that moment he threw his head back in laughter, revealing silver fillings. Cathleen took a secret pleasure at this revelation, she had never had a tooth filled in her life. His sudden outburst of laughter, had her saying in a haughty way, "Was it something I said?"

Jackie broke the sudden awkwardness, "Ah this is where we all are. How was dinner?"

Cathleen was pleased to turn her back on them and leave. When she got to the kitchen Simon was scraping plates and loading the dishwasher. "I'll finish up here, Simon, you go through to the snug lounge, Jackie's in there now."

"Ta, love. I'll take you up on that offer, it feels like I've been stuck out here all day. Still I've done the preparation for tomorrow night, so that'll help us tomorrow."

"Go then, go." Cathleen swiped at him with the tea towel, "Stop making excuses, I've said I'll finish up here."

"Did you say Jack's in the lounge?" "Yes, she's with the American and another couple that sat in the eaves."

Cathleen hurriedly dried up the last few bits and emptied the dish washer. She was eager to finish so she could get upstairs to read her letter again.

'Perhaps I will write to Tilly, it couldn't hurt and she might spill some light on these new developments back home.'

With the thought of home Ken came to mind, making it feel like her earlier lunch had dropped to the bottom of her stomach, *'I don't want him, so why shouldn't someone else have him?'*

Cathleen reminded herself of this over and over, but it didn't ease her blue mood that had settled over her like an eiderdown. She closed the kitchen door, putting the sign across which read in bold capital letters, No Entry. She popped her head in at the snug lounge

314

and called to Simon and Jackie, "Nunight all, I'm turning in early, I'm bushed. See you in the morning."

Jackie went to get up, "No, Jacks, stay there, I'm fine. It's just been a long day, that's all."

Once upstairs Cathleen closed her bedroom door relieved to have some time to reflect on her mother's letter.

*

Simon took his position at the bar. This was his favourite time of the day. The dinner was done and cleared, everything was laid out for tomorrow's breakfast, leaving him to enjoy a drink with the customers. Jackie had gone up early with one of her headaches, and Cathleen hadn't come down since leaving earlier. He caught sight of himself in the mirrored tiles that sat at the back of the bar, he pulled out the elastic band that held his hair in a ponytail. Running his hands through it he looked critically at his reflection. He pulled at his cheeks, *'I'm looking older, the hair has stayed in place, thankfully, but I look tired.'*

"It's quiet tonight." Simon recognised the American drawl without turning, "Yes, they're probably all reserving their energy for the dance tomorrow." He wiped down the bar with a tea towel, "What are you having?"

Laurence looked along the rack, "I'll have the same as you. What is it you're drinking?"

"Me, I'm on port." "Go on then, that's what I'll have."

Laurence had been coming to the hotel on business for over three years. "How long are you staying this time?" Laurence fingered the top of his glass, "I'm here till Wednesday, then off to London for four days." The conversation stayed with work, family and holidays, all the usual spiel. It wasn't until Laurence asked about Cathleen that Simon felt a stab of jealousy. He seemed a little too curious for his liking, and he thought perhaps Jackie was right, there had been a spark between them. "She's just a kid, Laurie. She's been here three months now, and she's a good little worker."

"I didn't mean that, Simon, she's a bloody beauty, hot! Even you can see that, can't you?"

"Well like you, I'm married, that puts a lot of things out of bounds."

"It doesn't stop you looking, surely, does it?"

Simon watched as Laurence downed his drink in one and left. He guessed he had upset him, but Laurence's comments on Cathleen had riled him. Simon heard the clock in the hall chime nine, it was still early, yet there wasn't an individual to be seen. *What's up with them all?"*

He took Laurence's glass and rinsed it out. Pouring himself another drink he went into the snug room to enjoy the last of the burning logs. He had just put his feet up on the pouf that matched the leather suite. His peace was broken when Cathleen plonked herself beside him on the big sofa, "Where is everybody?"

"Jackie's got a headache. Laurie was here, but he's gone up too, jet lagged, looks like everyone else is saving their selves for the dance tomorrow night."

"I could murder a drink, Simon. Can I get a Bacardi?" Without waiting for an answer she made her way to the bar. "Do you want a top up?"

He drained his glass and held it out for her. The feelings that he was trying desperately to bury were surfacing again, he just couldn't quell them. He had racked his brains trying to remember when he had first started to feel this way. When Cathleen had hopped off the coach back in November he had thought what a stunner, but that had been all. The stylish hair cut she had got made her appear older, but it wasn't then. He let his head lay on the back of the big leather cushion. He closed his eyes and relived the New Year dance. *That was it, it was then. The little minx had pulled me onto the dance floor and wriggled that firm little body against me. God, it had stirred feelings in me I thought had died.'* "There you go, Port and a slice of lemon." He opened his eyes and took the glass, patting the seat beside him. She plonked herself in heavily, sighing, Simon rested his arm across the back of the sofa, "What's up, love? You seem a bit down."

"I always get a bit unsettled when mum writes. Not that I want to go home, I said I never would, but I can't help missing them. It feels like they're all moving on without me… Can you understand?"

Simon smiled, dropping his arm on to her shoulders, enjoying the closeness, "You're a good kid, Cathleen. I bet no one's moving on without you, you're the one who's moving on. Look at you, twenty years old, and you've left home, making your own way in life. I bet they're all jealous of you." Tipping her glass back she finished her drink, "I don't think so, Simon, I think they're all glad to see the back of me."

He watched mesmerised as she put her cigarette in the holder they and bought her for Christmas and lit it. She took a deep long drag, and tipping her head back, blew out a stream of smoke. Simon watched, mesmerised, nothing had ever looked as sexy. This youthful creature sitting beside him made him forget how old he was, he wanted what he knew he couldn't have. It was dangerous, he knew that, but he couldn't let it go. She brought him back to the present, "I'm feeling a bit peckish, are there any of those little trifles left in the fridge?"

Pleased of the distraction, he jumped up, "I'll get you one, wait here." As he went into the kitchen he felt guilty for his thoughts. He had never been unfaithful to Jackie, the thought had never entered his head. They had worked side by side for the last thirteen years. He pulled open the fridge, there were three trifles left, *'Pull yourself together, man. Practice what you preach.'* It didn't help, he wanted her.

He wanted Cathleen. A young girl nearly eighteen years his junior, *What am I thinking?* ' He put a teaspoon in the silver dish, feelings of guilt didn't dampen the lustful thoughts.

Hoping his voice sounded steadier than his nerves, he held out the dessert, "There you go." He sat opposite, keeping her at a safe distance, it made no difference, as the spoon laden with cream reached her open mouth her tongue came out and licked her top lip. His own private thoughts stirred unwanted feelings, without realising, his own tongue was mimicking hers. The urge to hold her, open that flimsy nylon pink blouse she wore, and reveal the young soft pink flesh was driving him crazy. These thoughts were filling his day and night making thinking and sleeping difficult. He told himself over and over, it had to stop, it was crazy.

"Goodnight, Simon, thanks for that." She blew him a kiss, pushed the trifle dish across the table, unaware of his thoughts as his eyes followed her slim figure until it disappeared.

*

The Monthly Dance – January 28th 1967

Cathleen dressed with care. The dinners were served earlier than usual and everything was cleared by eight. The music filtered up the stairs to her room, the guests were already dancing. She had managed to put the unsettling news of Ken moving in a female lodger to the back of her mind.

Cathleen met Jackie on the stairs, laughing, she said "Well, Jackie, do you like Simon's hair cut? I think he looks years younger, don't you?"

She sensed Jackie was not happy about it, "Sorry Jackie, I was only joking. I like it though, I think it suits him better."

"I don't know what's got into him lately, he's acting very strange. If it's about age, I should be the one fretting, I'll be forty this year."

Cathleen told a little lie, "Forty, you don't look forty, Jackie."

"I'm feeling it, darling, Simon looks so much younger. Men age better than women, don't you think?" Cathleen reached out and touched Jackie's shoulder, "How old is he then?"

"He's nearly thirty eight, but he's still younger, and aging better than me."

"Go on with you, my mum says you're as old as you feel."

"As I said, I feel old these days."

The phone rang in the reception, "You go on through to the dance Jackie. I'll get this."

Cathleen was delighted to shake Jackie off, she wanted to make a grand entrance into the dance hall on her own, to witness the look on Laurence's face as she walked in. "Hello, The Three Chimneys, how can I help you?" It was someone booking for two weeks in the summer.

She stood at the double doors with the light behind her. The band were singing a Frank Sinatra hit, Strangers in the night, it couldn't have felt more romantic to Cathleen. Her heart seemed to miss a beat as Laurence looked over and gave her a half smile. As he moved across the dance floor she thought her legs would give way, she leant against the door frame for strength, unaware of how sexy she looked.

"Well, well, well. Do you dance as well as you look?"

She laughed, "Better." As he led her to the dance floor it felt to Cathleen like the whole room had disappeared.

Jackie stood with the crowd, watching, not Cathleen and Laurence but her husband. His eyes were on Cathleen, and it was at that moment she knew her biggest fears were reality.

*

Big Birthdays – 1967

Jackie's birthday had gone off a treat. Simon was glad of Cathleen's help, she had decorated the cake beautifully.

Simon draped his arm round Cathleen's shoulder, "Have you phoned your mum and wished her a happy birthday from Bournemouth?"

Cathleen's mood was not at its best, Laurence had left for London yesterday, promising he would phone, she hadn't heard anything from him yet. Her lack of sparkle was noticeable, "I will, I'll do it now if that's okay?"

Simon patted her back, giving her a mock push, "Of course it is, girl, go on, it's your mother's birthday, I bet she's been waiting by the phone all day for you." Cathleen made a half-hearted attempt at a smile "I don't think so, but I'll phone all the same."

Simon knew what the sad face was all about, but it didn't stop him feeling pleased that Laurie had gone. *'How come she was so smitten with him, what's he got, that I haven't?'*

"Jackie? You all right, love?" She broke into his thoughts, which caused a light blush to colour his cheeks, "Have you had a good day?"

She put her arms round his waist, "Hold me, Simon."

He held her back, concerned by the shake in her voice, "Hey, hey. What's brought this on?" Jackie's tears made his heart quicken, "Come on, Love, no tears. Not on your birthday. Don't you remember what your mum used to say? You won't grow." He was pleased when she tried to smile, "I don't know, being forty makes me feel old, I feel I'm leaving you behind." She looked up into his eyes, his pupils seemed large and dark, "Do you still love me, Simon, love me like you used to?"

He had married Jackie when he was just nineteen, life hadn't been easy. They had wanted a family, and when it hadn't happened they had bought the hotel. He thought that, with something else to focus on, a baby would just come along. Many tests later they had to accept it never would.

"Do I love you, what sort of question is that? I love you more than I can say, Jackie."

"But do you still want me, you know, want me… sexually I mean?"

His laugh was loud, too loud, but he followed it through with, "I still desire you if that's what you're asking? You still push all the right buttons, you must know that?"

"No, Simon, No I don't. I feel like I'm losing you."

He could feel her tears through his shirt, he felt like a mean fool, "Look Jackie, I think this big four O has you in a mid-life crisis." Trying to lighten the moment, he added, "Don't you start looking for someone else now, will you, trying to prove you're still attractive? Look at me, come on." When she raised her head her blue teary eyes shone with love, "You're my world, Jackie, surely you know that?"

His own guilt had him saying, "Is it Cathleen prancing around the place, do you think she's turned my head, is that it?" "I don't know, I think you can see she's lovely. I sense it…"

He held her at arm's length so she could see his face, his voice was stern as if speaking to a child, "You, stop that now. Yes, I'd have to be blind not to notice she's lovely, you must be able to see it. If you've noticed me watching her, it's because of Laurie. I've had my eyes on her, Jack, because…" Simon didn't want to tell tales, but he had to reassure his wife if it was the last thing he did, "Because she's been sleeping with Laurie, did you know?" Jackie shook her head, wiping her eyes with the back of her hand, "No, surely not." "Well, I saw him coming out of her room, he didn't see me, I was in the bathroom, but I heard." Simon was pleased Jackie seemed to brighten, "Silly girl. Silly, silly girl. Is that really why you've been watching her, Simon? Please don't lie to me." "Jackie, I can't help noticing she's a good looking young girl, young being the operative word here, but that's as far as it goes, promise. God, Jacks, her mum's your age. I'm old enough to be her father." "Yes Simon, so is Laurie but it hasn't stopped him, has it?"

Simon drew Jackie into him again, pleased she seemed reassured, "He obviously hasn't got as much to lose as me, now, has he?"

Jackie pulled away, so she could look him in the eyes, "I do love you, Simon, I don't know what I'd do if I lost…"

"No more, come on, it's your birthday Jackie. This is a good landmark, you know what they say, life begins and all that. Let's tell Cathleen she can man the bar, we're going up for an early night." "There's no one out there now, they've all gone up. Let her go off to bed too."

"No, what I have in mind might keep her awake."

He put his arm around her waist, kissed the top of her hair sprayed stiff wig, and told himself *'You've been a bloody fool, man. Pull yourself together.'*

*

Friday February 10th 1967

May couldn't settle. The house felt quiet, even though of late Prince had laid in his bed only moving if he had to. She filled a large bucket with boiling water and Dettol, and, pulling on her rubber gloves, she attacked the floor. She was still cleaning when Norman pushed open the back door, "I'm home, love." May didn't get up, she continued to scrub at the lino as if punishing it for what life had dealt her. She felt Norman's hand on her back, "Come on, love, come and sit down. I'll make you a cuppa."

"Oh Norm, I miss him already. I know it was difficult with his wetting, but he was ill." Tears fell into the bucket of disinfectant, "I've had a horrible day."

"Come on, May. This won't help, come and sit down and tell me all about it."

May sat in her chair trying to stem the tears. Norman handed her a cup of tea and sat opposite her "Tell me what the vet said, love, was there nothing they could do?"

May bristled, annoyance flashed in her eyes, "Of course there was nothing they could do or he would still be here, wouldn't he?" "Whoa, May, I'm only asking. Tell me all about it, come on."

Tears fell again, "I'm sorry, Norm, It's just...It was so awful. He had a tumour on his kidney. He said it was kinder to put him to sleep, I had no option. I held him while he slipped away. Oh Norm, it was like losing family. When I think what we've been through with that old dog..." "I know, May, I know. I could always get you another puppy, would you like that?"

May blew her nose, getting herself together, "No, Norm, we have a moving date. The solicitor phoned this morning saying we've exchanged contracts today, and we'll be moving next Friday. You'll have to sort it out with Perkins removals."

"Well, that's a bit of good news, eh? It'll be a new start for us, won't it?"

"I don't know, Norm, I'm feeling all confused. We had a letter from April Springs thanking us for the money we gave. I feel now that we should have given it all to them."

"Don't start that one. You were good to Rachel, we both were, and we loved her like our own. We took her in, gave her private education, an education we never even gave our own boys, so stop these silly thoughts now. A thousand pound is an enormous amount of money, and to be given to them by people they've never met. Pull yourself together, May, it's more than generous."

May wrung her hands in her lap, "I feel people are talking, you know, about the car, the new bungalow, I think they are making assumptions that Rachel came to us with money…" "Let them think what they like, we'll be gone from here next week, making a new start…"

May reached for her cup, "There's more on my mind, Norm. Tilly phoned today and said I won't have to rush over in the mornings anymore, as they've found a replacement for her at the school. I'm not needed to look after the boys now. I enjoyed it over there with her, Norm, it's like having our own boys back…"

Norman stopped May, "No, May, they're not our boys, but they're our grandchildren. When we move we'll do up the spare room, they'll be able to come and stay when they're older…" Excitement flickered in May's stomach, "Do you think Tilly will let us have them? I wanted to say this morning that I would still come over and help, but I didn't want to sound too pushy."

May watched as Norman ran his hand over his greased hair, "You women, you make life complicated. Why don't you just say what you feel? I'm sure Tilly would love the help. It isn't just the boys she has to contend with, Ed said Agnes has been having a few turns, it's all extra worry and work for the lass. I reckon if you'd asked, she would have welcomed the help."

"They're coming here for tea on Sunday, Norm, I'll ask Tilly then. I'll ask if I can still pop over and give a hand. Do you really think…?"

Norman stood up, "I don't know anything for sure, May, but it can't hurt offering, now, can it?"

May sat back, letting her shoulders relax into the chair. She closed her eyes, feeling better than she had felt all day. "Norman, can you take Prince's old bed to the allotment and burn it? It's no good to man or beast."

*

Sunday February 12th 1967

Ed and Tilly had taken their family over to May and Norman's for Sunday tea. Peter had started crying after his four o'clock feed, and May had nursed him for most of the afternoon. "We must make a move May, Rosie has school in the morning, and I need to settle the boys down for the night."

Ed put Peter, who was screaming in his carrycot, in the back of the van. Rosie and Angus scrambled onto the back seat giggling. "Come on, Tilly, the kids are in, what are you doing?" "Coming, just sorting out with your mum for next week."

Ed was in the driver's seat revving the engine when Tilly climbed in beside him, evenings were particularly difficult with the baby. Tilly said it was colic, but the constant crying drove him mad. "Did you give him some of that gripe stuff?"

"Yes, Ed, but he can't help it. Lots of babies suffer. It's not you who's out in the night, is it?"

Peter was good all day, but come his feed nearest to four o'clock he would start crying. "Your mum said she's going to come over next week and give a hand just the same. It's good of her, especially with the move and all."

Ed laughed, "I never thought I'd hear you say that about my mum."

"I know, Ed, but she's a good help. She's excellent with Angus, she takes him over the park for a good half hour and plays endlessly with him. When she's indoors she reads all sorts of stories to him..."

Ed squeezed Tilly's knee, "I can imagine, Tilly. She loved reading to us as kids, it's probably filling a void from losing Rachel, too."

Rosie sat forward, poking her head between the two front seats, "I agree with Tilly, Aunty May's much nicer now."

Ed turned his head to the child, "Is someone listening in on our conversation?"

Before Rosie could defend herself Tilly shouted, "Watch the road, Ed..."

He quickly corrected the steering, "Oops, there you go back on track. Peter obviously likes the rocky ride." Silence was bliss from the back, the motion of the van had sent him to sleep.

*

Lucy woke early, she knew Ken would have left for the market. She dressed in long trousers and a thick high necked jumper with two layers underneath. When Ken went to London she had to make her own way to the warehouse in Chichester. It was a long open road, and it was cold on the moped. Ken had said she could use the old bike from the shed. It had belonged to Harry, Ken's stepfather, and when he had died it had just got stored away, forgotten about.

It was at times like this when she had the house to herself that she would move from room to room, relishing the feeling she belonged somewhere. Ken had encouraged her to open up a savings account with the post office, and she had given this address as her permanent place of residence.

When she went downstairs, there on the table was the blue bowl Ken had bought her with a matching mug for Christmas. He had given her some Bromley lemon soap, and she had been so overwhelmed that she had kissed him. She had never kissed a boy before and she felt shy even though it was on the cheek.

When she had given him a pocket pen knife so he could open the boxes at work, he had kissed her, not on the cheek, but held her face between his hands and kissed her full on the lips, saying 'That's how it's done.' She knew she had blushed furiously, but she had liked it, so much so that when she lay in bed at night she replayed the moment over and over.

It was at times like this, while she was reminiscing, that she asked herself, *'Do I want more?'*

Lucy was looking forward to Saturday, May and Norman had moved to Selsey last Friday, and they were having a house warming this coming Saturday. Both Lucy and Ken were invited, and she was pleased at the prospect of seeing Tilly again. She hadn't seen her friend for a few weeks now. Since the children had arrived Tilly always seemed busy. No more foursomes to the cinema, or the local dances. Lucy knew, too, that Agnes hadn't been so well of late, Ed had said her medication was being changed, as her little turns she was prone to were becoming more frequent. This upset Lucy, she was fond of the old lady, while she had stayed with Ed Agnes had been very kind to her.

The phone rang, making her jump, "Hello?" she tingled at the sound of Ken's voice, "Lucy, there's been an accident on the Chichester road, it's still blocked. Come down Lagness road, but be careful the roads are full of sharp bends." "Okay, thanks for that, Ken. I'm just about to leave, if I can pedal that bike fast enough to make it kick start into action." She smiled as Ken's laughter tinkled down the line, "I'll see you shortly then, drive carefully."

Lucy pulled on her thick duffle coat, gloves and scarf, warmed by Ken's thoughtfulness and concern.

*

327

Sunday 26ᵗʰ February 1967

Pam sat at the dining table with her writing pad in front of her. She liked to write to Cathleen once a week, and Sunday had become her letter writing day. She twiddled with the pen, nothing seemed that important at the moment. The dramas on their road had quietened. Now May had moved she didn't really see anyone.

"Are you alright, Pam?" She looked up as Hal leant over her shoulder, "That looks a newsy letter." His laughter had Pam saying, "I don't know what to write, the scandal seems to have blown away…"

Hal took down an Encyclopaedia from the book case, "Tell her about our new neighbours, May's party, Tilly and the children. Come on, Pam, there's heaps to tell her. I am starting another job for the Covaxs', Hannah can…" "Okay, okay, I'll manage. Go on, get out of here. Leave me alone."

She could see him out of the corner of her eye settled in his chair reading.

Dear Cathleen

We have new neighbours now, a middle aged couple who have three children. He is a farm worker, and she seems to keep busy cleaning houses, privately. I'm tempted to get her in here. She lived in the town centre before they moved here, she caught sight of your photo on the mantelpiece and said she remembered you from working in Lesley's. So you might recognise her too?

We went to May and Norman's house warming on Saturday, the bungalow is beautiful. Everything is new including the building. Your dad was impressed, and we both felt quite envious.

Tilly was there with her family, she said you had sent her a card to congratulate them. She's going to write to you when she's got a minute spare. I think the baby is a handful. May is helping by the sounds of it, it's good to see their relationship so much improved.

328

Ken was there with Lucy. She seems a nice young lady, no one is sure what is going on between them but they seem happy and relaxed in each other's company. Ken certainly looks well, I know that will please you.

Agnes, has had several mini strokes. Tilly was saying they had upped her medication but with every little turn, she's becoming less able. This must add to Tilly's work load what with the little ones. Did you know she was the lollipop lady at the school? Well, she's had to give that up now she's a full time mum. It seems funny to say that, I can still see the pair of you running up the stairs giggling, scheming some plan or other.

Your father said to tell you he is starting a new job for the Covaxs', don't ask me why! – I think it is because I didn't feel I had any news worth reading. Everything seems pretty quiet here, and I should say, thank goodness. We miss you Cathleen, and would love a visit? I know you say you don't want to come back to Bognor but it would be lovely if you had a rethink on that front?

We all love you very much darling

Mum, Dad and Hannah XXX

Bournemouth

Wednesday February 29th 1967

Cathleen had heard from Laurence this morning, he was arriving in England on Friday, it would be Simon's birthday party. There would be a small gathering in the snug room taking place, and Jackie was organising a cake.

Laurence had been full of apologies for not keeping in touch, he hadn't been able to get to a phone in London, and by the time the meetings were over it was too late. Cathleen had wanted to ask where he had been for the last four weeks, but didn't want to spoil their reunion. It was a leap year, and she fantasised about asking him to marry her. She knew she was being foolish, but she couldn't help dreaming.

She knew from the beginning he was married, she had seen the gold band, Jackie had warned her, but Laurence, himself had made no secret of the fact. He was trapped, not just because of the three children, but the business he worked for was owned by his father-in-law.

Jackie appeared, making her jump, "Oh, someone looks happy."

This caused Cathleen to wave two letters at her, "Mum's written to me, and it looks like my old school friend has too. Can I get a coffee and have a read?"

"Go on, I'll man the desk for five minutes. You can bring me a cuppa through though."

Cathleen slipped off the stool and skipped off to the kitchen. "Coffee for me please, Simon, and one for Jackie."

She left him to it, and sat at the table in the café area. She read Pam's letter first, it was boring. The only bit that stood out for her was her mother's description of Lucy, nice young girl, who was still hanging round Ken. *'Why should I worry? I've got Laurie.'* It didn't matter how many times she told herself not to care, it kept niggling at her, like a fly.

When Simon came with her coffee she was lighting up her second cigarette, "Want one?"

He sat opposite her, "No, ta, I ought to get back to the kitchen. I've a heap of potatoes to peel. Unless you want to give me a hand?"

"Would love to, but I'm relieving Jackie from the reception, she might help?"

"Nah, no problems, Jacks will have cleaning to do. I just fancied a little bit of…"

Simon stopped speaking, Cathleen looked up to see Jackie approaching, "Come on, what's going on here then? I said a quick cup of coffee, not fraternise with my husband."

Cathleen stubbed out her cigarette, "Just coming, sorry Jackie. We were only talking, is…"

Simon had already scuttled back to the kitchen, Jackie laughed, "I'm only teasing you, darling, but I need to spend a penny, so can you take over again?"

Cathleen stubbed her cigarette in the ashtray, and went back to the desk at reception.

She still hadn't read Tilly's letter, her lunch break was brief, and the phone hadn't stopped ringing. Cathleen had a pile of filing to do, but with the distractions from people coming and going it lay untouched. She wished she could have helped in the kitchen; at least that had a finish time.

When Jackie popped her head round the door, saying, "We've finished dinners, how are you doing?" Cathleen showed her the bookings. "We've only just had the end of month dance, and already it's sold out for March. Easter's fully booked too." "That's all good, it keeps us in business, now come on through to the bar, Simon has poured you a port and lemon." "Jackie, I'll take it up to my room if you don't mind. I fancy a bath and some time on my own."

"Are you alright, nothings bothering you is it?"

Cathleen smiled, "No, Jackie, I'm just feeling tired. I've a letter from my mum I'd like to read again, and one from my friend I still haven't read yet. I just feel like reading them in private, you understand?"

"Of course I do, you go on up and I'll bring your drink up to you."

Cathleen closed down the reception, "No, that's not necessary. I'll come through with you, I'll have a quick ciggie, and then I'll go on up. I've also got that book to read that you gave me."

It was eight thirty before Cathleen opened the letter from Tilly. The front of the card was a picture of Wittering beach. Memories flooded as she recognised the sandy dunes. She didn't know why, but the sight of her friend's hand writing made her eyes water, blurring the letters in front of her.

Dear Cathleen

Thank you for the card you sent, it was good to hear from you. I know you left under a cloud, and I've felt for quite a while I hadn't been as fair to you as I should have been. I suppose what I'm trying to say is, you were brave to end your relationship with Ken, I can see that now. I think when all that business with you thinking you were pregnant blew up, I was just plain old jealous. I'm ashamed of myself for that now. It was easy to be angry with you, and blame you for hurting Ken, but I suppose, as you said, you wouldn't have looked at Michael if you had really loved Ken. I was so wrapped up in my own insecurities that it was easy to punish you by excluding you. So when I say I'm sorry, Cathleen, I really am, and I hope you can forgive me.

Well, with that out of the way let me tell you my news. Did you like the card? I chose it to remind you of our happy times spent on the beach. Do you remember, Cathleen, when Ed used to drive us to Wittering on a Sunday? Even then you used to lead poor old Ken a right old dance. Those days are long gone, I'm a full time mum now. Peter is the baby, he's just over three months, Angus is three, four in August, and Rosie, can you believe it? She'll be seven in July. She wants to go home to her mum. Ed is taking her to some fair in the Lake District. They all gather there in June. By all accounts the gypsies have some kind of group meeting, and Ed's going to combine the visit by looking up the woman who nursed him back to health when I was away in Canada. I am dreading Rosie leaving, but having the boys will help, I hope. I know in my heart it's the right thing for her, it was always only a temporary arrangement, but I feel she's my girl now, and I love her dearly. Having a baby is hard work, Cathleen, very hard work. He cries more than he smiles, which wouldn't be so bad, but my gran isn't as well these days. Our doctor has upped her medication and she now has to take two little pink pills as well as the blue, but it isn't just that, she needs help with dressing and undressing. I don't know if you can remember the layout of our new house, but just walking through to ours has gran panting for breath. I worry sometimes what I would do if anything happened to her, she has been like a mother to me. Now for Angus, he's a pickle. Full of energy, but would be easy if it was just him but when Rosie goes off to school I'm left with a screaming baby and a lively toddler. I didn't ever think I would say it, but thank goodness for Ed's mum, she's brilliant. She comes over most days and helps. Now I've given up my lollipop job at the school I take the pram and meet Rosie half way with the boys. May sits with Gran, and when I'm trying to do a hundred and one jobs, alongside looking after Peter, she helps amuse Angus. A godsend, Cathleen, I no longer call her an old battle axe! Do you remember the names we used to call her? On a sad note, you must have heard about poor Rachel, and the accident. It was terrible, Cathleen, but May held up well over that, and I think our boys have helped ease her pain. It was shocking for Michael too, to lose Christine just when the plans were all going ahead for the engagement. It was horrible, tragic, if I close my eyes I can still feel the horror of it all. I still take Rosie to the stables, but I don't stay myself and ride anymore, (no time) but I hear Michael isn't faring so well. He is drinking, Cathleen. I think there had been a row, things must have got pretty heated because she stormed off, and by all accounts she was driving like a maniac. It obviously wasn't all Michael's fault, but it's sad how we see things in grief. I actually feel sorry for him, he isn't the self-assured philanderer he always was.

I have so much to tell you, Cathleen, but I don't want to bore you. It feels good to be in touch. Thank you for breaking the ice. I don't hate you for what happened between you and Ken, I can see now you were right. Ken is happier than I have ever known him. There is an air of relaxed, contentment around him, if that makes sense.

I was speaking to your mum at May and Norman's housewarming, I expect she told you they've moved? It's really lovely too. All brand new. Anyway your mum says you were not planning to return to Bognor as you thought you were not missed. I miss you, Cathleen, it just took me a while to realise it. I'll sign off now and look forward to hearing your news. Look after yourself, and I say again I hope you find a reason to return someday.

Your old pal, Tilly X

Cathleen wiped the tears from her eyes. She had read the letter three times now, and each time it brought tears to her eyes. She wasn't sure if it was relief at having her long lost best friend back, or the sad news on Michael. She reminded herself how horrid he had been, and the shoddy way he treated her. She let her thoughts wander to Laurence. His love making is much more pleasurable, he's experienced, gentle and mature. She thought of the things Laurence had urged her to do to him, just thinking about it made her blush. She lost herself, recalling the moment, she could almost feel his hands on her. When she thought of Michael again, she couldn't help smiling. *'He was so funny, Blackpool had been hilarious until...'* as always the mention of that weekend brought back, how beastly he had been, and she knew he wasn't the lover Laurence was.

She read the letter again, finding her eyes falling to the last few paragraphs, Ken is so happy, content, relaxed, *'What is that supposed to mean?'*

Cathleen drifted off to sleep, holding the letter, her hair still damp, wrapped in a towel, while she dreamt of Wittering beach with Ken running beside her.

*

March 9th 1967

Jackie had been up early, she had ordered a sponge cake, cut and decorated in the shape of a champagne bottle.

Dinners had been served, and it was now eight thirty. The cake sat in pride of place in the middle of the table, surrounded by bowls of crisps, peanuts and finger rolls. A few of the guests had started to congregate in the snug room, attracted by the nibbles, unaware of the birthday.

"This looks nice, Jackie. Is there anything I can do?" Cathleen made an effort to smile, but Jackie knew her mood was low,

Laurence hadn't shown yet, and had been due to check in this afternoon.

"Come on girl, smile. We're having a party."

Jackie so wanted to dislike her for turning her husband's head, but knew it wasn't the girl's fault for being so young and lovely. "I'm okay. What time will Simon be back?"

"Anytime now, he'll love this, he loves surprises." Jackie slapped playfully at Cathleen's hand, "Stop fiddling with that holder, either light the ciggie or put it down."

"Laurence hasn't checked in yet, was his flight delayed, do you know?"

"I haven't heard, but plans change. I'm sure he'll turn up if he can." Jackie hesitated, "Cathleen… remember he's married… with children." Cathleen seemed to ignore her concerns, choosing that moment to light her cigarette. Her cheeks took on high colour, "How can I forget? He's unhappy, Jackie, he tells me he would like to leave…"

Jackie wasn't so sure about this, but didn't want to hurt the girl, nor spoil the celebrations so let the subject drop. "Okay, okay, I just don't want to see you get hurt."

Any further discussion was stopped when Simon appeared, the room became animated with the song, 'Happy Birthday to you'. Jackie kissed him on the lips, "We've been waiting for you. Come on, have a drink." The sound of the champagne cork popping caused a cheer. Jackie started filling the glasses, her eyes followed Cathleen, who moved over to Simon and took hold of his arms. She stood on tiptoe, and kissed him. She wasn't close enough to hear what was said, but the soft look that flickered in her husband's eyes caused her hands to shake with jealousy, and the champagne to spill on the tray.

It didn't matter what Jackie wore, or how she styled her wig, she felt fat, frumpy and old. Her mind did cartwheels, *'Perhaps keeping that young girl on after Christmas hadn't been such a good idea.'*

No sooner had the thought left her mind she watched as Cathleen squealed, running across the room. Laurie stood, case in hand, looking exhausted. Cathleen threw herself at him, and he had the good grace to catch her. It did look to Jackie as if he was as pleased to see her, as she was to see him. *'Perhaps the girl is right, he's unhappy and trapped at home?'*

Her eyes shot across to her husband, who was also watching this show of affection, the sick feeling returned, there on his face as clear as day, was pain, agony and jealousy. Jackie caught Simon's eye, and he had the decency to look sheepish. The smile he gave didn't reach his eyes. Jackie knew this infatuation with Cathleen was serious. *'Thank goodness for small mercies, she's set her sights at someone else's husband.'*

*

Cathleen was delighted, Laurie was staying until the end of March. Confiding in Jackie had helped their relationship too. They didn't have to creep around like criminals in the night anymore. Jackie seemed to be encouraging the relationship, giving Cathleen free time when Laurie appeared after business, late afternoons.

Simon was not as amenable, and some of the looks he gave made Cathleen feel uncomfortable. When she mentioned this to Jackie she had laughed it off saying, "He's acting like a father, darling. He thinks of you as his little girl."

Laurence's stay flew, three weeks had never gone as fast for Cathleen. They had been to see two films, walked along the beach of an evening with a late night feast, and made love in the moonlight hidden by the cliffs. Time was of the essence.

It was eight o'clock, Cathleen stacked up the leaflets on the desk, put the closed sign on reception and locked the main door. Tonight was Laurence's last evening, tomorrow he would leave for America. Just thinking about this made Cathleen tearful.

"Here you are, I should have guessed." Showing no shame, she draped her arms round his neck, kissing him on the cheek, "I'm up for an early night." There were titters at the bar about young love, and what did Laurie have that they didn't, and amongst all this jollity the two of them left for Cathleen's room, giggling like two silly children.

When she lay in his arms satiated, she told him she loved him, "I love you too, Cathleen, I've never loved anyone like this, you do know that, don't you?"

"Marry me, Laurie?" He laughed lightening the moment, "Ladies don't ask men, Cathleen.

"It's a leap year, and anyway I can do anything I want. Please say you will, if not now, later? "

"Oh, I wish I could, Cathleen, I wish I could."

"You can, you can leave your wife. You could get a job here, or I'll come to you. There is nothing to keep me in England, please say you will."

"Cathleen, I can't marry you, we've been through all this. I've always been honest with you, right from at the start. Don't spoil our fun, not on my last night."

Cathleen was stung, "Fun, is that what you think this is?" she managed to keep the edge out of her voice and asked questioningly,

337

"I'm not your plaything, Laurie. I love you. You said you loved me…"

Laurie reached over, cradling her naked body to his, "Hey, where's all this come from? Slow down, don't get too heavy, Cathleen, when I said fun, I didn't mean it like that. Come on…" He started kissing her bare shoulder, tracing his tongue down her neck, making his way down her body, Cathleen weakened as desire took over, she loved Laurie's love-making as much as she loved him. It was exciting and fulfilling.

Laurence left early on the Sunday, it was April fool's day, and Cathleen knew she had made a complete fool of herself. She had sobbed in her room, begging him not to go. When he had pulled free of her clutches she had dropped to her knees, holding onto his ankles, begging him to stay. He reassured her over and over, telling her, "I'll phone you, Cathleen, I promise."

When she protested, clinging on to him, begging that he take her with him, he had pulled himself free, "Come on, this is silly. You knew I'd have to go home. I'll be back at the end of the month. It'll go before…" her voice, desperate, had stopped him, "No, Laurie, you said you would phone last time, not once did you phone…"

Laurie had taken her in his arms, pushed her wet hair out of her eyes and away from her cheeks, and told her, "I love you, Cathleen, it's different this time, I promise. I'll phone you even if I have to walk to a phone box at midnight." He took out a card, "Here, this is my telephone number at the office, you can phone me. Make sure you don't phone me before Simon opens the bar of an evening, if you wait till then you can be sure I'll be at the office. If I'm not, say you're checking on my next booking, and I'll phone you back." Cathleen's tears had stopped as she scanned the piece of paper with numbers scrawled on it. He had seen his chance, and grabbed his jacket off the chair, "Now come on, let's go downstairs, and I want

338

you to wave me off smiling, so I can take that image of you with me, please?"

She had tried, but tears fell as his taxi disappeared.

Cathleen spent the morning cleaning, which was just as well, she couldn't face the guests with blood-shot eyes. She managed to serve the afternoon teas, but while she was helping Simon prepare dinner he took her in his arms, kissed the top of her head, and said, "He's not worth it, Cathleen, you deserve better. Despite her annoyance at his negativity, this show of kindness caused her to cry all over again.

*

Laurence Jackson replaced the receiver back on the telephone, Cathleen had phoned every day this week. He had the weekend ahead of him, this double life was making him uneasy. He had never played away from home before, but Cathleen had caught his eye, got under his skin. When he told her he loved her he believed he did. When he questioned if he could leave his family he knew he couldn't. He put his head in his hands, *'I wish I'd never set eyes on the kid. What's wrong with me, is this what people are talking about when they say they're having a mid-life crisis?'*

He looked up as one of the girls from the typing pool came through, "See you on Monday, Laurie. Have a great weekend." He watched as she left, knowing he should be shutting his own office up. Going home was difficult for him these days. Twice this week he had eaten out, pleased, when he had pulled into his drive to find his house in darkness, knowing he wouldn't have to make small talk. *'She must know something's wrong, surely?'*

How long he had sat staring at the work on his desk he didn't know, there was no one in the office now, but his mind was made up. He would end it with Cathleen. How? He didn't know yet, but he had no choice. He wanted to confess to rid himself of this guilt, but

339

would his life be worth living. *'No, I need to carry this one to my grave, the hard thing is going to be letting Cathleen go.'* Laurence wasn't one to be emotional, but he sat at his desk and gave way to the pain of letting go. *'You've been a bloody fool, Laurence Jackson, a bloody fool.'*

He put the key in the door of his home, two boys flew down the hall "Daddy's home, daddy's home." He caught them, and carried them through to the lounge, one under each arm and threw them on the sofa, leaving them giggling. His wife, Diana, came in, she kissed him "I let them stay up to see you. Alyson's in bed, she got too tired."

Guilt pulled his heart, he took Diana in his arms, "We'll go on a picnic tomorrow, we'll go to the lakes. I've neglected you of late, love. Things are going to be different from now on, I promise. For a start, I'm giving Bob the England contract, I've done with all this travelling."

"Really, why? Bob's up for retirement next year, will he want it?"

"He'll want it, he loves England. It had riled him when he got stood down. With hindsight he's the better man for the job, I'm not coping with it. Bob's an old hand, he'll enjoy the cut and thrust of it all. I've had enough. I want to spend more time here with you, with you and the kids."

The kiss she gave him held promise for the evening ahead, and he knew he had made the right decision. He offered to put the boys to bed, but she insisted he sit and eat his supper. He could hear the tales of Pickles the Pig and Lazy Lou, drifting down the stairs. He knew the story off by heart.

'I'll write to her, I'll write and explain.' His stomach lurched, taking his appetite, *'What did I get caught up in this for?'* The more he questioned himself the clearer it became, *'She's a beauty, I can't deny that, but it was Simon, yes, it was all Simon's fault. He fancied her, I could tell. He made me*

feel old, married, and tied down. When I joked about her in the bar that first night, I could see he liked her too. I wanted to rub his nose in the fact that he, with his bohemian looks and play boy image, might be a bit freer than me, but I still had the pulling power. Jesus, man, you must have needed your lumps felt." He stood up, leaving his supper half eaten, and poured himself a large Scotch, chastising himself for the task ahead, brought about by his own vanity, *'You stupid bastard, Laurence Jackson, you stupid, stupid, bastard.'* He downed his drink in one, and as he poured himself another Diana appeared, and his mind was made up, *'Monday I'll write. I won't take her calls, but I'll write, and hope she understands.'*

*

April 23rd 1967

Jackie wiped the tops down, put the last of the breakfast things in the dishwasher and put the kettle on the stove, "Once I've made these coffees I want you to relieve Cathleen from the reception, Simon. I need to talk to her." Simon raised his eyebrows, "What's up, what's she done?"

"Nothing, silly, I'm worried about her, that's all." Simon laid a tray up with cups and saucers, saying, "It's all this business with Laurie. She'll get over it, give her time, Jacks, you'll see."

"I still want to talk to her, she's a long way from home. I can't help but worry about her. She's pale, there's dark shadows under her eyes, and what's more, she's lost her sparkle."

Jackie was sitting in the snug room when Cathleen came through, the surprise could be heard in her voice, "Is everything okay?" Jackie patted the cushion beside her, "Come on, darling, I feel you need an ear?"

Cathleen sat opposite Jackie, who could see her eyes were already welling up. Cathleen was unaware of Jackie's own guilt at encouraging her to fraternise with Laurie. She had hoped it would turn her husband off the girl if he saw her throwing herself at a married man. "Have a coffee, darling, and tell me what's eating at you", when Cathleen sat quiet, looking at her knees, she added, "Come now, I can guess."

She watched as Cathleen flicked open her cigarette box. Her hands shook as she lit her cigarette. Taking a deep drag she exhaled, the words spilled out with the smoke, "He's finished with me." Cathleen put her cigarette in the ashtray and covered her face in her hands, "I hate myself. I wish I was dead. I've been a fool... again."

Jackie moved over beside her, she held her tight as she sobbed into her arms, "Don't ever wish you're dead, girl, you've got so much to live for, this is just one of life's learning curves, and you're no fool, Cathleen. You placed your affections in a bad place, but no, you're not a fool." She very gently pushed Cathleen's hair back off her face, "Come on, spit it out. Tell me all. A problem shared." When silence filled the room, Jackie urged her again repeating her words of encouragement, "Come on, girl, remember, we've been here before, you told me all about your fiancé." She stroked her arm, trying to encourage her to confide, "It had helped back then, hadn't it?" She was pleased to see the girl give a half smile. "There's a girl, blow your nose and tell me all." Jackie held out a handkerchief.

"He wrote to me, Jackie. He told me he couldn't leave his wife and family. He said he wished he could be in two places at the same time because he loved us both." Cathleen sniffed, blew her nose and finished, saying, "He said if it wasn't for the children it would have been a harder decision, but basically she's won."

"She hasn't won anything, Cathleen. She didn't know there was a contest, and you need to thank god for that, my darling. What I'm going to say to you now, Cathleen, isn't going to sit well, but Laurie has chosen his life back there, over you. You have to let him go. You're young, lovely and you've got a life ahead of you, you'll bounce back, you'll see."

342

When the sobbing subsided she held Cathleen at arm's length, trying to get eye contact, "Come on now, go on up to your room and wash your face. Take a while to get yourself together, and when you feel up to it come down. You've got to try and move on, go on, there's a girl…"

"Jackie?" Cathleen was hesitant, "I feel I want to go home. I know I said I never would, but I really do want to go. I want to see my mum, and old friends. I'm sorry if…"

"No, stop it. Easter's dealt with, we've got a few weeks before the summer. You go home, darling, take a couple of weeks."

*

The Rainbow

Chapter Twelve

Cathleen stuck down the envelope, it was a card for Tilly. She would be twenty one on Saturday. *'Twenty one, I wish we were fourteen again, running between each other's houses. Life seemed a lot simpler back then.'*

Cathleen lay back on the bed, *'I should go and post this if I want it to get there for Saturday, but I'm so tired these days, Laurie has knocked the stuffing out of me.'*

She had let her eyes close for a quick five minute doze, when she woke to a tapping, a voice came through her door, "Cathleen, I need you downstairs to man the reception, we're about to serve dinner."

Cathleen leapt to her feet, she looked at her watch it was ten to six. *'Blimey where's the time gone?'* She knew she had missed the post, and would have to pop it down there this evening when they had cleared up. She flopped back down on the bed, she had got up too quick and the room had started to swim. *'I feel bloody awful.'* She went to her washbasin and splashed cold water on her face, before she could reach for a towel she was sick, *'Oh god, I've got a bug, that's what's wrong with me.'*

The tapping on the door again made Cathleen jump, "I'm coming Jackie, I'm not feeling too clever." She opened the door so Jackie could come in, "I've been sick, it might have been something I've eaten or…" "I hope not, darling, or the whole place'll be down with it. Are you going to be able to work? We'll manage if you're not up to it?"

Cathleen put on a brave face, "No, I'll be alright sitting at the desk answering the phone, that's if you can manage the dinners?" The thought of smelling the food made her feel sick again.

344

"Good girl, come on then, let's get down there, Simon will be pulling his hair out."

It dawned on Cathleen that she hadn't served dinners with Simon for ages. *Perhaps my behaviour with Laurie sickened him, and he doesn't want me around?'* She didn't care, she preferred working in the reception area.

*

Saturday 5th May – Tilly's Twenty First Birthday

Tilly's birthday was to be a small affair. A close family tea which was to include Lucy and Ken. Her mother had phoned from Canada last night and she had spoken with her father and step brother Kevin. The postman had delivered a parcel three days ago which had strict instructions not to open it until today. There were a few cards that had come early, Tilly recognised Pam's handwriting and one from the Lake District which she guessed was from Brenda and Alf…

She could hear Ed in the hall downstairs, "No, Rosie, hold Angus' hand. You carry that, there's a good girl… No, I've got Petey." Tilly had hated the way Peter had become Petey, but the nickname had stuck with them all now, even May used it.

The bedroom door was pushed open, and there stood her little family. Ed had tea in one hand and the baby under his arm in what looked like a most uncomfortable position, "Petey, come to mummy. Oh, Ed, give him here, you'll drop him carrying him like that." Rosie leapt up on the bed, "I told him to give him to me, Tilly, but he wouldn't."

Ed tweaked her ear in play, "Tell-tale!" The laughter rang round the room, even Angus giggled, but couldn't have understood why.

Tilly had chocolates and talcum powder from the boys. Rosie had made her a pot from clay and painted it, which Tilly had said she would treasure always, and Ed said her present was downstairs. "It better not be a dog, cat or anything that needs any of my time..." "Tilly, come and see."

Tilly left the tea untouched on the bedside table and made her way downstairs carrying Peter. Ed came up behind her and put his hands over her eyes, "Steady on, no peeking. Open the door, Rosie." Tilly was guided over the step, "Careful, Ed, I've got the baby." Ed took his hands away so she could see again. There outside the house was a little black morris minor. "For me?" Ed laughed, "Well, it's not my birthday, is it?"

"Oh Ed, that's perfect, thank you, thank you."

She gave the baby to Ed while she opened the car door. "It's wonderful, I must tell gran. Oh, I want to drive it."

"Plenty of time, Tilly, let's go inside and have breakfast and sort getting your gran up. She knows all about it, and has been dying to see what you make of it." "What I make of it, I'm absolutely delighted. I could scream from the roof tops." She picked Angus up and propped him on her hip, kissing his cheek. She held out her hand to Rosie, then moved closer to Ed, who draped his free arm round Tilly's shoulders. "I've never been so happy in my whole life, do you know that, Ed? Ever."

Once indoors Tilly took the children into Agnes, "Gran, I've got a car. It's a little morris minor. When you're up to it I'll take you for a spin, I'll take you to see May and Norman's new bungalow. You'd like that, wouldn't you?" Agnes smiled, it was a weak smile that didn't reach her eyes, "I would, love, I would. Perhaps you could help me to the door so I can have a peek."

Tilly lay Petey on the middle of the bed, and helped Agnes to her feet, "Hold my arm, gran, Rosie, open the curtains, gran will be able to see from here." Agnes flopped back in her chair, "Lovely, Tilly, it's really lovely. You'll be able to get about now. Happy Birthday, love. There's something for you in that little box on my dresser."

Rosie ran over and picked up a box that had been decorated in shells, "This one, granny A?" Agnes seemed to fight for breath to answer, "Yes, that one, give it to Tilly, there's a good girl."

Tilly opened the box, and there nestled on cotton wool were two rings, Tilly picked up Agnes' bare hand "Gran, it's your wedding and engagement rings, you can't give me these."

"Oh yes I can. I want you to have them. Where I'm going I won't be needing them." Tilly put her arm round Agnes's shoulders, "I love them, gran, but please don't talk like that. Mum'll be coming home in the summer, you'll like to see her, won't you?" "Hush now, let's wait and see. I'm getting tired, Tilly. I wanted you to have my rings, love, that's all. Happy Birthday."

Tilly slipped them on her right hand together. They were too big for her finger, "I love them, gran. I'll treasure them always."

She watched as Agnes pulled Angus on to her knee. She could see the effort of lifting the child exhausted her. "Come on you lot, let's leave gran to get her breath." As she kissed Agnes on the cheek she said, "We're having a little tea party later. May and Norman will be here and Lucy and Ken, do you think you'll make it through with us?" Agnes held her chest as if it would help her breathe, "No, I'll stay in here if you don't mind. Pop me in a bit of cake. Perhaps May will come round for a bit? I'd like that."

"I can prop your door open if you like, so you don't feel so isolated." "No, love, you go and enjoy yourself next door. I'll be fine. I'll be watching my programmes."

Tilly knew this was a brush-off, it was obvious that Agnes' health was deteriorating, and the medication wasn't helping.

The tea party went well, Agnes managed to come through for the cutting of the cake, which made Tilly's evening. May went back in with Agnes for half an hour, but came back through at seven to help bath the boys with Tilly. It was at this time that the phone rang, Ed and Ken were outside with Norman, showing off Tilly's car, and Lucy was clearing the kitchen with Rosie. Tilly shouted down the stairs, "Can someone get the telephone?"

Lucy ran to the hall, bubbles still on her hands from the washing up, "Hello?" The voice on the other end seemed hesitant, "Is that Tilly?"

"No, sorry, it's Lucy. Tilly's just bathing the boys. I'll give her a shout, who is calling?"

"No, problem, I'll call again later."

Tilly appeared at that moment with Peter over her shoulder wrapped in a white towel, "Who was it?"

Lucy replaced the receiver, "I don't know, she hung up on me, saying she would phone later." "Oh well, couldn't have been important. Here, can you finish Petey off for me? His sleep wear is on the chair. I'll go and help May wash Angus' hair. He hates it."

With the children bathed and put to bed Tilly stood at the door and waved May and Norman off. Everything was cleared from the tea party, and Agnes was settled too. "Thanks for your help, May, and I love the necklace, thank you." She fingered the little silver cross they had given her, she had never really believed in God, but she found comfort from wearing this little symbol on her neck.

The phone rang again, "I'll get it, it's probably for me." Tilly picked up the phone, "Hello, Chichester 86156."

"Happy Birthday, Tilly, it's me, Cathleen. I'm so sorry about your card I..." Tilly interrupted "Don't be daft, it's good of you to call."

"No, Tilly, let me explain. I had it all here waiting, but I've not been too well, and I fell asleep. When I woke it was too late for the post.

You'll get one, promise." Tilly laughed down the receiver, "You are funny, Cathleen, that's fine, it's just good to hear from you."

"Have you had a good day, what did you get?"

Tilly couldn't wait to tell her old friend, "I got a car, Cathleen. You never know, I just might bring the boys down to see you in the summer. Gran gave me her wedding and engagement rings, which I've hung round my neck on a little silver cross and chain that May and Norman gave me. Lucy and Ken gave me a really pretty cake plate with a cake slice, she is funny; she taped sixpence on the handle to ward off bad luck at giving knives as gifts. From Mum and Dad I had clothes and a bracelet. There's three letters hanging off it, A, P, and R for my children's names…" Tilly stopped at the silence on the other end of the line, "Are you still there, Cathleen?" "Yes, yes, I'm just listening. You did really well…" "Oh but there's more, I had lots of cards and smellies. I'm so happy Cathleen, and you phoning has been the icing on the cake."

"I've got to go, Tilly, but have a lovely end of your day. You should get my bits on Monday, no, Tuesday, because of the May Bank Holiday." Cathleen finished her call with her own good news, "I'm coming back for a while, Tilly. I'm just sorting it out here. I'll see you soon. I've got to go now, its lovely to hear your voice. I'm feeling a long way from home these days. I'll write soon."

Ed looked up from the Monopoly board he had laid out ready for play. Lucy and Ken were fighting over the counters. "I want the hat."

Tilly said, "That was Cathleen, she sounds unhappy." Her comment seemed to fall on deaf ears as the arguing continued, "No, I'm the hat." Ken made a snatch at it, "No, I am." Laughter filled the room and Cathleen was forgotten.

*

349

Cathleen replaced the receiver, *'Lucy and Ken gave me.'* The sickening feeling in her stomach returned. *'Why do I care? I had my chance, I let him go. Why shouldn't he be happy with someone else?'*

Cathleen thought about Laurie, she had loved him with all her heart, she knew she had. She then questioned herself, *'Or was it because I knew in my heart I couldn't have him?'* She thought about her mother's early letters, and how niggled she was to hear that Ken was seeing this girl from the stables. She tried to remember what she looked like, *'She was a skinny, boy like creature. Surely Ken wouldn't fancy someone like that, she was just a kid, if I remember rightly.'* So much had happened she couldn't get a clear picture in her mind, and it bothered her more than she wanted to admit.

"Darling, there you are, Simon's serving drinks in the bar and there's quite a gathering in the snug room. Are you coming through?" Cathleen noticed the concern flick across her face as she said, "Not tonight, Jackie, I'm absolutely shattered. I don't know what's wrong with me these days. I might do as you say and go to the doctors on Tuesday if I don't pick up a bit."

Tears sprang to Cathleen's eyes as Jackie leant over and held her hand, "You do that, darling, that's a good idea. You haven't looked well for a while now. He might give you a tonic. You aren't still holding a torch for Laurie, are you?"

Cathleen wiped her eyes with a tissue, she hated these tears. She couldn't understand what was wrong with her, these days she cried at the silliest things. "I loved Laurie, Jackie. I won't get over him like I would a cold. It's time that's needed, but I'll get there. Don't worry about me, you go on through to the snug." She knew this was their best time of the day, she used to enjoy it herself, that was until this wretched tiredness had come to impact on her wellbeing.

*

May Day – Monday 7th May.

Tilly had had a bad night with Angus, he had been sick, and the bath was now filled with bedding that needed washing. She gave Ed a nudge beside her, "Ed, Ed, can you get a cuppa, I've been in and out of bed with Angus all night, he's got a tummy bug." Ed groaned, "What time is it?"

"It's cup of tea time! Go on, Ed, Petey will be awake soon. I just want a minute to myself." She was relieved to feel him swing his legs out, "Tea or coffee?" Tea, please, and can you take one into gran?"

She could hear the cups rattling and the kettle whistling as he moved about downstairs. She wanted to use the toilet, but didn't want Ed to hear her out of bed after she made such a thing about wanting to lay in.

Ed's hurried footsteps on the stairs told her something was wrong. She was already out of bed when he came in the room. His face was as white as a sheet, "Ed, what's up, what's happened?"

"It's your gran, Tilly." He reached out for her, "Tilly I think she's gone."

"Gone! Gone where?" Tilly was half way down the stairs, her dressing gown hanging loose at the sides, when it dawned on her. She realised what he had really meant. She tripped on the last step in her hurry. Ed was at her side when she entered her gran's room. Agnes was lying on her back as if fast asleep. Tilly fell to her knees by the side of Agnes' bed, "Gran, Gran." She shook her shoulder, the coldness told her what she already knew. "No gran, no. Oh gran, please…" Ed's hand on her shoulder made the situation feel more final, "Ed phone an ambulance, quick…" Ed lifted her up off the floor, "It's no use, Tilly…"

"Ed, she can't be, please…" Ed took her in his arms. "Come on Tilly we have to go back to our side. We've got to phone the doctor, but you know there's nothing anyone can do."

351

Tilly was guided back to their side of the house. She could hear Ed was still on the phone to the undertaker when the children woke. She opened the kitchen door, "Rosie, don't go into gran, in here please."

Angus sat at the table with two farm animals, he walked them along the table mat. She lowered her voice and told Rosie that Gran had gone to heaven with Rachel, she wasn't prepared for her answer. "I knew granny A wouldn't make the journey to say good bye to me. I felt it." Goose-pimples spread up Tilly's arms, she didn't know what to say, and was thankful for the distraction of Angus, who had got bored with the animals and wanted to eat breakfast despite his earlier sickness. "You can have a bit of dry toast." "I want Rice Crispies." "No, not today, no milk for you. It'll upset your poorly tummy." Angus started to create, "Angus…" Tilly was pleased to see Ed come into the kitchen, she passed the bread packet over to him, "Sort out some toast, I'm in no mood for tantrums today." She left them all in the kitchen while she went upstairs to make the beds, and get herself washed and dressed.

The Doctor arrived late morning and certified the death. What with it being a Bank holiday there was no one to collect the body. Ed shut Agnes' door, but the old lady's body lying lifeless had caused a dark cloud to settle over the house.

Tilly was grateful for the hustle and bustle of her children, they kept her mind on other things. She washed the sheets that had been soiled and left in the bath. She set to, disinfecting the toilets and rooms, keeping herself busy.

Ed had phoned his parents earlier, and at tea time they had both arrived, May had made cheese scones and a jam sponge. "Can I go and say goodbye to Agnes, Tilly. Would you mind?"

Tilly could see by May's eyes she had shed a few tears.

Once tea had been cleared, May offered to take the children home for her.

"That's really good of you, May, but will you manage them?"

May lifted Angus up on to her hip, "Can I manage them?" She tickled Angus, who seemed to have recovered from his bug, "I had two of you to manage at the same time, and both at the same age. Of course I'll manage, Tilly. Rosie will help me, won't you?" Rosie shook her head in agreement,

Tilly guessed she was appearing over-anxious, "I know, May, sorry. I'm not thinking properly, that's all."

"All the more reason for me to help out then, go on, Rosie, go upstairs and pack a few bits for the boys and yourself, there's a good girl."

"No, May, I'll go up and sort out the clothes, you won't want what Rosie thinks is suitable dress!"

May put Angus down, and took Peter off Tilly, "Go on then, you go up with her."

Tilly brushed the downy hair on Peter's head, "I'll keep Petey here with me, May. I'll go mad with nothing to do."

"As you like, Tilly, but they'll be plenty to do. Would you like me to come over in the morning?"

"No, May. Ed's taking tomorrow off, we'll sort out the necessary arrangements together."

"Does your mother know?" Tilly knew there was no love lost between her mother and May, and was surprised at May's mention of her, "Yes, May, Ed phoned her. She's coming home, my dad's getting her the next available flight."

"Good, good. You'll need your mum."

The subject was dropped, and no more was mentioned of her family. Tilly joined Rosie upstairs and busied herself filling a small bag with necessities for the children's stay.

When she closed the door after waving them off, she gave way to the tears. The tears that had been threatening to fall all day.

*

Cathleen woke again feeling sick. *'Urgh, thank god I'm not working in the kitchen.'* The moment she put her feet to the floor she ran to her basin in her room and retched. *'I don't need a doctor to tell me what my problem is.'*

At seven thirty she was sat at the desk, the heavy foundation didn't hide the dark shadows under her eyes. The smell of bacon drifted into the reception area making her feel queasy. She found sipping tepid water helped.

At eleven o'clock Jackie called out, "Coffee time, are you coming through?" As Cathleen made her way to the table, Jackie smiled, "You're looking a bit better. I said time's a healer."

'Looking better, I feel bloody awful.' But she said instead, "If you don't mind I'm going on upstairs, I've a couple of letters…" She didn't get to finish, "Oh come on, sit with me, Simon's made the coffee and gone into town. I could do with the company."

Cathleen didn't want to upset her, so plonked herself at the table, sitting opposite her. There on the table was a tray waiting with toast and marmalade. Cathleen couldn't face breakfast, nor coffee. Jackie poured herself one, "You having tea?"

"Not for me, I'll just keep you company." When Jackie leant back in her chair puffing out the smoke from her cigarette, Cathleen had the real urge for a fizzy drink. She could almost feel the bubbles just thinking about it, "Can I get a Coca Cola?"

"Of course, help yourself."

Cathleen couldn't believe how wonderful it tasted. It settled her stomach, and made her feel better than she had in weeks. If Jackie thought it strange, Cathleen was glad she didn't say anything. Jackie didn't comment either on the fact that Cathleen hadn't had a cigarette for over a week now. For fear of any awkward questions, she finished her Coke, saying, "I'll get back to the desk. I've got those invoices to tally. Do you want me to go to the bank later too?"

"Yes, that would be good, Cathleen. Have you made an appointment to see a doctor? You might look a little brighter, but you're not yourself."

"I'll call in at the clinic this afternoon and see if I can see someone. That's if I get these figures to tally and the banking ready. If not I'll be going home soon, I can go then."

She left to the sound of Jackie saying, "I'd rather you went home to your family looking better. They might not let you return if they think we aren't looking after you.

*

Friday 11th May 1967

Cathleen lay on her bed, the doctor had told her what she already knew. She was expecting a child that was due at the end of December. A Christmas baby. She hadn't cried, she felt numb. She thought about Laurie, and toyed with the idea of phoning him again. She hadn't, she'd told herself *What's the point?'*

Cathleen tried to convince herself that she didn't want him now. He had used her, like Michael had. This was the second time she had been made to look a fool. It didn't help either, knowing for sure she was pregnant. She had no idea what she was going to do about the baby, and as she lay on her bed she reassured herself with, *'I've got months yet.'*

The letters that had arrived this morning were still in her drawer, unopened. She rolled over on her side and took out the one from her mother. Her news was boring. Hannah had started playschool at Easter and had settled now, after a few weeks of tears. Her dad was doing a building job for houses off the Fairlands estate. It all felt very tedious, but she was looking forward to seeing them all. She was shocked to read that Tilly's gran had died, she thought about the old lady bent over her sewing machine. *'Dead, Tilly will be devastated.'* She put the letter on the side and reached for Tilly's. The pages revealed her friend's neat handwriting, which never failed to make her feel homesick.

Dear Cathleen,

I'm not sure you if you've heard from your mum, but my gran died. It was a terrible shock, despite the fact that she had been getting frailer by the week. I still can't believe it, I wake every morning thinking I must get her up, then I remember, and the pain of my loss starts all over again. I loved my gran, Cathleen, really loved her. To me she was my mum. I feel terribly lonely, which is silly as I'm surrounded with children, but her death has left a hole in my life. I'm hoping what everyone say's is true, and that time heals. She knew she was going to leave us, that's why she took her rings off and gave them to me. I feel she wanted to make sure I had them and not my mum. That makes me feel a bit selfish, but I always felt my mum resented the love that was shared between gran and myself. The funeral is on the Tuesday, the 16th, next week. Mum's arriving the day before, she'll be tired. It's a long journey, and takes a while to recover.

On a happier note, we're having the boys christened the following Sunday. The vicar said he would do them together. It will be good for my mum, as she will get to share in the celebration. I don't know if you know the little church in Hunston, Cathleen? But it's really pretty. There's a big pond opposite, I take the children there to feed the ducks. I bet my life sounds terribly boring to yours? I'm sorry Cathleen but I have become the typical housewife! But I love it. Ken and Lucy are going to be God parents, they seem delighted to have been asked. May has given me, Ed's christening gown. Luke's wouldn't fit Angus. I'm glad about that, what with Luke dying and all. Silly really but I wouldn't like to think of my little boy in it.

How are you? I expect you are out dancing, partying, and doing all the things I never got round to doing. Is there a new man in your life? I love your letters but I would really love to hear all! There must be more to your life than work?

How are the monthly dances going? What are your plans? You said you were coming home for a couple of weeks, when? That's great news, we'll have to have a good old get together. You're welcome to come to the Christening, if you can make it. Perhaps Ed can babysit of an evening, and we'll go to the cinema, just the two of us. Phone or write to let us know when you're coming. I'm loving my little car, it really has opened the door to freedom. Once we get gran's funeral over, I'm hoping things will settle. I'm waffling on a bit Cathleen, sorry.

Anyway for now, look after yourself, and I shall look forward to your letters, and thank you for your birthday card, it was lovely.

Love Tilly X

Cathleen sat up, folded Tilly's letter over and put it with her mothers. *'What did she write? Boring life, what I wouldn't give for a slice of her boring family life at the moment. I feel like going where her gran's gone.'*

Cathleen looked at her watch, it was eight o'clock, Jackie and Simon would be in the snug room now, enjoying a drink. The thought of the Coca Cola, it tempted her to get up. She slipped on a short, blue smock, not that she had a bump to hide, but it was a comfortable little dress.

She went into the snug room, Simon was sat with a glass of what looked like port in front of him. "Where is everyone?" Simon looked up, "Jacks has gone off to bed. You've just missed her. We thought you'd gone up for the night."

Cathleen pulled her hand through her short curls, "I fancied a Coke, is it alright if I get one? I might take it up if that's okay?"

357

"Oh, come on, keep me company. I don't get to see much of you these days. Do you like it working at the desk?"

Cathleen was at the bar getting herself a drink, she caught the gist of his question, and raised her voice in answer, calling, "Yes, it suits me. I always liked figures at school, but if you'd told me back then I would have done a job like this, I would have laughed at you." As she approached the snug room, she lowered her voice, "Do you know, I wanted to be a nurse?" Cathleen stood in front of him, putting her drink on the table, "Then I had ideas to be a hairdresser and eventually ended up in a café in the Bognor high street. Funny journey really, and here I am, not just a waitress, but a Jack of all trades."

Simon patted the seat next to him, "Come on, sit a while, It's lonely down here drinking on your own." She picked up her Coke and took a large gulp, enjoying the fizz, "I didn't know you liked Coke, Cathleen, I thought you liked a drink, drink."

She flopped into the seat beside him, holding the drink out in front of her in case it spilled. The leather suite seemed to swallow her up. "I've not been myself lately, what…"

Simon draped his arm across her shoulders "It's all this Laurie business, isn't it? I could kill him for hurting you like this. Jackie says you'll get over it…"

This sudden show of kindness brought the tears she had been holding back. The warmth of his breath could be felt as he kissed her head, "Come on, Cathleen, he's not worth it…"

The words fell from her lips, "I'm pregnant, Simon, pregnant, and I haven't got a clue what I'm going to do." She removed herself from his embrace and stood up. Simon leapt to his own feet, folding her in his arms. That is how they stayed, him cradling her like she was a child. She was grateful for the silence, she didn't need anyone to say how foolish she had been. There was no reprimand, just kindness and concern. Cathleen let herself melt into him, feeling safe for the

first time in weeks. "He's a fool, Cathleen, you're lovely, I…"
Simon moved his hand up her back, Cathleen recognised the sexual
desire attached to the movement, "Oh no, Simon, no! Not you too,
what do I have written across my face, easy, foolish, tart? Go to
your wife, Simon, I'm through with men, all of you. It's just one
thing you're all out for, you, you disgust me." She turned and fled to
the safety of her room.

Cathleen pulled her case out from under her bed and started
packing, thoughts whirled round her head. *'Not Simon too, poor
Jackie.'*

*

Cathleen, without saying goodbye to anyone, let herself out of the
hotel, pushing the key through the letter box. She gave no thought
to what Jackie would make of her sudden disappearance, Simon
could tell her what he wanted, *'He'll probably say when I told him I was
pregnant he kicked me out.'* She smiled to herself, *'It's so easy for men.'*
She got off at the coach park. She had managed to catch the last bus
leaving for Portsmouth, it was now ten thirty and daylight had
diminished.

She looked around for a connecting bus to take her to Chichester or
Bognor but it looked like there was nothing. *'Perhaps I should have
waited and gone in the morning. Slept on it.'* Simon's behaviour had
shaken Cathleen, and although she hadn't wanted to stay at the
hotel a moment longer, she now felt tired and nervous, *'what can I
say back home. What possible explanation can I make for arriving home at this
unearthly hour, two weeks early?'*

A man's voice brought her out of thought, "Move along missy,
there's a good girl."

The term girl made Cathleen feel young and vulnerable, and she had the urge to cry. "How can I get to Bognor this evening? I seem to have missed the last bus."

"It'll have to be train, but it's a good twenty minute walk to the station." Tears threatened again, "I'll phone a taxi, thanks." Cathleen made her way across to the telephones. She asked the operator for the number she wanted, and within minutes she could hear the phone ringing. Her heart quickened as she waited for an answer, relief washed over her when she heard the familiar voice, "Hello."

"Ken, Ken it's me, Cathleen. I need a big, big, favour. Can you please come and get me I'm in Portsmouth?" She could visualise him running his hand through his hair, "I can't now, Cathleen, sorry."

"Ken, I'm asking you as a friend, you know, for what we've shared. I'm desperate. Please, Ken. You're the only person I could think of."

"Cathleen, I've got to be up early, can't you phone your dad?" Cathleen leant her head on the side of the telephone box. Tiredness overwhelmed her, which made her voice wobble with emotion, "Ken, please. I wouldn't ask you if I wasn't desperate. I…"

"Okay, Okay. I'll come. Where are you?"

She relaxed against the door of the phone box, thankful. She filled him in with the directions of where she was, and he told her to make for the Guildhall, saying "I'll meet you there."

Cathleen looked at her watch, "What time, Ken? It's dark now, and I'm on my own."

"Cathleen, I can't fly. If you want me to come it's going to take a good forty five minutes."

"Okay, I'll be waiting. Please hurry, Ken." She paused before adding, "Thank you."

*

Lucy hovered in the hall as Ken pulled on a light jacket, it was a chilly evening. "Please don't go, Ken." "Luce, I've got to now, she's desperate, I could tell."

"She could phone her parents. You should have said no." Ken reached over and put his hand on her shoulder, "Hey, what's all this about, I'll be back by midnight. It's a lift that's all."

Lucy felt sick, "I don't like it, Ken, you'll get hurt again." She didn't like the wobble in her voice, "You won't bring her back here, will you?" "Of course not. Look I've got to go, she's on her own in the middle of Portsmouth."

Lucy reached out and grabbed his arm, "I'm sorry, Ken, but I'm scared. I'm scared you'll want her again."

"Come with me, Lucy, will that help?" She grabbed her coat, and while tugging it on, said, "Yes I'd like that."

It was cold in the car, she shivered. "Ken I don't want to sound bossy, but seeing you run like this to Cathleen's beck and call makes me feel uneasy."

"Why?"

"I don't know, it's just... I feel she only has to click her fingers and you go running to her beck and call." Lucy could see she had annoyed him, "I'm not making myself clear, Ken. I'm scared, okay? I don't know what I'd do if she wanted you back..."

"Hey, hey, stop. Where's all this coming from?" She could hear the amusement in his voice, "Don't laugh at me please. I'm trying to be honest with you. I'm frightened of losing you, losing your friendship." She felt his hand tousle her short hair, "That's music to my ears, Lucy. Do you think you just might care a little bit for me, not just as a friend?"

"I do care, I care a great deal. I don't know what this is I'm feeling as I've never had an involvement with anyone before, you know… Lucy faltered trying to find the right words, "I was never going to fall for anyone, and yet I think… if love has you feeling insecure, weak, and scared of losing, then yes I could be in love with you."

"Could be in love with me, does this give a man hope?"

Lucy started to relax, "I thought you didn't want a relationship again either?" Ken took hold of her hand and squeezed it, "I didn't initially. You've grown on me. I've wanted you since I kissed you at Christmas."

"Are you saying you love me, Ken?"

"Lucy, love is a strange word. I did think I loved Cathleen once, but you know what she was like to me, and I would have walked on hot coals if she'd asked me to, but it wasn't reciprocated. Everything about our relationship had me walking on egg shells. She made me feel I should be lucky to have her, I always felt she was better than me. I…"

Lucy interrupted him, "You were far too good for her. Everyone says it."

"Well thanks for that, Luce, but what I do know is, since I've met you I've been happy. Everything about you is uncomplicated. You're kind, easy going, fun and you make me feel liked, and good about myself. I don't know if that's loving, I do know though, for sure, I couldn't bear to lose you in my life."

"Ken, what if she does want you back, how would you feel?"

"Stop worrying, Cathleen will not want me back, and even if she did, I wouldn't risk hurting you."

Lucy sat quiet, mulling over Ken's words. She felt better, but she couldn't help the uneasy feeling that had settled in her stomach with the knowledge that Cathleen was going to be back on the scene. "Come on, Lucy, Cathleen is no threat to you. I'm picking her up because she sounded desperate. She hasn't anyone else…"

"She does, Ken, she has a family. Can I ask that from now on you don't bow down to her like this? You need to learn to say no."

"Lucy, Cathleen's been my friend for so long, there's no way I could've left her in Portsmouth at this hour of the night." When Lucy didn't answer he asked, "Could I?"

"Yes you could. You could have insisted she phone her dad."

"Let's not argue, I shall be eternally grateful to her now. I feel we have got our own feelings out in the open. Things will just get better and better for us."

*

It was eleven thirty when Cathleen saw the lights of a car pull up by the Guildhall, her heart sank when she saw it was a couple. *'Come on, Ken its bloody freezing standing here.'*

The sound of a horn made her jump. There was Ken standing with his door open, "Cathleen, over here." He came across and took her case, "Thank you, Ken, I owe you one." "You don't owe me anything, just get in the back. You can tell us all about it while we get you home." "Who's in the front then?" She knew without being told, and her heart sank. Lucy said hello as Cathleen got in the back." Lucy turned in her seat so she could see her, "you remember me, don't you?" Cathleen did her best to hide her disappointment, "Yes, yes I do. My mum said you were renting a room at Kens'. I suppose it was warmer than that caravan you were in."

Ken started up the engine, "Cathleen, you must remember Lucy working at the riding school?" "Yes, she was a stable hand, I remember that."

She was annoyed when her snub went unnoticed, and Ken asked, "What's all this about, why the hurry to come home. What's happened?"

She wasn't keen to air her problems with Lucy listening in, "It's complicated. I just had to come home. I was coming home in a couple of weeks anyway, but got homesick all of a sudden. Can I stay at yours tonight please? I can't turn up at home without any warning, and at midnight, can I?"

"You're going to have to, Cathleen. You must have a key?" "Ken, please. How can I? They'll wonder who's coming in at this unearthly hour. They'll think they're being burgled." Her annoyance turned to jealousy when Ken said, "No they won't. I'm dropping you off at yours. Lucy and I have to get up early tomorrow as Ed's off at the moment, you must have heard about Agnes dying…" Cathleen ignored him, she leant forward, "Lucy you wouldn't mind if I stayed for just one night. I won't be any bother. In the morning I'll make my way round to my mums. Please, Lucy."

"No, Cathleen, you heard Ken. I think it'll be better if you go home, better for all of us."

Cathleen sank back in the seat defeated, the earlier tears that had threatened, pricked again. She bit her lip, she didn't want to give this Lucy the satisfaction of seeing her cry. *'I should have stayed at the hotel, and left tomorrow, very early.'*

*

It was nearly midnight when Lucy and Ken finally got in. Ken had made hot chocolate, which they drank in the kitchen laughing at Cathleen's surprise when they dropped her off outside her house, and they had driven off, "It's mean to laugh, Ken, but she needs taking down a peg or two. Surely even you can see that, can't you?"

"Oh, I don't know, she's always been the same. She was an only child for so many years, and utterly spoilt. I suppose it gives her airs."

Lucy put the empty mugs in the washing up bowl, "Well I for one got great pleasure out of not giving in to her whims."

Ken put his arms round her waist, kissing her neck, "I could get used to this, it's like being an old married couple…" Lucy wriggled out of his hold, laughing, "Go on, you go on up, Ken, I'll finish here. Shout down when you're out of the bathroom."

She heard him mumble 'spoil sport' as he went up the stairs.

It was a good half hour before Lucy had finished in the bathroom, and was ready for bed. She tiptoed across the landing, stopping outside Ken's bedroom. She could feel her heart beating in her chest. She tapped his door, and it creaked as she pushed it open. He lifted his head off his pillow and eased himself up on his elbow, concern showed on his face, "What is it, Luce, are you alright?" "Is there room for a little one in here?"

Ken sat up straighter, "Plenty, are you sure?" Lucy moved over to the bed and pulled back the eiderdown, "Move over, I hate to think of you in this double bed all alone."

Lucy had no experience of loving, which caused her to feel more than nervous. Her stomach felt like it had a bag of kittens in it. What she had witnessed as a child through her mother's many lovers had made her feel sex was dirty. Pushing these memories to the back of her mind she kissed him, and snuggled closer trying to cuddle her way into his bent knees. The kisses were reciprocated and the deeper they became the excitement outweighed her nerves.

"Ken, I've never been with anyone, like this. I…" He kissed her nose, "I'm glad to hear it. I'm a novice too you know." He traced his hand over her body bringing it to rest on her breast, she felt the tingles of pleasure. "I didn't know it could feel like this. I want you, Ken, properly, you know…"

"Shush." He kissed her again, "I want you too." Ken moved his hands up and down her body, exploring every inch of her. She found the sensation exciting and the more he touched the more she wanted. As her excitement increased she found the confidence to reach down to explore his body. She guessed she was doing something right by the feel of his excitement. The more she fondled the more he groaned, "You're lovely, Lucy, have I ever told you that?" She kissed him in answer, and when he eased his body over hers, the pain she felt on penetration was swift, and then pleasure took over. Their bodies moved rhythmically together. When he pushed himself forward in a hard thrust, and then stopped, Lucy opened her eyes in confusion. Ken gazed down at her, his eyes were glassy and his breathing was heavy. She smiled at him, "What's up?"

"Sorry, Luce, it'll be better next time. I couldn't wait, I…" She felt foolish for not realising. She reached up and touched his face, she wanted to reassure him that it was okay. She let her finger rest on his lips, and whispered, "Shush, it was beautiful."

He reached for her, tucking her under his arm, "Marry me, Lucy? Please say you'll marry me." Without a moment's hesitation, "Yes please. I'd marry you tomorrow if I could."

Ken gave her a light kiss, "Before the year is out, I promise, you'll be Mrs Lucy Jarmes." Their kisses increased as they became one all over again.

*

Wednesday 16ᵗʰ May 1967

The funeral had been well attended. Tilly lay her leg on top of the covers, it was a stuffy night. She hadn't got used to seeing her mum moving around her house yet either. She stirred when Ed said,

"You awake?" "Umm just laying here thinking." Tilly turned over and cuddled under his arm, "Your mum and mine did well, didn't they?" She felt Ed's hand brush the top of her head, "You worry too much. Mum's heaps better than she used to be. I even heard the two of them laughing about the time they argued over yours and Cathleen's antics with my brother, which I might add I got the blame for." Tilly laughed, that seems so long ago now, doesn't it?" Tilly had something on her mind and was struggling to bring it up, "Ed, you know with Gran gone now, I think mum feels it might be a good opportunity for us all to move to Canada. I …" "No way, Tilly, we live here. Your mum can visit anytime she wants but the business is here and…" "You could start again there, it's a lovely country, lots of opportunities for the boys. Can't we see how we feel when Rosie goes next month?"

She felt Ed move away and sit up, "Tilly, I don't want to say, it's because of my mum, but think about it, it would kill her to lose us, especially now the boys have arrived. She loves you too, Tilly, I can tell. She's lost Luke and Rachel and to lose us…" Tilly put her finger over his lips, "Shush, I know. It's just when mum said, you know, I was tempted. It really is a beautiful country, honest."

"I'm sure it is, but this is our home, Tilly, our friends are here and our own little family. You never know, if we go miles away and Rosie ever feels the need to find us she won't be able to if we're in Canada…"
Tilly poked him in the ribs causing him to yelp, "That - is – blackmail, Ed, and you know it. We both know when Rosie leaves she will never come back. She'll go back to being that wild child she was when we first set eyes on her."

Ed lay back down cuddling Tilly to him again. He nestled his lips into her hair saying, "What do you make of Cathleen coming home? You said it wouldn't be for a couple of weeks, but by all accounts Ken picked her up from the station."

"I haven't given it any thought, what with the funeral. Have you heard anything from Ken?"

"No, I shall have to go to work tomorrow though. He'll tell me all about it, I can't believe she's just come home for a holiday, there's bound to be a saga…" Tilly gave him another elbow, "Don't be so judgemental, she's much better since she's been away. I've enjoyed writing to her. I just hope Lucy's okay with her coming back, she's smitten with Ken, and him her, it's just we're the only ones who can see it."

"Stop match making. Why don't you phone Cathleen and find out all the news?" Tilly sighed, "I might now the funerals over, probably tomorrow. I thought she would have been in touch with me, but perhaps she thought I would need this time with mum and all. I'll call her tomorrow, I'll invite her over for the boys christening on Sunday."

"Are you going to cope with all this entertaining so soon after your gran?"

"Ed it's sensible to do it while Mum's here. It'll be nice for her to be part of it, rather than hear all about it over the phone."

She felt Ed's grip tighten round her shoulders, "Okay, okay, you know best. Come on let's get some shut eye, Petey will probably wake soon."

She felt his kiss on the back of her head as she kicked the covers off her legs again, "Night."

Sunday 20th May 1967 - The Christening.

Cathleen dressed with care. Tilly had invited her to the Christening and she wanted to make a good impression. She had bought silver money boxes for the boys, and had put a pound in each, she knew this was generous.

She hadn't heard a thing from Ken since he dropped her off last week. She tried not to be rankled by the fact, but seeing Lucy sitting in the front seat dictating whether she was allowed to stay at Ken's had annoyed her more than she cared to admit. *'He can't really be interested in her, she looks like an underfed boy.'*

Cathleen stood outside the church waiting with the small crowd that had gathered. She felt uncomfortable amongst these people she didn't seem to recognise.

"Hello, Cathleen, how are you?" She looked up to see Tilly's mum, June, holding Rosie's hand. "Hello, it's really good to see a familiar face. How's Canada?" She spotted Ken arriving with Lucy, she tried to look engaged in conversation, but had trouble concentrating on what was being said. Tilly and Ed arrived and Cathleen felt sickened as the little boy ran to Lucy to be picked up. She was glad when June said, "Come on, Cathleen, we aught' to go in." The church seemed full and Cathleen perched herself on the edge of a pew next to an elderly lady, who said, "It isn't always this busy, there's a christening this morning." June made her way to the front where it seemed there were two rows of pews reserved for the event. Cathleen thought about moving down with them all, but her legs felt like lead. So she just smiled at the elderly lady without passing comment.

Her eyes followed Ed, Tilly, Lucy and Ken as they made their way to the front to join June and Rosie. She felt envious as she watched Tilly, who looked so natural holding the baby in her arms. This conjured up thoughts of her own predicament that was growing inside her. The vicar appeared, and the service took place with hymns and prayers, but for Cathleen it was lonely. She was sitting next to strangers at the back of the church, feeling excluded. Lucy was still holding the little boy, Angus, and Ken was trying to keep him amused. The more she watched, the lonelier she felt. The people in the front two pews made their way to the font. She recognised Ed's mum and dad, and thought how old May looked, and guessed she was struggling with the death of Rachel. The vicar spoke about godparents, which caused Lucy to give Angus to Ken as she took the baby from Tilly. This hurt Cathleen, tears pricked, *'I've been Tilly's best friend all my life, why am I not part of this little family?'*

Just when Cathleen thought she couldn't feel any worse, she caught sight of an engagement ring on Lucy's finger. She could hold her tears no longer, she took her hanky from her bag and blew her nose, telling herself, *'Get over it, you couldn't have Ken now, not even if you wanted to.'* As much as she tried to reason with herself she felt dreadful. *'Am I jealous?'* She couldn't be sure, but whatever it was, it hurt.

Once outside, Tilly threw her arms round Cathleen's neck, "It's lovely to see you. I didn't see you at the back. You should've come up the front. Oh Cathleen, I can't tell you how good it is to see you. We must catch up later, I…"

She watched as Tilly turned at the sound of crying, "Give him to me, mum, I'll take him now. He's hungry." She called to Cathleen, "We're having a small tea party at mine. You're coming aren't you?" All of a sudden Cathleen didn't want to be part of this happy gathering, but thought it would look churlish to decline. After all she had presents for both boys.

She felt better when she got to Tilly's, May spoke to her without any spiteful jibes, and June seemed genuinely interested in what she had been up to. Cathleen had the urge to ask how she had managed with a baby on her own, but knew she hadn't managed alone, there had always been Agnes. June had been lucky, Cathleen's mum wouldn't be able to offer that sort of support, her father was still living and there was Hannah still at home. *'No somehow I have to find a way on my own.'*

Ken came over and spoke, she found herself congratulating him on his engagement, hoping she had been mistaken. This thought was short lived when he dashed her hopes with, "Ooh, news travels fast. How did you hear?" "I didn't it was the bauble on her finger. I'm pleased for you, Ken, really pleased."

"I'm a lucky man, Cathleen. I didn't think so when you first called the wedding off, but I see now you were right to end it, and I understand." Lucy chose that moment to sidle alongside of Ken, her voice sounded slow and smug, "Hello, Cathleen." Cathleen felt like slapping the soppy smile off her face, when Lucy added, "Aren't the children lovely?" Cathleen didn't slap anyone, she found her voice, and managed a very polite, "Yes they are. Tilly's a natural little mum isn't she?" The small talk felt false and Cathleen distanced herself making an excuse she wanted to talk to Ed's dad. She knew she should have congratulated Lucy on the engagement, but the words stuck in her throat, "Hello, Norman, it's good to see you. My mum says you've moved to Selsey to live in a bungalow." If he was surprised by the sudden interest in himself he hid it well, "Yes, yes we have. May loves it, it's very quiet. Not that Bognor was noisy, it's just… what with the accident…" He faltered looking for the right words and added, "We needed a change." He moved away excusing himself leaving Cathleen feeling very alone again, *'No one seems to want to speak to me.'*

Tilly appeared carrying a tray of teas. "There you go, sugar?" Cathleen didn't want to be here a moment longer, "Not for me. I'm going to make a move, I'll pop over tomorrow, Tilly, we can catch up properly then."

"Sounds good. Sorry about now, it's hectic, but…"

Cathleen waved her arm, "Don't be daft. I'll see you tomorrow. Oh, and there's a couple of pressies for the boys, I've left them on the hall table." She kissed Tilly on the cheek, and left the gathering without saying goodbye to anyone else. She was desperate to get away.

Despite the warm weather of late, once Cathleen was out in the fresh air she felt cold. *'I'll phone dad, he'll come and pick me up'.*

She crossed the road and walked along the grass verge towards the shops. She took in a big deep breath, glad to be away from watching happy families.

The village seemed to be asleep, it was deadly quiet. There was a donkey in the field hanging his head over the fence. She stroked him, and he followed her until the wire barred his way. The sound of a horn had her look up, there was a man trying to cross the road, he was doing a V sign at a car. The man stumbled up onto the curb and stood still as if trying to get his balance, it was then that Cathleen recognised the figure, 'My god it's Michael.'

She caught up with him, and grabbed his arm, "Michael?" "Cathy Kay." She ignored his pet name for her, "Are you drunk, Michael?"

His eyes narrowed, "Don't you start, you haven't seen me in..? oh who cares, and the first thing you do is nag. Where are you going?"

"I was going home, I was going to phone my dad. Look at you, what's happened to you?"

He smiled that slow smile she used to love, "I'm a lost cause, haven't you heard?" She had heard he was drinking too much what with losing Christine, but she was still shocked at his dishevelled appearance. "I'm sure it hasn't been easy for you, Michael, but I haven't forgiven you for treating me so shoddily. You ruined my life, do you know that? You..." She reached for his arm as he stumbled again, "Oh it doesn't matter. Let's get you home before you get run over." She took out her cigarettes, "Do you want one?" When he refused, she lit her own and took a long drag. It was the first one she had had since arriving at the church this morning.

Michael was a shell of the man he once was, and she asked herself what had made her want to ditch her own wedding for this sorry sight.

Watching him stagger beside her made her forget her own problems, "Michael, I know you're upset about Christine, but look at you..."

"I'm alright, Cathleen. I drink because it helps me forget. I'm not as drunk as everyone thinks, but it stops people asking questions if they think I'm plastered."

"You're not alright, you look dreadful."

"It was all my fault, do you know that? Everyone blames me."

"No one blames you, silly, it was an accident. My mum wrote to me at the time, and Tilly. There wasn't a single mention that you were to blame." She wasn't sure if it was the drink, but she could hear a shake in his voice, "I killed her, Cathy, not directly, but I just as well have done. Then there's that little one, Rachel…" They had reached the top of Hunston hill, the canal was in view where there was a seat, "Come on, Michael, let's sit there a while." He followed her like a lamb and slumped down on the seat. She felt he looked more defeated than drunk. He sounded like a broken man as he continued his side of the story, "Innocent she was. Innocently coming back from a ride. It was all my fault." She was horrified to see he was crying, "Stop it, Michael, it wasn't your fault. It was an accident. These things happen."

"You don't know what you're talking about. I…" Cathleen didn't give him chance to confess, she second guessed what he was going to say. "I can imagine, I expect Christine caught you up to no good with another of the girls in the stables. When…"

"Shut up, Cathy, shut up." He stood, "You don't know nothing." She was horrified at the anger shining in his eyes as he stared down at her, "I wasn't with some girl as you say, that would have been easy, oh God so easy. No Miss Know All, do you want to know what I was doing?" Cathleen reached out trying to get him to sit for fear he would stumble backwards into the canal, "Let go of me, let me tell you what I was doing, then you can hate me too." She watched as he took a deep breath, "I was fucking the arse off a delivery man, and she caught me. There you have it, you thought you guessed - well you didn't guess that now did you? Not only that, but in Christine's anger she shot off like a bloody maniac, and killed not just herself but that little one too."

If he noticed Cathleen's face pale with horror, it didn't stop his next revelation spill from his mouth. She wanted him to stop, in her condition her stomach was fragile, what he was saying, and the implications behind it was making her feel sick. He didn't stop, it was as if he had been wound up and now released, "Cathy, the truth of it is, is that part of me was glad Christine was dead, it meant my guilty secret died too. I didn't have to explain myself to anyone…"

Cathleen had to stand, she needed a distraction. Michael read this movement wrong, he accused, "Go on, run. Leave me to rot. I…" She flopped back down the realisation of what he was saying still sinking in, bringing with it that sickening feeling back to her stomach, "Michael, why tell me?" He seemed to Cathleen quite sober now, "I don't know, Cathy, I think I had to tell someone, and you and I… well we are alike in so many ways. Stop looking at me like that, Cathy. I can't help it, it's the way I am.

Michael noticed Cathleen's face was ashen. But he drew a small comfort that she was still here, listening. "Thank you, Cathy, thank you for not running." When Cathleen sat quiet, he said, "It might sound silly, but I feel better for having said my guilty secret out loud." He reached for her hand willing her to say something, "Cathy, I've liked my own kind for…" He paused looking for an honest answer, and said simply "It feels like for forever." Cathleen still sat quiet, Michael tried to shake her hand trying to get a reaction, "Stop looking at me like that, I did love Christine, It was easy to love her, I'd known her all my life. Our being together was what was expected by our parents." Her voice was quiet, "But you liked me, we…" Michael put his arm round her shoulder, "I more than liked you, Cathy. You were fun. It was exciting, living dangerously, but I've always liked my own sex. It wasn't until I went to boarding school that I gave into my fantasy. I hoped by doing that it would pass, but it didn't. I would have married Christine, but..."

"Michael who else knows? What about..."

"Don't, Cathy, don't torment yourself. This is what I am. I don't like it..."

He watched as she put her head in her hands, "You ruined my life, Michael, you caused big trouble for me. Do you know that?"

He seemed sober now, and his voice was lighter showing the old signs of humour, "No, Cathy, you have to take responsibility for your own mistakes. If you're honest I probably did you a favour. If you'd married curly Shirley you'd be bored out of your brains by now." He watched her colour rise as her temper flared, "You don't know nothing, I..."

"Whoa there, the truth of it is, is that I've always liked your curly Shirley, even when we used to go dancing years ago." The slap across his face took the laughter out of his voice, he ignored the sting it brought, saying, "I'm sorry, Cathy, but that's the truth. You know how I was always ridiculing him, always finding fault with him, mocking. It was because I hated him for being normal, and I wanted him, wanted him like you had him. I think in some ways I took you as a way of getting at him."

"Please stop, Michael, I can't stand hearing this. I..." Michael ignored her, he rubbed at his cheek, it felt good to get this off his chest, and now he had started it was like a flood gate opening, he held her hands so as not to get another whack, "When you told him you had been with me, and he came for me that night with his fists, I took pleasure with every punch, it excited me but you wouldn't understand..."

"Stop it! Stop it! I don't want to hear any more of this. You, well... what are you going to do?" He could feel her relax, and he knew the fight had gone out of her. "I don't know, Cathy, I don't have

375

plans. If I'm honest I feel my dad knows, my mother's ignorant, she wouldn't want to see it even if I told her."

Cathleen swallowed hard, trying to come to terms with what he had been saying, "Homosexuality is legal now, Michael, you'll be able to find…"

"You're so naïve, Cathy. Yes it's legal, acted out in your own home. It isn't accepted, and it won't be for a long time. It's like sex before marriage, it's happening more and more openly what with the pill and the freedom movement, but it'll take years before the oldies accept it without frowns and gossip."

A swan stood up on the water flapping its wings. He noticed Cathleen looking at her watch, "Don't go yet, Cathy, come with me to the stables, I reckon my mother would love to see me entertain a lady again."

He was pleased to see Cathleen had better colour in her cheeks, "Your mum hated me on sight, I can still remember her."

Michael held his hand out to her, "No she didn't; she was just worried about anything upsetting the plans for the spring wedding. Come on, come with me, are you up for a ride?"

"Michael, I can't ride. I never could."

"Yes you can, come on, come for a ride."

"No! I must get home. You just don't get it do you? I was never that keen on the stables, I liked you… No, I didn't like you, I loved you. You were beastly to me, beastly."

He laughed, glad she had her old spirit back, "Don't start that again, I had no choice, when you started talking about marriage and all that heavy stuff, you frightened me off. You must understand a bit now, surely?"

"I'll walk with you to the stables, then I'll catch the bus at Mundham corner."

They walked the short distance to the Forresters drive, Michael leant forward to kiss her, she turned her head, and his lips caught her cheek. "Go on in, Michael. We'll talk again. I'm coming to see Tilly tomorrow, when I've finished there I'll come up to the stables. I've got my own revelations you can listen too."

He felt better than he had in months, he held his arm up in a wave, calling, "You're alright you are, Cathy. Cathy Kay, do you remember?"

*

Cathleen had gone to bed early, exhausted. This pregnancy might not show on her body yet, but the effects it was having on her wellbeing was very apparent. Today had been the first day she had not been sick, despite Michael's revelation.

Her mother had questioned her the other morning, and Cathleen had blamed the toothpaste, claiming it made her retch.

If Cathleen had been blindfolded she would have known she was home, she could smell it, it felt secure, and good. The day had started out horribly. She had felt excluded in the church, and in the way at the tea party, but despite Michael's disturbing confession it had been good to catch up with him, and as she lay in bed she felt happier than she had in a long time.

Tomorrow she would go over to Tilly's and give her the good news. She knew her friend would be delighted with the prospect of being given a baby. A new born baby, and her best friend's too. Cathleen felt her stomach, it was still flat but she cradled it in her palm, rubbing gently. *"My baby, Laurie's baby."* She lay thinking of Laurence, *'I loved you, Laurie, really loved you. I would have followed you anywhere if you'd given me the chance.'* Tears trickled out the corners of her eyes as she admitted to herself she had been foolish. She thought about Michael, and reminded herself he had used her, he had made a fool out of her too. She thought about their weekend to Blackpool, how sexy he had been, it was like he couldn't get enough of her, yet when she thought back to that time, and if she was honest with herself, she had chased him, and his lovemaking had been rough, nothing like Laurie's. *'How horrible he had been to me after Blackpool too, he made me feel like dirt. At least Laurie said he loved me, but couldn't possibly leave his family. He was sorry, which is more than Michael had been at the time.'*

It didn't change her feelings for Michael, she felt sorry for him, knowing now he liked his own kind, not only that, but he liked her Ken. *'But he's not my Ken, he's Lucy's Ken.'* Every time she let her thoughts wander to Ken and his engagement to Lucy, she had to acknowledge it hurt more than she cared to admit. As she drifted off to sleep her mind was troubled, *'These are the thoughts that nightmares are made of.'* She slept all the same.

*

Monday 21ˢᵗ May 1967

Tilly got back from dropping Rosie off at school pleased to see her mum had a cup of tea waiting for her. "Angus walked all the way home so hopefully he'll have an afternoon nap today, and we'll get a chance to have some us time."

June laughed, "I love the children, Tilly. You mustn't worry about me."

"I know, mum, but it has been pretty full on since you got here. Cathleen's supposed to be coming today, this morning I think. She left so suddenly I'm not sure. It was a bit hectic yesterday."

June put biscuits on a plate, gave one to Angus with a drink of milk and said, "I think somethings troubling that girl, she didn't seem right to me."

Tilly laughed out loud, "How funny you are, has Cathleen ever been right? She's fine, mum. She probably felt a bit out of it, what with

378

Ken being here with Lucy. You did know he was engaged to Cathleen once, didn't you?" when June nodded, Tilly said, "Funny really, Ken and Cathleen were together for what seemed like forever, and then she finished with him. I thought he would never get over her."

"People move on, love."

"Not always. You didn't, and I didn't. Sometimes there's only one person we want, and I did think Cathleen was going to be that person for Ken."

June sighed, "I shouldn't say it, but I think he'll have a happier life with the one he's chosen, Lucy seems a real sweet girl, you can't help but like her."

Tilly lifted Angus on to her knee, and wiped his face with her apron, "That's better. Go on, go and give these crumbs to Rookie, I don't think Rosie went out there this morning."

June stood up to look out of the window, she watched Angus running up the garden, "That bloody bird, he pooped all over my smalls this morning, I'd washed them by hand too. How did you come to get it?"

"Rosie found it, it had fallen out of a tree. She loves that silly old bird, but of late he disappears for weeks on end, and just when she gets used to not seeing him, he reappears."

The sound of crying coming from the pram brought the conversation to an end. June went out in the garden with Angus, leaving Tilly to feed Peter.

*

The bus was late which didn't help Cathleen's mood. She was disgruntled to find this morning when she tried to pull on one of her little skirts that the zip wouldn't do up. She had turned her body sideways to the mirror and she didn't seem to have even a ripple of a bump, yet this told her, her body was changing shape.

She sat on the bus watching as all the familiar places passed by, and admitted to herself it was good to be home. Her mother had said Jackie had phoned the house again while she was out yesterday. This was the fourth time Jackie had tried to make contact. Cathleen hadn't phoned her back, what could she say? She was only grateful that her mother didn't push for answers. She wasn't ready to reveal to either Jackie or her parents the real reason for her sudden departure.

Cathleen got off at Mundham corner, the weather was glorious, and she felt the walk would do her good. As she passed the stables she wondered if Michael remembered she would be calling in to see him later today. Her head was full of plans, she was desperate to see Tilly and tell her, her news. Cathleen had planned to give her baby to Tilly. *'I can't wait to see how excited she'll be at the prospect of being given a new born baby.'* She didn't relish the thought of telling her parents about her pregnancy, at least this time she knew it wasn't a false alarm. She was prepared, ready for it, ready for the flack. She loved Laurie, and she would have this baby no matter what anyone said.

Cathleen knocked on Tilly's door, squeals could be heard coming from the back garden, *'Everything seems so uncomplicated here.'*

Tilly filled the doorway, napkin over her shoulder, a pin between her teeth and a baby in her arms, she mumbled between her gritted teeth, "Cathleen, come on, come in, we've been waiting for you. I'm just sorting out Petey, go through to the garden, Mum's out there with Angus. I'll be with you in a minute." This isn't how Cathleen envisaged telling Tilly, she wanted it to be just the two of them, she wanted to witness Tilly's joy, to see on her friend's face how wrong she had been about her, and to realise that Lucy might be a nice girl, but she, Cathleen, is still her very best friend.

She watched Tilly kneel down on all fours and lean over the screaming baby, he was protesting at having to have his nappy put on. "It's bedlam in here, Tilly, I was hoping to have a quiet word with you. Is there any chance?"

Tilly found this remark amusing, "It's always like this these days, I think we should have named this house Bedlam! But I'll see if mum will take the boys to the duck pond. Angus has already walked this morning, but she can pop him in the bottom of the pram."

Cathleen was amazed at how her friend took all this mayhem in her stride, "Thanks, Tilly, it'll be good to talk."

"Everything's okay, isn't it?"

Cathleen looked down, unable to keep eye contact. She wasn't sure how much she wanted to tell Tilly, "Yes, it's just I haven't seen you in months, it would be good to catch up properly without all this noise."

Tilly laughed, "Is it that bad? I honestly don't notice it. Welcome to my world, Cathleen."

June didn't seem to mind when she was bundled off with the boys and the stale bread to feed the ducks with. She called out "Cheerio." And Tilly confided in Cathleen that she was dreading her mother leaving. "I've never been on my own, I've had Gran, now mum, and when she goes it will be just Ed and I. I feel a bit scared at how I'll cope."

Cathleen poo pooed this, "You'll be fine, you're a natural. Mum says Mrs Barrett's good these days, she'll help."

"Yes I know, and I'm sure you're right. Still let's not waste our time talking about my fears, let's hear all your gossip. I knew there was more to your letters than you were telling. Was there…"

"Tilly." Cathleen laughed, "No, there wasn't great news to tell you. It was a busy hotel and I was working, working hard. I loved it though, but…"

Tilly interrupted her, "I knew there was a but."

Cathleen reached out and placed her hand on her friends, she didn't feel as confident as she had earlier, "Please let me finish, I've so much to tell, and as you say we haven't got a lot of time." She could tell by Tilly's face she had her attention now, "I'll start at the beginning. I left here desperately unhappy, you didn't realise it, but I felt the whole world hated me. I think I hated myself. Going to the hotel was good for me, I worked hard and the owners liked me a lot." She thought about Simon, but didn't add, 'some too much'. "Please don't judge me when I say this, Tilly, but one of the guests caught my eye, he was American…"

Tilly leant forward smiling, "I knew it, I knew there was…"

"Tilly, please let me finish. His name was Laurence, Laurie, and he wore a big gold band on his left finger," the look on Tilly's face made Cathleen falter, "Yes, he was married, but what started out as a bit of harmless fun became serious. He gave me the age old story, how he only stayed with his wife because of the kids, but in the early days I didn't care. He came to England on business, and at first it was just fun, but over the months it all became so much more serious. The bottom line is, I loved him, and I still do. I believe he loves me, but he loves his wife more. On his last visit I got a bit too clingy, and told him how much I needed him, how much I loved him. The end result is, he left, and I got a letter a few weeks later finishing the relationship. He isn't coming to England anymore either."

Tilly reached out and took Cathleen's hand, "I'm sorry, Cathleen, that's horrible for you. It was a bit obvious that…"

"Stop, Tilly, there's more. When he left I was desperately unhappy, I phoned him every day for a week, I must have driven him mad as that was when he wrote to me, a letter, finishing our relationship. What he doesn't know is, I'm pregnant, Tilly, pregnant with his child. I can't get rid of it, it would be like killing a part of Laurie, but I can't keep it either. I've given this a lot of thought, and I want you to have it, Tilly, you and Ed. I couldn't think of…"

"Oh Cathleen, that's a lovely idea, but I can't have it. I've got Petey and Angus now, and…"

This was not the reaction Cathleen had anticipated, "Yes you can, Tilly, Rosie will be gone next month this one will replace her…"

"No, Cathleen, no. I believe you mean well, but I find the boys difficult. Rosie's easy, but the boys are hard work. No, I'm really sorry, but you'll have to find another way, as I say, it was a lovely thought, but not now."

"Tilly please. I want you to have it."

Cathleen couldn't hide her disappointment, she had convinced herself her old friend would be delighted, would have grabbed her hand off at the thought. This rejection had tears falling. Tilly seemed unaffected, she stood up saying, "Come on, Cathleen, I would have been delighted before I had the boys, but it's not for me now. Anyway I know when your little one is born you won't want to part with it, you'll see."

Cathleen sniffed trying to get herself together, "I would for you, Tilly, I promise."

When Tilly closed the discussion by filling the kettle with water and put it on the stove to boil, Cathleen knew she was defeated, and it didn't help when she said "You've a good mum and dad, they'll stand by you." Cathleen ignored her, which prompted Tilly to ask, "Is this why you came home early."

Cathleen didn't want to confide in Tilly anymore, her plans were dashed, and she didn't have a clue what she was going to do now. "Don't make me a cuppa, Tilly. I'm off tea. I'll wait for your mum to come back and then I'll make a move home, I said I'd help mum with the clearing of the back room."

The atmosphere felt stilted, and Cathleen was pleased when June got back and she could leave. When Tilly gave her a hug, Cathleen said, "I'm not leaving because you don't want my baby."

383

"Cathleen, I would love to be able to have it, but I can't, surely you can see how full on it is here?"

Tears threatened as Cathleen made her way down the path. She had to go to the stables now, but it was the last thing she felt like doing.

*

Michael looked at his watch, it was two thirty, and there had been no sign of Cathleen. *'Perhaps once she thought about my confession she isn't as okay with it as I thought.'*

Michael had woken this morning feeling better about himself than he had in a long time, it had helped sharing his problems with Cathleen, and she had listened. He thought back to the jive classes, he did like her, he had always been able to see she was a good looking girl, she stood out from the crowd. If he was honest he was attracted to her more than he had ever been to Christine. Cathleen had an edge to her, it felt exciting. *'Why haven't you come today? I was looking forward to seeing you.'*

Deciding not to let her absence spoil this new feeling of wellbeing he told his mother he was going for a ride on Blue. It had pleased her he could tell, he hadn't ridden since the accident, and with Lucy leaving they had had to employ a new stable hand. Roland, Roland was about forty, short and fat with not an ounce of patience with the kids, in fact they had had three more cancellations this week. Michael knew if this continued they would have no lessons running.

With his horse tacked up, he waved to his dad, "See you later." Michael wasn't met with the same pleasure he had received from his mother, "Oh, finding yourself fancying a ride are you? You could have waited an hour and taken the lessons. That would have been more useful." Michael ignored his father's sarcastic bellow that followed him as he trotted out of the stables, "You need to man up, boy, start looking at what you've done, and try and put things right, for…" the rest of it was lost in the wind. Michael was enjoying the sensation of riding his old horse across the road with the wind blowing in his long blonde hair. It felt good.

He bought the horse to a standstill when he saw a familiar figure pushing a pram. "Hello Tilly, how are things?" Michael leant forward and patted Blue's neck trying to keep him steady. The horse was expecting some exercise which was long overdue and was impatient to get going. Tilly lifted Angus off the pram on to her hip so he could stroke the horse, "I'm fine, Michael, how are you? She didn't wait for him to answer, "It's good to see you out and about again. I'm walking to the school to pick Rosie up, it's such a lovely afternoon."

Michael ignored the niceties, "Did you see Cathleen today? She said she was coming over this morning, and was going to call in on me too."

Tilly didn't want to discuss Cathleen with Michael, she didn't want to betray her friend's confidence, so just said, "Yes, she came over early. I think I may have upset… No not upset, but disappointed her. She left earlier than she probably intended."

"Where did she go, what time did she leave?"

Tilly popped Angus back on the bottom of the pram, "I don't know now, probably about eleven thirty, maybe a bit later. It's good to see you, Michael, but I have to get going. It's quite a stretch to the school."

Michael kicked the flanks of his horse, and felt happier knowing it wasn't down to him that Cathleen hadn't appeared. He turned the horse in to Church Lane and got Blue into a canter. *'It's good to be out like this.'* The horse's hooves made a clatter on the tarmac as he headed for the church, as he turned the corner he saw Cathleen. She turned at the sound of the horse, the picture she made took his breath away. She was knelt down watching the ducks on the pond, the sun seemed to light up her hair making it look red, and as she turned he had to admit she really was a striking looking young woman. *What's wrong with me? She really is lovely, and I do fancy her.'* He remembered their brief love affair and it brought about a stirring in his underwear. *'Christine never had this effect on me, but Cathleen has always stirred something in me.'* Michael knew he could get aroused at the sight of a pretty girl, but he couldn't escape from the fact that it was his own kind that caused more excitement for him. He slid off his horses back and walked towards Cathleen, how he wished things were different, there was something about Cathleen, she had guts, spirit and she was different, she seemed to have grown up. "Hello, there, I wondered where you were, you said you would pay me a visit." Cathleen stood brushing her skirt down, "Well the days not over yet, is it?"

Michael laughed, "You've always got an answer. Tilly said you left hers ages ago."

If Cathleen wondered how come he had been talking with Tilly, she didn't ask, but said "I stopped at Dunnaways, I bought a pasty for lunch, and he gave me some old stale bread. I've been sat here feeding the ducks. Thinking."

"Does this have anything to do with Tilly letting you down?" There it was, Michael witnessed the flash of anger in those green eyes, making her look dangerous, "Tilly didn't let me down, no one lets me down. I don't know what…"

Michael tried to steady the horse, it hadn't liked this show of anger, and Blue paced round in a circle, his hooves trying to take off. "Whoa there boy, steady on." Michael walked him over to the tree, dismounted and tied him up. Cathleen was already striding away. Michael had to run, "Steady on, Cathy, what's up? No one was saying anything, I was just concerned I hadn't seen you yet, and Tilly said…"

Cathleen turned, stopping, "Yes, and just what did she say?"

"Hey, hey, Cathy. Tilly didn't say anything, promise. What's all this about?"

Michael managed to steer her back to the duck pond where they sat on a big stone, "Come on tell me what's going on with you. I told you my guilty secret, surely you can trust me with yours?"

Cathleen stared out at the duck pond where she had sat for the past two and half hours, and told Michael all about Laurie. The predicament she had found herself in, and how she had hoped to give the baby to Tilly, but Tilly didn't want it. "See, she didn't let me down, I made an assumption and it back fired." She put her head in her hands, there were no tears, she said, "Everything I do goes wrong, sometimes I think I'm doomed."

Michael laughed, "You're not doomed, Cath. You take risks, I like that about you. How would you like to take a risk on me?"

"What do you mean?" Michael lay his arm across her shoulders, "I'll marry you, Cathy. I'll give this baby a name, and you too. What do you say? It'll stop tongues wagging about us both, it'll help us both."

"Michael, you would really do that for me?" He squeezed her tighter, "I would, I really would like to, Cathy."

"But what about 'your' liking for men? It couldn't work."

"I like you too, Cathy. If it doesn't work or you want out at any time, divorce me, I won't care. I want to help you, I want to do something good. I want…" When Cathleen went to stand, he was worried he had frightened her off, he tightened his grip, "That is more than good of you, Michael, more than good. The only thing is you can't have children, anyone who knows you will laugh at us, they'll be saying I'm tricking you, and you are being hoodwinked, and…"

"Let them say what they like. My mum will be delighted now. She wouldn't have been when Christine was on the scene, it was always to be me and Christine, but now I think tongues have already been wagging, and she would welcome a wedding, baby as well."

Cathleen kissed his cheek, "You make it all sound so easy, thank you, Michael, I'll bear it in mind. I'm not quite ready to face your mother yet, I can still feel her eyes burning in my back on our last meeting."

The two of them stood up and walked over to Blue, Michael untied the reins, "Do think on it, Cathy, you don't have to love me, you don't have to sleep with me, I'm offering you a name for the baby. I want to help you, I feel getting tied up with me was the start of your downfall, and this is a way of putting something right for you."

He mounted his horse, "Where are you going now?"

Cathleen patted the horse's neck, "I'll go and catch a bus back home. You go, go and ride. That horse looks like he's dying to run."

Michael kicked the horse in his sides and as it flew into action, he called over his shoulder, "Consider my offer, Cathy. It's genuine."

He didn't hear her answer, but as he steered Blue into the open fields that led over the farm, he eased himself up out of the saddle, standing in the stirrups as Blue took off into a gallop.

*

It was nearly five o'clock by the time Cathleen got home. Her mother was in the kitchen, and the table was laid for dinner, "Where's Hannah, Mum?"

Pam pushed her hair away from her face with her arm, she was stirring a pan on the stove that was boiling furiously, "She's next door, playing with their youngest."

"Shall I go and get her?" Pam poured the contents of the saucepan into a jug, "No she's having dinner with them tonight."

Cathleen didn't like being around her mum without a distraction, she was frightened of questions, as of yet she had given no explanation as to why after saying she would never return to Bognor, she is not only home, but home earlier than originally planned. "I'll go on upstairs and change, I've been walking in these clothes, and sitting down by that smelly duck pond in Hunston. I feel all sticky." Pam's voice was disappointed, "Oh, Cathleen, I was hoping we could have a little catch up, we haven't had chance since you got back, and your father won't be home until six."

Cathleen went over to the sink and kissed her mum's cheek, "I'll just get changed, and I'll be down. I don't want a cup of tea, I'll have a cold drink please." As she climbed the stairs, she told herself, *'Perhaps now's the time to confide in my mum.'* Her original plan had fallen, but she had a way out if she wanted it. Michael had been serious, she could tell.

"Cathleen, glass of orange down here for you."

She pulled on a pair of thin cotton trousers, and a baggy t-shirt. It felt good to be out of that tight skirt. She dropped into the comfy chair her father always sat in, and reached for the drink on the tray, "Thanks, mum, this is welcome."

"Now are you going to tell me what all this is about, love? I'm your mother and I know when something's bothering you."

Cathleen took a deep breath, "Mum, I… I don't know any easy way to say this, but I'm pregnant again, only this time I am pregnant, it's been confirmed." When Pam paled at Cathleen's revelation, Cathleen put her glass down and moved over to the sofa to sit beside her mother, "Mum, please, I know what you're thinking, but I loved this baby's father, really loved him. His name was Laurence, Laurie. He used me, and I got hurt. I'm not a child anymore, mum, I've lived away from home for six months, and I know what I want…"

"Oh, Cathleen, you don't know nothing. A baby, a baby is a full time job, it'll ruin your life, how will you manage, and on your own."

"I had hoped Tilly would want it, I could have given it to her, mum, but she said she has her hands full these days, she said thank you but no thank you. I met an old friend today, Michael, Michael Forrester, you know of him. It was the chap I had relations with before I went away to Bournemouth. He's offered to marry me, give my baby a name, and me. No, mum let me finish, I know his family will know it isn't his, as he can't have children, but he says if I want a divorce once the baby's born, he would go along with whatever I wanted. He feels bad about all the trouble he caused me last year, and for the way he treated me, you know, before I left Bognor."

Cathleen watched the confused look on her mum's face as she tried to process all this information, before she blurted out, "Good God, girl you can't do that. What about the father, the real father, does he know?"

"Mum, he's married. He finished with me when he went back to America. It's all so complicated, he wouldn't be interested, and I wouldn't want him now. He made a choice." This wasn't wholly true, Cathleen knew if Laurie came back claiming his undying love, she wouldn't be able to resist him. But she kept her facade, "I wouldn't marry him, mum, not just because I'm pregnant."

"Exactly, so you can't marry this Michael because you're pregnant, especially when it isn't his, and you don't even love him, and he doesn't love you. It's a recipe for disaster."

Cathleen was pleased, this was going better than she imagined, "Mum, Ken was going to marry me when I thought I was carrying Michael's child, you were all for it…"

"Only because you two had a history, he loved you, you had to be blind not to see it."

"Did he love me, mum, or was I a habit? He's soon moved on, hasn't he? He's engaged, did you know that?" When Pam wrung her hands together, it looked to Cathleen like desperation, "Look, mum, I don't want to live here, any more than you want me to, but could I, you know if I really had to?"

"Cathleen, I'm going to have to speak to your father, he's not going to be too pleased to say the least. I can't believe though that he would see you out on the streets, you were always his little girl."

"No, mum, I was once. I lost dad's respect after Ken and I broke up, I can still hear him ranting down here about my behaviour. I'm not ready for him to know yet, please."

Pam ignored her pleas, "Is this why you left the hotel in such a hurry, were they cross with you?"

"No, mum, they were not. I left on impulse because of Jackie's husband, Simon."

When Pam's chin dropped in horror, Cathleen's voice held irritation, "No! Wrong again, mum. Simon tried to comfort me when I told him Laurie had finished with me. When I told him I was pregnant, I can't be sure now, but it felt very much like he was coming on to me. I was disgusted. This was Jackie's husband, and she adores him."

Pam found her voice, "But you said you can't be sure, perhaps he was just being kind."

"He might have been, mum, but it felt sexual." Cathleen watched her mum blush at the word, "Mum, I'm nearly twenty one, sex isn't a dirty word. Anyway, I left the hotel that night. I didn't speak to Jackie, just gave Simon a piece of my mind, as I'm sure you can imagine. It just felt so awful. I was really happy with them, I felt liked, really liked for the first time in ages. Then for Simon to start some form of sexual groping, I couldn't take it, not just out of loyalty to Jackie, it was too soon after Laurie, Laurie had used me, and I was feeling cheap and dirty, and when Simon came on to me, he got the length of my angry tongue."

"You owe that woman an explanation, Cathleen. She has phoned this house four times now, and you haven't had the decency to answer one call." Cathleen picked up her glass again, "I can't, mum. What can I say? I don't want to hurt her, she's lovely, and she's been so kind to me. I've been a fool, I know that. I knew Laurie was married from the off. I went in with my eyes wide open, and I got hurt. I know even though you aren't saying it, you're disappointed in me. I'm sorry about that, mum, but you can't be any more disappointed in me than I am in myself." There were no tears, Cathleen felt surprisingly calm. She wasn't sure if it was Michael's proposal, because it had given her a safety net, or the fact that she really was growing up. She knew she had got herself into trouble, and somehow she knew she was the only one who could get her out of it whatever decision she made.

"I won't tell your father yet, love, but he'll have to know. After all we're going to be grandparents."

Cathleen kissed her mum's cheek, "Thanks, mum. I knew I could count on you."

"I will say, Cathleen, I don't want you marrying a man you don't love just to stop gossip. My shoulders are broad, we'll shoulder it together."

"In a funny way I do love Michael, mum. There's one problem though, he can't love me." Cathleen realised she hadn't been clear, and her mother made the assumption that after his fiancé was killed, he was struggling to love again. "People move on, Cathleen, he might love you, it's a very kind offer, he must have some feelings for you."

"Yes he does mum, he likes me. I think he even finds me sexy," there it was, that word again that had her mother blushing, Cathleen ignored it this time, "but believe me mum, he couldn't possibly love me like a man loves a woman. Trust me."

The back door opening had Pam up on her feet calling, "In here, love, Cathleen's home, Hannah's next door. Dinner won't be five minutes."

Hal appeared, "This is a sight for sore eyes, and how've my girls been?" He kissed Pam and keeping his arm round her shoulder gave Cathleen a wink, "Good to have you home, love, it's like old times."

*

Tuesday 22nd May 1967

Cathleen woke early, she was glad she had confided in her mother, but it didn't change the fact that her father was still to find out. That thought filled her with dread. There was a knock on her door, "Who is it?" It was Hannah, she was carrying her tiny tears dolly, and a book. "Can you read to me? Please." She dragged the please out in a pleading way which made Cathleen smile inwardly. "Come on up here. Then we'll have to get up. Hannah climbed up next to Cathleen and they lay together, while she read her little sister, Goldilocks and the three bears. "You don't do the voices like daddy. He reads them better." Cathleen tickled her sister, "Then perhaps he's the one you should ask to read to you then. I'm going downstairs, come on. I can hear mum's up."

Pam was just finishing a bowl of cornflakes, "Have we missed dad?"

"Yes, he was up and out before I even opened my eyes this morning." Cathleen noticed her mother looked tired, she hadn't brushed her hair and was still in her dressing gown. "Is everything alright, mum, you haven't told him, have you?"

Hannah tugged at her mother's dressing gown, "Told him what?" Pam pulled Hannah on to her lap, "Mind your own business," she

393

then looked at Cathleen and said, "No, no I haven't, but it was on my mind. I hate keeping secrets from him."

Hannah wriggled, "Mummy has a secret - mummy has a secret." Cathleen witnessed her mother's face heighten in colour, "Stop being silly, now go upstairs and get dressed. I'll do you some breakfast. You can have a boiled egg and soldiers, and I don't want to hear another peep of your nonsense." Once Hannah was out of earshot Pam said, "We are going to have to tell him, Cathleen, I couldn't sleep thinking about it. Hannah will say something, she always does."

Cathleen helped herself to a bowl of cornflakes, and sprinkled a good spoon of sugar over them, half of it went over the table, "I know, mum, tonight then. Can't we get rid of Hannah again, next door?"

"I'll try, but she was round there last night. I might ask Dorcas, you'll be needing an appointment with Geoffrey soon, best we keep in with them."

Cathleen was filled with dread at having to speak to Geoffrey about her pregnancy, it only felt like yesterday that she had sat before him telling him she was pregnant by someone other than her finance, this time she had to tell him she was pregnant with no father on the scene. *'Oh why should I care? Let them think what they like. This is only the start of it.'*

Hannah appeared carrying the post, "There's lots of letters."

Pam took them sorting through them. Most of them were for Hal, "There's one for you Cathleen, from Bournemouth."

Cathleen snatched it from her mother, leaving the last of her breakfast in the bowl. She went upstairs to read it in private. She knew without looking, it was from Jackie. Her hands trembled on the pink envelope as she eased the seal open.

Dear Cathleen,

I can't begin to tell you how much we miss you here. Simon has told me what happened, of course I'm angry with him, but the thing is I wasn't surprised, I saw it coming. I had watched my husband for weeks, darling, wanting what he couldn't have. The trouble is, men are programmed to look, they are red blooded, and they never seem to grow too old. I don't want to say Laurie didn't love you like you thought he did. What started out as a bit of fun, a silly competition between the two of them, has ended in heartache. Simon liked you and Laurie recognised it. Laurie being married with a family probably felt Simon had the edge on him, and he set about proving to himself he still had it in him to pull a pretty girl. I don't say this to be mean, darling, I want you to understand men. I do believe Laurie got caught out, I honestly believe he fell for you, but just couldn't leave his wife and family. I believe he hurt himself too.

I'm not worried about Laurie, darling. I'm worried about you. Both Simon and I want you to come back. I wish I had confronted Simon about my fears, but I felt what with turning forty, I was insecure. I am no match for your youthful beauty. I wish I had trusted you, as I know I pushed you with Laurie so as to keep you out of my husband's reach. We've all been foolish.

I don't know your plans with the baby, Cathleen. But if you can bear to come back, and give Simon another chance, I can assure you we will work round your pregnancy, and when the baby is here we will all pull together to look after it. I always wanted children, Cathleen, it never happened. When you arrived it was like having a daughter, I miss you so much. You don't have to worry about Laurie, he has resigned from the England contract, we have a Bob coming in his place - he's nearly sixty five. I'd like to say you're safe with him, but as I say, they never get too old to look!

I'd like to stay cross with Simon, but darling you really are a striking young woman, I really can't blame him for looking. He was wrong to take advantage of your vulnerability, but he has assured me it was all fantasy in his head. We've been married a long time, I'm not about to throw it away on one silly whim.

There is a lot here for you to think about, but if you want to come back, we will welcome you with open arms.

Please get in touch, Cathleen, if only to let us know you are well.

395

I finish this letter with a sorry,

With Love, and very best wishes

Jackie

Cathleen stared at the words on the page until they went out of focus. Things were unfolding with opportunities opening up without her having to try.

She had a hot deep bath, enjoying a soak in the bubbles. Every time the water cooled she topped it up with more, *'This is pure luxury.'*

When her mother tapped on the bathroom door, telling her to hurry up she wanted to get dressed herself, she made her mind up to speak to her father tonight. The thought of what she would say made her stomach feel weak, but she was determined.

Pam was curious about the letter, but Cathleen was not in the mood to share its news. There were things in there that Cathleen found hard to accept. The biggest was, she had been a game, some kind of contest. *'How could they?'* The more she thought about it, the more it stung.

When Cathleen told Pam she would tell her father tonight, her mother seemed to lose her complexion, "I think it's a good idea, it'll come better from you."

The letter played on Cathleen's mind, and the thought of what lay ahead made her restless. She practised how she would tell her father she was pregnant, but thoughts of his last outburst kept clouding her judgement. She had conversations with herself in her head, but her explanations got lost in too many words.

It was gone six when Hal came home, he called out as he pushed open the back door, "Hello, love, sorry I'm late. The delivery didn't turn up till ten this morning, it put us back all day."

Pam went through to the kitchen where he was washing his hands. "We've eaten, love, the girls were hungry, Cathleen's taken Hannah to the park, she'll be back shortly, she wants a word."

Hal raised his eyebrows, "Something I should be worried about?"

Pam kissed him on the lips, "She'll tell you in good time, but have your dinner first."

Hal was just finishing a second helping of crumble and custard when he heard Hannah and Cathleen in the kitchen. He strained his ears to the whispering, but couldn't make out what was being said. Hannah was first to appear, "Daddy, we've been on the swings, Cathleen pushed me really high." Before he could answer, Cathleen interrupted them, she kissed Hal on the cheek saying, "I'll be down in a sec, I'm busting."

Cathleen sat on the toilet not able to believe what was staring her in the face, the dampness she had felt in her gusset was not her desperate need for the toilet, but a thick brown discharge stared at her. "Mum! Mum!"

She heard her mother's footsteps on the stairs, Cathleen was up off the toilet standing in the open doorway, "Whatever's the matter love?"

Cathleen burst into tears, "Oh Mum, I'm bleeding."

Cathleen was helped into bed like an invalid. "I'll have to tell your father, you know that don't you?"

Cathleen was beyond caring, she was about to lose her baby. Laurie's baby, and all of a sudden she wanted it more than anything else in the world.

Doctor Covax arrived, he had that important look about him, towering over her, looking down his nose through his half-moon glasses, "Did you know you were pregnant?"

When she nodded, he said, "This isn't a good sign, Cathleen. You do understand that, don't you?"

When she nodded again, he said, "You're going to have to have complete bed rest, we need to get this bleeding to stop." He took her blood pressure, the silence felt scary. She relaxed a little when he smiled, "Well that seems all good." Without looking at her he asked, "Cathleen, do you want this baby?"

She didn't know how to answer, "I do, now…what I mean is, I think so. Things do seem to be settling, and I'm finding my way…"

"What about the father? Where's he, and what are his plans?"

"I'm, I… he doesn't know." Her blush could be felt on her cheeks. She was relieved to see her mum appear, "How is she, Geoffrey?" The easy friendship between the Doctor's family and hers made it all feel so much more embarrassing. She listened as he discussed her with her mother.

When she was left alone she turned on her side and cradled her stomach. There was a familiar, dull ache in her lower back, reminding her of her monthlies.

A tap at her door had her sitting up, "Come in." The grave expression on her father's face made her heart thump, "Dad I…"

He sat on the end of her bed, "You do beat all, girl, do you know that?" She couldn't answer he looked so sad, she thought for one awful moment he was going to cry. "Where did we go wrong, Cathleen? What is it with you? It's one disaster after another." Cathleen reached down for his hand, but he moved it away, pushing his hair back, "I'm sorry, dad…"

398

"Yes, Cathleen you always are, but you don't learn. Look at you, your mother says this bloke's married, it gets worse every time."

She had the good grace to blush, she had no words to defend herself, "I didn't think it was possible, Cathleen, but we gave you too much, too much of everything. When Hannah came along I know it pushed your nose out of joint, but we still loved you, even though you were difficult, a real trial."

"It's not Hannah, dad. I think I know now I made a mistake letting Ken go. It's him…"

Hal held his hand up, "Let me stop you there, girl? I'm only going to say this once, and I hope you learn from it. You have a habit of wanting what is not attainable. You could have had Ken, the kiddie loved you, he thought the sun shone out your backside, girl. When you had him eating out your hand you didn't want him, no, you played around with someone else's fiancé, worse than that, but I don't want to go there. Then you meet this chap, this American chap that's married, and he gets you in the family way. Well where is he? Back with his wife, that's where. Where he belongs. He was never going to marry you, Cathleen, never. You were just a bit of fun. It's the same old story, why buy the apple from the shop when you can scrump it off the tree for free? I don't want to be mean to you, but you cheapen yourself. You're a good looking lass, I might be a bit biased, but you are, and that is why you get all this attention. I should be angry with you, but I'm beaten. There you have it, beaten, girl, beaten. So over to you, you tell me your plans."

"Dad, I'm sorry, I really…"

"I don't want to hear it, Cathleen, I want to hear what you're going to do, and where you're planning to go. Your mum says you've heard from the woman at the hotel you worked at."

"I have," tears threatened as Cathleen read the disappointment that was as clear on Hal's face as if it was written in ink, "I have a couple of options, Michael the chap I had a fling with has offered to marry

399

me, take the baby on as his. Says I can divorce him if I want, but is happy to give me a name for the baby, stop the scandal a bit…"

"Do you love him?"

"I thought I did once, but not anymore." Cathleen knew she sounded dreadful, all her father's words seemed to be true, she only wanted what she thought she couldn't have. "I can go back to Bournemouth, Jackie said we could all pull together and look after the baby. I love it there, dad. It would save the gossip…"

Hal held his daughter's leg through the blanket, "You really think we're that shallow. I don't relish the talk, but our shoulders are broad. Your mother and I will want what is best for you and the baby…" Cathleen felt touched by her father's physical gesture, she could feel the warmth of his hand, "Last time dad, you said…"

"Let's not think about last time, last time was different. I want to shut that out of my memory and so should you."

Cathleen watched as her father stood, his movements were slow, and despite his kindness she could feel his despair. "Get some rest. Do what the doctor says, and when you're well, we'll take it from there."

When her bedroom door closed, Cathleen turned back on her side and gave way to tears.

*

Cathleen woke with a low, deep pain in her stomach, there was a screen round her, and she could hear voices. She remembered. Cathleen had miscarried and had had to have a dilation and curettage. It had been explained that it was a scraping of the womb to make sure that nothing was left behind, and to stop infection.

The screen was pulled back making her feel exposed, a nurse stood with a doctor, "How are you feeling?"

400

Cathleen explained her stomach was sore, and was assured it was all normal. "Your mother and father are here to see you, are you up for visitors?" Cathleen nodded, she didn't know why, but she felt tearful. This would have been an answer to her prayers four weeks ago, but as her father had said, when she couldn't have something, she wanted it more.

'I'm going to have to try, try and mend my ways.'

When Hal and Pam entered the side ward, Cathleen started to cry. Pam took her in her arms. She had been in this situation herself many times, which is why there had been a fifteen year gap between her two girls, Cathleen and Hannah. "You cry, love, let it out. We're here for you."

Hal shuffled his feet, Cathleen thought he looked uncomfortable. When Pam said, "Fill that beaker with water, Hal, she could do with a drink." He had done as he was asked, and then brushed his hand over Cathleen's head, "You'll be alright, girl. Give yourself time, you'll see."

*

Tilly packed the last of the clothes in the suitcase for Rosie. One week today and they would take her back to her mother. It didn't matter that she had the boys, the thought of losing Rosie filled her with dread.

She turned as her mother came in with Peter, "Didn't you hear him crying? The pram was rocking like a see saw."

"Oh give him here, mum, I was lost in thought. I hope Rhana's got room for all this stuff Rosie wants to take."

"What's her mum like, love?"

Tilly patted Peter's back, "Don't ask, every time I remember, I want to cry."

June reached out and gave Tilly's shoulder a squeeze, "I'll leave you to it. May and Angus will be back in a minute." June picked up a cardigan, folded it and draped it over a chair, "Do you want me to have the boys when you go to the Lake District?"

"I don't know yet, Ed's talking of taking us all up there. He wants to show his family to this woman, Hetty, who helped him when he was ill. I don't feel like I'm going to be very good company after losing Rosie, but I'll have to go."

June smiled at Tilly, "I've got some good news for you, love. I wasn't going to tell you till I was a hundred percent sure but I feel you need something to look forward to." She hesitated, "Well I hope its good news." Tilly looked curious, "Go on."

"Your brother, I mean half-brother, Kevin, has a job here with a big car company in London, and your dad's talking of selling up and coming to England. He misses you, Tilly, like I do. He reckons he'll easily get a job here as a mechanic. I was hoping we could stay in your gran's old room until we get a place, you know, sell up in Canada and buy here. It might take…"

Tilly grabbed hold of her mum with her one free arm, "That's the best news I've heard in a long time. Of course you're welcome. Kevin too if needs be."

The sound of the door told them May was back with Angus. Tilly went downstairs carrying Peter on her hip, "May, thank you." She looked down at Angus, "Did you feed the ducks with nanny?" She lifted him onto her free hip and kissed his fair head. He was an adorable child and she knew May was more than fond of him.

Tilly went into the kitchen to make coffee, while May and June went into the lounge with the boys. Tilly smiled at the sight that met her as she carried the tray through, Peter was laid on a blanket, and Angus was settled on the floor with his train set, and there were her mother and May chatting together like old friends, rather than the arch enemies they used to be.

Tilly told May all about her mother's plans to live in England, and the topic of discussion went from the move, the boys, to Lucy and Ken's plans to be married in the autumn, which had May saying, "That's a bit sudden. Is there a reason behind it?"

Tilly didn't rise to May's suspicions, and said quite simply, "No, May, it's not what you're thinking. They want to be married, why wait."

Tilly was pleased to see May looked embarrassed by her thoughts, and the conversation was steered to Rosie's departure. They finished their coffee with the sorry tale of Cathleen, and the fact that she had been discharged from hospital yesterday.

Laughter rang round the room when May said, "To think I used to believe Cathleen was a much better choice for my Ed, oh how wrong I've been. You did a good job with your Tilly, June. I'm only glad she found it in her heart to give me a second chance."

Tilly stood up, gathered the mugs, and gave Angus a biscuit off the tray, "May, I don't know what I'd have done without you lately. You've been a brick."

*

Saturday 2nd June 1967

Michael pulled up outside Cathleen's house, he felt a little nervous, but walked up the path with his head held high in a confident manner. Pam opened the door, "Yes?"

"I've come to speak to Cathleen, please."

He was shown through to the dining area, he liked what he saw. The home was immaculate, clean and modern. He could hear voices in the kitchen, and when Cathleen appeared wearing a baggy t shirt and shorts with not a smidgen of makeup on, Michael thought he had never seen her look so beautiful, *'How I wish I could love this woman.'* He witnessed the blush that crossed her cheeks as she

403

recognised her visitor, "Michael, I wasn't expecting you, or anyone for that matter." She looked down at her choice of dress as if in explanation, he laughed, "You look great, lovely legs!"

The awkwardness was gone, and when Pam left a jug of lemonade on the table she sat and told him what had happened. Michael put his glass down, and took her hand, "That's such a relief Cathleen," he spoke fast, not wanting to be misunderstood, "not your loss, but… you know, I thought you'd decided to just get rid of the baby."

"Michael I could never have done that. I know people think I'm out for myself all the time, but I was prepared to own up to my responsibilities."

"Cathleen, would you have married…"

She stopped him, "Michael." He watched her hesitate, "Michael, I want to thank you for your support, I…"

"Would you have married me? If I hadn't…"

"I don't think so Michael, not because of what you told me, but it wouldn't have been fair on you or me. It did mean a great deal to me though. You've turned out to be my very best friend, and I shall love you forever for that."

"What about Tilly? Where does she fit in in all this?"

Cathleen poured herself another drink, "Tilly is my friend, and a good one, but we've changed, both of us. I'm leaving here Michael, I think you should too."

"What with you?"

He smiled as she laughed, "No Michael, but you need to find yourself, like I need too. I'm taking a job in Wales, that's if I get it. With the reference Jackie and Simon have given me, they'll think they're getting an angel."

It was Michael's turn to laugh, "Well let's hope your wings don't fall off."

Michael stood on the Hill's front doorstep holding Cathleen in his arms, he wished again he could love this woman, love her like a man should love. He kissed the top of her head, "Be happy, Cathleen. Keep in touch, and you never know I just might come to Wales for a visit."

Cathleen kissed him full on the lips, "Do that Michael, I shall write to you, promise."

He climbed into his car, his lips still tingled from the kiss. He was warmed, that despite what she knew about him she could still show affection. *'Perhaps she's right, I should get away from here, find myself too.'*

His engine purred into life, he felt better than he had in months. Since Cathleen's return, things had been better at home, and he hadn't been seen in the Spotted Cow pub, once.

*

The Lake District – Appleby Fair

Rosie sat on her bed, looking out over the park. School had closed on Friday for half term, but she knew there would be no going back after the holidays. Sadness swept over her as she realised she was really leaving. She kept thinking of her mother, hoping to instil some happiness to the situation. "Rosie, tea's on the table. Come on! That's the second time I've called you."

Rosie didn't want to admit to anyone she was struggling to leave this house, but the prospect had taken her appetite. *'I'll be okay, once I sees me mam.'* She closed her eyes trying to visualise what she looked like, but it was difficult. *'How could I have forgotten me mam?'*

She turned from the window at the sound of Tilly's voice, "There you are. Whatever's the matter? You've got beans on toast downstairs and its going cold."

Rosie burst into tears, "I'm frightened, me tummy feels funny." Tilly took the child in her arms, "I can imagine, it's fear of the unknown. Once you see your mummy you'll forget all about us."

Rosie's face heightened in colour, "I aint ever gonna forget you. I loves you Tilly, I feel like I wants to stay, but I have to go, I have to go to me mam."

Tilly brushed Rosie's hair away from her eyes, "You're not back yet, and you're forgetting how we taught you to speak."

"Can I come back Tilly, if I don't like it…?"

"Rosie you can come home anytime, you know where we live, don't you?"

Rosie hopped off the bed, "I'll eat me tea now."

"I'll eat my tea now. Go on young lady, Angus is in the garden calling for you."

*

Monday 4th May 1967 – Bank Holiday

Tilly put the last box in the back of Norman's car. "You can't get another thing in, good job you bought an estate."

Rosie had clung to June begging for reassurance that she would feed Rookie, her bird, should he reappear. It had brought a lump to Tilly's throat when she heard Rosie tell June, she wasn't her nanny J, she already had a nana Jay. Tilly's mother had got down on one knee and looked Rosie in the eye, saying, "I don't care how many nana's you have with the same initial, I'm your nanny J too, and don't you ever forget that." There had been tears from both, but once they were all settled in Tilly's little car, Rosie was up on her knees looking out the back calling, "Bye nanny J, bye."

*

The closer they got to the Lakes, the heavier it seemed to rain. The weather suited Tilly's mood, she felt desperate. They had stopped twice already, she had used the ladies, fed the children, but had been unable to manage anything but a cup of tea. She felt sick to the pit of her stomach.

The sight of mixed coloured horses being exercised, and some being washed in the river was a good indication they were in the right place.

Tilly looked out of the window, and then at Ed, "Why are we stopping?"

"I'm going to get dad to wait here, I need to find Rosie's mum first. You never know she might not be here, or she might not be in a position to..."

"I'm coming too." Rosie was reaching for the handle of the car, showing no fear of leaving this family.

Tilly turned round, "Rosie, you're Rainbow now."

Ed placed a hand on Tilly's shoulder, but spoke to them both, "I don't think we should say who Rosie is to anyone until we find her mum. It might not be possible for her to stay. It'll be easier if we say we're looking for a friend, rather than Rosie's mum, after all, that maniac you told me about might still be around."

Tilly spoke in hushed tones, "Don't Ed, you'll frighten her." The truth was the thought of that man, and this place terrified Tilly.

She watched as Ed got out of the car to speak with his parents, they agreed to have the boys on their laps while Tilly and Ed went to explore with Rosie. May had pulled out Rosie's wellingtons, "She'll need these. Those new shoes will get ruined in this mud." Tilly smiled inwardly, but she knew it was sensible.

Rosie held on to Tilly's hand, the rain had stopped but the ground was thick mud. Ed pushed open the gate, the noise was horrendous. There was a mixture of laughter, cheering and music. They could see a scuffle taking place, a group of men were stood in a circle while two young lads were fighting with their bare hands. The taller, thinner one wasn't faring as well as the other, and Tilly gripped Rosie's hand tighter, trying to shield her from this violence. "I think Ed's right, don't say you're Rainbow yet, let's find your mum first." Rosie didn't say a word.

Someone grabbed Ed from behind, he lost his balance in the mud. When he tried to stand he was kicked back down, "What're the likes of yours sniffing round 'ere for?"

When Ed managed to stand, the man screwed the collar of his coat up in his fist holding him in a vice like grip, "Well?"

Ed was genuinely scared, he didn't like what he was seeing. "We've come to see an old friend." This caused loud laughter, "Hey Duke, this toffee 'ere has come to see an old friend." Ed found himself pushed towards the circle where the fight was taking place.

Rosie had started to cry, and he heard Tilly's high pitched voice above the shouting, and jeering. "Please, we need to find Rhana." This seemed to halt their fun. The man who had grabbed Ed at the start said, "An' who's asking?"

"We know Rhana from the fair, she used to read the cards in Cornwall."

Ed found the reprieve was short, he was being punched in the back of the head by different people and every time he swung round to defend himself, someone else punched him from behind. He couldn't win, it was as much as he could do to stay upright in this mud. There was laughter as they mocked Tilly's voice. Ed was trying hard to defend himself as well as keep an eye on Rosie and Tilly.

"Come on toffee, shows us what yer made of."

With the next punch Ed lost his balance. He tried to stand up, but was kicked down. He could hear Tilly's screams, but there was nothing he could do, these were not his sort of people, and he was never a fighter.

*

Tilly grabbed at a passing woman, and in a desperate state said, "Please help us, we're looking for Rhana, and my husband's being set upon by that lot." She pointed to the scuffle that was getting louder by the minute.

"She's over there somewhere, see that wooden caravan, that's 'ers."

The laughter was deafening. Tilly couldn't move, she couldn't leave Ed here being beaten. "Rosie run to the caravan and get Rhana, get her to help Ed." Rosie didn't move, she gripped Tilly's hand tighter than ever. Tilly, not knowing where her courage came from, moved into the circle still holding Rosie's hand, "For God's sake, we came here as friends, what is it with you people?"

There was more mocking of her voice, and choice of words, but Tilly's intervention gave Ed chance to find his feet. Seeing Ed covered in mud, angered Tilly, "You should be ashamed of yourselves, frightening our little girl…" her tirade was lost in more jeers and laughter.

Someone stepped forward which caused the mob to quieten, "Pack it in." He seemed to cast his eyes over the sorry sight the three of them made, and said, "You looking for Rhana?"

Tilly nodded, unable to find her voice. He pointed to a Romany caravan that sat at the edge of the field. This led to Rosie saying, "Where's the rainbow?" Before Tilly could quieten her, the man answered, misunderstanding her question, "That van got burnt with the old lady."

Before Rosie could ask any more they headed for the beautiful wooden van that had a horse tethered at the side.

The door opened at the back and standing there was a woman that Tilly vaguely remembered. She looked years older. Her beautiful long, red hair that had flowed down her back was cut round her ears as if hacked, and her eyes were lost in dark shadows. Tilly could sense Rhana's mind working quickly as she took in the sight before her, and amongst the noisy atmosphere she whispered, "Rainbow, my rainbow." Rosie was out of Tilly's grip and into her mother's arms. "I'm home mum, I can read me letters… my letters. I can do all the things you wanted for me, I even knows me sums."

The two of them stayed holding each other. When they drew apart, Tilly could see Rhana was crying. She seemed unaware of the state of them, "Come in, come on. It's small but I can make you a cuppa."

"We can't stay, we've two children waiting back at the gate with family. Rosie, I mean Rainbow wanted to find you. We went to the fair at Chichester and were told you'd come back with your own kind."

Rosie looked around, "Mummy where's Jimmy?"

"Jimmy died shortly after we got 'ere. Ee didn't fare so well after that trouble… I lost me nana Jay earlier this year, an' I 'ave 'er van now."

Rosie ignored this information, "I've got lots of stuff mummy, I got books, and clothes. Shoes and boots, I've had everything, Tilly…"

Tilly stopped Rosie, "Come on, let's go and get your belongings, and say your goodbyes. You've got the rest of your life to show mummy what you have, and to say what you've been up to."

The four of them made their way to the top of the field again, thankfully the sun was trying to peek through. Tilly got nervous as they neared the group that had set about Ed earlier, but they barely turned in their direction.

*

Rhana felt in awe at the posh looking lady and gent in the car waiting. The gent got out, "What the hell happened to you lad?"

Ed shrugged, "Fell over, it's a quagmire in that field." Rhana could see he wasn't convinced, but Tilly intervened, introducing her as Rosie's mother, and corrected herself saying Rainbow.

Rhana watched in awe as the posh lady got out of the car, she carried a small boy with blonde hair who reached out for Rainbow, and she watched as her daughter took him in her arms saying, "I'm going back now, back to me mummy, Angus. I'll miss you, I will, I'll miss you all."

Tilly introduced the posh lady as May. Rhana could not only see the disapproval on her face, but she could feel it.

Rainbow said her goodbyes, they were all tearful, but when Tilly took the child in her arms, it looked like she would never let her go. This show of love brought a lump to Rhana's throat. She couldn't hear what was said between the two of them but she heard Rainbow say, "There's no one in the whole world like you Tilly, I'm always gonna love yer, no matter where I go."

The older gent broke the moment, when he opened the back of his car. The seats were laid down, and the boot was full. Rhana stepped forward, "We ain't got room for all this stuff Rainbow. Pick a box, an' that's yer lot."

411

Rosie stamped her foot, and held her arms at her side indignantly, "I've got to bring it all, it's me pretty things, and me learning books, I've brought it all."

Rhana looked round at this family, they were good people. She spoke to Tilly, "Where yer goin now, from 'ere like?"

"We're visiting friends nearby, why?"

Rhana felt a wind. It blew up around her, bringing with it the second sight she had been gifted. She could feel it, she could see it, see it as clear as a picture book. "I need time. I need er bit er time to make room for all this stuff. You saw the van, it ain't kitted out for pretty clothes, or learning books."

Rosie was crying, "I want my stuff, Tilly packed it all for me. She said I had to keep learning." Rhana noticed every single word the child spoke was perfect English. This is just what she had always wished for her. The only problem was, she could see it had separated them.

"We'll leave 'ere on thirteenth, how long you's all staying in these parts?"

Tilly had hold of Rosie's hand, "We're here for four days. We can hold the bulk of this stuff, that'll give you time to make room, will that help?"

Rhana sighed with relief, Rosie let go of Tilly's hand saying, "Yes mum, that's what we'll do, we'll make room."

It was agreed. On the dot of nine, Friday morning, Rhana and Rosie would be waiting at the gate.

*

Rosie stood in the entrance of the van with Agnes' old carpet bag she had given her, and her mother carried a small box. "Where am I going to sleep?"

Rhana dropped the box in the middle of the floor which filled the space immediately. "Up there, we'll put a blanket over the seat.

"I'll need a room, a bed of me own."

"Not now, Rainbow, not now." There was a bump at the side of the van, Rhana opened her door, "Watch where you're bleeding going, stupid bastard."

Rainbow felt scared, she started to cry.

Rhana sat on the built in sofa, "Come 'ere, Rainbow, come 'ere. Stop that silly noise, you's home now, I've dreamed of this day I 'ave. Come let's sort some space, you can 'ave me room if you wants."

Rosie didn't like this angry place, her mother hadn't been like this when they lived at the fair, "I don't like these people mummy, they're scary."

Her mother took her in her arms, and held her tight, Rosie could hear her breathing in the scent of her hair, "I missed yer so much my lovely, I wanted yer yer know, I walked for days along that pier looking for yer…"

"I'm home now mummy, I'm home." Rosie didn't feel like she was home, this wasn't the place she had been brought up in, and her mum was different. She took a book from her bag, it was Enid Blyton's famous five. "I'll read to you mummy, would you like that?"

The noise outside was deafening to Rosie, she didn't like it, "Why didn't you stay with the fair? I liked it there."

"I couldn't, Jimmy was hurt, real bad. I 'ad to come and find me own. Nana Jay looked after me for a while, then she got sick."

Rosie ate little at tea time, she said it tasted funny. She climbed in to her mother's bed with her, and hoped in the morning things would feel better.

Rosie woke early, the sun was shining. She washed in the lake with her mother, and many others from the camp. She noticed she was introduced as just Rainbow, not a mention that this is my daughter. Rosie guessed it had something to do with that maniac man who she had had to run from. In the sunshine her new surroundings seemed better. It felt good to be back with her mother. Everybody seemed friendly today, not so frightening, and the noisy shouting had stopped. When she told her mother this she had said, "It'll start up later, animals some of 'em are, you'll get used to it. It's the drink."

Rosie still wondered where all her stuff would go. When she broached the subject, Rhana had said, "Plenty of time, we can always ask one of the other vans to hold it for us. Rosie hadn't dared to say she didn't want her nice things going anywhere but here. There was an old horse tethered up outside her mother's van, his name was Bruce. Rosie had made friends with him already.

By Thursday, Rosie had settled. She had made many friends. One in particular was a scruffy girl called Beverley, who lived in a van two down from them, she had become Rosie's shadow. Rosie felt superior to her, as Beverley couldn't read. Rosie had read a few of Enid Blyton's stories to her, and had said she would teach her to do her letters, and her numbers.

There was a lot about being back with her mother that Rosie liked. She was enjoying the amount of freedom she was given here. She liked the horses, and sleeping with her mother. All these good things didn't outweigh the strange feeling in her stomach when she thought of Tilly. Tilly, Ed and her brothers, and her own bedroom. With these thoughts came excitement, *'They'll be dropping all my things off tomorrow. I'll be able to see Angus and Petey again.'*

She didn't want to think about them all going back to Hunston, or the fact that she would never see her other family again. To stop this feeling of sadness, she kept telling herself what fun it was here.

414

It was a bit noisy, and she didn't like the men, they didn't seem able to talk like normal people, they were always shouting. Her mother shouted too. She couldn't remember her being like that before.

"Rainbow, Rainbow." A boy of about ten ran towards her, "Come on they're racing, they'll be down in a minute." All thoughts left Rosie as she rushed to the bottom of the hill.

*

Rhana looked out of the window when she heard a tap on her door. It wasn't raining, but there was a chill in the air. It was Alice, Rhana spoke to herself as she moved to open the doors at the back of the van, *'What the bleeding 'ell does she want?'*

She forced a smile of welcome, "Alice?" Rhana looked out past her, "Is everything alright?"

Alice made to move in the van, but Rhana blocked her way, "I'm a bit busy, making room, what with my friend's guest staying."

Alice's voice was sharp, "You ain't kidding any of us, that's your kiddie, an' you knows it." Rhana gave her a blank stare. She couldn't answer because she couldn't think of one believable reply, "She's a Murphy, I can sees it, and so'll they when they puts two and two together. Yous ran away from 'ere, what... must be seven year ago now, your granny got a hiding over it, I remember. You's were having the bairn, I knows it, you knows it too. I'll tell you this, when rumours get out, them Murphys'll know it too. You don't have a chance in hell of keeping her from them... I"

She shut the door in Alice's face. Rhana was physically shaking, and knew her actions would have clarified Alice's suspicions. She had to trust and act on her second sight. There was only way forward to save her child.

*

Rosie hadn't gone home for lunch. Joey's mother had given her a sausage and a hunk of bread, and she had played with Joey and Susan round the bonfire, poking sticks in it, watching as they caught alight. It wasn't until the horse racing had finished that she made her way back to her van. She pushed open the back door horrified to see her mum's tear stained face. "Mummy, what's happened, what's wrong?"

"Come an' sit with me, Rainbow. I need to talk to yer." Rosie's heart beat fast in her chest, but she sat quiet, frightened of what she was going to hear. "Yer know when people are sick, like yer granny Jay, and Uncle Jimmy… and yer said with yer new family yer lost yer granny Agnes?" Rosie nodded, still unable to speak. She could sense something bad was going to happen, but didn't know what, where or when? "What I wants to tell yer is, I'm ill, Rainbow, I has a growth, right 'ere in me chest." Rosie found her voice, "Can I feel it?"

"No, no yer can't, but I can, an' it's growin', growin' by the day. It's called a depression and it's killing me. Yer won't understand this now, but yer will, when yer's older."

Rosie threw her arms round her mother's neck, "It's good I came back, I can look after you, you won't die, mummy, you'll get better, you'll see."

"No I won't, Rainbow. Think 'bout when I'm gone, yer be left with this lot. Yer don't belong 'ere no more. You never did, you's a show girl, yer belong with the fair. These people 'ere are different. Believe me, I wish fings were different, but as I see it, you 'ave one option, and that's if that good family'll take yer the morrer, yer gotta go."

Rosie started to cry, "I wanna be with you, you me mummy, you love me."

"I do love yer, that's why I want yer to go with em. They want yer, Rainbow. I can see it, I can sense it, and I can feel it. I'm gonna be gone from this world by end of the year, I can feel that too. Then what, what 'appens to yer then, eh? Yer done real well since yer been with them. If yer stays, yer would soon be like this lot, I don't want it for yer, I want yer to be somebody, it's for the best."

Rosie started to sob.

"Stop it now, this is silly. I could see yer were gonna to miss em all, yer just want now what yer can't ave. I couldn't have 'ad your things 'ere either, it's only just big enough for the two of us. An' where yer gonna sleep, yer can't sleep with me forever. Yer'll understand one day, but for now I want yer to be a big girl an' do this fer me 'cause' I aint gonna be able to care for yer, and God only knows I don't wanna leave you to the 'ands of this lot."

*

Friday 8ᵗʰ June 1967

Goodbyes

Tilly had shed many tears with Ed in the privacy of their room, and despite everyone saying they had done the right thing, it didn't help. She missed Rosie more than she ever thought possible. "You saw what sort of people they were, Ed, what will become of her? I almost feel like not going back, I don't think I'll be able to stomach seeing the change in her."

Tilly was pulled into Ed's arms, "I'm sure she'll be the same old Rosie." She couldn't hold back the tears that were always threatening, and they fell again, "These people are worse than the ones she lived with at Farleys Fair, surely you can see that? I was frightened for your life at one point." Although Ed said she was exaggerating, she knew it had shaken him up at the time.

"Come on blow your nose, we have to say our goodbyes here first."

The two of them went down stairs, where Norman and Len were talking about cars. Norman was saying how he liked to drive the estate, it was solid, and roomy. May and Hetty were amusing the boys, Peter was able to sit up on his own now, and was taking an interest in everything. Ed dragged their two cases into the kitchen, "We're ready. Can you fit these in yours, mum?" May was up on her feet, "Yes we'll make them fit. Once we drop off Rosie's stuff we'll have heaps of room. I'll be glad to get home now, won't you?"

Tilly didn't answer for fear of more tears. Ed pushed forward, "Come on, let's make a move, I want to be back before six tonight, I promised I'd help Ken in the morning."

After many thank you's for having them, and goodbye's, they were glad to be on the road, "Put your foot down, Ed, I don't want to be late. The last thing I want is for you to have to go in that camp again."

He laughed, "Do you think I relish the thought? No, Rhana will be at the gate, she promised."

Tilly wasn't so sure. She had seen the tiny living space, and knew that fitting in Rosie's stuff was going to be difficult. *'Perhaps she'll have a trailer?'*

*

The sun was shining, but it felt damp in the air. They arrived at the camp on the dot of nine, and Rosie and Rhana were waiting for them as promised at the gate. Rosie was immaculate. Her hair was tied back in a ponytail, and she was wearing a pink frock with white open toe sandals and short white socks, "Bloody hell! Look at her, she looks better than when we dropped her off" Angus shouted in the back, "Buddy hell, buddy hell." Tilly hit Ed's leg and tried to distract Angus with the horses grazing in the field.

Tilly got out of the car and Rosie threw herself at her, "I'm coming home Tilly, I'm coming home with you, Mum can't have me. You said I could if I wanted…" Tilly squeezed her to her, which stopped any further explanations. "This is the best news ever, darling." Tilly raised her eyes in question at Rhana, "She do best with the likes of yer an' yours. I ain't doing so well, and she woulda missed yer, all of yer."

Rosie ran across to Norman and May as they pulled up behind Tilly's car. "I'm coming home with you all, I'm not staying with me mummy. I'm going to be Tilly's girl."

What May said, Tilly had no idea, for she had moved across to Rhana, and held her in her arms. When she found her voice, she said, "Thank you, thank you so much. I'll do my very best for her, always, I promise." Rhana nodded, but said nothing.

When Rosie had finished telling Ed, Angus and Peter that she was coming home with them all, she stopped and looked round for her mother.

*

Rhana stepped behind the gate distancing herself from the scene. When she heard Rosie call, Mummy wait, wait." It felt like her heart was breaking. She turned, saying, "No, Rainbow, yer mus go now. Go with yer family".

Rhana could feel the pull. Her child was torn between her love for her new family and her loyalty to her mother.

Rhana held the gate closed to stop Rosie entering the field, but the child climbed up on to it not worrying about her pretty clothes getting dirty. She threw herself into Rhana's arms. "I love you mummy," tears fell as she clung to her mother's neck, I'm always gonna love you, always. I'll not forget…"

Rhana prised Rosie off her, "Yer just look for the Rainbow, that's where I'll be. Now go, go on, go."

As she watched Ed lift her child off the gate, she thought, '*That's my Rainbow. I'd called er that, not only because it suited er, but for the colour she brought to my life. I must let er go now, let er go with these good people who've given er a chance.*'

She could hear Rosie calling goodbye from the car, but she didn't look back.

*

Tilly couldn't believe it, they were all going home as a family. Rosie was sitting in the back of the car with Angus, and Tilly sat in the front with Peter, who wouldn't sit still. Tilly was pleased that although Rosie had shed a few tears, they had stopped quicker than she had expected.

Rain started to fall on the windscreen, Ed put on the windscreen wipers, "Well we're glad to have you back Rosie, Tilly's been a right wet blanket since we said good bye to you." Rosie's next words made Tilly go all goosepimply.

"Auntie May said they was to be Nanny and Grandad now, so can I call you mummy and daddy, like Angus?"

Tilly felt Rosie's little arms creep round her neck, "Can I, Tilly, can I call you mummy too?" "I feel like the luckiest mummy in the world." There was laughter when Ed said, "Me too."

"You're not a mummy." Even Angus laughed, but they guessed he didn't know why.

*

It felt to Rhana like the heavens had opened as rain lashed down, soaking her long white smock. She made her way to the lake, the same lake where many years ago she used to meet Rainbow's father,

420

Flynn Murphy. How she had loved him as a girl, that was until he had raped her, raped her not far from where she stood now, gazing into the lake.

She waded into the water letting her thoughts wander to her Nana Jay, and Jimmy. Jimmy from Farley's fair. He had loved her, really loved her, but her heart had been wrongly placed. The decision she'd made was right, she had felt it when that family dropped her off. Her Rainbow, her precious little girl would find her way.

She eased her body further and further into the water, stretching her arms out, embracing its abys. The rain briefly pattered on her back, but as the lake claimed her body, and soul, she could no longer feel it.

*

The Rainbow

The rain continued to beat on the windscreen, and Ed had the wipers going full pelt, making the children laugh at the squeaking noise.

The unsettled feeling Rosie had had in her tummy felt better. She enjoyed listening as Tilly chatted away to them all, then said, "Come on let's chase the rain away with a sing song?"

Rosie giggled, she had loved all the singing on the long journey up here. With this thought she realised again how good it felt to be going home. The noise of the rain beating on the car was drowned out with , "There was an old man called Michael Vinnegan…" Rosie stopped singing. There it was, one of her feelings. She could feel it, she could see it. It was like opening one of her story books, but this was a book only she could see. A picture drawn for her eyes only. It seemed with her vision the rain eased, and the sun peeked through the dark clouds making them appear blue. She wriggled forward so she could look out of the windscreen, and there it was, a rainbow arching over the sky, a rainbow you just couldn't miss.

Rosie knew, her mother had gone.

The End

The final book in the trilogy is Glass Houses. I hope you enjoy reading it.

The Rainbow

Sequel to The Other Half of Me

Acknowledgements

Special thanks to Monica Maloney. Someone who touched my life, and left all too soon despite reaching the grand age of 102.

I would like to thank the writing club 'Pen to Paper' particularly Steve Mann. The group has kept me on track giving fair criticism.

A big thank you to John Ainger for helping with my crime scene. This was excellent guidance.

I want to thank my daughter Christie who took a photo of my granddaughter, Amelia, and designed the front cover. Also, Christie, thank you for your constant support of my creative writing.

Last but not least, my husband, who never fails to believe in me, but more than that, he endures getting ignored while I tap away on my lap top getting these chapters out of my head on to paper. Thank you Keith.

Third Edition 2018

Author

Sharon Martin

Lives in West Sussex with her husband.

Sharon has two children, Christie and Mark and

Five grandchildren

Amelia Grace Finnegan, Josephine Ann Finnegan, Evania Rose Checketts, Jensen George Checketts and Ottile Rose Martin

Praise for The Rainbow

Wendy Devonshire – Editor of local magazine "I was a captive audience when I read this book as I was convalescing after an operation. I had the best excuse for not being able to put it down. This is no sugary sweet novel with everything working out perfectly for the 'goodies', it is quite realistic in that way and that is what I like about Sharon's writing. The storyline twists and turns making it difficult to predict. It follows on very well from her first book, The Other Half of Me, and by the end, all the various strands are neatly sewn together. Given how many narratives there are, this is quite an achievement. I really enjoyed reading this book and hope many others will too.

Printed in Great Britain
by Amazon